Girls

on

Film

Iain Cameron

To find out more about the author, visit the website:

www.iain-cameron.com

DEDICATION

For my daughters, Lucy and Amelia.

ONE

'Look at me, Maggie look at me...that's it.' The shutter clicked. Cindy adjusted the exposure on the camera a half-stop and tilted the light away from her subject, trying to harden the look. 'This time Maggie, don't smile, look serious. Face me but don't look at the camera. Great, that's it. Hold it.' The shutter clicked again and again.

In between pose changes Cindy Longhurst glanced at her watch. She did everything fast when she was 'in the zone'. Five to seven. Bugger. She needed to wrap this up soon. Her daughter was appearing in the school play this evening and she couldn't be late.

'I just need a few more, Maggie, all right?' she said.

'Sure thing.'

Maggie Hyatt was a self-employed businesswoman, a recently divorced mother of two with a superb figure and legs that a stocking manufacturer would drool over. Maggie wanted to change the pictures displayed on her promotional material and website for something more professional, whilst still emphasising her considerable assets.

'What if I sit on the couch again?' Maggie asked.

'Okay.'

Cindy re-positioned the camera and walked over to

adjust Maggie's clothing, a fetching green dress that hugged her figure.

Before she got there, the door of the studio flew open and two men barged in looking as if they owned the place. Cindy turned to face them.

'Boys, if you could please wait outside, this is…Hey, what are you doing?'

One of the men, large and barrel-chested with a pockmarked face, grabbed her arm, slapped her cheek and frogmarched her into the office at the rear of the building. At the same time, his smaller and thinner companion ushered Maggie Hyatt out the door without a word.

'What's the meaning of this?' Cindy said, trying to regain her composure, her face stinging. 'What are you doing in my studio?'

A fist came flying towards her, knocking her backwards over the desk.

'Shut the fuck up lady. You talk when I ask a question.'

The two men rifled through the drawers of her desk and the filing cabinet, searching for what, photographs? They were wasting their time as she worked digitally, saving her photos on hundreds of little SD cards, all backed up on various portable hard drives which she stored off-site.

'Where are they?'

'Where are what?'

'Don't play innocent with me or you get another smack, understand? You know what I want. The pictures you took of the girls. I want them.'

'I take lots of pictures of girls.'

In one stride he reached out, grabbed her blouse, pulled her towards him and punched her again.

'Where do you keep the pictures we come here for?' he shouted into her face.

She groaned, her eyes filling with tears. Had she always known it would end like this? 'Filing cabinet...bottom drawer...blue box,' she muttered.

The skinny guy walked to the filing cabinet. Reaching into the bottom drawer, he threw a load of SD card boxes that were in his way onto the floor before hauling out the blue box. A bunch of old pictures she took at a little studio she used to own in Portslade.

'This one?' he said holding the box in the air.

'Yesh,' she slurred. The punches to her face left it swollen and throbbing, neither aids to good diction or vision.

The big guy opened the box. 'These are camera cards,' he said to his companion.

'We can look at them there,' he said nodding at the computer.

The big guy shook his head. 'No time. The other woman will call the cops. What we gonna do?'

'Shut up, I'm thinking.'

'Make it quick.'

'Ok. I decide. We take her with us.'

The big guy walked over to Cindy, pulled a gun from his jacket and pointed it at her head. 'Any shit from you, you get this, understand?'

TWO

'More wine, sir?' the waiter asked, lifting the bottle from the ice cooler.

Detective Inspector Angus Henderson, Surrey and Sussex Major Crime Team, declined. He was on-call this evening and it was never a smart move to meet a distraught witness or a fearful victim smelling of booze and unable to think straight.

The waiter filled his companion's glass before replacing the bottle in the cooler and walking away.

'I like this place,' Henderson's girlfriend, Rachel Jones said.

They were seated in the Blue Marlin, a seafood restaurant in St George's Road, Brighton. They'd eaten there once before, but at prices that wouldn't shame smart restaurants in London, they didn't do it often.

In the last few months, Rachel had changed jobs and locations. She'd left the soft pastures of country and environment reporting for a promotion into general news. Not with a specific brief to cover crime, but on occasion, their professional paths did cross. In addition, *The Argus*, the newspaper where she worked, moved out of Hollingbury, the place where Henderson used to be based. His unit had been relocated to Malling House in Lewes and the newspaper to Manchester Street in the centre of Brighton, giving Rachel the option of a walk first thing in the morning instead of a drive.

'I like it too,' he said. 'It's only a short distance from the house, meaning we don't need to bring the car and spend twenty minutes trying to find a place to park the blooming thing.'

She put down her wine glass. 'We were talking about this in the office the other day. Why is it when they build a new block of flats, they only give the owners one parking space? If a couple live there, they might have a car each and if they have any grown-up kids, they'll have one as well.'

'Aye, it's the same on new housing estates. With smaller houses, there's often no garage and if there is, it's single with no room to park more than one or two cars outside.'

'I suppose it's because we live on a small, congested island.

'You say that, but it's not so small or congested where I come from. The problem isn't so much about space but that a large proportion of the population is shoehorned into London and the south east of England. It encourages builders and developers to use computer programs to squeeze as many houses into a piece of land–'

His phone rang. He pulled it out and mouthed 'sorry' to Rachel.

'Henderson.'

'Detective Inspector Henderson, Lewes Control here. We've received reports of a suspected kidnapping. A patrol car is on site. Can you attend?'

Henderson sighed, yet another night-out with Rachel spoiled. 'Yes. Get hold of DS Walters and tell her to meet me at the scene. What's the address?'

He finished the call a minute or so later and looked over at Rachel. She looked peeved. Her tetchiness was a recent development as in the past, she seemed to take such interruptions in her stride.

'You need to go?'

He nodded.

'What is it this time?'

'A suspected kidnap.'

**

Henderson called DC Sally Graham and DC Phil Bentley on the way. From what little he knew, information would be at a premium and he would set the two detectives on the task of finding witnesses.

He reached Hurstpierpoint, a small village about ten miles north of Brighton. It boasted a decent selection of local shops and pubs, but was best-known as the location of Hurstpierpoint College, an expensive co-ed private school boasting a host of famous alumni.

He drove through the village centre and turned down a narrow road called Langton Lane, which looked as though it didn't see much traffic. A few moments later, he turned into a driveway but didn't need to check the address. Despite the darkness of the cold January night and the absence of street lights, he saw a police patrol car and a small gaggle of neighbours standing in a huddle shivering under

6

hastily grabbed jackets.

He got out of the car and approached the cop who was guarding the crime scene from encroaching neighbours and any journalist who might appear. He pulled out his warrant card.

'Evening sir.'

'Good evening, constable. I was told this incident took place in a photographic studio. Where is it, in one of the rooms inside the house?'

'No sir, it's a building out back. Follow the path there,' he said pointing, 'around to the back of the house. You can't miss it.'

Famous last words as he falls into the duck pond. 'Thanks.'

Henderson made to move away but stopped for a moment to look at the house. It was constructed from grey stone with large bay windows, perhaps with four bedrooms inside and two or three large reception rooms. 'Substantial' was the word that came to mind. Lines of trees on either side separated it from any neighbours. To the side of the house, in the place where many would build a garage or site an extension, it was paved and tarmacked, a drive-through for customers of the studio, he assumed.

He continued walking. At the rear of the property stood a large, brightly lit wooden building with sweeping lines and masses of glass. It was so striking and elegant, it wouldn't look out of place in an architectural magazine.

Inside, a cop was gazing at the photographs stuck on the wall. There were many, some huge and others passport-sized, arranged in such a way to make this provincial studio resemble a photography exhibition in an arty part of Paris or Milan.

'Good evening, constable. DI Henderson, Serious Crime Team.'

'Ah, evening sir,' he said turning around.

'What can you tell me about what happened here?'

The constable reached into a jacket pocket for his notebook. 'We received a call at eight-sixteen from a Ms Maggie Hyatt,' he said reading from his notes. 'She said two men came into the studio while she was being photographed. One of the men ushered her out while another manhandled Ms Longhurst into the office at the rear.'

'Who's Ms Longhurst?'

'She's the photographer: Cindy Longhurst. She owns this place, I'm told.'

'Ok. Go on.'

'Ms Hyatt went home but later became worried about what happened to Ms Longhurst and decided to come back. She found the studio as you see it now, lights on, doors open but no sign of Ms Longhurst. She then called us.'

'Why didn't she call us earlier.'

'Initially, she believed it to be a personal matter and none of her business.'

'Fair enough. Anything else?'

'I've found one other witness. Mrs Lidia Rathbone lives down the road and was walking her dog down the lane. When she passed the end of the driveway, she saw two men bundling Ms Longhurst into a car and driving off.'

'Why didn't she call us?'

'I don't know, sir. Maybe she thought it was a prank or they were messing about.'

'Did she note down any details about the kidnappers' vehicle?'

'No, sir. She's quite elderly and doesn't know anything about cars.'

'Anything more?'

'No sir, that's about it.'

'You've done some excellent work tonight, Constable Murphy. Well done.'

'Thank you, sir.'

'Where are the two witnesses?'

'Ms Hyatt is sitting in the waiting room over there,' he said pointing, 'and Mrs Rathbone has gone home. Too cold for her, she said.'

'I assume you noted her address?'

'Yes sir.'

'Good. I'll take a look around here and then I'll speak to Ms Hyatt. You go over to the driveway and direct my detectives to this place. They should be here in a few minutes.'

'Yes sir.'

Henderson didn't know much about photography. He'd been inside a couple of studios, the family having photos done when he was married to Laura in Glasgow, and he'd been in the place where police photographers worked when not attending crime scenes. This place looked to be on a different level.

The room where he stood, a sort of ante-room with six Apple iMac computers, led into a huge open studio with portable room dividers to section off the space, floor-standing lights, light-deflecting umbrellas, numerous cameras and a variety of reflectors and screens to create different effects and backgrounds.

He walked from the studio into an office at the rear with a desk, filing cabinet and personal pictures of a girl and boy. With strewn papers and a floor scattered with SD cards and other bits of debris, it looked as though someone had started a fight in here.

'Evening sir.'

Henderson turned to see Detective Sergeant Carol Walters coming towards him. 'Evening Carol.' He looked again. Gone was the usual shapeless trouser suit and anorak, replaced with a smart, dark patterned dress, light black jacket and, a rarity, eye make-up and lipstick.

'Did I drag you away from something more appealing than a photographic studio in the sticks?'

'You did, but I won't hold it against you.'

'Do I know your date?'

'Not unless you've been looking for a man on Tinder.'

'You don't expect me to respond, do you?'

'Then the answer is no, you don't know him.'

'Have you been briefed?'

'The super-efficient Constable Murphy out there told me about two witnesses, and a car driving off with our victim inside.'

'It's all we have at the moment. Let's go and talk to one of the witnesses.'

They walked through the studio. 'This is some place,' Walters said. 'You can still smell the newness.'

'It should feel familiar to you as you're forever redecorating.'

'True.'

They walked into the room he'd been in earlier, which he knew from a sign above the door was called the Video Production Suite. From there, they came into what looked like a waiting room with soft chairs, a coffee machine and a television hung from the ceiling.

'Ms Hyatt?' Henderson asked.

The woman sitting there stood and extended her hand.

'I'm Detective Inspector Henderson and this is my colleague, Sergeant Walters. Thank you for waiting. We'd like to ask you some questions about what happened here tonight.'

'Fine with me,' she said retaking her seat.

'Can I get you anything?' he said nodding towards the drinks machine.

'I'll take a black coffee.'

'I'll do it,' Walters said. 'You want one, sir?'

He nodded.

Maggie Wyatt was in her early forties, with thick, wavy brown hair, a pretty unmarked face and a figure a twenty-five-year-old model would be hitting the gym to try and achieve.

'If you can repeat the story you told the constable earlier,' Henderson said, as he took the cup from Walters.

After hearing her account and waiting as she dabbed her eyes with a handkerchief, he asked, 'Why were you here?'

'I run a health food business on the web: Maggie's Farm. You might have heard of it?'

Henderson shook his head.

'Oh, you should take a look. Some of my products can prevent razor drag,' she said looking at him. She then looked at Walters, 'and there are others to reduce spots caused by using too much foundation.'

'I'm sure it's all good quality stuff.'

'It is, and I was here to get some up-to-date shots to put on the website. It hasn't been updated for a few years. You've got to freshen it up now and again, haven't you?'

'So, you were in the studio getting shots done when two men came in. What time was this?'

'Around seven.'

'Could you describe them?'

'Not well as I only glanced round before one of them grabbed me and bundled me outside. The one who grabbed Cindy and slapped her was a big guy with a crew-cut and acned face, and the other, smaller and skinny, weaselly as my mother would say.'

'Did you notice the car they drove?'

'It was black, a big 4x4, maybe a BMW or Mercedes, I don't know. I didn't look too closely.'

'What made you come back?' Walters asked.

'Initially, I thought it was none of my business. She's very capable is Cindy and I thought she could handle it. Later on, after I'd thought about it and remembered the angry faces of the two guys, I came back. Maybe it's got something to do with the finance to build this place.'

'Doesn't she own it?'

'I don't know if she does or she doesn't, but if you saw her old place in Portslade, it was a shoe-box compared to this. To leap from there to a place like this takes a shed load of money, don't you think?'

'So, you came back,' Henderson said, 'expecting to find what? Cindy distressed or maybe beaten up?'

'Yeah.'

'When you didn't find her, you called us?'

'You got it.'

'Have you tried calling her?'

She nodded. 'Numerous times. It rings but she doesn't answer.'

'What do you think has happened to her?'

'I really don't know. I can't think of any reason why someone would try and hurt her, she's such a sweet person. Gave me a shoulder to cry on when my husband buggered off, and helped a lot to publicise Maggie's Farm.' She dabbed her eyes again.

'You've obviously known Cindy for many years, do you know what she does when she isn't working?'

'Now there's a story,' she said. 'She's very righteous is our Cindy, campaigning against anything and everything. It could be fracking at Balcombe, the council's treatment of Afghan refugees, building on the green belt. Any protest and Cindy is out there supporting it. I might be doing her a disservice as she must see some logic in the things she protests about, but I can't.'

'Is she married, does she have children?'

'Christ, children! Who's picking up Molly?'

'Who's Molly?'

'Cindy's daughter. When she divorced from that useless specimen of a husband, Greg Jackson, the boy went with him and she kept the girl. She's a pupil at

Hurstpierpoint College and Cindy told me she's appearing in a play there tonight.'

Henderson turned to Walters.

'I'm on it, gov,' she said, getting up to leave.

'We'll send someone over to the school to pick her up,' Henderson said.

'Good,' Maggie replied. 'Make sure she goes to her father, useless as he is. I don't think Cindy would be happy with her going into social services.'

'Do you have her ex-husband's address?'

'Cindy has a black book of all her main contacts and stores it in the top drawer, right-hand side of her desk. He'll be in there.'

'Thanks. Is there anyone to look after the studio in Cindy's absence?'

'She's got an assistant, Annie Heath. She works four days a week. She should be here in the morning.'

'If not, I assume her name is in the address book?'

She smiled, the first. 'You got it.'

Henderson said goodbye to Maggie Hyatt a few minutes later and headed back into Cindy's office at the far end of the building. He edged around the room, careful not to disturb anything as he hadn't yet decided to call in a forensics team. It was then he noticed the blood on the desk. He wouldn't have spotted it on the wood of the desk, but some had marked nearby papers.

Using tweezers, he carefully lifted some items out of the way and his curiosity was rewarded when he spotted a button, small and opaque, from a shirt or a blouse.

He heard Walters come in.

14

'I've sent Sally Graham to pick up Molly from her school,' she said, 'and I told Phil Bentley to talk to our other witness, Lidia Rathbone. He's good with the old ladies, he's been out with enough of them.'

'You leave Phil alone.'

'He deserves it.'

'Look at this,' Henderson said, pointing at the blood and button.

'Do we know what Cindy was wearing?'

'No. Give Maggie a call and find out.'

'What do you think? She got thumped and fell back on the desk, spilling the blood?'

'Maybe a tussle with someone grabbing the front of her blouse followed by a smack.'

'Do you think she's been raped?'

'It's a messy desk, but there's no evidence to suggest it. I've been debating whether I should get forensics in here, but seeing this, I've decided I will. With luck, it'll also clear up the 'R' question.'

'Fair enough.'

'If Lidia corroborates Maggie's story, it establishes that Cindy is a kidnap victim. By whom and for what reason we don't yet know. My hope is when the forensics boys come in here, they will find something to help us, otherwise there's a busy private and professional life we need to trawl through.'

'I'm up for it.'

'Even with a new man on the scene?'

'I won't miss a beat.'

THREE

Greg Jackson took off his jacket and hung it with care on a peg in the hall. It wasn't as if he was trying to look after an expensive item of climbing gear made by the likes of North Face or Rab. It was a thin, crappy thing, bought from a department store, but he couldn't afford to buy another.

His son, Jamie, seventeen and heading for the same aimless lifestyle he lived if the boy's recent academic results were anything to go by, was out at a party tonight. It wouldn't be with a girl as these modern teenagers, or at least Jamie and his friends, didn't go in for this sort of thing. He'd seen some of Jamie's female classmates when he used to drop him off at school, and he couldn't help but be mystified by his voluntary abstinence. The poor boy had to be gay or stupid.

It was good job his son was away this evening as otherwise Greg would only take out his bad mood on him. His boss at Harris Manufacturing where he worked in Burgess Hill, Gary Richardson, had been on his case all day. If it wasn't about the price of raw materials, not his fault, the cost of temps in their Hassocks warehouse, partly his fault, it was about the high levels of scrap. He worked in Accounts not Manufacturing, the stupid prat.

He took a beer from the fridge, noting he needed to buy some more, popped the ring pull and took a seat in the lounge, contemplating another Friday night alone. Time was when he would be upstairs taking a shower, getting dressed in his best togs and dashing out the door with whatever food he could eat while walking. The evening would then be spent with his mates in a pub in the centre of Brighton followed by a late-night session in a noisy night club.

His youth hadn't quite passed him by, but he didn't feel he'd experienced enough of it. He'd had his share of one-night stands, but as soon as some attraction developed, he'd fall into a long-term relationship with all the enthusiasm of an American evangelist preacher. Before he knew it, a couple of years had passed with nothing much to show for them.

Following a few relationships like this, he met and married Cindy. They were happy together for ten years and, looking back, had lived a good life. He'd been at the early stages of his accountancy career, studying for exams and looking forward to qualifying in the not too distant future. Cindy opened a small studio in Portslade and it was steadily growing in popularity. What went wrong, he couldn't put his finger on, but when they split, she was making plans to move to a bigger place and he was facing a future as a dogsbody having flunked his exams and been sacked from a good job for incompetence.

He often felt like this on Fridays. A day that promised so much with the end of the working week and an opportunity at night to unwind and leave all the problems of life behind. Now, all he had to look forward to was Saturday supermarket shopping in Tesco and a weekend in front of the telly, as Jamie spent most of his time in his room.

He put the beer can to his lips but found it empty. He crushed it, annoyed for drinking so quickly as he had only one left. It took an effort to get up from the settee and walk back into the kitchen. He dumped the can in the bin and opened the fridge, not to remove the remaining beer, but to see what he could cook for tea.

Despite being badly paid and not able to afford to put his son into the same school as his daughter, Molly, he would not economise on food. He had learned to cook while married to Cindy as she frequently went out to meetings or discussion groups where the zealots would plan their next day of protest. He was happy to support Cindy on marches, but he refused to sit and listen to a load of old windbags moaning about the government, big business, capitalists, the Americans or any number of protagonists responsible for screwing up the lives they wanted to lead.

If he ever did attend such a gathering, he would tell them it wasn't anyone else's fault they hated everyone, it was their own. If they hadn't messed around at school, smoking in bike sheds, staring out of the window and haranguing teachers with their stupid questions, they might have made something of themselves. Then, they would have something more important to worry about than fracking or somebody else's refuse collections. How did he know this? He'd made the same mistakes himself.

He took out a paring knife from the drawer and sharpened it. He pulled over the vegetable rack where he removed a carrot, cabbage, peppers and an onion, and over the next ten minutes, shredded the lot. He put the wok on the cooker, lit the gas and turned it up high. While waiting for the oil to heat, he took out a thigh of uncooked chicken from the fridge and cut it into pieces. When the wok reached a suitable working temperature, he scooped up the chicken pieces and placed them inside, the sizzling drowning out the radio in the background. When the chicken was cooked, he tipped in the vegetables.

A few minutes later, he carried a tray into the lounge with a delicious-smelling meal and his last can of beer. He put the tray down and switched on the television. He refused to pay the exorbitant charges for Sky or cable and made do with Freeview, but being so indiscriminate in his tastes, he could usually find something to while away a few hours.

He started watching a crime drama. It was fine for the first hour, by which time he'd finished the stir-fry, the last drops of beer and a plate of ice-cream and fruit. However, when the plot alighted upon a fraud taking place at the office where one of the main characters worked, he lost all concentration as it brought it all back.

He'd been sacked from his previous job at Mathieson Transport, not because he'd done anything wrong, but he'd failed to spot the thieving activities of two men working there. Their job was to empty the huge forty-tonne articulated lorries that brought goods into the UK from all over Europe, but in doing so, they were helping themselves to some of the merchandise. During the rancour and recrimination that followed, it didn't help his case when he accused, with some justification, the owner of Mathieson Transport, Ted Mathieson, of having an affair with his wife.

For a while afterwards, he couldn't get another job, driving a further wedge into his relationship with Cindy. After months of trying he ended up at his current place, Harris Manufacturing, a small producer of bespoke items for the aerospace industry, and there he would stay. It wasn't a bad place to be if he could ignore the huge amounts of money being made by his boss and his two direct reports.

The negative thoughts were making him feel agitated and he couldn't remember what had happened in the crime drama over the previous half hour. He walked into the box room at the back of the house, euphemistically called a study, lifted his laptop and headed back into the lounge. He switched it on, put it to one side to allow it to boot-up and carried on watching television.

Five minutes later it was ready. He turned down the sound on the television and picked up the laptop. Loading his web browser, he selected a website from his list of 'favourites', an adult dating site. If a woman had expressed an interest in his profile, he would have already received an email, a text and probably a 'Halleluiah! Someone's Interested!' alert on his phone, so that wasn't his reason for logging on. He wanted to see if any new women were on the site.

While browsing, he searched for a woman in his

office, Debbie Payne, as he'd overheard her telling someone she'd recently joined the same dating site. He found her after a time but the reason it took so long was the photograph on the screen didn't look a bit like her. She was a reasonably attractive woman, mid-forties, a bit overweight with thick dark hair, but the woman on the website was a cracker; young, early thirties and blonde. The bio read like the woman he knew, even if she was gilding the lily a touch when she claimed to spend her free time hill-walking and dancing, as he knew she preferred watching television and going to the cinema.

He stopped to consider if this was something he needed to do, post a flattering younger picture of himself. Not that he owned many pictures of himself unless he went back at least seven years to the studio shots taken by Cindy. He opened the 'Photos' app on the laptop and scanned some of his old pictures. He spent the next couple of hours looking at photographs, some memories making him smile and others leaving him melancholy. In the end, he found one he liked and loaded it up on the website.

He looked at the clock and decided to shut the laptop down. He went into the hall, grabbed his jacket and headed out to the car. He felt happier than he often did on a Friday night and wondered why he hadn't thought about doing something like this before. He'd dated a couple of women from the site and noticed they never looked the same as their pictures. He assumed at the time they'd used an old one as they didn't have anything more recent, or they'd been members of the site for a while and hadn't updated their picture, but he knew Debbie in the office hadn't been doing it for long.

It was approaching midnight by the time he parked outside the house of Jamie's friend, Alex. He was under strict instructions not to come to the door. He wouldn't dream of it, as the sight of a seventeen-year-old with pecs bursting through a tight t-shirt, a nubile young thing on one arm and a bottle of beer on the other would age him faster than Mother Nature could.

He was on the point of phoning, an activity designed to give him something to do as Jamie would never pick up, when the front door opened and the boy himself strolled out, walking like a gangsta rapper. His son never 'strolled' anywhere, as he was introverted and had self-confidence issues, so Jackson knew he'd been drinking or taking drugs. His behaviour had been a problem ever since the divorce, but now combined with teenage angst and anxiety, it had mushroomed.

He missed the car's door handle at the first attempt and after succeeding, fell inside the car and made it into the passenger seat more by accident than design.

'Hey,' he slurred. His usual complexion was white with an array of angry red spots, but in the sodium light of a Burgess Hill street it looked pasty-grey. People were hospitalised for less.

'Drive on, driver,' he said, a stupid grin splitting his face.

'Aren't you forgetting something?'

'Eh?'

'Seat belt.'

'Ah.'

He watched as Jamie, with one eye closed, tried to spear the tongue into the buckle without success. After a few further attempts, Jackson got fed up waiting and plugged it in himself.

'Ah was gettin' there,' Jamie said, his alcohol-laden breath a little too close.

'When?' he asked as he drove off. 'Next Wednesday?'

'Ha, ha you made a joke.'

Jamie laughed, not the sarcastic laugh of the boss when he heard a delivery would be late, but the hearty chortle of the inebriated.

There was no point in asking him how the party went, he would have to wait until morning and hear the more comprehensible version. They drove in a sort of silence, the radio playing low and Jamie talking to himself. It was the gibberish of the plastered, not the coherent conversations he used to have with his imaginary friend, Eric, aged twelve or thirteen.

'Can you go slower, Dad?' Jamie said, 'I feel a bit sick.'

'I'm going no faster than the speed limit. Don't you dare throw up in my bloody car, or you'll get the job of cleaning it.'

'Yeah, I can see me...'

He'd lost the thread and rested his head against the window with his eyes closed. They made it back to the house without incident. Jackson was so busy trying to get his son out of the car without him falling face-first on the pavement, he failed to notice the police car parked across the street or the copper walking towards him.

'Good evening, sir.'

He looked up. A woman stood there, conservatively dressed in dark trousers and zip-up jacket, pretty face, her blonde hair tied back in a ponytail. Wicked thoughts of his dating website sending women out for personal visits stopped when he noticed the police ID she was holding up for him to see.

'Detective Constable Graham, Sussex Police.'

Shit, he'd only drunk two cans of beer and didn't remember doing anything wrong, except maybe not indicating as he turned into his street as there wasn't anyone around.

'Are you Greg Jackson?'

'Ye...yes. Why do you want to know?'

'Are you the former husband of Cindy Longhurst?'

'Yes, I am. Why?'

Jamie seemed to lose interest and wandered off, walking unsteadily towards the front door of the house. If he had trouble opening the car door handle, he would need some luck finding his key and trying to fit it into the little keyhole.

'Can we step inside for a moment?'

'What's this about?'

'Can we just move inside, sir?'

He racked his brains. He was the law-abiding sort, but the huge money made by bosses at the place where he worked did rankle. They drove big saloon cars and took holidays at the MD's villa in Barbados. Those on the shop floor could barely afford two weeks in Mallorca.

Over the years he'd helped himself to the laptop he used at home, paper for the printer and about six months ago, he'd pocketed a payment sent to the company in error for five thousand pounds. The copper's face gave no indication if she was here to breathalyse him, arrest him for stealing or give him a medal for getting his teenage son home in one piece, albeit in an inebriated condition.

Jackson walked towards the house, the front door ajar to the vagaries of all four winds. Jamie could award himself ten marks for dexterity in the face of a severe impediment, but zero marks for energy conservation. The copper instructed him to sit in the lounge. He'd seen enough crime dramas to know what comes next. She was here to deliver some bad news.

'I'm afraid to say, sir, we believe your ex-wife, Cindy Longhurst, has been kidnapped.'

'Kidnapped? Why? How?'

'We don't know all the details as yet, sir. Can I get you anything to drink, a cup of tea maybe?'

'No, no thank you, officer there's no need to get me anything, I was just taken aback to hear you say she's been kidnapped, is all.'

He'd almost burst out laughing, the relief at finding out the police weren't here to arrest him.

He paused, searching for the right words. 'How can I put this? Me and Cindy have been divorced for seven years and even though I don't wish her any harm, she means nothing to me now. I've moved on.'

'I understand sir.'

If Cindy had a current boyfriend, not that he would know as they didn't speak often and when they did, it was usually about the kids, it was his responsibility now. Jackson made to get out of his chair, giving the cop her cue to leave.

'One more thing.'

Oh no, here it comes, the handcuffs, Lewes Crown Court, Wandsworth Prison.

'We've got your daughter, Molly, in the back of the car.'

Damn! He'd momentarily forgotten about her, preoccupied as he was about going to jail, or not.

'She needs a place to stay.'

FOUR

On a Saturday, without a major case to investigate, DI Henderson could sometimes be found looking through the offerings in the furniture shops of Brighton with Rachel, but on every second Saturday, he would be at the Amex watching the football.

Henderson and a Sergeant from Brighton's main police station in John Street had treated themselves to a season ticket to watch Brighton and Hove Albion play at the American Express Community Stadium. Alas, this Saturday Henderson was in the office as he did have a major case to investigate, but he wouldn't miss a match as Albion were playing away this weekend.

He opened the thin file on Cindy Longhurst and flicked through the contents. It crossed the mind of all detectives investigating missing persons or kidnap claims, cases without a subject and no obvious motive, that it all could be a hoax or a tasteless birthday surprise. The information on this one was sketchy and the recall of two witnesses, one clear although she hadn't seen much, and the other, a distance away on a dark night, variable.

However, just as the police response to a missing person case was based on its merits, for example, all the stops would be pulled out for a child or a vulnerable individual, he couldn't see an innocent explanation for this one. The kidnappers had smacked Cindy in the presence of Maggie Hyatt and the blood on the office desk suggested further violence had taken place inside. Alternative scenarios proposed by DS Walters that she would be found wandering around the fields outside her studio, dazed following a rape or lying dead in the bushes, didn't hold water. A walk around the extensive grounds last night, a search of the nearby house and the sightings of their two witnesses of Cindy being bundled into a car, discounted them all. He closed the file, left his office and walked towards the Detectives' Room.

'Quieten down,' Henderson said to the assembled group of officers, a few annoyed to be working the weekend when their roster said they didn't need to.

Henderson tapped the picture of the victim he put up on the whiteboard behind him. 'This is Cindy Longhurst, a thirty-nine-year-old divorced mother of two and owner of Longhurst Studios in Hurstpierpoint. Two men kidnapped her at her photographic studio yesterday around seven in the evening. The men, according to one of our witnesses, Maggie Hyatt, who was having her picture taken by Cindy at the time, drove a black 4x4.'

'That narrows it down a bit,' Phil Bentley said.

A few laughed.

'A forensic team will be attending the crime scene this morning as DS Walters and myself found evidence of a violent struggle. Afterwards, they'll move on to the house. You've all got a copy of Maggie Hyatt's statement. Phil, how did you get on with our other witness, Mrs Rathbone?'

'She might be eighty-one,' DC Phil Bentley said, 'but she's sprightly. She goes swimming twice a week and walks her dog every day. She confirmed that when she walked past Cindy's driveway she saw Cindy being man-handled into the back of a car, the previously mentioned 4x4. Her dog Sandy, a small terrier, had taken a liking to some smell he detected and she was standing in sight of the house when she saw the incident.'

'Didn't all this activity make the dog bark?'

'He's an old thing, she says. Doesn't see or hear too well.'

'I presume she got out of the way before the kidnapper's car drove out?' Henderson said.

'As soon as the car door shut, she hurried back to the road and stood in the shadow of a bush until they disappeared.'

'Which direction did they take?'

'Towards Hurstpierpoint.'

'Sally, you picked Cindy's daughter, Molly, up from her school?'

'Yes, I did sir,' DC Sally Graham said. 'I took her to her father's house in Burgess Hill.'

'How did he respond to the news?'

'He looked shocked at first and then said she was nothing to do with him as he'd moved on.'

'Charming. No indication of any animosity?'

'Quite the opposite I would say.'

'Interesting. Okay, you've all heard what we know so far. Now, there are two ways to approach our search for the missing woman and we'll cover them both with two teams. The first team will trawl through Cindy's background. DCs Graham and Bentley will manage this. You're not trying to write her biography,' he said, eliciting a few weak smiles, 'but to uncover a motive for her disappearance. Look through the financials of her business for debts, her customer correspondence for angry or aggressive emails and for any evidence that she might have upset someone during the numerous protests she attended.'

'It could be a long list,' Graham said. 'I remember the fracking protest at Balcombe angered a lot of people.'

'So did the demonstrations outside the Thales electronics company in Crawley about arms sales to Israel,' Bentley said.

'Cindy was involved in that one too?'

Bentley nodded. 'This is according to our elderly witness, Mrs Lidia Rathbone. She says she knew Cindy well, and once camped out herself at Greenham Common to protest about the US siting nuclear-tipped cruise missiles in the UK.'

'It looks like you'll have your work cut out, but be careful not to get sidetracked. Members of those groups can be quite persuasive.'

'Yes sir.'

'The second group will be fronted by DS Wallop and DC Young and focus on the physical search for Cindy. I want her picture plastered up in all Sussex police stations, on the website, in newspapers and on television and in every patrol car going out in our region. Also, run a check by local hospitals, make sure she hasn't been admitted.'

'Will do boss,' DS Harry Wallop said.

Henderson bent down and finished his coffee, now cold. 'DS Walters and I will talk to Cindy's assistant, Annie Heath, and Cindy's ex-husband, Greg Jackson. We'll meet again at six-thirty to review progress. I apologise for buggering up everyone's weekend but if we find Cindy alive and unharmed, it will all be worth it.'

**

Seeing the photographic studio again on a crisp January morning had no less effect on DI Henderson than it had the previous night. He still marvelled at the dramatic architectural touches, the way the large windows were positioned to maximise natural light from the south and west, and the way the colour of the wooden frame of the building blended with neighbouring woods.

In common with the previous night, Cindy's Range Rover stood at the front of the house, the lights blazed inside the studio, but two new vehicles were now parked there: a van he assumed belonging to the SOCO team and a grey VW Polo.

'There's money in this photography lark,' Walters said as she got out of the car. 'Just look at the size of this house, the big car and the studio.'

'She's probably studied hard and worked the hours to achieve it.'

'I'm not sure you need to study much to do photography,' she said as they headed towards the studio. 'I think it's more about having a flair for the subject and a good eye for what will look great in a picture.'

'Any students I know, like my daughter, are dismissive of anyone not studying for an academic degree. It just shows you looking at all this, what do they know?'

Henderson pushed open the door of the studio into the waiting room and headed in the direction of the office. Leaning against the doorframe with her back to them, they saw a young woman watching the activity going on inside and chatting with members of the SOCO team.

'Morning,' Henderson said quietly as he approached, hoping not to make her jump.

She turned slowly and Henderson could see why she had trouble moving. She was pregnant and, based on the size of the bump, wasn't far away from the big day.

'Hello there. Can I help you?' she asked.

Henderson introduced Walters and himself.

She held out her hand. 'I'm Annie Heath, Cindy's assistant. I didn't expect to see anyone this morning. I cancelled all of Cindy's appointments as soon as I heard the news.'

'Are you not able to take over in Cindy's absence?'

'I worked closely with Cindy until a few months ago, but ever since I've grown to this great size it's been too difficult. I'm expecting twins you see, and the little buggers kick like blazes. I find it too awkward getting around the studio and I can't lift all the equipment. Some of it is quite heavy.'

'I'm sure.'

'We should move to the waiting room,' Walters said. 'You can sit down there.'

'Good idea.'

They walked back to the waiting room where Henderson dispensed water for Annie and made a coffee for himself and Walters before sitting down.

'It's terrible what's happened to Cindy,' Annie said. 'I'm not sure it's really sunk in yet.'

'It is and we're doing our best to find her,' Henderson said. 'Do you know or suspect who might be behind it?'

'I've only just heard the story from your people in Cindy's office. I've been racking my brain to think who could be behind it ever since.' She sighed. 'Despite being a sensible person before pregnancy, sometimes my head feels like mush and I can't string two thoughts together.'

'Let's talk about her background, it might help you remember something.'

'Okay.'

'Tell me about this place? Did Cindy buy it like this or did she have it built?'

'She bought the house and land about five years back and had the studio built to her own specifications.'

'Did she finance it herself or borrow the money?'

'Ah yes, I know this,' she said, as she moved heavily in her seat in an effort to get comfortable. 'Cindy's ex-husband, Greg Jackson, used to work at Mathieson Transport in Newhaven as an accountant or something. They used to socialise with the company's owner, Ted Mathieson, and his trophy wife

Tamsin. A former Miss Lithuania, if you will. Over time, Cindy and Ted became friends, one of the reasons why she and Jackson split, as a matter of fact. When Cindy came up with plans to build this place, Ted lent her the money.'

'All, or some?' Henderson asked.

'I think it was about half. It's all above board. She pays him every month. I'm sure she gets a preferential rate, but hey, what are friends for?'

'Were Cindy and Ted romantically involved?' Walters asked.

'For a spell, but I think he was a sympathetic ear for Cindy when she and Greg hit a rocky patch, and it was another notch on the bedpost for Ted. I think he fancies himself as a lady's man.'

'You mentioned her ex-husband, Greg Jackson,' Henderson said. 'What's he like?'

'I've always found him a bit wet, if you know what I mean. See, Cindy's a real live wire, constantly busy doing something but as Greg got older, he couldn't be bothered with protest marches and heckling politicians at party conferences. He'd rather sit at home watching telly and drinking beer. They sort of drifted apart as many couples do. It didn't help that he never completed his accountancy qualification.'

'Any particular reason?'

'He said he couldn't find the time to study because they were always away, taking part in demonstrations and sit-ins. The way he tells it, he can't get the best jobs as they only go to qualified people, so he ends up working for people younger than him, and he hates it. Over the years it's sort of ground him down.'

'What about boyfriends? Is Cindy going out with anyone?'

With some effort, Annie got to her feet. 'I must go to the loo, the little buggers in there are pressing down on my bladder. I'll be back in a mo.'

'Annie's given us another name to add to our list,' Walters said. 'Ted Mathieson.'

'Yes indeed. Money's every bit a motivator as jealousy or envy. Phil and Sally are looking at the financials but I'll make sure they catch sight of the agreement between Cindy and Ted Mathieson. See if they're both keeping to their sides of the bargain.'

'The name Mathieson rings a bell,' Walters said. 'How about you?'

'Nope, can't say it does.'

'I think his name came up in an investigation about a year or so back, but I can't remember in relation to what.'

'Check it out when we get back to the office.'

'Will do. Oh, hi Annie, how are you feeling?'

'Much better, thanks but don't worry, I'll be doing it again in another twenty minutes.'

'Would you like more water?'

'No, I wouldn't,' she said as she slumped into the seat, 'it would just make it worse.'

'Before you went out,' Henderson said, 'we asked if Cindy had any boyfriends.'

'You did, didn't you?' she said, the previous effort leaving her breathless. 'Now wait a minute, what was his name? Yeah, she used to go out with this guy called Mike Harrison. He's some sort of builder or handyman and they got on well together for a few months despite him being not her usual, shall we say, intellectual standard. In the end, she got shot of him for being too controlling.'

'In what way controlling?'

'Calling her up at all times of the day, not in a friendly way to see how she was, but to find out what she was doing and see who she was with. He got angry if she took photographs of men. She used to tell him they were old guys or just young boys or he'd go ape-shit. Oops, sorry I swore, it just comes out on its own. I swear it's the hormones.'

'Do many men come here?' Henderson asked, his personal curiosity roused.

'Sure, I'd say about thirty per cent of our clients are men. In the main they're self-employed people, models, those with a big social media following, and singles on dating sites. All sorts. We also get a lot of people coming here to use our video services which can be accessed on the Apple Macs next door, the likes of pop bands, web bloggers and small-business owners.'

'Interesting.'

'I was saying about Mike Harrison. When they spilt, he wouldn't leave Cindy alone. He'd turn up here at all hours and bombard her with texts pleading with her to come back. He said he loved her and I think he did, but he had a weird way of showing it. In the end, it turned Cindy off. Now that I think of it, if you ask me who kidnapped her, my money's on him.'

FIVE

The Scania 620 with the twenty-four-pallet trailer turned into the yard at Mathieson Transport in Newhaven. The brakes hissed as George McDuff, the driver, lined it up, before the big sixteen-litre engine roared into life once again and reversed into the loading bay. A few minutes later, the brakes hissed again and the engine sighed as it was switched off.

Managing Director, Ted Mathieson, watched the lorry arrive from his office on the first floor and terminated his phone call. He left the office and walked downstairs, headed in the direction of the loading bay. The lads working in there started to look busy whenever he appeared, not only because he paid their wages, but he could walk-the-talk as he'd driven an HGV as big as this one and over the same routes as McDuff had done.

He found his driver sitting on a ledge outside having a smoke.

'Hello George.'

He turned. 'Hullo there, Ted. Good to see you. Are you here to see me or cadge a smoke?'

'If you're offering, I'm cadging.'

'I wasn't but what the hell, you're the boss,' he said, holding out the packet. 'Fill your lungs.'

'Cheers,' Mathieson said as he sat beside him.

He always made time for George McDuff. They were similar in age, forty-seven, they both liked Scotland, George as he came from there and Mathieson because he enjoyed shooting grouse. George had been his first employee. In a way he reminded Mathieson of what he might have become without the ambition, aggression and abilities he possessed. Still a driver, taking the big Scania out to Austria and back. Mathieson didn't mind driving but he would miss his big house in Telscombe Cliffs with uninterrupted views of the Channel and the Ferrari parked out front.

'Your missus still on her health kick?' George asked.

'With renewed vigour, I would say. She slips bran into my breakfast cereal.'

He laughed. 'She's a devil that one. I would say she'll be the death of you, but if she gets her way you'll live to be a hundred.'

'Not smoking these things, I won't,' he said holding up the white stick between his fingers.

'Ach, we've all got our vices. I mean, wanking makes you blind, puffing these will give you cancer, pork pies lead to a heart attack. If you try and avoid all those, where's the bloody fun in life?'

'Shagging a twenty-seven-year-old comes near the top of my list.'

'It would in mine too, but there's no need to rub my face in it.'

'How did you get on at Calais?'

'Your money's safe this week. I drove fast past a big bunch of illegals about a mile from the port, and closer in, the police were keeping them away from the waiting areas. I think these new locks on the doors make a big difference. They can't sneak in when I'm having a break at a service station.'

'I'd take a gun and shoot the bloody lot of them if I could. A couple more fines and we'll be branded a trafficker and the supermarkets will scarper like rats from a sinking ship.'

'They must see the measures we're taking to try and prevent it.'

'The market's too competitive, George,' he said, before sucking a final drag from his cigarette and stubbing it out in the bin. 'One black mark against our reputation and they'll replace us in a flash. What we do, a hundred companies can do.' Mathieson stood and stretched. 'See you later, mate. Thanks for the smoke.

He returned to his office upstairs in a thoughtful mood. The illegals had been a thorn in his side for the last couple of years, and now the authorities were fining trucking businesses and the driver up to two thousand pounds for every illegal immigrant found in their truck at Dover.

The tricks they tried were becoming ever more daring and dangerous. They laid obstacles in the road to slow the trucks down or engaged drivers in an altercation at a service station, allowing time for their pals to break the locks on the trailer and jump inside. If they couldn't get into the truck, now made more difficult with the sophisticated locks that he and other truck companies were using, they hung on to wheel axles or laid themselves flat on the roof.

He was running a business and didn't want to be fined, money he could put to better use buying fuel or warehousing racks, but he and his drivers were human too. For all his bluster, he didn't want to see any of them killed, crushed under the wheels of an HGV or dropping from the roof while it sped along the motorway at seventy miles an hour. He wished they would all go back to where they came from. The ineffective meddling of politicians was, as always, at the heart of such problems and it was up to them to find a solution.

He picked up an industry report about the issues companies like his would face when the United Kingdom exited the European Union, when his phone rang.

'Ted, good afternoon to you. Jim Levitt, Clifton Oak Furniture in Manchester.'

'Good afternoon Jim, how are you?'

'Good. Yourself?'

'Excellent, couldn't be better. What can I do for you, Jim?'

'Did you see the response I sent about your proposal?'

'I did. My secretary's drafting a reply as we speak. In short, you like everything we offer, but not the rate.'

'Got it in one.'

Levitt waffled on about tight margins, competitive industries, fickle customers, the whole nine yards. Mathieson wanted their business. They needed twenty trucks a month to go out to a hardwood furniture manufacturing facility in Croatia, and bring wardrobes, sideboards and dining room tables back to their gigantic furniture warehouse in Chorley. The goods would be vacuum-wrapped on pallets, easy-peasy work, and if Mathieson played his cards right, very profitable too.

'If I'm not mistaken, do I detect a man who would like a little something from the deal to treat his wife or girlfriend to a night out once in a while?'

'You might say that.'

'How about five hundred–'

'Wait a minute Mathieson, you don't get me so bloody cheap.'

'- a month.'

'Now you're talking, but I was thinking closer to a grand.'

'No can do. The union are expected to demand a 3% pay rise for drivers about the middle of this year. It could wipe out any profit I make on this arrangement at a stroke.'

'You're breaking my heart. Seven-fifty.'

'Jim, just remember my company's delivery time hit rate. I bet it's the best of all the companies bidding for this work. When the furniture comes into Chorley bang on time, week after week, that alone will make you look good in front of your bosses. Six-fifty. It's my final offer.'

'You're a hard bastard, Mathieson and no mistake. You've got yourself the business.'

He put the phone down a few minutes later and rubbed his hands together in satisfaction at a deal well done. Deals like this where the customer believed they were getting one over the supplier didn't fail to give him pleasure. Most of what he said to Jim Levitt was lies, but once they'd signed a contract it wouldn't matter. He'd researched Clifton Oak and knew a lot about what they did and how much money they made. In essence, Levitt needed something to show his bosses what a good job he was doing, and Mathieson, like a good soldier, had just handed it to him.

He worked until nine, sustained or otherwise by a tub of cold chicken, rice and peas prepared by his lady wife this morning. It didn't taste bad, but for a guy who could take part in a pork pie or doughnut-eating contest and expect to be competing for a top three place, it didn't satisfy. He was about to extract a Snickers bar from a catering-sized box he kept in the office when he heard a truck drive into the yard.

Mathieson Transport drivers arriving after six in the evening usually parked in the yard, making sure the perimeter gate was locked before leaving for home. If the loading bay was empty and open, they backed inside, leaving the crew coming in at seven in the morning to unload.

Tonight, Ted Mathieson had deliberately left the loading bay doors open, and the driver, Steve Hedland, backed the big lorry inside. Steve had just driven back from a dry food packing facility in southern Germany with sixteen pallets of tinned peas, baked beans, soup and coconut milk.

When Steve climbed out of the cab Mathieson was waiting with a mug of coffee in one hand and a Mars bar taken from his box in the office in the other.

'That was some fucking drive,' Steve said taking the drink and chocolate bar from Mathieson.

'Problems with the law?'

'Nope. Accidents. It seemed every motorway I joined was congested with some pile-up or other.'

'Some parts of southern Germany get a thick early fog. It takes most of the morning to clear.'

'Sounds like it. Any way I'm here now.'

Steve was young, good-looking and smart, not the attributes often associated with long-distance lorry drivers. He wore his hair short and kept his facial hair trim, looking more like a businessman than a commercial driver. Mathieson knew some drivers who liked to wear their hair long and grow bushy beards. Despite the well-publicised 'war on terror' they couldn't understand why their trucks were habitually stopped as they tried to enter the UK.

'No problems with the load?'

'The main or the special?'

'Both.'

'Nothing at all. Want to take a look?'

'I'll wait until you're finished.'

'How's business going?'

'Great. I think I just bagged Clifton Oak Furniture. They're an out-of-town outfit in Chorley.'

'Good to hear. Age and the demands of a pretty wife haven't robbed you of your touch.'

'Cheeky bastard.'

'Clifton want us to do what?'

'Bring wooden furniture they're having in a factory in Croatia over to their main warehouse in Chorley.'

'Pallets?'

'Yep. Fancy it?'

'Not me. I like what I'm doing and so do you.'

'Too right, mate.'

'Ok,' Steve said, screwing up his chocolate bar wrapper and scoring a hole in one when he threw it over a two-metre distance into the bin. 'Let's do this.'

They approached the truck, a Volvo FH, still looking good despite over sixty thousand miles on the clock and after completing a round trip to Southern Germany.

Steve grabbed a set of ladders and positioned them at the side of the cab on the passenger side and climbed up. Leaning behind the wind deflector, he used an electric screwdriver to remove recessed screws and open a compartment not in the original spec drafted by the vehicle's designers in Gothenburg.

He removed the lid and put it to one side.

'How's Otto?' Mathieson asked as Steve worked.

'Getting fatter.'

'I don't think such a thing is possible.'

'He blames Oktoberfest. He can't resist another glass of beer from one of the pretty girls, he says.'

'The toad. He wouldn't know what to do with it if one of them took a shine to him.'

'Couldn't find it under all those layers of fat, I suspect.'

'I'm surprised he hasn't been topped by the Albanian gang he deals with, the way he talks about them, calling them cabbage farmers and pig shaggers.'

'Yeah, that's what he tells us, but to them, he's probably good as gold.'

'You could be right.'

'Here we go, first one out,' Steve said, easing a

large bag out of the long, shallow compartment, high enough and wrapped in oil-soaked paper so the dogs at Dover wouldn't get too excited.

Mathieson caught the bag without trouble. He'd been a fly-half in amateur rugby until a broken collar bone stymied a stellar career, but he was still a solid catcher. He got plenty of practice as the two men had played this gig many times before.

They unloaded six bags, same as last time and the time before. Inside each bag, cocaine, the drug of choice for bored housewives and middle-class dinner parties. They didn't need to do anything more tonight except lock the bags away in a secure box. At five-thirty tomorrow, before the loading bay crew arrived, he would remove the bags and meet his buyer, a dealer from Brighton.

On the street, the twelve kilos of premium coke could be worth anywhere between one-and-a-half to two-and-a-half million pounds. If the buyer doctored it with glucose powder or benzocaine, much more. However, it didn't do to be greedy. The five hundred grand the two men shared every six weeks or so suited them both just fine.

SIX

Henderson stretched. The previous night he'd tossed and turned, the numerous possibilities behind Cindy Longhurst's disappearance flipping around his head like the inside of a washing machine spin programme. At least now he could discount the innocent and frivolous: the hen party, birthday prank, surprise weekend away and a whole raft of other possibilities, as this was now day four.

No one in their right mind would leave a photographic studio open to the elements for this many days, not after spending so much time and money developing it. It was winter outside and strong winds and frost would soon make mincemeat of her room dividers and lighting rigs. The studio also contained other expensive equipment such as cameras, portable lighting units, coffee machine and computers, all easy to sell in the car park of a pub or from a stall at a street market.

The computers, he now knew, were for the use of independent photographers and filmmakers who could hire the studio for a day or a week to make their own videos or film their own photo-shoots. When finished, they used the editing software on the computers to view and amend their work. Someone from a production company might have kidnapped

Cindy, and they had been added to their list of people to talk to.

The forensic team started work in the office at the studio on Saturday morning but found no suspicious fingerprints, suggesting her assailants wore gloves or didn't touch much. The blood on the desk had been analysed and matched to Cindy, no surprise there, but what piqued his interest was Annie Heath telling him that a box of SD cards was missing.

In one scenario running through his head in the wee small hours, the two men went there to retrieve pictures taken by Cindy. In which case, he could understand the removal of a box of SD cards if they believed it contained the pictures they were seeking, but why did they need to take Cindy as well?

In many respects, the results of the forensic team analysis posed more questions than it answered, but in this type of work, not every risk paid off. He grabbed the file and headed off for his eight-thirty meeting.

'Phil,' Henderson said to DC Phil Bentley when the hubbub in the Detectives' Room subsided. 'The investigation into Cindy's background. Did you find anything interesting?'

'Her emails and other correspondence drew a blank. Sure, we found some heated exchanges between her and the Managing Director of the company proposing to drill for shale oil at the Balcombe site, but nothing you could call malicious or threatening.'

'What about other protests she's been involved with?'

'Nothing. Balcombe seemed to be the one she took the most interest in. The others looked like she was making up the numbers. A face in the crowd.'

Henderson sighed. 'A dead-end.'

'Yep, sorry boss. Better news on the financials, though.'

'Let's hear it.'

Sally Graham lifted her papers. 'Six years ago, Cindy received an inheritance from her grandmother of almost half a million pounds.'

'Whoa,' Harry Wallop said, 'that's a lot of loot. My granny left me a photo album and a shit-hole in Dereham to clear out.'

'She moved from her house in Portslade to the house at Hurstpierpoint. Plans for a new studio were drawn up a few months later. It cost a few thousand shy of two hundred grand. Cindy put up half and Ted Mathieson the other half.'

'Does Mathieson own a share in the business, or did he give her a loan?'

'It's a loan. There's a formal agreement between them and Cindy is up to date with her payments. Her studio makes a healthy profit and it's her money rather than her ex-husband's that pays for her daughter's expensive school fees.'

'I checked out Mathieson,' DS Walters said. 'If you remember, gov, a couple of days back I thought his name had cropped up in some previous investigation.'

'And did it?'

'Yep. Operation Skylark was coordinated by the Met in an attempt to put a stop to the flood of methamphetamines coming into London. They raided dozens of addresses including one owned by Brighton drug dealer, Charlie McQueen. There, they found some of Ted Mathieson's business cards. McQueen said it was because his mother was shipping some stuff abroad, but the team came across no evidence to back up his claims. They talked to Mathieson, but without a warrant, which they didn't have any grounds to demand, Mathieson gave them short shrift.'

'As he was entitled to do,' Henderson said. 'They went fishing without a rod.'

'Quite.'

'Sally, did you manage to examine Cindy's other financials, her credit cards and bank accounts?'

'I did and it turned out to be an easier process than normal. She kept all the statements in her office but I found nothing to ring any alarm bells.'

He sighed 'Another one off a rapidly depleting list. We've still got the forensic search of the house, the interviews with her family, ex-boyfriends and the photos to come but I'm loathe to even think of looking at the photos. We've no idea what we'd be looking for and if the kidnappers found what they came for.'

This elicited relieved laugher from several of those present. No one fancied undertaking such a mammoth and thankless task.

'One area we haven't discussed is the questioning of Cindy's customers. We've got people who come in for a sitting, such as a family, or in the case of Maggie Hyatt, individuals. We've also got businesses that hire the studio and gardens for the day or the week and bring in their own people. With the non-businesses,

Sally, check their names against the PNC and see if anyone's got form. For businesses, and with a bit of luck there won't be as many, you'll need to find out the names of the employees who came on-site. Run them against the PNC, and check out the company, see if they're being investigated by any agency.'

The Police National Computer, PNC, contained a record of all criminal acts. Names could be entered to determine if suspects had previously committed an offence and if any prosecutions were pending.

Sally Graham nodded as she took note.

'Before you say it sounds like a lot of work, I agree. Gerry Hobbs, as I'm sure you all know is now a DI in the Drugs Unit, has agreed to lend us some bodies.'

'Good,' Graham said, 'we could use them.'

'Right,' Henderson said, emitting an audible sigh, frustration evident at not finding a lead. 'Over to you, Harry, for an update on the search.'

DS Harry Wallop lifted the papers in his hand. 'For reasons I suspect are something to do with the fact that the missing woman looks, how should I say—'

'A cracker,' Phil Bentley said.

'Photogenic, I was about to say, the papers have lapped it up. Her picture's been all over the local rags and she's even been on the telly, on South Today.'

'Good work, Harry.'

'We've had a number of calls, the more credible ones we've responded to, but so far nothing worth pursuing.'

'It's a shame we still don't have *Crimewatch*. What about hospitals?'

He shook his head. 'Dead end I'm afraid.'

'Is her picture out with patrols, on notice boards and so on?'

'It is. We're even getting cooperation from a couple of councils who've put it up on their websites and social media accounts.'

'Good. Keep the pressure on with the appeals and follow-ups, it might just jog someone's memory.'

'Will do.'

'Continue pushing this one, people,' Henderson said as he gathered his papers together. 'I'm convinced Cindy is still alive but we're running out of time. I'll see you all again at this evening's update meeting. Six-thirty, sharp.'

Henderson walked back to his office, a sense of foreboding at the back of his mind. There had to be something more they could do to give them a clue as to why someone would kidnap Cindy Longhurst: a successful photographer with no apparent enemies. He knew from previous experience of kidnaps, the longer this went on, the less chance they had of finding her alive. When the kidnappers had got what they wanted, be it sex, money, information, they would most likely kill her. He put the time period at a couple of days not weeks.

'Ah, there you are, Angus,' Detective Chief Inspector Lisa Edwards said as she came striding towards him. 'It's early and yet you look harassed. Where have you been, a team meeting about the Longhurst case?'

'Got it in one.' He walked into his office and threw the folder he carried on the small conference meeting table and sat down. Edwards took the seat opposite.

CI Edwards was a tall, stocky blonde from West Yorkshire. While blondes were reputed to open their mouths before connecting with their brains, women from her part of the world had a reputation for talking straight, if not on occasion downright blunt. The hair today was tied back in a ponytail. This not only emphasised the tiredness and lines around her eyes, the result of manpower shortages, a burgeoning overtime bill and a crap time over the Christmas break when her husband walked out and failed to return.

'What's the latest?' she asked.

'I'd love to tell you why I think she's been taken, never mind by who, or where, but I can't even do that.'

'No dodgy deals with back-street financiers, jealous ex-husbands or angry disputes with neighbours?'

Henderson shook his head. 'She's no wall flower, building a successful photographic studio after her divorce and still finding time to protest about a host of big issues. Having examined her finances and the people she associated with, only one sticks out. He's an ex-boyfriend who bombarded her with texts.'

Okay, and what about this Ted Mathieson character? In my time I've known a lot of dodgy guys in the haulage business.'

'It was Mathieson who lent Cindy some of the money to finance the building of the studio. She wasn't in arrears with the payments.'

'Maybe he needed to get his investment back pronto and she refused, or couldn't come up with the cash.'

'According to Cindy's assistant, Annie Heath, they were the best of friends. He'd come over and see her every month or so and take her out to lunch.'

'A true gentleman. There's not many of them about,' Edwards said, a dark look passing across her face. 'Maybe he wanted something more than a business relationship and she didn't.'

Henderson smiled. 'If he did kidnap her, it's a hell of a queer way to try and impress a woman.'

'Aye you're right, it's a bit too caveman for me too. Talk to Mathieson, find out what he's got to say about her disappearance.'

'I intend to.'

'Where do we go from here? Her picture's everywhere, if anyone spots her they know we're looking for her. Hospitals, what about them?'

'Harry's group ran a check on those in Sussex, Surrey and Kent. No sign.'

'Okay. What's next?'

'We'll continue to plug away with wall posters and newspaper updates. On the research side, we're all set to trawl through her customers. We'll also be talking to her ex-husband, ex-boyfriend and of course, Ted Mathieson.'

Edwards stood to go. 'It sounds like you've covered all the bases. Just as well as I've got a bad feeling about this one.'

'What makes you say that?'

'I investigated a similar case in Leeds three years back involving a woman in her early forties. The killer kept her in captivity for five days, raped her time after time and beat her up almost as often. When he'd finished with her, he dumped her lifeless body in a quarry.'

'You caught him?'

'Oh, yes. A neighbour, three doors down. Let's hope here,' she said with a sigh, 'we don't see the same result. See you later.'

SEVEN

'What goes on in this place?' Walters asked as she closed the car door.

'The manufacture of engineering products for industry, their website says, but don't ask me to explain what it means.'

They had driven into an industrial estate in Jubilee Way, Burgess Hill, and were now standing outside a long, grey building with the name Harris Manufacturing Ltd in bold blue letters above their heads. Along the walls of the building sat broken pallets and metal cages containing all manner of rusted junk.

'Do you think I'm going to need overalls and a hair net?'

'Cindy's ex is an accountant, not an engineer.'

They walked inside and Henderson realised Walters's earlier question about clothing didn't sound so fanciful. The Reception area looked grubby, as if the folks out in the manufacturing floor, which could be seen through a large and scratched Perspex window, came traipsing through here regularly. Out there, he could see a huge machine and inside it, a tool spinning at fantastic speed, sheering millimetres off the surface of a static piece of metal.

'Detectives Walters and Henderson to see Greg

Jackson,' the DI said to the receptionist when the phone was no longer clamped to her ear.

'I'm not sure he's free. Our Managing Director, Mr Richardson, is trying to expedite an urgent order.'

'I don't care how busy he is,' Henderson said, 'I want to see him now.'

'I don't think—'

'Listen, Ms Fenwick,' Henderson said, following a glance at her name tag. 'If you don't call him now, we'll head upstairs ourselves and take him back with us to Lewes. With luck we might return him in about three hours.'

'There's no need to take that tone with me. I'm only doing my job,' she said, her exaggerated body language conveying more than her words. She picked up the phone, 'I'll see if he's available.'

A few minutes later they were seated inside a small meeting room. The walls were coffee-coloured, the table and seats looking as though they'd been rescued from a second-hand furniture shop and the room exuding all the charm of an undertaker's waiting room.

'What a dump this place is,' Walters said, taking a seat with some reluctance. 'If they're making any money, they sure aren't spending it on the meeting rooms.'

'They're making money all right but I think the MD and senior managers are creaming off most of it. Did you see the cars around the side of the building?'

'I thought they belonged to the company next door.'

'No, they're parked in spaces reserved for this

place.'

'The big Merc and a couple of BMWs?'

'They could be leased, of course, but the website listed all the big airlines they dealt with and talked of a full order book.'

'I take it back then.'

The door opened and a man walked in wearing the harassed face of someone who'd got out of bed on the wrong side or wished he'd stayed there.

'Hello. I'm Greg Jackson,' he said holding out his hand for the officers to shake.

'Detective Inspector Henderson and this is Detective Sergeant Walters, Surrey and Sussex Police, Major Crime Team.'

'You said on the phone this has something to do with my ex-wife, but for the last few years I've had nothing to do with her. She not my responsibility any more. So, if you don't mind, I'd like to get back to my department. My boss is going ape-shit and some of my colleagues are in tears.'

'Mr Jackson, close the door and come and sit down. This will take as long as we need. We are here on an important matter which takes preference over any issues your boss may have.'

'Try telling that to Richardson,' he said as he closed the door.

'I will if he dares to interrupt.'

Jackson was of average height, with light brown thinning hair, and wore a tired grey suit that had seen better days. He spoke in a West Country accent with the added texture of a pronounced nasal tone, indicative perhaps of a sinus complaint. In

Henderson's experience on meeting one side of a divorced couple, it was often the woman who didn't look to be wearing well, but based on the many pictures he'd viewed of Cindy, the roles here were reversed.

'Mr Jackson, I'm sure you're aware that your former wife, Cindy, has recently gone missing, believed kidnapped?'

'How could I not be? My daughter was dumped on my doorstep by one of your lot and the story's been all over the front pages and television for days. On social media people are taking about nothing else, some suggesting I must be hiding her in my basement or some other rubbish.'

'Are you?'

'What, keeping her in my basement? You're having a laugh. I live in a crappy new-build in Burgess Hill with such a small garden the trees next door block out the sun. So, no, I don't have a basement.'

'Garden shed, maybe?'

'Nowhere. I was glad to get shot of her if you must know.'

'Surely not, sir,' Walters said, a mischievous tone in her voice, 'when she received such a large amount of money in her grandmother's will?'

'You know about that?'

She nodded.

He sighed, perhaps loath to re-visit painful memories. 'We've been divorced for seven years and about a year after it happened, her grandmother died and left her a shed-load of money. I told her that me and Jamie deserved half. For sure, we'd split the finances at the break-up, but I visited the old woman as much as she did.'

'How did she respond?'

'She said she was putting some of the money in trust for Jamie when he reached twenty-one but she told me to get lost. As far as she was concerned, we settled all the financials during the divorce.'

'You didn't agree.'

'Too right I didn't bloody agree. I even took legal advice. As I said, I liked the old woman and went to see her as much as Cindy did.'

'What did you think when she invested the money in a big house in Hurstpierpoint and a new studio?' Henderson asked.

'I felt well pissed when I first heard, but despite not giving us a bean she's a great photographer. I didn't doubt she'd make a success of it.'

'Do you think she has?'

There was a loud rapping on the glass and Henderson turned to see a man in a tailored suit, perfectly cut to fit his portly frame, tapping an expensive-looking watch and walking away.

'That's Richardson telling me to hurry up.'

'We won't keep you much longer, sir.'

'I hope not or it'll make him even madder than he is now.'

'We were talking about Cindy's studio,' Henderson said.

'Yes, I think she's made a success of it. The place is always busy and it's the go-to studio for video makers who use the fields outside to film adverts for butter and yogurt and all that crap.'

'How are the children taking the news?' Walters asked.

He sighed. 'It's hit Molly really hard. Not only is her mother missing, she's not in her own house with her own things. Jamie, who's seventeen, didn't take our divorce well. Maybe that's how all teenage boys behave, I don't know. He hated my wife for splitting us up but I didn't turn his head. Let's just say he's less upset about the current situation than his sister, and secretly pleased to have Molly around.'

'Can you think of any reason why someone would want to kidnap your ex-wife?' Henderson asked.

'To shut her up, she never stops talking. Now that I think about it, that could be counter-productive as she'd never stop haranguing the kidnappers over the injustice of it all.'

'Was she in debt to anyone, did she do drugs?'

'She's got no debt that I know about and didn't drink. She didn't agree with drugs.'

'Is there anything in her past you think might come back to haunt her?'

'No, I don't think so...but wait. About four years ago, she was involved in a bad car accident. She knocked a guy off his bike, crushing his legs and leaving him in a wheelchair.'

'Sounds serious. Was she hurt?'

'No, she wasn't hurt and the accident wasn't her fault. It was a filthy wet night in Brighton and she was driving along the Old Shoreham Road.'

He looked up, distracted at something going on in the outer office. With an annoyed scowl and a flick of the wrist he indicated to whoever was outside, clearly not his boss, to go away.

'She hadn't been drinking,' Jackson continued, 'and driving at less than the speed limit when a cyclist came out of nowhere. He was coming down Park View Road, no lights and it didn't seem like he was braking. He skidded under the front wheels of the car crushing his legs. She hadn't been drinking like I say, but the cyclist tested positive for cannabis. The police didn't charge her.'

Henderson couldn't recall hearing anything about this in their discussions about background checks. Perhaps with no charges being brought, no details were documented. He would ask someone to look into it.

'It's an interesting story,' Henderson said, 'but I would imagine it would be difficult for a bloke in a wheelchair to kidnap anyone.'

'I'm not so much talking about him, but his family. His dad, Tony Mitchell, is a builder and his other two sons are built like brick shit-houses. They were very bitter when they heard the police verdict, telling the papers that no mistake, sometime in the future Cindy would get her just desserts.'

**

They left the meeting at Harris Manufacturing five minutes later. Greg Jackson showed them to the door, but on the way, he got collared by the MD who gave the hapless accountant a dressing down for keeping him waiting.

'I wouldn't want to work for a tyrant like him,'

Walters said as she climbed into the car.

'Me neither. He just about tore the man's head off.'

'What did you make of–'

Henderson's phone rang. After a brief conversation, he dropped the phone back into his pocket, reversed the car and shot out of the industrial estate while still clipping up his seatbelt.

'What's the big rush?'

'Harry Wallop received a call a few minutes ago from a dog walker. Yesterday evening in Wild Park, from a bit of a distance away mark you, the caller said she saw a bloke lift a large bag from the boot of his car and drag it into the woods. It looked heavy but she thought no more about it until she picked up last night's paper at breakfast and read an article about Cindy Longhurst's disappearance.'

'Christ, it took her until this morning to put two and two together? I thought her picture was all over the place.'

'It is, but at least now it sounds like we've got a positive lead.'

'Positive, yes if it points us to our missing woman, but negative as it means she's dead.'

'I know, but we need to confirm it one way or another.'

Morning traffic was light and they made the journey from Burgess Hill in less than twenty minutes. By the time they parked close to three police vehicles, the search was only just getting underway. At over 140-acres in size, it was the biggest park in Brighton. He hoped the search team had a specific area to focus their efforts on, otherwise it would take more than the twenty-odd officers Harry had deployed to find anything.

It looked to Henderson as if the woman holding the leash of a glossy Cocker Spaniel, now talking to DS Wallop, was their witness. She had obviously just remembered the place where she saw the man the previous evening, because Wallop lifted his radio and seconds later, the search team changed direction. They were now focussing their efforts on a narrow band of ground on the north side. He approached the pair.

'Morning sir.'

'Morning Harry.'

'This is Mrs Jenny Davis, the lady who saw someone unloading a heavy object last night.'

Henderson shook her hand, hoping it wasn't the one used to pick up the dog's poo, evidenced by the blue bag in her other hand.

'Thank you for contacting us Mrs Davis.'

'I wish I'd called you last night. I knew about the missing woman, but I didn't make a connection with the car in the park until I read an article in *The Argus* this morning.'

'Good job you did.'

'I said to my husband, Eddie...'

Henderson was half-listening as he watched the activities of the searchers. In a wide line, they were now making their way slowly into thick woods.

'...he said to me, Jenny, you need to pick up that phone and call the police. So, I did.'

'Thank you for doing so. Harry, I'll take a walk over there and join the search team.'

'See you later, boss.'

Henderson walked towards the trees, Walters beside him.

'You extricated yourself expertly there, gov, she's the type who could buttonhole you for a couple of hours.'

'If the mischief took hold, which it didn't, I was about to suggest you could look after her and take her statement.'

'Good job you didn't.'

They parted the branches and dipped inside the cover of trees. It looked to be a dense wood from a distance, but they found they could walk easily between the trunks as they were spaced a few metres apart, and the thick composition of the canopy overhead left the undergrowth sparse and easy to negotiate. It took a few minutes to catch up with the search team as they were making rapid progress too.

'I can't see a guy dragging a heavy bundle much further than this, gov.'

'I'm thinking the same thing.' Henderson reached for his phone to call Wallop to tell him this didn't look like the right area, when he heard a shout.

Many of the officers broke away from their regimented line to locate the voice, Henderson and Walters followed. A minute or so later, they found the search team gathered around what appeared to be a hollow about four metres across. Henderson pushed through the crowd of bodies to see what everyone was looking at.

At the base of the hollow, a pile of broken bricks, wall render, smashed glass and bent pipes, into which a couple of coppers were carefully sifting.

A few minutes later one of the officers looked up and saw Henderson. 'There's nothing under it, sir. Some bastard has littered this fine park where I take my kids every Sunday with all the crap from a demolished conservatory.'

EIGHT

Henderson parked his dirty Audi estate beside a sparkling clean and beautiful red Ferrari 488 GTB. Ignoring the protests by DS Walters about the cold and biting wind, he stood for a moment to admire the gleaming paintwork, the stunning lines of the body styling, the alloy wheels and its sumptuous interior.

He wondered if all the accessories he could see, the satnav, digital radio, leather seats and all the rest were included in the one hundred thousand pounds plus list price. With every car he'd ever looked at, the enticing quoted price was thousands of pounds less than the final price paid after installing a range of 'optional accessories' that many owners considered essential.

'Can we go inside now?' Walters said, exasperation evident in her voice. 'I'm freezing my socks off out here.'

'It's a good job the car doors aren't open,' he said as they walked towards the entrance of Mathieson Transport, 'then you'd never get me away.'

'Praise be.'

The receptionist had been expecting them and, without much delay, led them upstairs to Ted Mathieson's office. On seeing the officers approaching, Mathieson put the phone down and came out to meet them.

'Can I get you anything before we sit down,' he said after introductions. 'Tea, coffee, water?'

'Coffee for me,' Henderson said.

'And for me,' Walters said.

'Three coffees, Andrea, and close the door behind you. Oh, and Andrea, hold my calls.'

'This is a nice office, Mr Mathieson,' Henderson said, taking a seat facing Mathieson's desk. It was a bright and airy room with modern furniture, television on the wall, glass-fronted cabinets and not an unpleasant view over the tops of neighbouring businesses, the grey sea lurking in the distance.

'It's not bad. Most people think of offices in transport companies as being small, an in-tray full of grubby invoices, a bin overflowing with empty paper cups and girlie calendars on the wall. We've got one of those. It's called the Dispatch Office, but it's downstairs.'

Mathieson was a sharp dresser, a chubby figure neatly attired in a well-trimmed blue striped suit, white shirt and a patterned tie, suitable attire Henderson imagined, to sit behind the wheel of the expensive vehicle outside. However, the stylish accoutrements couldn't disguise the face: a hard expression, one not familiar with smiling. When added to the hawk-like eyes, it gave an overall look that wouldn't seem out of place in a police mug-shot.

'We're here, Mr Mathieson because we are investigating the disappearance of photographer, Cindy Longhurst.'

'Bloody odd it is. Cindy's the last person someone

could hold a grudge against. She's kind, generous, would help anyone in trouble. You've probably heard about her protest activities, well it just sums her up. She can't just sit on the sofa stuffing her face with biscuits and watching soaps like most people. When she sees something out there that she perceives as an example of injustice, or indifferent government, she'll let people know she doesn't agree with it. Ah, here's the coffee.'

Andrea's timing was good as just then, the loud roar of a lorry gunning its massive engine filled the air and rattled the windows of Mathieson's office, making conversation impossible. A few seconds later, the noise faded into the distance when the truck left the yard and made its way towards its destination.

'What's your relationship with Cindy, Mr Mathieson?' Henderson asked after Andrea had left the room and closed the door.

Mathieson sat back in his chair, comfortable to be asked an easy question.

'I gave her a loan to help start her business.'

'How did that come about?'

'If we wind the clock back eight, nine years, her ex-husband Greg Jackson used to work for me.'

'Yes, we know.'

'You maybe didn't know he doesn't work here now because I sacked him.'

He was right, Henderson didn't know. 'Why did you do that?'

'Incompetence, pure and simple. A couple of people in the loading bay crew, I won't mention their names, were on the fiddle. Anything and everything, it didn't matter, they nicked goods from lorries, diesel from the store and personal stuff from the lockers of other drivers. Jackson, as my finance guy, should have spotted it earlier but he didn't. At first, I suspected he was in collusion with the thieves and trying to cover it up, you know, but I realised he was too dumb and scared to be involved in something like that.'

'So, you sacked him.'

'Him and the two thieves, but not before the other members of the crew got a hold of them and handed out their own form of justice.'

This was a story he no doubt told down the pub on a Friday night, the aggrieved drivers getting their own back on the guys with the temerity to steal their things. 'You don't expect me to condone the taking of the law into your own hands, do you, sir?'

'I suppose not.'

'Was it through Greg that you met Cindy?'

'Yeah, before the fiddling started, myself and my wife, the one before the current Mrs Mathieson, used to socialise with them. Cindy's great fun and she and I get along like a house on fire. After a time, she realised her husband didn't like going out in a foursome and neither did my wife. So, the two of us would meet for lunch or dinner whenever the notion took.'

'How did the investment in her business come about?'

'She bought a big house in Hurstpierpoint after she received a large inheritance from her grandmother...' He looked over at Henderson who nodded.

'The house came with a couple of acres of land and

one day she came up with the idea for a studio. Not just a room to take photos, but a fully-equipped photographic suite where filmmakers can come and shoot videos and make adverts. I must admit, I was sceptical at first, but Cindy can be persuasive when she sets her mind on something, and right from the off, she made it work. It's now one of the main studios in the south and profitable too.'

'It's a bit of a departure from this,' Henderson said, casting an arm around the office, 'to a photography studio.'

For a moment, Mathieson looked shifty, as if a feeling of guilt had passed over. Maybe for not telling his new wife about the loan, although Henderson doubted she would notice. Mathieson didn't look short of money.

'Sure, it's the first time I've spent big money on something outside the world that I know, transport and distribution. However, I invested not so much in the photography business, which I admit I know bugger-all about, but in her. I invested in Cindy. She told me she could make it work and I had faith in her.' He tapped his forefinger on the desk. 'She pays me on the nail every month.'

'Where were you on the night she disappeared: Friday 26th January?'

He picked up a fat desk dairy, and even at this early stage in the year, it looked to be well used.

'Ah, I was there,' he said smiling. He snapped the diary shut. 'I don't know if you remember, but there was a big outbreak of flu just before Christmas. Half the buses in Brighton weren't running because of it.'

Henderson nodded. 'We were short-staffed too.'

'I've got a nine-year-old. I've got two grown up kids as well by my first wife, so it's second-time round for me doing all this school stuff again, but to tell you the truth, I love it. A load of teachers and pupils at my daughter's school came down with flu a week before the Christmas break and couldn't put on the big play they'd been rehearsing. The night Cindy went missing, I was watching Snow White do her rescheduled thing with her seven little men at Hurstpierpoint College.'

This rang a bell in Henderson's head. Cindy's daughter, Molly, also went to Hurstpierpoint College.

'Can anyone verify your attendance?'

'Sure, I talked to a number of people that night. I'll write down their names if you like.'

When finished, he handed the paper to Henderson. The DI glanced at it before asking, 'What do you think has happened to Cindy?'

'Christ, I wish I knew. I'd tie them to the back of one of my lorries and drag them around Newhaven for an hour. Cindy's a dear, dear friend of mine and I hope to God you find her soon, safe and well.'

Five minutes later, the detectives left Mathieson's office and walked back to the car.

'I believe him,' Henderson said.

'Me too. I think the sincerity he showed back there is hard to fake.'

'It is. However, I'm tempted to take a look into the financials of his company and find out how profitable this business really is. I've always believed transport companies ran on tight margins, especially if they're working so closely with national supermarkets as

Mathieson does.'

'Me too.'

'If so, how come,' he said as he started the car and headed back to Lewes, 'he's got such a fantastic car, smart office and, no doubt, a very expensive house?'

'You said you're only tempted.'

'I think it's a distraction we can all do without.'

'Maybe you could–'

Henderson's phone rang. He pressed 'receive' on the steering wheel and the voice of DS Harry Wallop boomed through the car's speakers.

'Morning, sir.'

'Morning, Harry.'

'I hate to say it, but we have another sighting.'

'What is this,' Henderson said, looking at Walters in amazement, 'Groundhog Day?'

'What do you mean?'

'Yesterday when you called about the Wild Park sighting we were on the point of leaving Harris Manufacturing after talking to Greg Jackson. Today you've called as we're coming out of Mathieson Transport after seeing Ted Mathieson. What is it this time, a load of old cars?'

'It's another sighting I'm afraid, sir, but I guarantee it's not another pile of rubble. There's a body and I think it's our missing woman.'

**

Henderson had driven through Saltdean numerous times but he couldn't recall ever stopping there. This part of East Sussex from Rottingdean to Peacehaven was dotted with thousands of bungalows and hundreds of retirement homes. They were occupied in the main by the aged, living on the south coast to benefit from the sunshine, sea air and bracing walks along the tops of spectacular cliffs.

The naked body of Cindy Longhurst lay at the bottom of one of those cliffs. He knew it was Cindy as soon as he saw her; he'd looked at her picture every day, every working hour, for the past week. He needed to look hard, mind you, as her face and body were bloody, bruised and battered, not from falling off the cliff tops some forty metres above his head, but from being beaten before receiving a bullet to the head. This wasn't his theory, but the educated initial assessment of the pathologist, Grafton Rawlings, currently kneeling down on the pebbles beside the corpse.

Henderson felt sick. Despite being aware of the low probability of finding her alive due to the violent nature of her abduction, he had harboured a measure of hope that they would. Call it blind optimism or something about the case that gave him hope, he couldn't say, but the sight of her broken and battered body lying on the stones hit him hard.

He could see Walters standing on the under-cliff walkway, talking to the person who found her, a dog walker with a lively pooch that couldn't keep out of the water despite the cold temperatures. Once again, Henderson knelt down opposite the pathologist.

He didn't say anything for a few minutes before he looked at Henderson.

'I would say she hasn't been here long, perhaps

dumped a few hours back when it was still dark. She has a number of injuries and maybe a few broken bones, but I can't be sure until I get her back to the mortuary. What I can say with some degree of certainty is her injuries didn't kill her. The bullet to the head certainly did.'

'Has she been in the water?'

'No. So, we can rule out being transported here by the tide. She was definitely dumped here.'

He heard a crunching noise and looked up to see two people approaching.

'Here come the stretcher bearers.'

Henderson stood and stretched his tired muscles.

Walters finished talking to her witness and walked over to join the DI.

'There's no vehicle access down here, according to our witness,' Walters said. 'Therefore, he or they must have dragged or carried the body all the way down here.'

'It might be restricted access for the public, they don't want cars driving up and down the under-cliff walkway and annoying pedestrians and running over dogs, but vehicles must be able to get down here. How else could they build and maintain the walkway?'

'I didn't think of that, but if they did come down here in a vehicle in the middle of the night, who would notice one car or a van? There wouldn't be anyone around.'

'Yeah, especially in winter. Call the office and get some more people down here. We need to know how they did it. Once we've established the where and the how, get a team moving door-to-door and see if there are any insomniacs in the houses nearby, or if anyone was woken by the noise of a vehicle at some ungodly hour.'

'I'm on it.'

'In many respects, it's not a bad place to dump a body. In winter, only a few people walk along the beach, especially if the weather's inclement. Come high tide, the sea will help to wash away clues and aid decomposition. Maybe by finding the body before that happened, we've bought ourselves a slice of luck for a change.'

NINE

Mike Harrison loved to paint. He could turn his hand to most things: plastering, woodwork, bricklaying, but painting was his passion. Not only did it give him time to do some daydreaming, as pushing the roller up and down didn't require much concentration, but the results were instantaneous, ergo one happy customer.

In his line of work, a self-employed handyman, he could be anywhere in Sussex, Surrey or Kent doing a job. The cost of fuel not only ate into his profits, but with each new piece of work he didn't know what he'd find until he got there. It could be a flooded house, the limb of a tree embedded in a smashed roof, or rotting windows and rotting everything else.

What he liked, and what every other self-employed tradesman he knew wanted to get their hands on was a steady job. He'd worked at Hillcrest House, near Shermanbury, for almost a year. The house was built in the 1800s but had been considerably remodelled since the businessman who owned it bought it ten years ago. Despite the extensive renovation, any old house required regular maintenance, and with a customer as fastidious as this one, all the little updates and changes he wanted created plenty of work for Harrison.

He finished the first coat of Peachy Pink but didn't

step back to admire his handiwork. He knew how good it would be without looking, and in any case, he was desperate for a fag and a cup of tea. He tidied up his workspace in the event someone should walk in, not that anyone would, the owner was at work at his wine business in Brighton while his wife, Julia, would still be in bed. Julia was what his barbed-tongued elderly mother would call a 'soak'. A woman who would spend the morning buying clothes, enjoying coffee with her friends before cracking open a bottle of Sauvignon Blanc while watching the afternoon soaps.

He didn't know for sure, he didn't come to the house every day, but piecing together her morning-after face, the empty bottles and occasional pieces of broken furniture or a door he was required to fix, she would often be drunk by the time her husband came home. Harrison had been married and his ex-missus liked a drink, but he would've given her hell if he ever came home and found her drunk. She couldn't drink in the afternoons anyway, tradesmen like him weren't paid as much as self-made businessmen, and she had to work for a living, teaching special-needs children how to read and write.

Harrison wouldn't put it past the husband to give her a good smack now and again. He'd never seen any evidence of this, but it didn't stop him speculating. He liked to gossip as much as the next man.

Julia Webster was a good-looking woman with wavy shoulder length blonde hair, a slight frame and the most piercing blue eyes he'd ever seen. Once or twice he'd found himself standing outside her bedroom door, his hand inching towards the handle.

Her bedroom was down the hall from the spare room he was painting and it would be a simple thing to do, turn the handle and walk in. She liked him, he knew she did, and wouldn't be fazed by his presence, but he was wary of her husband.

Today, he walked past Julia's bedroom without a sideways glance and headed downstairs. The housekeeper nodded a curt 'hello' as she dusted a mirror, but never did he receive a smile from the miserable cow. He opened the back door and took his familiar seat on the bench facing the fields. He never tired of the view: woods to one side, open and rolling hills in front and more woods on the other side. It changed from season to season and now in early February, the grass was covered in a silver sheen and the trees all huddled together in the breeze as if trying to keep warm.

He filled a cup with tea from his flask and sparked up, sending out a large cloud of smoke and condensation into the air. In the early days of his apprenticeship as a painter, the old guys used to warn him about the danger of having open flames near oil-based paints and spirits. It was good advice as he'd once seen a couple of guys become engulfed in flames and he'd heard that fumes absorbed by clothes could become a fire hazard even when the painter returned home. It wasn't a worry nowadays, most household paints were water-based and didn't produce any fumes, inflammable or otherwise.

He put down his cup and pulled a newspaper out of his pocket. The first few pages were politics which he ignored, unless it was something about the pernicious influence the EU were having on this country, and turned to the news section. He almost set the paper on fire after dropping his cigarette into the middle when the main story on page five hit him like a hammer. Cindy Longhurst had been found dead.

He couldn't believe it and read the short article again and again. He knew how reporters worked. Stories like this were penned from the scant information they could glean while standing behind police tape and thrusting their recorders into the faces of stoic policemen. The story would fill out in a day or two as by then they'd have attended a press conference and received a press release. Then, if he bought several newspapers, they would all be carrying the same story, often with the same bits of the press release quoted word for word.

He sat back, the newspaper on his lap, the cigarette burning un-smoked between his fingers. He knew Cindy well. They'd met here, at Hillcrest House, he repairing some glass in a conservatory window, broken by a pissed Julia or high winds, and Cindy taking photographs of the family and the house.

She had been cool towards him at the start, in his experience women often were, but when she got to know him and saw his true self, a relationship developed. They'd been happy for about three months but it ended on a sour note, even by his standards. He was bereft and it devastated him to lose the best, most intelligent, most driven woman he had ever known.

His subsequent errant behaviour when he bombarded her with texts and calls was due to grief at losing this fabulous woman, but also the anger he felt at being used. He couldn't put a finger on the reason why, but looking back, it felt like she'd flicked a switch when they'd first met. After three months, when she'd had her fill of his bad jokes, his poor hygiene and lamentable parsimony, she turned the switch off and walked away.

In truth, the relationship didn't always run smoothly. Whenever she stayed over at his place, she complained about how he lived, the food he ate and, first thing in the morning, commandeered the bathroom. All his shaving gear was shoved to one side and more than once, he had to rescue his caffeine-infused shampoo, designed to thicken his rapidly thinning hair, from the bin.

The noise of dogs barking reminded him of something else. In the woods, he'd been told, were a long line of kennels where the owner bred dogs, pit bulls she said. Cindy had asked him about them a number of times and teased him when she found out he hated dogs. He wouldn't dare go near them.

She'd only spent a couple of days at Hillcrest House, but whenever Harrison returned from working there she would often ask how often the owner visited the kennels, did other people go there, had he looked inside the kennels? Cindy was an avid political campaigner and her concern for dumb animals was touching, but he'd tell her, no, no, no. He'd never been there and would never go near so many dogs even with someone pointing a gun at his head.

He looked at his watch and realised he'd been sitting outside longer than intended, not that it bothered him. He was paid for work completed, not for how long it took. It only mattered now as he felt cold. He walked inside, his body shivering.

'How are you getting on upstairs?'

Julia stood there, leaning against the door frame of the kitchen, her slim figure encased in a tight dress, emphasising every curve. She must have gone easy on the sauce last night as her face looked normal, beautiful even, with none of the puffiness in her cheeks and bags under her eyes that he'd often see.

'The first coat is done,' he said. 'I'll do some of the woodwork now and in the afternoon, I'll give the walls another coat.'

'Will it be finished by the end of next week? My sister's coming for a few days and I want to put her in there.'

'Oh, no problem.'

'Will the room smell of smoke?'

'What? Why would it?'

'Because you stink of it,' she said, before turning and walking back into the kitchen.

'Bitch,' Harrison muttered under his breath as he climbed the stairs.

He reached the top floor, his anger seething as he walked past her room thinking he should go in there and steal something that would break her heart to lose. He stopped and turned, determined to do that very thing, when his phone rang.

It was a number he didn't recognise, not unusual in his game but for once he wished it was from someone he knew.

'Mike Harrison.'

'Mr Harrison, good morning. This is Detective

Constable Sally Graham, Surrey and Sussex police. I hope I haven't caught you at a bad time.'

He'd felt better, but he would take his revenge on the acerbic Julia Webster later. 'No, it's fine.'

'We'd like to talk to you about the kidnap and murder of Cindy Longhurst. When are you free?'

TEN

'How are you getting on with that problem you had with your landlord?' DC Phil Bentley asked his car companion, DC Lisa Newman.

'Which one? There's been so many.'

'The leaking shower from upstairs.'

'Oh that, we've been nagging him for so long about it, I've almost given up.'

'Haven't you got a big hole in your ceiling?'

'Yeah,' she sighed, 'it's now a talking point when anyone comes round. He says he's got so many other properties to deal with, he'll get to me eventually.'

Lisa Newman was the newest and youngest member of the team, taking the age accolade away from Sally Graham, who at twenty-three now spoke like an old-hand. Newman was fast-track, a university graduate with a post-graduate diploma in criminal law. Bentley had done it the hard way, worked his way up from uniform, and tended to resent the fast-track kids who knew the theory but with bugger-all life experience to back it up. For reasons he couldn't explain, he didn't feel the same way about Lisa. She was smart and savvy and good-looking to boot.

'Where did you go to uni?' he asked.

'Imperial College.'

'Did you live in halls?'

'God no, I couldn't afford to.'

'Didn't your parents...'

'Nope. My dad's a taxi driver and my mother can't work because of her arthritis. I'm one of the many unwashed with a bloody great student loan to pay off.'

'You don't need to pay it back if you work abroad, do you?'

'That's right.'

'After a couple of years in Sussex, you could get a transfer to Europol or Interpol.'

'Trying to get rid of me already?'

'No, no I'm just...I don't know, just talking.'

'I could do, but it would only be for a few years. When I came back, they would start charging me all over again.'

'Another good Bentley idea down the toilet.'

He guided the car through a left turn before the satnav piped up and told him he had reached his destination.

'Not bad looking houses around here,' Newman said. 'I thought the areas around Portslade and Southwick were full of first-time buyer houses but some of these are huge.'

They drove slowly along The Green in Southwick looking for the house belonging to the Mitchell family. Mum and Dad would be at home as Bentley had called ahead and made an appointment.

'There it is,' Newman said. 'It stands to reason a bloody builder would own the biggest house in the area.'

'It's not a bad place to live,' Bentley said as he parked the car. 'Detached houses away from neighbours and a fine view of The Green.'

'It depends on where you live and what happens out there at night,' Newman said as she got out of the car. 'The place where I used to live in East London, on a summer's evening on a patch of grass as big as this, people would be shooting-up, dealers would be everywhere, kids would be tearing up the turf doing wheelie turns on their bikes and dogs with no obvious owner would be taking a dump.'

'I don't think they see much of that around here,' Bentley said as they approached the house.

'It's Friday night. We'll see when we get back to the car if it's still there and in one piece.'

Tony Mitchell greeted them at the door and without offering much in the way of a greeting or a handshake, invited them in. He was a big guy, about six-two and well-built, but what might have been muscles in his twenties and thirties had turned to fat now. All the same, Bentley wouldn't fancy being on the receiving end of one of his fists. They looked like the business end of a couple of sledgehammers.

A traditional style of house on the outside gave way to a modern looking place on the inside, with wooden floors, a large, flat-screen television hung on the wall and pieces of art, watercolour views of landmarks along the Sussex Coast, dotted around.

Tony Mitchell slumped into a chair, not tiredness Bentley suspected but a big frame to manoeuvre, and slapped his big fists on the arms. He faced them, not with downright hostility, but something not far from it.

'I said on the phone,' Bentley said, 'we wanted to

talk to you about the disappearance of photographer Cindy Longhurst–'

'Good fucking riddance I say, that bitch didn't win any medals for good behaviour. I tell you–'

'Tony, what the hell are you playing at?'

In walked, Bentley presumed, Mrs Mitchell, a diminutive lady about the size of an average thirteen year-old and weighing less than the slim DC beside him.

'How do you mean, love?'

'I mean being rude to those two detectives. They're only doing their jobs and you didn't even offer them a drink.'

She walked over and shook their hands. 'I'm Polly Mitchell, Tony's better half.' She spoke with a Sussex accent, a hint of Irish in there somewhere.

'Now,' she said, 'before we talk any more, what can I get you? Tea, coffee or something stronger?'

'No, nothing for me,' Bentley said.

'Don't be daft, I'm making a coffee for myself anyway. You want one?'

'Go on then,' Bentley said. 'I'll take a white coffee, no sugar.'

'Same for me,' Newman said.

'Coming up.'

'I'll give you a hand,' Tony said levering himself out of the chair.

'Good job she came in,' Newman said after the Mitchells retreated into the kitchen. 'The way he was sounding off, we would have been out on our ears in the next thirty seconds.'

'Yeah, and he'd probably give us a cuff around the

head for good measure.'

Tony and Polly returned a few minutes later, coffees for Bentley and the two women and a beer for the big man. In Bentley's experience, alcohol didn't calm people like him, it only made them more belligerent.

'You were saying?' Polly said, looking at Bentley.

He put down his cup. 'When I called, I said we're part of a team investigating the disappearance of photographer Cindy Longhurst, kidnapped from her studio two weeks ago today.'

'We saw the story in the paper,' Polly said, 'didn't we Tony?'

He grunted something which sounded like agreement before taking another swig from the beer bottle.

'We've upgraded it from a kidnapping to a murder. Her body was discovered yesterday.'

'I didn't get a chance to look at this morning's paper,' Polly said, 'but it's terrible news, so it is.'

'We are in the process of interviewing everyone who knew her, trying to put together a picture of her life.'

'So, you thought you'd come here,' Tony said, 'because she crippled my son and, using copper's logic, you assumed we might be behind it.'

'You did make threats against her after the police decided not to press charges.'

'Of course I did, I was fucking angry. Who wouldn't be after what she did?'

'Tony,' Polly said, the expression on her face one of outrage, 'do not use that sort of language in this house. They are only doing their jobs. Any more of your outbursts and they'll think you did it.'

'Aye, well maybe I was tempted.'

'Where were you on Wednesday night?'

'Why the fu...? Why should I tell you?'

'To eliminate you from our enquiries.'

'Maybe I don't want to be eliminated from your enquiries. It might be a good idea for me to be arrested and get my picture on the front of every bloody newspaper. People would then ask why, and I could tell them about how she crippled my son.'

'Tony, don't be a fool,' Polly said. 'All the publicity in the world won't bring Alex's legs back, will it?'

'No, but it would make me feel a whole lot better.'

'What, losing three day's work until you can prove your innocence and having to eat all that sloppy jail food?'

'When you put it like that,' he said smiling for the first time, 'I would miss your cooking. On Wednesday,' he said, turning to eyeball Bentley, 'I came home about six, went down to the pub overlooking The Green, *The Cricketers*, for a couple of pints and came back here for my dinner.'

'He did go out for a bit, and after we cleared up, we watched a film,' Polly said.

'You didn't go out later that night?'

'No.'

There was a noise, a soft clunk against the door before it opened. Expecting a child to enter, Bentley was surprised when Alex wheeled in.

'I thought I heard voices.'

'It's two policemen, love, talking about the woman

who died.'

'The one who knocked me down?'

'Yes.'

'I read about her, tragic, it is.'

Alex was young, early twenties with short black hair, a trim beard and a smiling, open face. He was clearly well used to the wheelchair as he manoeuvred it expertly around the coffee table and chairs.

'These people are here,' Tony said, 'to find out if we killed her.'

'Why would we?' Alex said. 'I don't bear any animosity towards her.'

'Well, maybe you should,' Tony said, his voice raised, sounding as if he was going over a point aired many times before. 'How many times did we ask her to at least apologise for what happened? She didn't have the bloody manners to say it.'

Alex waved a hand dismissively. 'Give it a rest, Pop. I told you I don't want her apology. It's all water under the bridge now.'

Tony leapt out of his chair with surprising alacrity. He pointed a finger at his son. 'This is not done, not by a long chalk.'

He turned to face the detectives. 'Are we finished?'

'I think so,' Bentley replied, 'for the minute.'

Without a word Tony strode off. Seconds later, the detectives heard the sound of the back door opening and closing.

'I better go and see if he's okay,' Polly said.

She stood. 'It was good meeting you both. Alex will see you out.'

Bentley and Newman stood. 'It's fine, Alex, don't

bother. We can see ourselves out.'

'Don't worry, I'm used to it.'

The hallway was wide and it was easy for Alex to turn the wheelchair and reach for the door handle.

'Please excuse Pops, he gets like this whenever my accident is mentioned. All he ever wanted was for Longhurst to apologise, but what was she going to apologise for? It was my own fault. Accidents do happen.'

'Maybe he's disappointed you couldn't follow him into the family business,' Newman said.

'You've hit the nail on the head, trust a woman to spot it. I've got two brothers who work there, but they're not as smart as me and could never end up running the show. I mean, I work in the office but I get respect as the boss's son, not because I used to do the job and know what it's like.'

'How is it around here for wheelchair access?' Newman asked.

'Woeful. High pavements, bumpy surfaces, pubs with hard-to-open doors. I could go on.'

'At least you've got a decent-looking pub close by,' Bentley said.

'What, *The Cricketers*?'

'Yeah, I imagine it would only take you three or four minutes to wheel along there.'

'It's not a bad place, but I don't go there. I go to another pub about ten minutes away.'

'Why?'

'We all got barred from there. Pops had a big argument with the owner and swore he would never darken their door ever again.'

ELEVEN

Charlie McQueen paced up and down the floor in his study. His wife called it a study, but he hadn't studied anything since leaving school at sixteen. Even then, one of the reasons he left school earlier than some of his contemporaries was because he didn't do much studying while he was there.

Despite being born in a poor part of Glasgow, his alma mater wasn't some skanky inner-city institution whose catchment area was a sink estate full of single parents on benefits, staffed by idealist young teachers with Marxist leanings. His adopted parents had sent him to a smart fee-paying place out in the country.

The phone call he received not more than five minutes ago had upset him. He wanted to take a look at one of his storage facilities, but as he was in the middle of serving a one-year ban for drink-driving, he needed someone to take him there. Rick said he would do it, but he'd called a few minutes ago to say a consignment scheduled to arrive in two days' time was coming in tonight and McQueen agreed Rick should go and deal with it.

In his place, Rick was sending Liam McKinney. McQueen and McKinney had been best mates at one time and, over the years, the Irishman with contacts all over Brighton had pulled in a lot of business. Lately though, his attitude, methods and foul mouth had gradually got on McQueen's nerves and a few months back he started to put a bit of distance between them. It sounded like the parting of two lovers, but it wasn't. In the drugs world, there are only friends and enemies with nothing in between. At the moment, he wasn't sure into which category he would place McKinney. The old adage of keeping enemies closer didn't apply in this dirty business. Friends you rewarded, enemies ran away or they were killed.

He heard a car draw up outside and after shouting a loud 'goodbye' to his wife walked out into a frost-tinted night. He lived in a smart part of Hove, his neighbours' driveways cluttered with up-market German marques: Audis, Mercedes and BMWs. One of the rewards for being one of Brighton's biggest drug dealers. McKinney's own set of wheels, a black Chevrolet Camaro with a red lightning stripe, stuck out like a monk at an atheist convention.

'Evening Charlie,' McKinney said smiling, the result of an earlier snort of coke and not the natural bonhomie of an easy-going character.

'You still driving this heap? The neighbours will stop talking to me.'

'It's a collector's piece, and anyway, you said yourself, you don't like your neighbours.'

'I didn't say that, ya prick. I said, some of them get up my nose. There's a difference.'

McQueen still spoke with a Scottish accent that became more pronounced when it suited him or whenever he got drunk. It was useful when buying dope from Russians and Bulgarians as it made him sound hard and similar to them. No matter where his suppliers came from, they could all relate to a minority being oppressed by a larger neighbour. In their case, the oppression was real as several came from poor areas of the Ukraine, Iraq and Afghanistan, but he was faking it. He'd left Glasgow at the age of eight and had lived in Sussex many more years than Scotland, but the accent had been useful at boarding school and it was useful now.

Charlie McQueen owned a number of buildings dotted around Sussex. Some were labs making crack-cocaine, spice, and growing cannabis, while others were simply warehouses where he stored drugs which had been bought in bulk. No one in his organisation knew all his suppliers: McKinney knew a couple, Rick knew a few, but only McQueen knew the lot. If one of his crew wanted to take over and tried to kill him, or ratted on him to the law, they wouldn't even have half of the business that he had now.

This was another reason he didn't want McKinney driving him tonight, it could add another location to the Irishman's repertoire. McQueen didn't programme the car's satnav and so avoided leaving an accessible record, plus he took him on a circuitous route. The sap's head was so coked, he probably wouldn't remember where he'd been.

Outside a hamlet called Brook Street, they turned up a farm track. In the daylight, visitors could see a rusty sign beside the gate indicating Ratner's Farm, but at night, no chance. He was renting a barn from Gabriel Ratner, a cereal farmer whose family had owned the land since the 1820s. This wasn't a case, popularised in newspapers, of a poor farmer having to dream up new ways of making a shilling due to falling prices, or the vagaries of the British summer.

Ratner made his fortune by anticipating cereal market changes with a high degree of accuracy. He did this by keeping a close eye on dieting, fitness and celebrity magazines and making extensive use of social media. He then grew crops demanded by the changing tastes of a fickle public. Nor did he mind renting his barn to a well-known drug dealer, as Ratner had been a customer of McQueen's for many years.

The barn lay some distance from the cluster of farm buildings making up Ratner's Farm. This suited McQueen fine as even though he didn't fear interference from the farmer, it stopped nosey visitors from taking too close an interest. It wasn't a working lab so people didn't come and go every day.

Instead, when a consignment arrived, like the one Rick was checking on tonight, they delivered it here and, now and again, one of his guys would show up and remove some bags. They would be taken to one of his labs in Brighton where heroin and coke would be doctored with a similar looking powder to reduce its potency. It wasn't good for business to kill his customers.

He got out of the car and without another word to McKinney, walked over to the barn and opened up. Switching on the lights was squeaky-bum time, the fear of finding the shelves stripped clean by rivals or, as happened to another storage facility, an infestation of vermin. A colony of rats had got in and ripped open bags of cocaine, scattering the contents over the floor before dropping dead from ingesting huge quantities of the product.

The barn hadn't changed from his last visit. The floor area had been fitted with several lines of heavy-duty metal racking. The first sets of racks, the ones to catch the eye of an intruder or a farming inspector, contained bags of nitrate fertiliser. They effectively screened the bags behind it, sealed inside plastic storage bins.

McQueen walked inside, casting an expert eye along the shelves, looking for the slightest anomaly. Finding none, he called McKinney over.

'Shift these boxes up there,' he said pointing, 'and I'll do the same on the other side. The consignment Rick is bringing in tonight needs a lot of space.'

He would shut up now, he'd told McKinney enough, but by the faraway look on the daft bastard's fizzer, he could have told him they were in Homebase and he would believe it.

It took no more than five minutes to tidy things up and he was sure they'd made enough room for Rick. He took a final look round and walked to the door. McKinney was already outside, drawing on a fag as if it was his last. McQueen wouldn't let anyone smoke in the same room as the product. He killed the light and locked the door.

It was a fine, clear night and if not so bitterly cold, he might have stopped for a moment to look at the stars. Few subjects at school grabbed his interest but astronomy did, and the school he attended not only had a dedicated club but a decent telescope too.

Initially, he did it to get away from the Hooray Henrys in the dorm, talking about their rugby prowess and the number of runs they scored in cricket, but in time, he fell in love with the subject.

At home in Shirley Drive, he had installed a telescope in the attic and frequently went up there to stare at the tails of comets and gaze at the International Space Station. The calm of the night was interrupted when McKinney started the Camaro, a rough animal noise akin to a belch from a hippopotamus. He'd never been a flashy driver, preferring an anonymous 4x4 when he could legally drive. He equated his position to that of a lottery winner, it was fine that his fortuitous circumstances were known to those he worked with, but make it public and every Tom would start sending him begging letters.

He got in the car and closed the door. They'd only been in the barn for less than ten minutes so the car was still warm inside, good job as he'd only worn a light jacket this evening and the short walk from the storage facility to the car left him shivering.

They drove back through the untidy array of farm buildings, out to the road and headed back to Brighton. He didn't know what made him look back, a noise maybe, a premonition, but he did, and saw two black 4x4s turning into the farm. They turned fast and something told him they weren't being driven by a team of silage experts from the Ministry of Agriculture.

'Stop the car!'

'What?'

'Pull in up there and turn around. We're going back to the farm.'

McKinney did as he asked. 'Why, have you left your phone behind or something?'

'Didn't you see?' He knew as soon as he'd said it he was wasting his breath. McKinney could only see enough to drive him here and back to Brighton. He didn't look in his rear-view mirror and his peripheral vision was non-existent.

'No, what?'

'Two cars, big 4x4s, just turned into the farm. I've got a bad feeling about this.'

They headed back to the farm. McKinney hadn't said a word since being told, clearly the words didn't make sense or he was taking his time processing such a large amount of information. In five minutes' time the penny might drop.

'Don't drive to the barn, park your car up there. Keep it out of sight.'

'It's bloody miles to the barn from here.'

'Don't talk crap. It's no more than three hundred metres. In fact, it would be better if you stay here and watch the car.'

'What? I wanna come, see what's going on.'

'No, you don't. If this is what I think it is, you'll only be a fucking liability. Stay here.'

McQueen strode off along the rough road leading to the barn. He pulled out the gun from his waistband and made sure it was ready to fire.

When he caught sight of the barn he moved off the track and did a wide semicircle towards it. On reaching the far side, away from the 4x4s parked outside, he couldn't see what was going on. Whoever was in the barn hadn't switched on the lights. He could hear activity going on. *Bang-bang-bang*. They were in there with hammers or baseball bats, smashing the place up. The bastards.

He approached the intruder's cars. He couldn't take on six or eight heavies with only one gun, but he could make it difficult for them to get home. He lay on the grass and fired a succession of shots at the large tyres on the nearest Mercedes. He hit a couple, but just then, someone he didn't notice standing close to the cars, opened up with what sounded like a Mac or Uzi sub-machine pistol. Fucking hell! He looked around but there wasn't a whole lot of cover to hide behind. Luckily the shooter mistook the location of his shots and was firing at an area over to his right.

He needed to get out of there fast before the wreckers came out of the barn and came looking for him. He got up and ran, increasing the distance between him and the track. He heard another burst of fire, but the shooter was firing blind. In any case, he believed he would be out of range of the short-barrelled weapon, but no way did he want to test his hypothesis.

He heard voices behind him, Russian, but didn't yet hear the sound of their undamaged vehicle's engine starting up. He ran and ran and when nearly at the farm buildings, ventured a look back. Not content with smashing up the inside of his storage facility, the barn that contained some three or four million pounds' worth of product was now engulfed in flames. Now he heard one of the Mercedes cars start up.

He reached the Camaro and hauled the door open, startling McKinney who looked to have been snoozing.

'Drive!' he shouted.

'What?'

'Drive the fucking car.'

'Are we in a hurry or something?'

'McKinney, if you don't drive this fucking car right now, so help me, I'll stick this gun right up your arse and pull the trigger.'

TWELVE

'You're a difficult man to track down, Mr Harrison,' DS Walters said.

'Am I?'

'It took several calls before you answered your phone and you don't reply to messages. How do you run a business if you don't answer your phone? I might have been a new customer with a big job for you.'

He shrugged. 'It's hard for me to take on any more business at the moment. I'm almost full time with one client.'

Sitting across from DS Walters and DC Seb Young in an interview room at Malling House was Mike Harrison. A building handyman, he was a former boyfriend of Cindy Longhurst and, according to Annie Heath, one she couldn't shake off.

'We're members of the team investigating the murder of Cindy Longhurst.'

He nodded but didn't show any emotion. Walters imagined any boyfriend of Cindy's to be youthful, handsome with sensual eyes and a cheeky smile, but Harrison looked age-ravaged, with thinning hair, a wrinkled face and a pallor not far from sickly. She knew he was forty-four but he looked several years older.

'How did you two meet?'

'Let me think. I was doing some work for this big client I was telling you about when she turned up at the house. He'd spent a lot of money re-modelling the house and wanted professional pictures done.'

'Who's the client?'

'Constantin Petrescu at Hillcrest House.'

'Why was Cindy there?' Young asked.

'I don't know, to take pictures of the house and family. The usual stuff.'

'What happened between you and Cindy?'

'We got talking and I asked her out.' He paused a moment or two for effect, but he was a crap actor. 'No, I should have said, I didn't ask her out, she asked me.'

Curious, Walters thought. Harrison didn't look a catch in her eyes, but friends and colleagues often accused her of being too fussy.

'How long did the two of you go out together?'

'About three months, I think.'

'How would you describe your relationship?'

He looked thoughtful, perhaps wondering how to position this to stop the detectives asking the obvious. 'Good I would say. I was sorry when we split up.'

'You were more cut-up than you're suggesting, Mr Harrison. According to reports, you wouldn't leave her alone. You turned up at her studio unannounced and bombarded her with texts.'

'Hold on a minute. Don't bloody accuse me of bombarding her with anything. We broke up and I wasn't happy about it. So what? I wanted her back, there you go, I admit it.'

'No need to raise your voice, sir. Annie Heath told

us–'

'Annie Heath? She's an interfering busybody. She tried to put the boot into our relationship right from the start, telling Cindy I was no good and all that crap.'

'Why would she say that?'

'Because she doesn't fucking like me. Does she need another excuse?'

At this point, Walters would often step in and tell the witness or suspect to calm down. It appeared as though he'd moved beyond the point of thinking straight, but Harrison seemed like one of those people who were born angry.

'I assume Cindy finished with you and not the other way round?' Young asked.

'I can see why they made you a detective, son. Why would I hassle her if it was me who told her to bugger off?'

'Maybe you'd made an error of judgement and you regretted it later.'

'There was no error of judgement, mate. When she decided to finish with me, bang,' he said, thumping the edge of his hand on the table, 'decision made. I got the proverbial boot in the arse.'

'Where were you on the night Cindy was kidnapped?' Walters asked.

'Which night are we talking about?'

'Friday, twenty-sixth of January.'

'On Friday, any Friday I stop work at five and drive to my local boozer for a few jars until seven. I then buy a Chinese or tandoori on the way back to my house and watch telly until eleven.'

'Which pub is your local?'

'The County Oak in Patcham.'

'Can anyone vouch for your presence there?'

'Sure. I meet my mates, Trevor Stevens and Billy Sinclair on Friday nights and we play a bit of pool, but why would you think I kidnapped Cindy and killed her? I loved her for christsakes. We had a good thing going.'

'It could be your revenge for her dumping you,' Young said.

'You're pulling my chain, pal. Why would I? And where would somebody like me get a gun? I wouldn't know how to use one. I'd probably blow my foot off trying to figure it out.'

'You must come into contact with a lot of people in your business. One of them could find you a gun, I'm sure.'

'You guys don't have a clue who killed her, if you did, you wouldn't be talking to me. Did Annie Heath see me anywhere near the studio? No. Did Cindy call out my name when she was being dragged out to the kidnapper's car? No. And let me tell you, the essential word there is 'drag.' Cindy wouldn't go down without a fight, not Cindy. The answer to all those questions is no because I wasn't there.'

'Where do you live, Mr Harrison?'

'What's that got to do with anything?'

'Just answer the question.'

'Up the road from the County Oak pub in Patcham.'

'In a house or a flat?'

'A semi-detached house.' He smiled but without

humour. 'I know where you're going with this, but let me tell you, if I brought a screaming and kicking Cindy Longhurst back to my house, even in the middle of the night, my fucking nosy next-door neighbour would recognise her and call you lot. Her picture's been in all the papers, even in the rag that old bitch reads.'

'Where do you keep all the materials for your work?'

'I've got a shed out back and, before you ask, it's filled with plasterboard, wood, paint and bags of cement. You couldn't swing a cat in there never mind hide a grown woman.'

**

'What you're saying is it doesn't sound like Harrison is someone we need to put under surveillance,' Henderson said, looking at DS Walters and DC Young across the meeting room table.

'Nope, he's loud and full of bluster,' Walters said, 'but underneath it all, I think he was hurt when she gave him the old heave-ho.'

'Nevertheless, follow up his alibi and talk to his two mates in the pub. I don't often like to rely on pub alibis, but as this one is early evening there's a chance their memories will be a bit more intact.'

'Will do.'

'The thing I don't see, based on your and Seb's description of the man, is what she saw in him in the first place. He's a tradesman, not very bright by the sound of it and not committed to any of her causes.

Added to the mix, it appears he's also got some anger management issues.'

'Maybe she likes a challenge. Greg her ex, didn't strike me as her type either.'

'Greg's different. They got together when they were both young and he kept up with her at the time. When he got older, he wanted a quieter life but she didn't. Harrison, by way of contrast, looks, maybe not a loser, but a poor bet right from the off.'

'You're right,' Seb Young said, 'they do appear mismatched, down to their standards of dress. Cindy, in pictures, always looks smart, her hair regularly cut and styled and make-up deftly applied. He, on the other hand, still looks like a tradesman despite not wearing his work clothes.'

'Could it be,' Henderson said, 'Cindy teamed up with him for a specific purpose and when she'd achieved it, let him go? Don't forget her high moral compass and support for the underdog. Maybe he had something she wanted and perhaps when she got it, the sudden termination of the relationship caught him off guard and part-way explains his subsequent reaction.'

'It's no way for a normal person to treat an ex but having met him, I can understand how he behaved like he did.'

'If she was using him, what could it be for?'

'The obvious one is sex,' Young said.

'If that was the case, I imagine he would get wind of her displeasure before the big chop. There would be complaints in bed, the odd sly comment when they were out socialising, perhaps.'

'What if,' Walters said, 'Harrison wasn't the target at all, but the guy they were both working for?' She picked up her notebook and flicked to the most recent page. 'Constantin Petrescu.'

'I know of him. He owns the wine warehouse in Portslade I sometimes buy from.'

'I've been there too. Same guy don't you think?'

'He owns more than the Portslade warehouse and by the speed with which he opens new premises, I don't think he's short of a bob or two. A large house in the country sounds about right, plus it's hardly a common name in Sussex.'

'True.'

'Remind me what they were both doing at his house,' Henderson said.

'He was there as a handyman and she as the photographer of the family and the house. It seems the owner is the fastidious type, Harrison told us the house had only been recently remodelled a few years back and here he was re-painting walls and re-laying wood flooring.'

'So, she takes a fancy to the owner of this large house, who we think is much more in her league than Harrison, but first she targets Harrison and spends three months with him trying to find out more about Petrescu. I don't buy it.'

'Me neither,' Walters said. 'Maybe she wanted to get closer to Petrescu, not in a sexual way, but for what he stands for or something he's involved in.'

'This sounds a bit more like Cindy, as she's quite the righteous campaigner. If this guy owned, for example, a company in the fracking business or a manufacturer of firearms, maybe she wanted to get friendlier with him to find out more about his activities, or to try and influence him. I don't know him too well, but any time I have spoken to him it's usually been about the drinks business.'

'Maybe it's not about the owner at all, but about the house,' Young said.

'How do you mean?'

'Maybe she wanted to buy it or was sounding him out for a friend.'

'An interesting angle,' Henderson said. 'Let's run with it and see where it takes us.'

'Maybe she wanted to use the house as the location for a photo shoot,' Walters said.

'Or the house possesses interesting features she wanted to photograph.'

'Could be there's some new development taking place in the area,' Young said, 'like fracking or a new road, and she wanted to elicit his help in opposing it.'

'She might have been interested in all those things,' Henderson said, 'and targeting Mike Harrison made sense as it would keep her in touch with the owner. But, I can't see how her involvement in any of those could lead to her death.'

'Me neither,' Walters said. 'We're back to the owner.'

'Ok,' Henderson said. 'See what you can find out about him Carol, the businesses he owns, if he's got a criminal record, anything at all.'

'Shouldn't we bring him in for questioning?'

'What for? Hiring Cindy to carry out a short photo session a couple of months back? No, it's not enough.

He'd be within his rights to tell us to get lost. The connection we know about is between Cindy and Mike Harrison. Find out why she targeted him and we'll be on the way to solving this.'

The two officers left Henderson's office a few minutes later and Henderson returned to his seat behind the desk. They'd uncovered a new name, Constantin Petrescu, but he didn't hold out high hopes. The links between him and Cindy were too tenuous. It had to be for some other reason that Cindy targeted Mike Harrison, but at the moment, he couldn't think what they might be.

THIRTEEN

Henderson returned to his office, a cup of takeaway coffee in his hand and his head full of Grafton Rawlings's comments from the post-mortem. A minute or so later, Carol Walters and Phil Bentley came in and sat down in the visitor's seats.

They had been his companions at Brighton Mortuary along with the photographer, the coroner and the Mortuary assistant. He half-expected to see the Chief Constable in attendance, as an hour or so before the P-M, Henderson and the CC appeared together at the Cindy Longhurst kidnap press conference. It seemed most of the UK media, and some European and American networks too, were also there. This case had gripped the public conscience like no other he could remember in the last couple of years, partly due to Cindy's good looks and the fact that she was succeeding in a business dominated by men. The CC told him he was keeping a close eye on developments.

'How are you feeling, Phil,' Henderson asked, 'after the P-M? I looked round a couple of times and thought you weren't feeling well.'

'A lot better now than when Mr Rawlings ran his scalpel around her skull. My face must have been green.'

'What do we make of his findings?'

'The cause of death didn't come as a surprise,' Walters said. 'We all know the effect of a bullet to the skull, but I couldn't get my head around the marks on her ankles and wrists, indicating she'd been tied up.'

'Not only tied, but the marks and abrasions on her face and body suggesting she'd been beaten. Also, the dirt and grime on her clothes, hair and nails, evidence she's been imprisoned in some grotty place since being kidnapped.'

'I didn't hear Mr Rawlings say that,' Bentley said. 'I was probably too busy trying not to throw up.'

'So, we're back to the question we've been asking ever since we became involved in this case. Why would someone kidnap Cindy Longhurst, and now, why would someone beat her up before putting a bullet in her head? She's a portrait photographer, not a bloody drug dealer, for God's sake.'

'It has to be someone or something she took a picture of rather than someone who didn't like her,' Walters said. 'We've talked to the two dodgy people in her life, Mike Harrison and Tony Mitchell, and while Mitchell's alibi isn't sound and needs another interview to clarify, neither men look a good fit.'

'I agree but taking pictures of what?'

'Perhaps a well-known person she photographed in a compromising position.'

'I would be more interested if she worked for a tabloid newspaper or a photographic agency and spent her time hanging around outside a nightclub waiting for celebs to appear. It doesn't fit with the image I have in my head of a portrait photographer.

Her job, it seems to me, is working in her studio at Hurstpierpoint, taking photographs of people like Maggie Hyatt.'

'You're right,' Bentley said, 'but don't forget, when she went on those marches and protests, she always took her camera.'

'How do you know?'

'In her office there's loads of photos on the walls and I looked through some of the cupboards. It's the same sort of thing you see in newspapers: a group of people all linking hands and singing, or the crowd having a bit of argy-bargy with the boys in blue.'

'Maybe one time when she was out protesting,' Walters said, 'she might have taken a picture of someone or something they didn't want her to take.'

'Could be.'

Henderson stood and walked to the window. 'What did she see that could be so bad it would get her killed? Why go to the bother of beating her up first? What were they trying to find out?'

'Maybe they wanted know the location of the originals of the pictures she took,' Walters said.

'Yes, and remember Cindy's assistant, Annie told us she thought the kidnappers took away a box of SD cards. In this age of digital photography, they're the originals.'

'Okay, but what if they looked through the box and found it wasn't what they wanted and beat her up to find out where she kept them.'

Henderson nodded. 'The kidnappers maybe didn't have time to look through the SD cards individually when they came to the studio, and didn't come back as they thought we'd be there. The fact we haven't heard reports of it being wrecked or burnt down suggests she might have told them where she'd stored them.'

'And maybe they killed her,' Walters said, 'because she was the only person who knew where they were and what they contained.'

'What if,' Henderson said, 'the pictures they took away from the studio weren't the ones they wanted and so they beat her up to reveal their location. They killed her, not because she revealed their whereabouts, but because she refused to do so.'

'Which means...'

'Which means the pictures they killed her for are still at the studio.' Henderson returned to his seat. 'I think the time has come for us to start searching through her pictures.'

'I agree with the conclusion,' Walters said, 'but there's so many it would take twenty people a year to complete. Even then, we don't know what we're looking for.'

'Maybe it won't be so bad.'

'I'd like to know how.'

'She must operate some sort of cataloguing system. If so, we can put aside anything that looks like her day-to-day work: portrait pictures, shots for catalogues and the stuff she does for adverts. We only need to look at what's left, which might be five per cent or less of the total.'

'True, but how do we recognise the important pictures when we come across them?'

'I don't know, but it's clear whoever we have looking at them needs to apply a certain degree of common sense. We're trying to find a picture or pictures that are so awful, embarrassing or extreme that someone will do anything to ensure they're never published. Something like this shouldn't be so hard to recognise, should it?'

'When you put it in those terms, no.'

'Good,' Henderson said. 'Carol, I'd like you to get this organised.'

'Ok.'

'Now, where are we on forensics?'

'Ah, Angus, I'm glad I've caught you,' Detective Chief Inspector Lisa Edwards said as she walked into his office. She nodded to the other two, 'Sergeant Walters, Constable Bentley. I'd like to introduce a new addition to your team, Detective Sergeant Vicky Neal.'

A few minutes later, after Edwards returned to her office and Walters and Bentley to their desks, he sat down at the meeting table facing the new Detective Sergeant. He knew of her impending arrival, here to replace Gerry Hobbs, now a Detective Inspector in the Drugs Unit, but a couple of emails and a curriculum vitae could not replace a one-to-one discussion.

'What made you want to move to Sussex from Manchester? I would have thought there was enough activity in their serious crime unit for any new DS.'

'It was a personal issue rather than a work one,' she said, her Mancunian vowels coming thick and hard. 'You're right, we've got it all there: gun crime, big drug deals, people trafficking and all the rest but it's relentless. Every week, another shooting, every fortnight a major drugs bust. Like a factory conveyor belt, they just kept coming.'

'Your DI has said some complimentary things. It sounds like they were sorry to lose you.'

'How can I put it, I brought a bit of intelligence to the unit. They're all good detectives, don't get me wrong, but not many have studied criminology like I have.'

Henderson noticed this on her CV. After a degree in Psychology from Reading, she completed an MSc in Criminology and Criminal Psychology at Portsmouth. If asked, Henderson took the view that only detectives with a lot of experience under their belts really benefited from studying Criminology at degree or post-graduate level. Vicky didn't have any experience when she started the course as she'd joined the police straight after completing her studies.

'He said your contribution in solving the Salford Poisoner case was key. Tell me about it.'

'Did it make the nationals? I don't know if you'd have heard about it down here.'

'No, I didn't, I saw something about it on an internal document.'

'Okay, some bloke in Salford was going into off-licences and corner shop grocers, replacing Coke bottles with one of his own, laced with a rat poison that made people, mainly kids, vomit.'

He watched her as she spoke. She was tall and slim, with shoulder-length, dark brown hair, and brown intense eyes. The overall effect was attractive and perhaps the reason Phil Bentley went gaga when first introduced. He didn't think her good looks would present a problem around the office, but her forthright attitude might ruffle a few feathers.

'With your DI's glowing recommendation and your qualifications, you could have the pick of where to go next. Why Sussex? As far as you could get away from Manchester?'

She smiled, but not warmly. 'Something like that. I know I sound like a died-in-the-wool Salford lass, but I've got a couple of relatives in this area. I used to come down to Worthing as a kid to visit my grandmother.'

'What do you know of Sussex from a policing perspective?'

'I know it's a mix of big towns like Brighton, Worthing and Crawley, plus Gatwick Airport, and small towns and villages. There's crowd control issues with events at the Amex stadium, not as big as Old Trafford or the Etihad, but still a big football match to police. Plus, pop bands, celebrities and political conferences at the Brighton Centre.'

'I see you've done your homework. Where are you staying?'

'I'm renting a flat in Lower Rock Gardens, near the seafront.'

'I know where it is. You're about a mile along the road from me, although I don't think you'll get much time to settle in. You've joined us right in the middle of a murder investigation.'

'I don't mind, sir, it's what I came here for.'

Henderson went on to explain about the kidnap and subsequent murder of photographer Cindy Longhurst.

'I know something about the case,' Neal said, 'I've been reading *The Argus* on-line for the last few weeks.'

'Good. You might also know we don't have any strong suspects. This is despite interviewing her ex-husband, ex-boyfriend and her business partner, although I intend re-interviewing the father of a disabled man Cindy knocked off his bike four years ago. We're now of the opinion the answer lies in a photograph or photographs she took, but as you can imagine over the course of a near twenty-year career, there are tens of thousands, perhaps millions of pictures to sift through.'

Neal paused for a moment. 'You've looked at her customers, I assume. Someone might have tried it on with her and maybe it left lingering resentment.'

'We're doing this at the moment. It's a long list of names and all we can do at the moment is run their details through the computer and see if anyone has form.'

'What about forensics? Did they find anything?'

'I was about to get an update when you and CI Edwards walked in. Why don't we go through to the Detectives' Room where you can meet the rest of the team and we can get the forensics status at the same time?'

FOURTEEN

At five o' clock in the morning it was still dark outside. Ted Mathieson walked through the house to the integral garage. Upstairs, he'd left his wife, Tamsin, sleeping. Despite her liking for the morning workouts she did with her personal trainer, 'early' for her was more like nine or ten. His daughter wouldn't be perturbed by his early start either, as she boarded at her school, Hurstpierpoint College. It would be a couple of hours before she would be woken up by boisterous girls talking excitedly about their boy-infested dreams or a discussion about which moisturiser they should use today.

He hefted the holdall into the back of the car and slammed the lid shut. Ted Mathieson yawned as he eased his wife's VW Golf out of the garage. Friends had come around to the house for dinner last night, more like business acquaintances if he was being honest, so neither he nor his wife knew them well. At times, the conversation turned quiet or sounded stilted, but his legendary depths of hospitality didn't disappoint and to compensate for the lack of spark, they'd all drunk too much.

As the owner of Mathieson Transport, he didn't need to work the long hours he used to. He had a trusty colleague in Brian Everett, his commercial

Director and right-hand man. With the exception of negotiating contracts, Brian could easily manage the place while he was out, and with such a good deputy in place, Mathieson could work part-time if he chose to do so. His wife didn't think too hard about those sorts of issues and it was easy to palm her off with an explanation that his early-morning start was due to the pressures of work. However, his daughter, despite her tender years, was as sharp as a tack. It was a good job she was boarding.

The bag in the boot contained four kilos of high quality cocaine. Their contact in Germany, Otto, came up with the goods every eight weeks with the same regularity as the tick-over of a BMW six-cylinder engine. A couple of weeks after receiving their last big delivery, Otto told Mathieson's driver, Steve, he could get them some more if they wanted it. He gave him some spiel about a bumper crop in Columbia, the cartels working overtime, less product being seized by the American authorities, blah de blah de blah.

Did he take them for a couple of fucking tosspots? He'd done his homework on Otto and far from being the congenial beer-swilling fatso he wanted them to believe, he was a razor-sharp property developer. He was ploughing all the dough he made from his drug dealing business into new property developments in Bavaria. The 'extra' coke he offered was not manna from the gods, as he suggested, but some from his private stash to provide the readies to finish off a sports centre being built in Nuremberg.

Mathieson's buyer, Charlie McQueen, sounded non-committal about the extra product, citing low prices and for a moment Mathieson considered selling it to someone else or reducing his next order from Otto. Again, Mathieson had done his homework and knew McQueen's operation was coming under severe pressure from the authorities, first the local drugs squad and, rumour had it, the National Crime Agency. They hadn't scored any big successes against McQueen's organisation yet, only the closure of a few 'crack' houses and the seizure of a few kilos, but recent statements made by the police sounded as though they were getting close.

McQueen was also under pressure from Russian gangs, keen to grab a share of the lucrative UK drugs market. Over the weekend, *The Argus* reported the fire at a rural barn near Brook Street. A propane heater was most likely the cause, according to the farmer who owned it. Mathieson asked around and knew the Russians had hit McQueen. Assuming he'd lost a fair amount of product and perhaps some vital laboratory facilities, would the result be higher prices for street buyers or would he try and squeeze his suppliers?

He liked McQueen but didn't trust him. Glaswegian sounding and street-wise by nature, meaning he would use anything to hand, be it a gun, knife, bottle, beer glass, or his fists to clear any obstacle blocking his path.

In a way, he was an entrepreneur like Mathieson with the same issues about people, product supply and cash flow, but this was where the comparisons ended. If the authorities suspected Mathieson of any wrongdoing, his business could be raided by the forces of Her Majesty's Revenue and Customs armed with calculators and laptops. If McQueen was fingered, he would have his doors kicked in by big lads wearing Kevlar vests, armed with Heckler and Koch machine guns and with the menacing clatter of a helicopter overhead.

He turned up the road towards Devil's Dyke, a high point on the South Downs and one used frequently by hang glider pilots. There wouldn't be any hang gliders around at this time of the morning, it still being dark and cold, and he didn't often see anyone else up here except the occasional dog walker. He stopped the car in the car park close to the café and waited, leaving the engine idling to keep warm. When meeting Charlie McQueen he liked to arrive ahead of time. They had a good thing going and it wouldn't be his lack of commitment that would spoil it.

He enjoyed listening to the radio at this time of the morning. He reckoned the stations put on their less experienced disc jockeys and due to them having little repartee to draw upon, and with no army of fans to canvas their opinions on last night's television or the football, they played lots of music.

The soft rolling hills of the Downs were coated in a fine covering of white frost, glowing red with the first rays of winter sunshine. The view would make a spectacular picture if he could paint or take photographs, but he could do neither. Thinking of photographs reminded him of Cindy. He thought about her often, almost as much now as he did when she was alive. He loved her like no woman before or since and would continue doing so, he suspected, until the day he died. His one abiding regret was she didn't love him in return.

They'd met when Cindy's former husband, Greg, started work at Mathieson Transport. At the time, they were a small outfit with only three lorries, all working regionally. Greg's skills as a bookkeeper were fine up to this point, but as the business grew and they got into bed with national supermarkets, he didn't grow at the same pace. When two scroats were found stealing, it gave Mathieson a good excuse to get shot of him.

It didn't stop him seeing Cindy as her daughter was in the same year as his little one at Hurstpierpoint College, and he made a point of talking to Cindy any time he took Jasmine to school or to a hockey match. They became lovers for a spell, but while his heart was sucked in like water spinning down a drain, her heart was like a dam, effectively blocking the stream of his allure.

His small bout of introspection came to a halt when he spotted a car coming up the hill. He grinned when he saw it; a black Chevrolet Camaro with a red lightning stripe along the side and a roaring exhaust. A better advert for a drug dealer he couldn't imagine. He was surprised McQueen would be so stupid to jettison his normal mode of transport, an innocuous Toyota Camry.

The Brighton drug dealer was currently banned from driving for a drink-driving offence and if he wanted to get stopped, even at this early hour of the morning, that car was perfect. He decided he would rib him about it. However, when the car drew alongside his and came to an abrupt halt, he realised neither Charlie McQueen nor his right-hand man, Rick, were inside.

The guy who exited the vehicle was no Glaswegian or brawny yank with a McDonald's-sized gut asking for directions to the American Car Show, but a badly dressed scrawny bloke with a mop of untidy black hair. In common with his German supplier, Mathieson had done his research on McQueen's business and knew it wasn't a cop or someone working at the Devil's Dyke pub. This was one of McQueen's people, Liam McKinney.

'Charlie couldn't make it,' he said by way of greeting, 'and sent me instead.'

'No problem.'

'You got the gear?'

Mathieson opened the boot of the VW and unzipped the holdall. 'Take a look.'

So far so normal. With McQueen, they didn't take the dope or the money out of the cars until the sale was agreed and both bags were zipped up. You never knew who was lurking nearby or focussing a zoom lens.

McKinney looked in the sports bag and fingered the drugs with the skill of an experienced dealer.

'Four kilos?'

'Yep.'

Mathieson was good with Irish accents as he followed rugby and often went over to Dublin to watch Saracens on tour or England in the Home Internationals. McKinney was a Belfast lad and if someone twisted his arm, he'd say a catholic from the

Ardoyne.

'Good. Zip her up.'

Mathieson zipped the bag, carried it over to the Camaro and slung it into the boot beside another similar-looking holdall. He unzipped the other holdall and counted the cash. He didn't count it note-for-note, he wasn't a bean counter and it didn't pay to hang around with so much dope and a bag full of cash. Instead, he counted the bricks; the thousand-pound piles, and flicked through each pile to ensure it contained currency and not Monopoly money or photocopier paper.

Despite being in business with these guys for over a year, a time scale that ordinarily would build confidence and empathy with suppliers in the transport industry, he still didn't trust them. Not only did they possess the brashness and over-confidence of youth, but they were more used to playing dangerous games than him, selling to users and the enormous risks they took on the street every day.

'Hey,' Mathieson said, 'what's going on? You're eighty grand light.'

'It's supply and demand, mate. You brought the stuff to us when we've got plenty.'

He could see it now. McQueen, the fucking coward, sent his underling to try and undercut him, but he wasn't having it.

'That's not what I heard. These raids by the law and the Russians those last couple of months hitting your business hard. Reports say you're hurting.'

McKinney shrugged. 'Fuck do I know, I just work

123

there. This is the price, mate, take it or leave it.'

Mathieson grabbed him by the lapels of his bomber jacket. 'You fucking liar. You're trying to squeeze me. Who do you think I am? Some sort of street punk you can short change?'

'Take your dirty paws off me you shithead.'

'Who are you calling a shithead?' he said raising his fist.

McKinney punched him in the gut. He'd been punched in the gut before but never like this. It made his legs and arms go weak and he was forced to release his grip.

Mathieson fell to the ground clutching his gut and only then did he realise he'd been stabbed.

FIFTEEN

C'mon people,' Henderson said. 'Let's have a bit of order here, we've got a lot to get through today.'

DI Henderson and the murder team were gathered in the corner of the large Detectives' Room. After the kidnapping of Cindy Longhurst had developed into a murder inquiry, the group had expanded and he now counted eighteen officers either sitting on chairs or perched on the edge of desks.

'I suspect many of you haven't heard the news,' Henderson said, 'but early this morning Ted Mathieson was found stabbed. He's in hospital but the wound does not appear to be life-threatening.'

'Quiet now, quiet now,' Henderson said as everyone tried to talk at once. 'He was discovered at Devil's Dyke at six-thirty this morning. We've no idea how or why he was stabbed but somehow, he managed to crawl the short distance to his car and press the horn. The noise alerted an early morning jogger who called an ambulance. He's currently undergoing surgery at the Royal Sussex. If the operation is successful, he is expected to make a full recovery.'

He left them a moment or two to talk about the news while he reached for his coffee.

'Right,' he said putting the cup down. 'This unit wouldn't normally involve itself in a stabbing, these sorts of cases are more the preserve of detectives at John Street, but as Mathieson's name has cropped up in an active murder investigation, we will make an exception. DS Neal will be in charge of this one. DC Graham will assist DS Neal and make sure she doesn't get lost.'

Vicky Neal smiled, clearly happy to be leading her own inquiry so soon.

'For now,' he said tapping the whiteboard behind him, 'let's concentrate on the murder. We know forensics didn't come up with much, so I need an update on how we're getting on checking her customers and examining the photographs in her studio. You first Harry.'

DS Harry Wallop puffed out his chest and opened the papers in front of him. 'As you can all imagine, the list of customers at the studio ran into thousands. By the end of last night, every last name has been run through the PNC. Twenty people were found to have criminal records.'

'Good work, Harry. You're excluding businesses at this stage?'

He nodded. 'Yep, but that work is more Phil's baby. There's a lot less of them, maybe about forty, but we need to bring some measure of savvy into that inquiry. We first need to identify which staff members were involved and then isolate those who might have come into contact with Cindy.'

'I understand. Forget about them for the moment.'

'Right. The twenty individuals with records have been sorted into two groups: 'minor' and 'other crimes.' Officers are working their way through the interviews, principally those who fall into the 'other crimes' category.'

'I take it the reason you're not highlighting anyone today is because no one as yet has sprung to your attention?'

'Correct.'

'Keep it going, Harry and let me know the minute you get a bite.'

'Right, sir.'

'DS Walters, how's the review of Cindy's photograph collection progressing?'

'Slowly. She does everything digitally which means we need to wait for each SD card to load before we can view the pictures. Give me photo prints any day of the week.'

'If she used a film camera, chances are she wouldn't keep a printed copy of every photograph she took. Those she didn't print would most likely be on contact sheets, requiring magnification to see properly. So, don't knock digital so readily.'

'Just me having a little gripe.'

'How many computers do you have over there?'

'Three.'

'Rustle up a few more and the officers to man them. I'll sign it off.'

'Will do.'

'Does her cataloguing system help?'

'It does, but when we come across a pile of SD cards with the labels, 'weddings' or 'family portraits', we need to sample a few to make sure they contain what we think they do.'

'Fair enough. Have you found anything yet?'

She shook her head. 'No such luck, but with a few thousand to go, hopefully we'll find something before we finish.'

He nodded, confident they would. 'Right, to other lines of enquiry. We've spoken to Cindy's former husband, Greg, as you all know, and while I mark him down as bitter for missing out on a share of Cindy's grandmother's inheritance, I don't think he's twisted enough to kidnap or kill her. What's your take, DS Walters?'

'When officers went to his house to tell him about Cindy's death, he was more concerned about how he was going to pay for his daughter's school fees than the passing of his ex-wife. On balance, I'm of the same opinion. I don't think he's behind it.'

'We've also spoken to the ex-boyfriend who Annie Heath claimed had been hassling Cindy, Mike Harrison. He vehemently denies any involvement in her abduction and murder and you Carol, were checking his alibi.'

'His alibi checks out, sir with his mates from the pub and I also took a look in his shed. Full of painting and building stuff like he said.'

'Have we established if there is a more recent partner on the scene?'

'Cindy didn't have a current boyfriend,' Sally Graham said.

'DS Neal, call the Royal Sussex and find out when Ted Mathieson has returned to the land of the living. We need to speak to him, see if he's somehow connected with this. That's all for now. Update at six-thirty.'

**

'Ted Mathieson got knifed?' CI Edwards spluttered, almost spilling the cup of coffee in her hand. 'What the hell for?'

'Wish I knew,' Henderson said.

He liked Edwards's office. It was bright and airy and almost gave out an optimistic air, something in short supply in modern-day police work.

'You don't think it's connected with the Longhurst murder?'

'I don't see how, but I remain open to a different interpretation. I think transport businesses sail on the edge, some as clean as other companies, others as dirty as old snow. It's the perfect cover for bringing into the country prostitutes, drugs, guns, contraband cigarettes and anything else worth selling.'

'It is too. You think his stabbing is connected to his business?'

'I think it's more likely than anything although his name did crop up in an earlier case.'

'Oh really?'

'Operation Skylark, it was called, a big drugs operation by the Met. Mathieson's business card was found at premises owned by Charlie McQueen.'

'There's tenuous and there's tenuous, Angus. A business card found in someone's person or premises is right on the edge.'

'I agree.'

'In which case, we should hand the stabbing over to John Street. We've got enough to contend with.'

'I want to keep it and give it to DS Neal. See how she handles it.'

'Canny as ever, Angus. Good idea, let her cut her teeth on something meaty. I wanted to ask you, how's she settling in?'

'Fine. No concerns to speak of.'

'Doesn't her, how should I say, forthright manner rub some people up the wrong way?'

Henderson smiled. 'She's got a few back's up, but I don't think it will cause too many problems.'

'Good. I found out what happened in Manchester. No wonder we got our hands on a good officer at such short notice. I know you don't go in much for office gossip but would you like to hear it?'

He nodded.

'She worked at the station in Stretford and unbeknown to other officers there, she was seeing the Superintendent, a forty-two-year-old married man with four children.'

'Oh.'

'Yes, it elicits that sort of reaction, doesn't it? A few weeks after it started, his wife came to the station with two of their kids in tow and, in Reception, engaged her husband in a stand-up row, leaving no one in ear-shot in any doubt what he and DS Neal had been up to. A couple of days later, the two of them had an altercation in the locker room, leaving him with two broken teeth and a bruised face when he fell against a wooden bench.'

'An ignominious end to a tawdry affair. Boy, has she left some debris behind.'

'She's done that, for sure. Not long after, the Super

picked up a censure for his troubles and, unable to stand being the butt of a thousand jokes, transferred to my old nick in Bradford.'

'An interesting story.'

'It's more than just a story, Angus, it's a warning across the bows. Take heed. How are you getting on finding Cindy Longhurst's killer?'

'Slow and steady, I'm afraid. Nothing came out of forensics.'

'I can't believe no one saw a car dumping a body in Saltdean at two or three o'clock in the morning. I thought elderly people needed less sleep and were usually up in the night having a pee.'

Henderson shook his head. 'We've talked to residents about a hundred yards either side of the dump site and nobody heard or saw a thing.'

'How can this be?'

'I think it's because the lounges of most of the houses along the seafront face the sea to maximise the view, and the bedrooms are at the back of the house, overlooking the garden.'

'Makes sense, I suppose, especially if you add in a bit of deafness and poor eyesight. Nothing from the body?'

'Nope. All we know is Cindy was kept in captivity, she was underfed and beaten before being shot. No prints, no DNA.'

'Who the hell would do this to a photographer? I can understand people not liking tabloid photographers who wait outside nightclubs and try to catch celebrities in short dresses climbing in and out of cars, but someone taking pictures of families and middle-aged women trying to re-launch their careers? It defies logic.'

'It doesn't make much sense to me either. We're now reviewing her customers and looking through her vast collection of photographs, looking for an anomaly.'

'Talk to me about the photographs.'

'We believe Cindy's kidnappers came to the studio to recover a series of photographs. They wanted the pictures as we believe they show something they didn't want publicised. They wanted her, because she witnessed it.'

'Which assumes it was always their intention to kill her.'

'Yep, it seems that way. However, once they looked at the SD cards they took away from her studio and found they weren't the ones they wanted, I think they beat her to find out where she'd hidden them.'

'I wonder if she coughed up.'

'Who knows, but if Cindy held out and refused to tell them where the pictures were, you would think the kidnappers would have come back to the studio for a second look. If they suspected they were still at the studio, they might have tried to burn the place down.'

'Which they couldn't do as we had people there, but what if she told them and they'd retrieved the pictures from a different place. Another studio for example.'

Henderson shrugged. He'd debated the same issues with the team numerous times. 'Maybe.'

'So, if the pictures aren't there, we're wasting the time of...how many officers do we have down there?'

'Six.'

'We might be wasting the time of six officers looking through old wedding photos and thousands of family portraits of Mum, Dad and two-point-four children.'

'It's one way to look at it, but what if she held out and the pictures are still there? Maybe the kidnappers believed they couldn't return to the studio because of us or they assumed we'd removed all the pictures as evidence.'

'It's a thin straw, Angus, and will cost us dear if it leads us down another blind alley.'

'But you're not against us looking?'

'I don't see you've given me much choice. You don't have any better leads to follow, do you?'

Henderson sighed and shook his head. 'Despite interviewing her ex-husband, business partner and ex-boyfriend. We only have Tony Mitchell left.'

She leaned across the desk towards him. 'Just remember the size of the crowd of journalists at yesterday's press conference. This case is high profile. With some reservations, I don't care what you do or how you do it, as long as you get me a quick result. Am I being clear?'

SIXTEEN

'Interview timed at ten-fifty,' Phil Bentley said.

Henderson looked across at their interview subject. Tony Mitchell's arms were folded and on his face he wore a scowl. The arms were large and tattooed but Henderson couldn't be bothered trying to read or decipher them, although he did notice a heart with an arrow through it, and the name 'Polly' inscribed in the middle.

'Mr Mitchell do you know why you are here today?'

He said nothing; the lined and stubble-marked face impassive.

'No? Well, let me enlighten you. You lied to my officers. You said when they asked where you were on the night Cindy Longhurst was murdered, you went to *The Cricketers* pub. We know you didn't.'

'Did I fuck lie to you. I said I went out for a couple of pints. If I said *The Cricketers* it was through habit.'

'How can you say that? You haven't stepped foot in the place for over six months.'

'You know what I mean.'

'No, I don't know what you mean. If you didn't go to *The Cricketers,* where did you go?'

'A pub along the road from there called *The Ship Inn.*'

'You sure?'

'Of course I'm sure.'

Henderson nudged Phil Bentley beside him.

'No, you didn't, sir,' Bentley said. 'We also checked with *The Ship Inn* and even though they know you and your son as regulars, they didn't see you or your son on the night in question.'

'How would they remember us? It's a busy place.'

Henderson could think of a few reasons. A large intimidating man pushing his son in a wheelchair, for one.

'Let's put the question to one side for the moment, Mr Mitchell, and talk about Cindy Longhurst.'

'What's there to talk about?'

'Tell me about her.'

'There's fuck-all to tell. She crippled my son, end of.'

'She did, there's no denying it, but your son was riding recklessly on his bike on a wet night when visibility would be poor and stopping distances greater.'

'Yeah, but she was going too fast, if she had been paying attention she could have stopped.'

'Not according to the officers who investigated the accident.' Henderson reached into a file and pulled out the accident report, turned it around and pushed it towards him. 'There it is in black and white, it couldn't be any clearer. She hadn't been drinking and her speed was less than the speed limit.'

He chucked the paper back at him. 'A bloody whitewash.'

'How can you say it's a whitewash? Cindy had no connections with the police. She didn't work for us and none of her family did.' Henderson sighed, before speaking slowly, giving the obdurate man in front of him time to absorb the meaning. 'Why don't you get it, Tony? Your son was injured in a car accident, tragic as it might be, but it wasn't the driver's fault.'

'I don't believe it.'

'You weren't there at the accident scene and, according to my officers who came to your house a few days ago, your son even believes it was his own fault.'

'You won't change my mind.'

Henderson looked at his face and saw something else; was it guilt, or regret? 'I think there's something else going on here, Tony. Tell me there isn't?'

His face was impassive again, the big shovels for arms and hands folded in an, 'I'm not talking to you' gesture.

He didn't know how to get him to talk, so he decided to throw a few contentious ideas at him and see how he reacted. 'You knew Cindy Longhurst before the accident, didn't you?'

No reaction.

'Something was going on between you and Cindy Longhurst, am I right? What was it? Were you two having an affair?'

'Don't be soft, I would never cheat on my wife.'

'I think you knew her before, Tony. You're a builder, did you do some work at Longhurst Studios? Lay the tarmac for the car park, improve the drainage, maybe?'

'It was my fucking company what built it.'

The nail had been truly hit on the head. 'Now I see.'

'See what?'

'What happened? Did she refuse to pay you? Did she become too demanding?'

'Nothing like that.'

'What then? Tell me.'

The arms unfolded. 'Construction of the studio was started by Wright-Carson. Remember them?'

Henderson shook his head.

'In the building trade on the south coast, they were the dog's bollocks. They got all the big contracts and the likes of us picked up the bones and scraps. Well, they took on a big contract to refurb a former power station in Thanet and found all this asbestos and radioactive material when they started clearing the site. It cost millions to sort and when, at the end of the job, they went to the client for payment, he refused. They sued, but with the time it was taking to go through the courts, they ran out of cash and went belly-up.'

'Was the demise of Wright-Carson good or bad news for you?'

'Good, because we picked up a lot of jobs they abandoned which made up for the many times in the past those bastards did us over.'

'Including Longhurst Studios?'

'Including Longhurst Studios.'

'What happened?'

'I don't know if you understand much about the building trade but, often as not, you just can't take over a job from the last guy, hoping to carry on where they left off. They'd done a lot of the ground work but they'd taken short cuts, you know?'

'Which would cost money to fix.'

'Right, but in addition, Wright-Carson under-priced the job and loads of others, probably another reason why they went bust.'

'I assume you discussed this all with Cindy before you started work.'

'Sure I did, but she insisted we come in under budget as it was all the money she could spare.'

'You could have walked away.'

'We could, but I thought we could make it.'

'Did you?'

'No, the job went over by twenty grand and she refused to pay.'

'Couldn't you reach a compromise?'

'Nope, she still owes me twenty grand.'

'Whether she owes you money or not, doesn't detract from the studio itself. You've done a terrific job, it's a magnificent building. You should be proud.'

'You think so?'

'Yes, I do.'

He sat more erect, the chest inflated and almost cracked a smile. 'Thanks.'

'Going back to the anger you expressed about Cindy Longhurst, twenty grand doesn't do it for me, Tony. You're a successful builder. You probably make that much on a quiet Friday afternoon.'

He clammed up again and Henderson knew he was on the right track.

'C'mon Tony, there's something else you're not telling me. I think you knew Cindy better than you're saying.'

The arms unfurled and he clumped his big mitts on the desk with a thump, making the desk vibrate like the start of an earthquake.

'We had a fucking affair and she dumped me when I thought we were about to move in together. Does that do it for you, Inspector?'

**

'This is like Manchester,' DS Neal said.

'I've never heard Brighton called that before. In what way?' her driver DC Sally Graham asked.

'You've got the city back there which I admit isn't as big as Manchester, but you only need to go a couple of miles outside and you're in the countryside.'

'I've been to Manchester and I know what you mean, but in the Pennines, the countryside is wild with no houses for miles. Here, there are few wild places, if any, and everywhere else that isn't built on is partitioned by big fences.'

'I don't see many buildings around here.'

'No, because here at Devil's Dyke,' she said pointing, 'the land to the left and right, is part of the South Downs and designated as a National Park. It's not easy to get permission to build in a National Park.'

'Right.'

Graham parked the car in the large car park, busy even on this dreary Wednesday afternoon. In her experience, many cars would be owned by 'weekend' walkers, people who would go for a half-hour walk and reward themselves with a large coffee and a chocolate muffin in the café. The detectives came to Devil's Dyke to allow DS Neal to see the place where Ted Mathieson had been stabbed with the added bonus of improving Neal's geographic knowledge of Sussex.

Neal walked away as if she had spotted something and by the time Graham collected her handbag and locked the car, she was some distance ahead. She ran and caught her up.

'What is it?' she asked the sergeant.

'Look.'

She followed her arm and saw a hang glider approaching. The pilot looked experienced, gently pulling the strings on either side of him, trying to put the giant kite where he wanted it to go. He landed without drama and rapidly gathered in the material behind before the stiff breeze whisked him back out over the valley.

'I like watching them,' Neal said as they walked back to the car park. 'What they do is so elegant.'

'Don't you fancy a go yourself?'

'No, not me. I can't do heights.'

'Right, the crime scene,' Graham said, pointing at the car park downhill from the café car park. 'Mathieson's car was parked over there. At the time he came here in the morning, it would have been deserted. Now, anytime I come for a bit of bird watching, I use the car park at the top, which is on the far side of the restaurant over there. There's always someone about. More often than not, another bird watcher.'

'Maybe he didn't care to have other people around him to see what he was up to.'

'Could be.'

'Two things still bother me though,' Neal said. 'Number one, there must be a dozen places where he could go for a walk between here and his house in Telscombe Cliffs. I was looking at a map last night.'

'For sure, there are some great cliff-top walks and under-cliff walks, he could access the South Downs close to where he lives and there's the Marina and Brighton Promenade as well.'

'My second reservation comes after speaking to DS Walters. Mathieson doesn't look or sound to her like a guy who goes on early-morning walks. He drinks, smokes and he's overweight. People I know like him have trouble getting out of bed in a cold morning, never mind coming to places like this for a bracing walk.'

'So why did he come here?'

'If we can find that out, I'm confident we'll find out the reason why he was stabbed.'

SEVENTEEN

DS Carol Walters drove through the village of Hurstpierpoint. Like many larger Sussex villages, it had a selection of small shops: newsagent, co-op, post office, café, each forced to up their game by the competition now coming from the web, in addition to the number of large supermarkets situated within a five-mile radius.

At least this village had more than one pub when many other villages had lost theirs. Like shops, they needed to do something different, and some were offering themed nights such as 'beers from around the country' or the 'best pies in the world.' Many around the county were also improving their food selection, shifting the focus from the drinking dens of the past into genuine competition for restaurants.

She turned down Langton Lane and took a left into Longhurst Studios.

'Whoa, look at this place,' DC Seb Young beside her said, 'it's straight out of an architectural magazine.'

'You sound like the boss, but I don't understand the appeal of all this wood.'

'It must have cost a packet.'

'It did.'

They got out of the car and walked quickly to the studio, the wicked, cold wind whipping across the fields in the distance didn't encourage lingering.

'Hello Annie,' Walters said when she spotted Annie Heath tidying up inside.

'Hello Sergeant, are you here to check on your team?'

'I am. I hope they're not bothering you or interfering with business.'

'No,' Annie said, 'they're tucked away in the office all day and don't bother me. Sometimes I think you become invisible when you're pregnant, you know? To be truthful, there's not much going on at the moment. I can't take over from Cindy as I can't stay on my feet for too long. Looking ahead, I don't know what's going to happen to this place.'

'I expect Ted Mathieson might try and employ a contract photographer until he can decide what to do with it. Did you hear what happened to Ted?'

'Terrible, isn't it? Do you guys think it's connected with Cindy's murder?'

'We don't think so, but we won't know for sure until we get a chance to speak to him.'

'It seems a heck of a coincidence if it isn't, but I don't see how Ted could be involved in anything, you know, illegal. He's a bit coarse and rough on the outside, but he's a teddy bear on the inside. If you could see the way he treated Cindy. He was lovely and she never had a bad word to say about him.'

Walters edged away, fearful of becoming embroiled in one of Annie's long reminiscences. 'I must get on, Annie. See you later.'

'She's so big,' Young said in a hushed tone as they reached the office door. 'Is she expecting quads or whatever the medical expression is for five?'

'Quintuplets, I think it's called. No, it's only twins. I just hope it doesn't all kick-off when we're around.'

She opened the door and the smell of stale coffee and a variety of body odours filled her nose, no wonder with six people all sitting at whirring laptops shoehorned into a small room ordinarily occupied by one.

'Morning all.'

'Morning Sarg.'

Six officers, including detectives Graham, Bentley and Newman from the murder team were spaced out around the desk, the others making use of any flat surface or trying to balance the computer on their knee.

'You've briefed the newbies?' she asked DC Sally Graham.

'I did, as much as anyone can for an inquiry like this.'

Walters looked around. Each officer had a box of SD cards. They slotted an SD card into the laptop, waited for it to load before skimming through all the pictures, making sure it matched the description on the index card. She stood behind Sally Graham and could see hundreds of images of a woman and her two kids.

'She's taken a ton of stuff like this,' Graham said. 'Hundreds of pictures of one person or a couple. It's the beauty of digital, you can take as many photographs as you want. I do it when I'm bird watching and delete the crappy ones when I get home.'

'I had a family photo done once,' Young said. 'My mother wanted a picture of the four of us and in a few good shots, my brother had his eyes closed. On pictures where he didn't, my mother did. What the photographer did was lift a decent picture of my brother and merged it with a photograph where the rest of us looked good. It's the one she now has on her wall.'

'Clever.'

'It is, and that process of trying to find a photo with a few of the people looking good probably accounts for a large portion of the pictures you're seeing here.'

Walters walked to the filing cabinet and opened a drawer. Cindy operated a comprehensive indexing system and Walters would bet the photographer could lay her hands on a specific set of images in a matter of minutes. Problem was, none of the headings suggested anything malicious, something so bad that it would encourage kidnappers to take her away to beat her up and murder her. The headings instead hinted at normality, ordinary people recording key moments in their lives: birth, graduation, birthday, confirmation, marriage, Bar Mitzvah, golden wedding.

Young was looking over her shoulder.

'It's all ordinary stuff here,' Walters said, 'if we believe what's on the labels.'

'Maybe she kept the serious stuff off-site.'

She considered this. Putting herself in Cindy's shoes, would she keep something secret, never mind her lifetime's work in a wooden building? Pretty as it was, it would be less secure from the standpoint of fire, burglary and adverse weather conditions than the substantial stone-built house next door.

She looked at Young. 'Let's ask, shall we?'

They left the office and were rewarded with a blast of cooler but fresher-smelling air as they stepped into the studio. They found Annie, leaning against a wall, her face contorted in pain.

'Are you all right?' Walters asked.

'Yeah, I'm fine. I think the little buggers are having their gym lessons at this time of the morning.'

A minute or so later, Annie's face returned to normal and her breathing to a regular rate. 'What can I do for you?'

'Did Cindy keep copies of her work off-site?'

She sighed. 'She made me promise not to tell anyone, but I suppose it doesn't matter now. On a Friday, she would transfer everything she did in the past week from SD to a portable hard drive and stored them away from the studio.'

'Where did she keep them?'

'In the house.'

'If you can tell us where they are, we'll go over there and get them.'

'I'm not a cripple, sergeant. C'mon,' she said levering herself away from the support of the wall, 'and I'll show you.'

They followed the waddling Annie over to the house. She unlocked the front door, pushed it open and headed into the hall to silence the alarm.

'No one's been in here since Cindy was kidnapped, except your forensics people and Greg to pick up some of Molly's things,' Annie said after the buzzing stopped. 'It's a shame, this is such a lovely house and

146

Cindy was always entertaining.'

Young and Walters walked into the house and Annie directed them to a small library.

The shelves were not made of dark walnut so beloved of film makers when they wanted to show a quintessential English setting, but a light wood which she thought was ash, lightly coated with a non-translucent varnish. The shelves were also not filled with reams of dusty old books that no one would ever read, but a huge selection of crime, romance, thriller and literary novels as good as could be seen in a small bookshop.

'Cindy loved her books,' Annie said. 'She'd rather immerse herself in a good story than sit mindlessly watching telly, she often told me. Personally, I would miss all the soaps and crime dramas that I like to follow, but when there's nothing on the box except rubbish or football, I do like to read a good book. Cindy let me borrow any book I wanted from here. I don't suppose I'll get much chance to pick up a book or anything else when those two come along,' she said patting her stomach.

'Your own private library,' Young said.

'It is really.'

'The back-up disks?' Walters said.

'See if you can spot them. The forensics guys didn't until I showed them, but then they didn't spend much time in the house.'

'Where are they, on the shelves?'

'Yeah.'

Walters scanned the lines of neatly ordered novels, hardback books about photography, art and travel but she couldn't see anything that didn't look like a book.

'Do you give up?'

The detectives both nodded.

Annie pointed to a shelf. 'Do you see them now? You'll need to do the fetching as I can't stretch.'

Walters could see them, slim, grey, about the size of a novel, anonymous in a sea of similar-sized items and well hidden from prying eyes. She reached up and removed five portable hard disks drives.

'They're a couple of terabytes each. Cindy buys new ones every year as she says storage prices are falling and a new one holds more and is faster than the one before. It must be true as she was doing more work than ever before and yet three years ago it would take seven drives to do her weekly back-up.'

'It's good having those,' Walters said, 'it should speed things up. Shall we go back?'. She didn't want Sally and the rest of the little crew in the office looking through more SD cards any longer than necessary, as plugging in one hard disk drive would be quicker and easier than loading and unloading a pile of SD cards. In addition, she believed Cindy might have copied any incriminating files straight to one of those, so if her kidnappers ransacked the studio or set the place on fire, the secret pictures would still be safe.

They were walking towards the front door of the house when Annie stopped and let out a loud groan. She leaned against the wall for support. When she didn't return to her usual self a few moments later, Walters asked, 'Annie, are you all right?'

'No, I don't think so,' she said breathing hard. 'I think my waters are breaking. Can you call me an ambulance?'

Walters helped Annie into a chair in the living room while Young called for an ambulance.

'Are the police trained to deliver babies?' Annie asked.

'No, it's more to carry out first-aid and treat trauma wounds, but many of us have been in this situation before.'

'With twins?'

'There's always a first.'

Annie groaned, the spasms coming at regular intervals. Walters soon found the kitchen and returned to the lounge with a bowl and a cloth and started to dab Annie's brow as her temperature was rising. She took her hand and instructed her to take deep breaths.

Young was standing at the living room door, motionless.

'Are you all right, Seb?' Walters asked. 'You're looking a bit pale.'

'No, I don't have a clue what to do with something like this,' Young said.

Me neither, she was about say, not with twins anyway. 'Don't look so startled, it's only babies. I tell you what you can do, walk out to the end of the driveway and direct the ambulance. This place isn't so easy to find.'

Young, grateful for the chance to escape, disappeared out the door without saying another word.

Ten minutes later the ambulance appeared. Annie's contractions hadn't restarted and, in some respects, she looked and sounded the same as when they'd met her earlier. The paramedics told her that labour hadn't started yet, but as her waters had broken, they would take her into hospital.

'It puts you off having kids,' Walters said as they watched Annie being helped into the ambulance.

'What, all the pain and the lack of mobility?' Young said.

'No, doing a job like this. I don't see how anybody can be pregnant in the middle of a murder investigation.'

EIGHTEEN

'Where are we going?' Henderson asked the pool car's driver, DS Neal. 'I thought you said Ted Mathieson was still in hospital?'

'He is.'

'The Royal Sussex is the other way.'

'He's been transferred to the Belvedere, a private hospital in Hove.'

'Ah, right. The NHS not good enough for him?'

'Apparently not.'

'I hope the satnav is programmed. I don't want us getting lost.'

'Don't worry, it is. I'm usually good with directions, but not having lived in Sussex too long, I'm not yet confident of knowing my way about.'

'There aren't many tall buildings or landmarks around here to help get your bearings, but if you can see the sea, at least you'll know which way is south.'

'Makes a change from Manchester. People give you directions based on football stadiums and pubs.'

'Sounds a bit like Glasgow.'

They turned into the Belvedere Hospital in Hove and, first impressions, the building didn't have the look or feel of a place like the Royal Sussex. The detectives didn't need to drive around a massive car park looking for a parking space and there weren't any ticket machines to rob them of all their change. Inside, it looked and smelled like a hotel, the illusion extending to the Reception area where they were met, not by a nurse or a charity volunteer, but by a smartly-dressed receptionist.

Henderson leaned over the desk and showed her his ID. 'DI Henderson and DS Neal to see Ted Mathieson.'

'Ah, good morning detectives, Mr Mathieson is expecting you. You'll find him in Room 34.'

They walked down a corridor past private rooms for the privileged few to recover in peace, cossetted with the accoutrements he could see through an open door: HD television, remote-adjustable bed and a mini hi-fi system.

Henderson knocked on the door of Room 34. He gave the occupant and his guest, if one was inside, a second or two to shout out if they were indecent or otherwise indisposed. He opened the door.

Ted Mathieson was alone and lying in bed, one end slightly raised where the addition of two fat pillows supported the patient's head. He was watching television while picking at a punnet of grapes. He could keep the television as Henderson failed to see the attraction of daytime viewing: game shows, films and the re-running of old soaps, but he wouldn't mind a few grapes.

'Good morning Mr Mathieson.'

'Ah, it's you lot. I was wondering when you would show up.'

'I can see your brush with death hasn't softened your attitude to the police.'

Henderson took a seat to the patient's left while Neal stood at the base of the bed, beneath the television.

'Do you mind if I help myself to a few grapes?'

'Fill your boots.'

'So, how are you?'

'I tell you, whoever did this to me must be having sleepless nights. If they don't know what I'm capable of, they're in for a mighty surprise.'

'You can forget any thoughts of retribution, leave this investigation to the police. Turn the television off. I'd like to talk to you about what happened.'

Mathieson reluctantly picked up the remote control lying on the bed and switched it off. He was wearing pyjamas, partially open at the front where Henderson could see a broad bandage around his torso. His pallor didn't look so bad for man who had been stabbed.

He'd seen other victims in the past, spread out on the pathologist's table, ready to be dissected, or those barely living and looking like Banquo's ghost having just come out of surgery where a spleen or a kidney had been removed. The difference between a successful and unsuccessful outcome depended on three factors: the size and cleanliness of the assailant's blade, the location the knife entered the body and how quickly the patient could be seen by medical professionals.

'Mr Mathieson, first of all, can you explain your presence at Devil's Dyke at six o'clock on a Tuesday morning?'

'I can go where the hell I like. It's a free country the

last time I looked.'

'Mr Mathieson, let me start at the beginning for your benefit. When anyone is assaulted like you have been, it is the job of the police to talk to the victim and witnesses, investigate the incident and bring the perpetrator to justice. This is what we'd like to do now without hearing any frosty comments from you. So, I'll ask you again. What were you doing at Devil's Dyke at this early hour of the morning?'

Mathieson's face looked grumpy and his body language would have mirrored his mood except that when he tried to move, he winced in pain. 'I'm not a good sleeper and often I wake at five or six in the morning and can't get back to sleep. When I do, sometimes I go out for a walk.'

'Do me a favour, in the dark?'

'Yes, in the dark. I like to be outside when the sun comes up.'

'Very lyrical, I'm sure. What happened next?'

'I got there and went for a walk around Devil's Dyke. When I came back to my car someone appeared behind it and pointed a knife at me. He told me if I didn't give him my money and my phone he'd stick a knife in me.'

'What did this person look like?'

'He had wavy black hair, green eyes and wore a black Adidas tracksuit.'

'Any distinguishing marks?'

'A scar above his right eye.'

'Age?'

'Twenty-four, twenty-five.'

'It's a good description. It will give us something to

go on. What happened then?'

'I told him I didn't have my wallet on me, only my phone. It was the truth, I only intended going out for a walk. Nothing is open at that time of the morning, so there's no reason to bring any money. He got agitated at hearing this, probably a druggie itching for a fix, and made a grab for my wrist to see if I was wearing a watch. I took a chance and went for him and we tussled. It was then I got stabbed.'

'What did your assailant do?'

'He ran off.'

'Did you notice if he came by car or was he on foot?'

'I don't know, I was too busy trying to stay alive to see if the bastard made it home safely.'

'What did you do then?'

'I crawled to my car, opened the door and pressed the horn. A passing jogger heard the noise and called an ambulance.'

'You're lucky anyone was about. I think the cleaners at the restaurant at the top of the hill don't start work until eight. You'd have been in a sorry state by then.'

'I might have died,' he said with dramatic effect, 'according to the paramedic.'

'Do you think you were targeted or are we looking here at a random robbery?

'How do you mean targeted?'

'If you're in the habit of walking around Devil's Dyke in the early hours of the morning, perhaps someone noticed your presence and was waiting for you.'

'I see what you're getting at. Nah, I don't go there regularly, random I would say.'

'You are aware we are in the middle of an investigation into Cindy Longhurst's murder.'

'How could I forget? You already know that Cindy was a good friend of mine.'

'Do you think,' Henderson said, posing the main question he wanted to ask today, 'your assault is in any way connected?'

'You're having a laugh, Inspector. Cindy was kidnapped and killed by a serious team of villains. I was attacked and stabbed by a pathetic junkie desperate for cash to secure his next fix. If you can get a connection out of that you're a better man than me.'

Henderson had met many junkies in his time and none were early risers. Most were lucky to be out of bed by the early afternoon. In addition, Devil's Dyke was several miles outside Brighton, requiring the use of a bike or a car. If a habitual drug user owned anything valuable, they usually sold it in the early stages of their career.

'I'm being serious,' the DI said. 'We find Cindy Longhurst with a bullet in her head and a few days later her principal business partner is found stabbed. Can you not see why we might think the two events could be related?'

'Well, I think they're not.'

'How can you be so sure?'

Mathieson opened his mouth to speak and closed it. Perhaps the temptation to utter the real reason for his early morning jaunt to Devil's Dyke being overruled by an innate desire to keep his nose out of trouble.

'I'm an investor in Cindy's business, but I don't know what she gets up to on a day-to-day basis or even month-to-month. I don't work with her and she doesn't work with me. We're not connected at the hip.'

'You said when we first came in about taking your revenge on the person responsible for your injuries. In order to do so, it assumes you know the name of the individual who stabbed you. Would you like to tell me who you think it might be?'

'You're twisting my words, Inspector. I didn't say I know them, but if I were to find out the name of the guy who did it. In any case, it was anger talking. I don't know the name of this junkie bloke any more than you do.'

A few minutes later, the detectives walked back to their car, once more out in the cold after the warm, fragrant air of the Belvedere.

'It's your first time meeting him, Vicky. What did you think?'

'He's aggressive and spikey, but that may be due to the injury or the drugs. However, his story didn't ring true.'

Henderson laughed. 'Why not?'

'I can't see a druggie or even a serious mugger being around Devil's Dyke so early in the morning. I also think he goes there more often than he suggests, maybe to meet a woman or to sell contraband. The story about a mugger is no more than that, a story.'

'If you're in any doubt, pick up yesterday's *Argus*, a copy of which I noticed on Mathieson's bed. Inside on page three or five, I think it is, you'll see an article about a bloke who robbed a bookmaker in Hollingbury. The description of the culprit caught on CCTV matches Mathieson's assailant, down to the make of tracksuit and the scar above his eye.'

'The crafty sod.'

'When we get back to the office, find DC Graham and the two of you get over to Mathieson Transport and talk to the people there. With Ted Mathieson out of the frame for a few days you might, if you're lucky, get the chance to take a look around. See if you can find out what he's been up to.'

'Shouldn't we apply for a search warrant and turn the place over?'

'On what grounds?'

She shrugged. 'Suspicions of criminal activity?'

'We've no evidence to back it up. For the moment, Ted Mathieson is a victim and our job is to find out what took place at Devil's Dyke. You said yourself, he might be going there to meet a woman. What if her husband showed up with a knife? However, if you do find anything incriminating when you go to Mathieson Transport, I'll happily apply for a search warrant.'

On the way back to the office, he instructed Neal to take a detour. A few minutes later they turned into the car park at the Regency Wine Warehouse in Portslade.

'I'll be back in a minute,' Henderson said as he got out of the car. 'I just need to pick up something.'

He entered the vast building, stacked high with wine from every corner of the globe, some from places that he didn't know made wine. The owner came from Eastern Europe and this explained the large selection of bottles from Serbia, Croatia and Bulgaria, not often seen in other wine shops.

This morning he didn't have time to dawdle, not that looking at wine labels held much interest anyway, but despite being predominately a wine warehouse, they stocked a fabulous collection of Scotch whisky. The other booze establishments in the chain were similarly equipped, creating an inviting haven for people like Henderson, and all because the boss liked to drink the stuff himself.

The following night, he and Rachel had been invited to the home of Rachel's new boss, a large house in Tongdean Avenue in Hove, for a dinner party. He knew a newspaper editor's salary didn't stretch to a house in such a good area, but his wife was rich, her father a millionaire businessman. As a consequence, the sort of wine he and Rachel drank over Sunday lunch, a five quid bottle of own-label, didn't hit the mark. He was under strict instructions to buy a couple of bottles of decent Californian Zinfandel.

Balking at the high prices, he finally selected two bottles at twenty pounds each and carried them to the counter. There, a pretty assistant by the name of Tamsin, who looked too young to drink alcohol herself, wrapped his purchases in tissue paper while he reached for his credit card and inserted it into the machine.

'Angus. I haven't seen you for ages.'

Henderson turned. 'Simon,' he said sticking out his hand. 'It's good to see you again. How are you?'

'I'm great. Glad I left, to tell you truth. The station

was doing my head in.'

'What are doing now?'

'Security consultant.'

Henderson spent a few minutes catching up with his former colleague before saying goodbye. No matter how much ex-Detective Sergeant Simon James tried to put a gloss on his departure from Sussex Police, he couldn't hide the trembling hand and the bottle of whisky held discreetly at his side.

The former DS had a serious drink problem in the latter stages of his career at John Street, and it looked as if the new job hadn't changed him. Looking at his own habits, Henderson often met narks in pubs, the team celebrated successes there and he and Rachel could usually be found in one. Habits like this, forged in the harsh environment of a tough job didn't always go away when the job disappeared, as Simon James proved. It was a warning which Henderson would be a fool to ignore.

NINETEEN

'What do you do, Angus?'

Henderson took a moment to consider the question. Depending on who he was speaking to, he might say 'cop', 'security consultant', or if making a real effort to keep a low profile, 'government employee.' None of which were a downright lie.

He and Rachel were at the house of Rachel's boss, News Editor Gary Richardson. The person posing the question was one of Gary's neighbours, Steve Gatson. The owner of a burglar alarm business, a man more likely to respect the police than hate them, so instead he said, 'Detective Inspector, Sussex Police.'

'Interesting. Do you deal with house burglary and shoplifting or are you involved in the more serious stuff?'

'I'm in Serious Crimes.'

'I imagine the big case of the moment is the murdered photographer from Hurstpierpoint.'

'You're right, but before you ask if there are any suspects in custody, the answer is no. Not yet.'

Henderson lifted his wine glass, a deep red Barolo with strong cherry hints, according to his eulogising host earlier, and took a drink. Most people would turn away at this point and start talking to someone else, unwilling to continue a conversation that could expose them to the dark underbelly of the place where they lived, but to Henderson's surprise he didn't.

'I suspect the job must be harrowing at times.'

'You're quite right, it can be.'

'How do you cope? I suppose you develop a bit of a thick skin after a time.'

'For sure you do, and the way you measure it is when you come across an awful sight like a multiple stabbing or a fire. I look at the youngest and newest constable. You see, I might be analysing the scene dispassionately, trying to establish how they died and looking for clues, but chances are they're throwing up their guts.'

'It shows how other people are responding to the crime even though you might be trying to block it out.'

'Yes, but it's a difficult path to navigate. We're human like everyone else, and if I was to imagine a loved one in such a situation, I'd fall apart, right?'

'Sure, but it wouldn't do for detectives to fall apart when talking to relatives of the victim.'

'I can't say it's never happened.'

'I bet.'

'So, on the one hand, we've got to be dispassionate and analytical in the way we conduct the investigation and how we deal with members of the press, like Gary over there,' he said nodding across the table to the man opposite. 'On the other, we need to have sympathy and compassion for the grieving family.'

'It must put a strain on marriages and health, with people working long, unsociable hours.'

'It does but it's not only the long hours, it's the junk food eaten late into the night to keep us going and the booze consumed at the end of a hard day or week.'

'The point Steve raised about relationships is a valid one,' a woman at the far end of the table said. Henderson hadn't drunk much wine as he was on-call, but he'd been slow to realise the other eight occupants around the table had stopped talking and were listening to the conversation between him and Gary Richardson's neighbour.

'She's a marriage guidance counsellor,' Steve said in his ear.

She went on to throw around statistics about the level of divorce within the Emergency and Social Services, how they were higher than the national average and similar to those found in the emergency services of other Western European nations. He'd read the same thing many times before himself, and when encountering such an article in a magazine or newspaper, it often ended up in the bin. He preferred to concentrate on the successes in his life, not the failures.

He was saved from further analysis-paralysis when his phone rang. He excused himself and walked into the hall.

'Is this Detective Inspector Henderson?'

'It is.'

'Lewes Control, Amanda speaking. How are you this evening, sir?'

He knew Amanda and made a point of talking to her whenever he spotted her smiling face in the staff restaurant.

'I'm not bad. You rescued me from a potential ear

bashing.'

'In which case, I suspect you've now moved from the frying pan into the fire. We've received a report of a body on the Castle Hill National Nature Reserve.'

'What's the location?'

She gave him the coordinates and, turning to face the wall, his phone jacked to his ear and his notebook held up against the smart, expensive-looking wallpaper, jotted down the details.

'The body was found by a passing driver, who stopped to take a leak. The pathologist has been called.'

'I'll need a SOCO team with a portable lighting rig, and can you call DS Walters and ask her to meet me there?'

'Will do. Anything else?'

'No, thank you. Bye Amanda.'

'Bye sir.'

Henderson knew the place Amanda was talking about, a large area of open farmland to the east of Brighton, a Site of Special Scientific Interest, with few trees to break up the undulating landscape. He turned to find Rachel standing there.

'Who's Amanda?'

'An operator at Lewes Control. She's mid-fifties, three kids and twice the size of you.'

'Are you leaving?'

'I'm afraid so.'

'How can you? My boss is in there. How will it look with me just moving into a new job?'

'It will look fine. Gary works with news journalists, he knows what it's like being on-call.'

He reached forward to put his hands on her shoulders but she pulled away.

'Don't. You leaving will spoil my evening.'

'Rachel, I can't stand here and discuss this with you. You knew when we first started going out things like this could happen.'

'Well maybe I didn't think hard enough.'

'We'll talk about this later. I need to go. Can you apologise to the folks in there for me?'

He looked at her; stony face, hands on hips, lips in a tight line.

'Bye,' he said.

That went well he said to himself as he opened the car door. Luckily, Rachel's boss owned a large house with a driveway big enough to accommodate all the cars outside, as he didn't want to waste any more time by asking those inside the house to shift their vehicles out of the way.

Gary lived in Hove and it didn't take long for Henderson to make his way to the A27. At Falmer, he took the turn-off towards the American Express Community Stadium, the Amex as it was known to Brighton and Hove Albion supporters. About half a mile past the stadium, where in the daylight drivers would see little more than rolling fields to the left and right, a featureless landscape in winter but full of life in the summer, he slowed and pulled into the side of the road. He parked behind two vehicles, one a police patrol car and the other the VW Golf belonging to DS Walters.

'You got here before me for a change,' he said to the approaching DS as he got out of the car.

'I didn't have so far to drive when the call came.'

'Out with the new man?'

'No, he's attending a conference in Vienna.'

'What's the story here?' Henderson said as he opened the boot of the car, took out a protective plastic suit, shoes and gloves and put them on.

'Nathan Farrell, the guy now sitting in the back of the patrol car, got out of his car, which he's moved up the road to let our vehicles in, to take a leak. He walked over there,' she said pointing into the field, 'so passing cars wouldn't see him.'

'I don't see much cover.'

'I guess if he moved in about five metres, car lights wouldn't pick him up.'

'Okay, so he walks into the field. Did he trip over the body or did he spot it?'

'He was standing there peeing, looking back at the road when he saw it. First, it was picked up by a car's headlights, and a minute or so later he went over to investigate.'

'You know my next question.'

'Did he touch the body? No, he got such a fright he immediately ran back to his car and called us.'

'Last question. Why did he need to stop for a leak? Has he been drinking?'

She nodded. 'Over the limit.'

'Ah shit.' Breathalysing a witness and then telling him, if he didn't already know, he was about to lose his licence and being hit with a hefty fine didn't make for a cooperative witness. For some people, it could mean they couldn't continue doing their current job and, in addition, when they finally got their licence back, their insurance premiums would rocket, that is, if they could find an insurer willing to take the risk at all.

'Let's take a look at the body.'

The verges on both sides of the road were covered in coarse grass and weeds to knee-height. The body lay even further below the verge in what looked to him like a drainage ditch, making it invisible to passing cars. In some ways, it was a good place to dump a body. Cars zipped past at fifty to sixty miles an hour without stopping and those who walked in this part of the South Downs were instructed to stick to designated paths.

By the light of the torch he could see it was a woman and looking closer, a naked young woman, perhaps eighteen or nineteen with brown wavy hair. It was obvious she was dead without him checking, which he did with a gloved hand on her neck. Her skin was as pale as a ghost, no colour on her lips and her eyes were open and staring vacantly at weeds.

'A pretty girl if not for the bruises and scratches on her face and around her ribs,' Walters said.

'Indeed,' Henderson said, 'and—'

'Who is this interfering with my crime scene?'

'It's not me, gov, honest,' Henderson said. He stood and stretched.

'Hello Angus,' Grafton Rawlings, the pathologist, said, as he walked towards him.

'Hello Grafton. I didn't hear the familiar growl of your car's exhaust.'

'This is because I parked it up the road on a paved section. Can't have the Healey sitting on damp grass.

What have we here?'

'A young woman who looks as if she's been badly beaten. The cause of death isn't obvious.'

'Give me a few minutes and I might be able to tell you.'

Rawlings bent down and with a practiced hand, felt all around her head and down the contours of her body.

Henderson stepped away and approached Walters. 'The bruises worry me,' he said.

'Me too.'

'Are you thinking what I'm thinking?'

'They look similar to those on Cindy Longhurst?'

He nodded. 'They do, but I'm hoping it's something else.'

'What, you'd rather we had two murderers running around Sussex than one?'

'No. It would be easier with one killer for sure, as two crime scenes can be compared and differences identified. I was thinking this might be something we can sort out quickly, like a domestic.'

'I think you're clutching at straws, boss.'

'Angus, can you give me a hand to turn her?' Rawlings asked.

Henderson walked towards the pathologist but stopped when he heard a noise behind him.

'Where do you want the lights, gov?' a deep voice said.

In the dim light Henderson could make out two members of the SOCO team carrying a portable lighting unit.

'Over here,' Henderson said pointing at a point

near Rawlings, 'but make sure the beam is angled down and facing into the field. We don't want it blinding passing drivers.'

'Right oh.'

 Henderson knelt down beside the body. He placed his hands on the dead woman's back and the top of her legs.

'On the count of three,' Rawlings said, 'one, two three.' Henderson heaved and they rolled the inert figure from lying on her front to her back.

With a click, the tragic scene before them became bathed in a cold, white light, further emphasising the paleness of the cadaver's skin. Not only did the lighting rig brighten the area, it illuminated the bullet wound he could now see at the side of the dead woman's skull.

TWENTY

DI Henderson stood outside the door of Assistant Chief Constable Andy Youngman's office. A few moments later, the man himself came out to join him and they both walked in the direction of the conference room.

The murder of the girl found on the Castle Hill National Nature Reserve had caused palpitations around Sussex. The similarities between her death and Cindy Longhurst's were not lost on anyone, including the press, who were already warning young women not to venture out alone at night.

What they were cautioning them against, Henderson didn't know. He didn't know if the murders were the work of a sadistic serial killer, stalking the streets and country lanes of the region, or something else. If they were seeking a serial killer, he would applaud such advice, but a number of other possibilities also came to mind. Problem was, he didn't have the hard evidence to counter the growing hysteria.

Youngman walked into the conference room, a large auditorium with seating for over two hundred, Henderson in his wake. In the seats and standing along the aisles, not the jaundiced faces of weather-beaten cops, none too happy at having to listen to the

ACC banging on about another racial equality initiative or anti-drugs campaign, but the nation's media. Looking closely, he could see print journalists, online reporters, television news and a couple of German and French television crews.

ACC Youngman, the officer with ultimate responsibility for the Major Crime Team, took centre stage both in seating position and in stature. Six-foot-four and built like a useful centre-half, Youngman was two years away from fifty-five, police retirement age, but the bald man with the eagle-eyed stare, was a dedicated keep-fit enthusiast. He eschewed fast-food and alcohol, late-night staples for most of those under his command, and could outrun many men much younger than him.

Youngman arranged the papers in front of him and then stood, a cue for those in the hall to be quiet. 'On Friday, at around eleven in the evening, the body of this young woman was found at the edge of Falmer Road, close to the American Express Community Stadium.'

Behind Youngman's large frame, the screen lit up. The first image displayed the murder scene followed by the best photograph Grafton Rawlings could arrange of the victim's face after she'd been cleaned up. With a little make-up, she looked less pale but it couldn't disguise the bruises around her nose, cheeks and ear, although the blood-matted hair around the side of her head had been washed and tidied, leaving no trace of the bullet's deadly entry.

'We have been unable to identify this girl from the Missing Persons Register and therefore I would like to appeal to all your readers and viewers to look closely at this photograph. If anyone can identify this young woman, I would ask them to contact our helpline.'

The telephone number of the helpline appeared on the screen.

'I would like to assure all callers to the helpline, their calls will be treated in confidence. I would like now to hand over to Detective Inspector Angus Henderson, the Senior Investigating Officer on this case.'

Henderson stood. He took a moment to look at his audience. It wasn't a dark room as favoured by pop bands and comedians, the floodlights obscuring all except the front row. Ten-thirty in the morning, all ceiling lights blazing, they could see him and he could see them. He clicked the little device in his hand and the screen behind him came alive with a photograph of the murder scene.

'As the Assistant Chief Constable said, the body of this young woman was found at the side of the Falmer Road, about half a mile from the Amex Stadium. I say at the side of the road, but due to the height of the grass and the shallow ditch where the body was located, it would have been completely obscured from passing motorists and walkers.

'The cause of death was a bullet wound to the side of the head. The bruises on her face and body indicate she had been beaten before being killed. The time of death was approximately twenty-four hours before. We believe the body was taken to the place where she was found shortly after she was killed, between two and three o'clock the previous morning. I would appeal to any motorists travelling along the B2123, Falmer Road, in the early hours of Thursday morning to come forward. They may have seen something that could help us.'

Henderson paused for a moment or two to let them digest the information, but not long enough for them to believe his stint was over and they could now bombard him with questions.

'Forensic tests have been carried out on the body and ballistics are examining the bullet which killed her. Enquiries are continuing.' Henderson re-took his seat.

'We have time for a short question and answer session,' Andy Youngman said. 'Before asking your question, please state your name and the organisation you represent.'

Before Youngman finished speaking, the clamour to ask a question was the most animated Henderson had seen.

Youngman pointed at a woman in the first row, blonde with crimson highlights and red lipstick designed to dazzle.

'Shirley Fairbrother, *Sky News*. Can I ask Detective Inspector Henderson, does he see any similarity between this murder and the abduction and murder of photographer, Cindy Longhurst, at Hurstpierpoint in late January?'

'The similarities,' Henderson said, 'between the two victims are this: both are women, both were found bruised, and both had been shot in the head. There's not enough information to say if they both have been killed by the same person or not, and I would ask you not to speculate.'

'Can't you tell from the bullets recovered from both bodies? Sorry, Bill Crowley, *Independent*.'

'You're quite right, we can,' Henderson said. 'Two bullets fired from the same gun will display uniquely identifiable properties. We are in the process of analysing the bullet which killed the current victim. We will have more information when this analysis is complete.'

'Steve King, *The Times*. Is it right for members of the tabloid press such as the *Daily Mail* and the *Sun* to ask the women of Sussex to stay indoors?'

'Newspapers are free to print what they want, I can't stop them. However, I believe there is no need to panic. People, as always, should be careful when going out and report to the police anything they think looks suspicious.'

'Rob Tremain, *The Argus*. Are you any closer to finding out who killed Cindy Longhurst?'

'If I can answer this question,' the ACC said. 'DI Henderson's team have spent significant time and resources tracking back through Ms Longhurst's life, her considerable photography career, and interviewing most of her friends and associates. Enquiries are continuing and we are confident of apprehending the offender soon.'

Youngman called a halt a few minutes later. For high profile cases like this, calling for a Q&A could turn into a bruising and counter-productive mistake, but it offered those present a snapshot of what journalists were thinking and what might be appearing on tonight's news bulletins or in tomorrow's newspapers.

Clare Park, the Sussex force's Media Coordinator stood. 'All the photographs presented today are included in your media pack. If you require proofs, I can supply them. My number is also in the pack. Thank you all for attending.'

Henderson and the ACC filed out, the officers to the right, the journalists to the back of the hall. Intermingling was asking for trouble and the police forces that tried it often found themselves with a brawl on their hands and, of course, photographers and camera crews were already primed and ready to record every last detail.

'You did some good work in there, Angus,' Youngman said in his clipped, military delivery as they walked together. 'You sounded decisive but didn't let slip too many details.'

'Thank you, sir.'

They headed out the back door of the building where they would part, Henderson to his office, Youngman to his.

The ACC turned to face him, the eagle-stare much in evidence. 'You saw them in there, Angus, they're like a pack of wolves. If we don't get a result soon, they'll eat us alive. I'm counting on you but listen: if you don't feel you're up for it, tell me and I'll appoint someone else.' He poked a finger at Henderson's chest. 'This has got to be sorted ASAP for all our sakes. Understood?'

**

Henderson returned to his office after the press conference, the Assistant Chief Constable's voice still ringing in his ears. His bosses wanted results, the press wanted results, his team wanted results and so did he. They were all aiming at the same target but what the media didn't know and his bosses didn't care to consider, was some cases were more difficult to solve than others. If anyone harboured any doubts, he could point to the large pile of 'cold cases' which any police force could produce.

He pushed the paperwork he intended doing to one side and stood leaning on the front of his desk and stared at the whiteboard. There, he'd marked up the names of the main men in Cindy Longhurst's life: Ted Mathieson, Greg Jackson, and Mike Harrison. He needed to get Youngman's voice out of his head and focus on this. He took a deep breath and walked closer to the whiteboard, looking closely at the small pictures tacked up there.

Ted Mathieson, the rich transport company owner who'd burned a candle for Cindy and who wanted to marry her but she had turned him down. His reason for killing her would be what? If he couldn't have her, no one else would? It sounded plausible and was a motive cited in several killings he knew about, but Mathieson didn't strike him as the overwrought, part-unhinged, impetuous type, characteristics of the murderers in those sorts of cases. He appeared cool and calculating and was more likely to say, 'If she doesn't want me, fuck it, I'll find someone who does.' A former Miss Lithuania didn't sound like a bad second-choice.

Greg Jackson, Cindy's former husband, a man whose life was passing him by as Cindy's went from strength to strength. A man in a poorly paid job with a boorish boss and a teenage boy to bring up, it wasn't a surprise when he talked about money; or rather the lack of it. However, Cindy's demise wouldn't make him any richer. Her estate wouldn't go to her ex-husband, who said himself he had cut all ties with her, but more than likely to her two children. If not about money, Jackson might have been jealous of her success, or did he do it to get his own back on Ted Mathieson, a man who loved Cindy and the one responsible for firing him?

It had a ring of truth about it, but having met the man, he didn't think him capable of killing anyone. In any case, where would he find two heavies to drag her from her studio and bundle her into a car? In the engineering business where he worked? Getting two people to do your bidding required either a powerful and persuasive personality and plenty of money. Greg Jackson had neither of those.

Mike Harrison looked more promising, not because he was an interesting character, but because he needed to understand what attracted Cindy to him. Some tradesmen he knew couldn't wait to get out of their work gear and were smart, snappy dressers who could impersonate a banker or a lawyer if they put their minds to it. Others fell into the 'scruffy' class with traces of paint and plaster in their hair, their clothes stained and their fingernails permanently dirty.

Harrison belonged in the latter category, a guy

whose trade could be determined on a first meeting. Why did Cindy, a woman with taste in fine art and a strong moral conscience, feel the need to date a man never happier than when reeking of paint and holding a pint of beer in his hand?

His thoughts were interrupted when his desk phone rang. He leaned over, grabbed the handset and tensed, half-expecting it to be Andy Youngman with round-two of his *Find the Murderer* pep-talk.

'Henderson.'

'Hello sir, it's Sally Graham.'

'Hi, Sally. How's it going over at the studio?'

'Shurrup you lot in there!' she hollered, 'I'm on the phone to the boss. Sorry sir, I didn't mean you. With so many people in this small room, if anyone makes a noise—'

'Or farts,' he heard someone say.

'We all hear it,' Graham said. 'I'm moving outside.'

'How are you getting on?' Henderson asked when the background noise subsided. 'We held a press conference for the second murder victim this morning and I'm keen to make some progress at the studio and free up some members of the team.'

'I don't think it's going to happen soon.'

'What makes you say that?'

'I think the murders are connected. You know the picture we've all got a copy of?'

'Which one?'

'The second victim. Castle Hill Girl.'

'Yes.'

'I've found a picture in Cindy's photos of a woman who I think is her double.'

TWENTY-ONE

Henderson walked to the car, the photographs and scant information about the girl they were calling Castle Hill Girl in a folder under his arm.

It was a couple of hours after the press conference, but he wouldn't be surprised to find a few journalists still hanging around, hoping to thrust a digital recorder under his nose and pick up an exclusive scoop. Instead, he reached the car without being molested, perhaps the biting wind overruling the needs of a demanding editor.

He wondered if Rachel had been in attendance at the press conference, she being a news hound now, away from the backwater of environmental and horticultural reporting. He'd seen and heard *The Argus's* chief crime reporter, Rob Tremain, but she wasn't beside him. With such a large crowd in the conference room, Lord Lucan could have been there and no one would have noticed.

He hadn't seen much of Rachel over the weekend as he had been working and when he wasn't, she didn't have much to say. He wasn't sure if she was still sore about him leaving the dinner party early or annoyed at her own show of petulance now the real reason for his absence had revealed itself.

He could understand the reasons as everyone was

entitled to a decent social life, uninterrupted by phone calls and the demands of others. Unfortunately, anyone working for the emergency services was in the same boat: doctors, ambulance drivers, fire fighters. Due to the demands of a twenty-four-hour economy, this also applied to security guards, computer operators, television news reporters and a host of other seemingly unrelated jobs, such as those who maintained retail websites or manned important government installations.

The journey to Hurstpierpoint sailed by in a blur. One moment he was driving out of the Malling House car park, the next, coasting through the village. This was perhaps a symptom that Rachel was getting to him or he'd been to Hurstpierpoint too many times. Whatever the reason, he had to concentrate now as a delivery van was blocking the road and he had to wait several minutes before it was safe to overtake.

He turned into Longhurst Studios, this time not to gaze admiringly at the architectural style but to be shocked at the number of cars. He shouldn't have been surprised as, despite having so many officers working in the office here, not one of them would think of calling one of their colleagues and offering them a lift.

He walked into the studio, looking neat and tidy with most loose items stowed away, but with a closed-down feel. No photographs had been taken lately and he doubted if they ever would be. There was no sign of Annie, no doubt sitting in hospital wishing her own personal ordeal would soon be over.

He pushed open the door and almost backed out as

the stale smell hit his nostrils.

'Afternoon sir,' a few of them said.

'Afternoon,' Henderson said.

It was post-lunch and many looked to be off-duty with ties askew and buttons undone, lounging in chairs or leaning against walls as if having just devoured a large feast. He couldn't blame them, it was hard work looking through thousands of photographs with no aim in sight.

'Sally,' he said to DC Graham, 'bring your laptop and anything else you need into the waiting room. I don't think there's room enough for me in here.'

'Sure thing.'

She lifted the laptop up in one hand and carried the portable hard disk drive attached to it with the other.

They walked through the studio towards the waiting room.

'I don't suppose you fancied the hum in there,' the DC said. 'A few of the guys went out on the piss last night and we're all suffering for it today.'

'It's a consideration, but as well as the lack of space I don't want to create a false hope by finding whatever we discuss on the front cover of tomorrow's newspapers.'

'I know what you mean. There's only me and Lisa in there but the guys are worse than us for gossiping. Oh, I meant to tell you, Annie gave birth.'

'That's great news. What did she have?'

'Twin boys.'

'Oh my, she'll have her work cut out. Mother and babies doing well?'

'Yes, no problems.'

'I'm pleased to hear it.'

When they reached the waiting room, Sally put her things on the table while Henderson walked to the coffee machine.

'I need a coffee before we start,' he said. 'Do you want anything?'

'No thank you, sir, all I've done today is drink coffee. I'll be lucky to sleep tonight.'

With his drink on the table but pushed to one side, and the laptop and portable hard disk drive in front of him, he sat down. Sally took the seat beside him. She clicked the mouse on the laptop and opened a file, before selecting one of the pictures from the press conference, a facial of the Castle Hill victim.

'Right, that's the picture we all have. Now if I open this file on the portable hard disk.'

'What's on the disks?'

'The SD cards in the filing cabinet are backed-up here. Now, if she wanted to hide something that she didn't want anyone else to find, myself and Sergeant Walters think she would have hidden it in here.'

'Why? What makes you say that?'

'Every Friday, Cindy backed-up all the work she did in the week onto these disks, and stored them in the house. If she took a series of controversial photographs, she could load them onto the disk from the SD card as normal, but destroy or reformat the card, leaving no trace of the photographs in the studio. If someone broke in, or like the kidnappers who came here to retrieve them, they wouldn't find any trace of them.'

'So, if we're trying to find this mysterious series of photographs, we could pick up a box of SD cards and compare the names of them with the names on the hard disk. If any files don't have a corresponding SD card, bingo.'

'It's exactly what we've been doing, with the added complication of having to take a look at all the files to confirm what they contain.'

'Got it.'

'Now take a look at this.'

She pushed the laptop towards him.

He looked intently at the pretty young woman before him. She had brown, wavy hair touching her shoulders, brown eyes, dark eyebrows, small nose and an engaging smile with a row of perfect teeth. The deep blue sky and fly-away wisps in her hair suggested the picture had been taken outside.

Now, he compared it to the photograph of their latest victim, as she had been laid out on the mortuary slab. This girl also had wavy brown hair and brown eyes but the thick eyebrows sold it. 'You're right Sally, it's the same girl. What a great spot, well done. Who is she? What do we know about her?'

Henderson's mind started racing. A picture of the Castle Hill murder victim had been taken by Cindy, therefore the two women were connected, but how? Had she been a customer of the studio? Did this mean someone was picking off Cindy's customers one-by-one, a list running into thousands? It was a crazy notion which he dismissed; it didn't bear thinking about or make much sense.

'The file doesn't contain many photos and only a

few of her. Look at this one.'

She was standing outside a house but her frame obscured the house number. The newness of the patio slabs around her feet and the colour of the brickwork behind her suggested a new development, but he couldn't discern much else.

'The others of her are simply variations on this one. Different poses standing beside the same house. There are four in all which include her.'

'Only four? You were bloody lucky to find her.'

'I know.'

'What's her name? Do we know it?'

She shook her head. 'I don't know.'

'No indications on the file or the photo?'

'I'm afraid not.'

'What about analysing the data included on the photo file? Don't digital cameras stamp some information on a photo? Like, where it was taken, the date, the camera used and so on?'

'They do and you can normally see something by right-clicking the photograph, but don't forget, Cindy's a professional photographer. If she didn't want anyone seeing information about this woman or anyone else, she'd have the skills to hide it.'

'Makes sense, but I want you to send a copy to the tech boys at Haywards Heath and see if they can find something. We need to find out as much as we can about this woman. What about the other pictures on the same file? What's the connection there?'

'I'm not sure there is any. Take a look for yourself.'

She'd reduced the pictures to thumbnails and he could see from the count at the bottom of the screen the file contained twenty-seven photographs.

'Double-click any you want to enlarge.'

He scanned the thumbnails at first and counted seven different young women.

He double-clicked one. Same as before, a charming full body shot but nothing to indicate where the model and photographer were located. He did the same to a few more.

'I don't think it's by accident, but do you notice how none of the images give any indication as to where the photographs were taken or which house they're standing outside? It's almost as if Cindy wanted a picture of the women but was conscious of someone in the future finding them and locating the girls if she gave away too much.'

'I see what you mean. Perhaps it's a secret family she didn't want anyone to know about.'

He thought for a moment. 'I think Cindy's too young for it to be her grown-up daughters. It could be nieces or friends.'

'Perhaps it's women she knows from a club or perhaps some protest group.'

'Could be, but what they all have in common is they're young, slim and pretty. You'd be hard pressed to find that many in a knitting circle or at an anti-fracking protest.'

She laughed. 'You're right.'

'What if it's something a bit more insidious: women rescued from a life of domestic abuse, drugs or prostitution, say?'

'I don't think they're drug users. They look too healthy. A few are showing their bare arms and I don't see any scars or track marks.'

'Good point. These pictures are posing more questions than answers, but I certainly think it's a major step forward.' Henderson stood and stretched. 'I'd better get back and talk to the team. Sally, send the pictures over to the High-Tech unit as we discussed, and brief the other members of your little group in the office about what you've discovered and what they now should be looking for.'

'Will do.'

'Also, reinforce the 'no leaks' rule. I don't want to see any of these pictures leaked to *The Argus*. I'll remove anyone from this investigation who does.'

'No problem.'

Henderson's phone rang.

'The more pictures we find, the better,' he said to her. He lifted his phone. 'Henderson.'

'Afternoon gov.'

'Afternoon Carol. Sally's found some great stuff over here at the studio. Pictures of our second victim are on one of Cindy's back-up drives. I'm coming back to the office to brief everyone.'

'Fantastic news. I've just heard something else that should help us too.'

'Excellent. What is it?'

'Are you sitting down?'

'Yes.'

'Liar, I bet you're not. I've just taken a call from the ballistics lab. The slug extracted from Cindy Longhurst's skull matches the one found in Castle Hill Girl.'

TWENTY-TWO

The pub was busy for a Monday night. Liam McKinney finished the dregs in his glass and walked to the bar to buy another. He nudged a guy out of the way, too engrossed in something on his phone and leaned on the bar.

'A pint of lager when you get a minute Barry,' he called to the barman as he poured drinks for a gorgeous looking blonde. She looked about thirty with a fabulous figure, squeezed into a tight blue dress. At twenty-four, McKinney imagined she was too old for him, but if this was an example of how older women looked after themselves, perhaps it was time to lower his expectations.

Barry did as he was told, emitting a few tuts from a couple of geezers beside him, but the barman knew on which side his bread was buttered. McKinney came in here three, four nights a week and not only did he drink there, he transacted business there, so Barry also benefitted from the largesse of McKinney's customers.

McKinney retook his seat in the corner. He was waiting for his customer, a guy called Rick who said he wanted to buy fifty grams of coke. His antenna rose when he first heard: a big sale, lots of dough, but why so much? Was he trying to set himself up as a rival dealer? Rick said he lived in Crawley and wanted it for himself and the football supporters' club where he was a member. This was cool as McKinney operated only in the Brighton area. If in the future he wanted to expand into Crawley, it wouldn't do any harm to cultivate some contacts and maybe move into partnership later. If Rick didn't fancy a joint-operation, McKinney would bring up some mates and force him out.

The alcohol was warming his cockles, as his father used to say, and making him think shite thoughts, as the young McKinney would say. He didn't do partners, he'd taken a knife to the last two and preferred being on his own. Charlie McQueen was a sort of partner, he sourced the goods while McKinney worked the streets, pubs and clubs, selling to the next level down in the food chain.

He'd been avoiding McQueen for the last few weeks and refused to answer his phone after the man screamed and shouted into his ear the last time he called. He'd gone ballistic when he heard McKinney had stuck a knife into the gut of his fat bastard friend, Ted Mathieson. McQueen had told him that Mathieson wouldn't like his money being cut and McKinney had been instructed to 'take no shit', as the Russians were hitting the business hard and impacting cash flow. McKinney did as he was told, so why was McQueen so mad?

His ruminations, disguised to the other punters in the pub as a man reading *The Argus*, had agitated him. When he felt this way, he drank, and if he indulged too much, his agitation would turn to aggression and someone would pay the price. He reached for his pint and discovered the glass empty. He looked around at the table on the left and the one on the right, but no one was stealing his beer. He was about to go up for another when a bloke came into the pub. He knew at once this was his guy, the voice on the phone said he would be wearing a black leather jacket.

The man walked towards him. 'Liam?'

'Sure. You Rick?'

He nodded and stuck out his hand which Liam shook.

'You wanna drink?' Rick asked.

'Sure. Pint of Heineken,' he said holding up his empty glass.

'Coming up.'

Rick headed to the bar to buy McKinney a pint; number five or could it be six? It was more than he usually drank when making a sale as he liked to keep a clear head, at least until the deal was done. He didn't know this guy, but the set-up felt good. Rick looked the way he sounded on the phone, a big fella, but soft around the edges, with a bit of a beer gut, jowls on the face and flecks of grey in his hair. Someone he could take easy if the exchange went sour.

Rick came back with the beers and sat down. He lifted his glass and nodded to McKinney, 'Cheers,' he said.

'Cheers,' he replied.

'Do you follow football?' Rick said, nodding at the copy of *The Argus* lying on the seat, the football pages uppermost.

'Sure, the Albion, got a season ticket.'

'Me too. Where do you sit?'

'East stand.'

'You're opposite me.'

'You don't support...what's their name?'

'Crawley Town? Nah, I'm not from there. More Haywards Heath, me. I've always followed Brighton.'

He felt a prat. He knew what they were called, every footie fan in the south east knew the names of all the clubs in the area. The booze was playing tricks with his memory.

They chit-chatted for another five minutes before Rick picked up his glass and finished it. 'Wanna make the trade?'

The cogs inside Liam's head did a little spin. Trade? What bloody trade? Christ, for a minute he thought they were two old mates having a bit of a get-together. He needed to get a grip.

He finished his drink and they walked outside. McKinney took a right into Montreal Road. 'The car's right up here, the gear's in the boot. You got the dough?'

'Yep,' he said tapping his jacket pocket.

Some drug dealers, when faced with large sums of money, like the fifty big ones Rick had with him, would try to roll the punter and keep the cash and hold on to the drugs. They were the penny-pinchers, hand-to-mouth sort of guys who took drugs themselves and needed a steady supply. McKinney was a wholesaler, and it didn't make sense to steal from his customers when trying to build a business, and Charlie McQueen would cut his ears off if he ever found out he was doing so.

McKinney had got rid of his Camaro after the Mathieson incident and while awaiting the delivery of a new Porsche 911 Carrera from a dealer in Burgess Hill, he'd bought a little run-around, a BMW 3 Series with lowered suspension, black alloys and a thick yellow stripe down both sides: class.

He beeped the alarm and reached for the boot release lever.

'Leave it, McKinney,' Rick said as he jabbed something hard into his side. 'I'm holding a Beretta 92 fitted with soft tip ammunition. If you don't want your guts plastered all over the paintwork of your pretty motor, you'll do as I tell you.'

Another geezer appeared from nowhere, blocking his intended escape route through the gap in the parked cars.

'Nice and easy Liam,' the other guy said. 'Get into the back seat of the car.'

'What's this about? Is it money you want? I got money.'

'Shut the fuck up and get in the car.'

He climbed into the car and the new guy got in beside him. He also had a gun which he poked into McKinney's ribs. Rick drove. He headed down Southover Road to the Lewes Road and on reaching The Level, turned into St Peter's Place and joined the A23 heading north.

'Where are we going?' McKinney asked.

Both men ignored him.

They cruised past Preston Park, dark and empty at this hour of the night. What he wouldn't give to get out of this car, run across the grass and hide in the trees at the far side. A few minutes later at the roundabout marking the junction between the A27 and the A23, they turned left up Mill Road, the place where Albion fans used to park when the team didn't have a ground of their own and were forced to play matches at nearby Withdean athletics stadium.

'What do you want?'

No response.

He needed time to think, but the beer in the pub, a couple of whisky chasers and the snort of coke he'd taken before coming out to steady his trembling hands, were messing with his brain. He was armed like those two clowns, but with a knife. No matter that he always kept it sharp, a knife was no match for two Berettas.

They turned up Devil's Dyke Road, heading in the direction of the place where he and Ted Mathieson fell out. It suddenly came to him. McQueen would be waiting in the car park, trademark baseball bat in hand. He'd seen him do it in the past but he wouldn't try and beat his brains out, would he? They'd worked together for nearly three years and by virtue of McKinney's contacts and his tireless pounding of Brighton streets, together they'd made millions.

The car didn't turn up the little road that led towards the car park but continued to follow the road past The Dyke Golf Club, and he practically wet his pants with relief. If these chancers weren't McQueen's men, who the hell were they?'

'Who are you guys? Where are we going?' McKinney asked.

'You'll see soon.'

Halleluiah, the gunmen did have voices. A minute or so later the car pulled into a layby and came to a halt. Rick switched off the engine.

'Why are we stopping?'

'Shut the fuck up and get out the car.'

He did as he was told and was tempted to make a run for it, but before the idea fully formed in his head, both men appeared at his side and blocked the escape route.

'This way,' Rick said, nodding in the direction of the trees beside the lay-by. The thicket looked dark and foreboding in the pale, yellow light of the moon, but he walked towards it and soon found they were tramping along a path.

Few people had used it since autumn as it was partly overgrown with weeds and he could feel branches of overhanging trees combing through his hair. He couldn't stop to push them out of the way or rub his leg after a branch whacked it, because if he did he received a jab in the back from the barrel of a gun.

He raised his one arm as if about to scratch an itch, but instead intending to reach for his knife, when a whack in the back stopped him. 'Hands where I can see them, McKinney. Any fancy tricks, mate, and all I do is pull the trigger.'

They walked for a couple of minutes and came to a small clearing no bigger than could accommodate five or six people.

'Stop here.'

'What's this?' McKinney said, his voice higher than normal. 'No meeting with Charlie, no chance to state my side of the story?'

He grabbed Rick's arm, not in an attempt to wrestle his weapon away but trying to plead his case. Rick pushed him back with ease and smacked him in the face with the butt of the gun, knocking him to the ground.

In the moonlight, he saw Rick look over at his mate, who nodded. Rick pointed the gun at McKinney and before he realised what was happening, the gun spat its venom.

TWENTY-THREE

Henderson returned home late, a meeting with the team to discuss the connections between Castle Hill Girl and Cindy Longhurst had kept him at the office. The facts were irrefutable: the two women had been killed by the same gun, and pictures of the latest victim appeared on Cindy's computer.

The same gun suggested the same shooter and the similar state of the two victims' bodies, both beaten and kept in similar dirty conditions, implied they were both kept in the same place. The team had also bandied about motives for the killings; drugs and prostitution, as discussed with Sally Graham, plus money laundering, blackmail and all the rest of the headings from the serious crimes handbook.

The exercise wasn't such a waste of time because not knowing the name of the shooter, if they could find out the activity he or she was involved in, the team would be half-way towards discovering their identity. Alas, one main motive did not present itself. They didn't know if Cindy and their new victim were killed for the same reasons, or if Cindy was killed for photographing something and Castle Hill Girl for being involved in something else.

They needed more and he now focused the

investigation on two fronts. One, a team would continue looking through the photographs in Cindy's studio, trying to find some unguarded pictures of their second victim and her companions, something to try and identify their location. In essence, trying to uncover the revealing photographs they believed the kidnappers were trying to find when they kidnapped Cindy.

The second focus of the investigation was on trying to discover the identity of their new victim. Fingerprint analysis had uncovered nothing on the database so, at great expense, and bringing a frown to the face of CI Edwards, she authorised the victim's DNA to be fast-tracked. If it didn't trigger recognition by the PNC, they would circulate her details to European police forces as PC Phil Bentley, the team's expert on the female form, believed she looked East European.

'What time do you call this?' Rachel said as he stopped in the hall to take off his jacket.

'I was delayed. We've had a new development in the case and the team meeting went on longer than expected.'

'I was expecting you home hours ago, your dinner will be stone cold.'

'I'll stick it in the microwave.'

'Do what the hell you like,' she said walking back into the lounge.

He headed into the kitchen. It looked clean and tidy as if nothing had ever been cooked there, his plate of whatever it was sitting beneath the protection of a sheet of kitchen paper. He lifted it to find a large helping of chicken in a tomato sauce with a pile of penne beside it. Heating a dish of pasta in the microwave hadn't worked for him in the past as it usually came out too hard, but he was too tired to think of a better solution.

While waiting for it to heat, he took a seat at the table and reached for a copy of *The Argus* lying there. It was the evening edition, time for journalists and editors to digest the details of this morning's press conference. The main part of the article quoted verbatim large sections of the press release and he knew if he went on the web now and looked at the same story in another half-dozen newspaper websites, it would be the same.

To their credit they didn't say they believed both women were killed by the same person, but reiterated their previous warning, that with two victims dead, women should refrain from going out or if they needed to, they should be accompanied. It was the usual knee-jerk scare tactics of newspapers. They had no evidence the streets were any more dangerous than before. Cindy had been kidnapped in her studio, in reality her home, and the latest victim, from God-knows-where, but not the same place as Cindy.

The microwave pinged. He grabbed a tea towel, removed the steaming plate, and set it down on the table. He picked up a fork and tried eating a piece to see if was hot and decided it would do. The pasta didn't taste too bad either.

They didn't often eat in the lounge and he wouldn't do so with this sort of meal. One false move and the whole lot would slither off the plate on to the carpet like a jellyfish on a fishmonger's slab. Rachel knew he wouldn't come in to the lounge and if she couldn't be bothered walking into the kitchen to talk to him, he wouldn't force the issue.

It was the same problem annoying Rachel now that broke up his marriage to Laura in Glasgow. His ex was a stoic individual but her legendary patience frayed to breaking point when he didn't turn up for a friend's birthday party, her parent's silver wedding anniversary and at least two Christmas celebrations. The icing on the cake, or more accurately, the straw that broke the camel's back, came when he arrived home at midnight to find the house had been full of friends, a surprise party laid on for him after receiving his promotion to Detective Inspector.

He opened the newspaper looking for other news, trying to free his mind from the Cindy Longhurst case and the troubles at home. A fifteen-year-old lad had gone missing from his house in Bevendean, an off-licence had been robbed on Preston Road and someone was sounding off about refuse collections, this time because the crews were being noisy and had left a mess on the pavement.

He was about to chuck the paper away in disgust when he noticed the name of the journalist who penned it: Rachel Jones. He smiled. Perhaps her editor, Gary Richardson, miffed at Henderson departing his dinner party early, had got his own back by assigning Rachel a bum assignment like reporting on refuse collections. No wonder she was walking around at the moment with a face like a baby with colic.

In order not to soil the spotless kitchen, he put his plate and cutlery in the dishwasher and closed the door. He reached for a short glass and after pulling out the bottle of Glenmorangie from the cupboard, poured a generous measure. He stood for a moment and took a swig, before walking towards the lounge.

'What are you watching?' he said, taking a seat in the armchair.

'Quiet, this is a key bit.'

He watched the screen for several moments and inwardly groaned, yet another cop drama. He understood why television programmes needed to be action-orientated. The times he had to sit for hours filling in forms, disciplining a rookie DC for some stupid error of judgement or waiting for the results of a forensic test wouldn't interest anyone.

What he couldn't understand was even in the dramatic scenes, they couldn't capture with any accuracy how these incidents often played out. Murders in real life were more heart-wrenching, grief-stricken and life-changing than could ever be portrayed on the screen, and wounds like knife slashes, gun shots and punches, were more painful and debilitating. In addition, the fear felt by officers at the start of a raid or searching a seemingly empty house could be palpable.

At ten, the credits rolled. He had to admit the dialogue was good and he loved the music playing throughout, a synthesised melody over a rocking beat.

'I enjoyed that,' Rachel said.

'The bad guys were caught but will they serve any time in jail?'

'What do you mean?'

'From what I saw, the slip-shod way the investigation team gathered evidence would be enough for the case to be thrown out by the CPS. The baddies will probably sue for wrongful arrest.'

It was his attempt at levity but it didn't penetrate Rachel's stony scowl.

'You're always demeaning the programmes I enjoy. I'm away to put the dishwasher on.'

'Don't you think we need to talk?'

'No.'

She walked out of the room leaving him facing the BBC newsreader. He gave it another ten minutes, stories about European politics, a crisis in the Middle East and bad weather in the Far East, but when it turned to a missing Polar exploration in the Arctic, he switched channels.

Rachel returned to the lounge some time later and announced she was heading to bed.

'It's only what,' he looked at the clock, 'ten-twenty-five.'

'I'm tired.'

'Come in and talk to me.'

She pushed the door closed and sat down.

'What do we have to talk about? You're married to your job. There's no room for me in your life.'

'I admit the job does swallow me up at times, but not all the time, as you know. In between big investigations it goes back, maybe not to a nine-to-five, but certainly to more regular hours.'

'Well maybe the slower bits between enquiries don't compensate for all the missed meals, cancelled dinner dates and party invitations.'

Henderson sighed. This sounded like an old recording, one played many times at the house he once shared with Laura.

'Are you still sore about me leaving Gary's dinner party early?'

'Of course I am. I was embarrassed to go back in there.'

'Why? Because you had to sit there on your own? The bloke I was talking to, Steve, was also there on his own and so was Sue the marriage counsellor, a worse advert for marital union I couldn't think of.'

'Trust you to demean the conversation.'

'Why were you embarrassed? They're your people. You work beside most of them.'

'I've only started working beside them, there's a difference.'

'You think me leaving spoiled what, the impression you were trying to create?'

'Didn't you notice? They're all men. I'm trying to prove to them that I can hack it in the world of hard news.'

'And me leaving–'

'Stop trying to change the subject. It's not my job that's the problem here but you, and your damned job.'

'The work I do isn't going to change, it's always going to include intensive highs and quiet lows. I don't have any control over it.'

'Maybe you should look for another job.'

'Within the force you mean?'

'Maybe.'

He shook his head. 'It's not much different anywhere else. The detectives in John Street get called out at all hours to domestic disturbances and street fights, and the unit Gerry Hobbs has moved to are carrying out drug busts once or twice a week, usually in the middle of the night.'

'I bet his wife isn't best pleased.'

'She isn't.'

'If not the police, you could do something else.'

'Do you think I'd feel better doing a regular nine-to five in an insurance office? I don't think so. In any case, who'd hire me?'

'There's bound to be something you could do. Your problem is you won't look.'

'Why should I? I'm not looking for anything else. I do this job because I think I can do some good and make a difference. Do you think I'd feel the same if I sold pensions or life insurance policies?'

'If you did, you would be helping people by protecting them and their property, but I know you won't even consider it. You're too selfish.'

'How the hell can say that? If I was making millions trading bonds or selling shares or something, I would accept what you're saying, but risking my neck and those of my team to find murderers and kidnappers, it's anything but.'

'You're not going to change, I can see you won't. Well, maybe it's time for me to think about *my* future. Goodnight.'

TWENTY-FOUR

'You want to see me, gov?' DS Vicky Neal said, standing at the entrance of DI Henderson's office.

'I do Vicky, come in,' he said.

She took a seat across the desk from the DI and watched as he tidied the pile of papers in front of him, pushing them to one side to clear a space. She didn't know him well but she had enough female nous to realise he wasn't as up-beat as she'd seen him over the last few weeks.

She'd asked her regular companion on the Mathieson stabbing, DC Sally Graham, if he was yet another dour Scot, as she'd met plenty of them in Manchester. Up there, they could blame it on the dismal Pennine weather, which at times made even the cheeriest soul feel miserable, but what would be the excuse here in the sunny South of England?

Graham said no, she didn't regard Henderson as sour-faced or temperamental. He got angry when most people would, particularly when things weren't going well, but for the majority of the time she had always found him even-tempered and approachable. In which case, it had to be trouble at home, but the self-assured DC assured her it couldn't be. Neal was a nosey bugger and wouldn't let it rest; she needed to dig deeper.

'I mentioned at the meeting yesterday about a body discovered near Devil's Dyke?'

'Yes, male aged about twenty-seven with gunshot wounds to the chest and head. Discovered by a group of hikers.'

'Yes, him. He's been identified as Liam McKinney, a known drug dealer from Brighton. The way he was killed and his chosen profession makes me think, with a strong degree of certainty, his death is drug-related. Therefore, no connection to the Cindy Longhurst inquiry.'

'A fair comment, I think.'

'In which case, I could legitimately hand it over to the Drug Unit, as it's within their jurisdiction.'

'I understand your logic, although I think I can hear a 'but'.'

'The Cindy Longhurst enquiry started before you arrived and I know how hard it is joining a team in the middle of any investigation, especially with you not being familiar with all the players. I gave you the Ted Mathieson stabbing, but as there's not much happening there at the moment, I want you to handle the Liam McKinney murder for me.'

'Thank you, sir. I'd be happy to.'

'I know you'll do a good job as you've seen plenty of similar action in Manchester.'

'Some months we were dealing with one a week.'

'McKinney's murder will be investigated separately from Cindy Longhurst as there's no connection that we know about, and to do so would only cause confusion. Agreed?'

'Fine with me.'

'I'll exempt you from attendance at the Cindy Longhurst meetings. I think you'll have enough on your plate with this. When you need them, you can use DC Deepak Sunderam and DC Seb Young.'

'Right.'

'Here's the file,' he said passing a manila folder over to her. 'There's a few things in there for you to get your teeth into: the SOCO crime scene report, the post-mortem and a profile of McKinney, generously given to us by the Drugs Unit. Despite his chosen career path, I don't want any short-cuts taken. Drug crime in Sussex isn't like Manchester, we don't find bodies of dealers every day of the week, or even every month. His death might be a sign of an impending gang war or a new outfit moving into the area, so it's important for you to dig deep and find out who's behind it.'

'I'll do my best, gov. Anything else?'

'No, the lecture's over,' he said giving her what looked like a forced smile. 'Enjoy your reading.'

She left his office carrying what felt to her like treasure. She'd worked on cases like this before, but after moving to Sussex she expected a slower pace of life and felt pleased to be blooded so soon. Despite DI Henderson being the Senior Investigating Officer on the McKinney murder and ultimately responsible for its progress, he was too preoccupied with the Cindy Longhurst case and she believed she could run this investigation how she wanted.

She sat at her desk and flicked through the contents. She started with the post-mortem report. The first thing she noted was the amount of alcohol and drugs in his system. The drugs sounded to her like a toke before heading out, while the booze indicated a decent drinking session in the pub just prior to his death. Perhaps attacked by enemies when they spotted him the worse for wear.

The gunshot wounds were interesting: one to the chest and one to the head. Chest wounds often occurred when a gun was in the possession of a poor shot or a novice, someone only capable of hitting a big target, or a rapidly taken round fired by a fleeing gunman. If trying to kill, it was a slow method, more likely to puncture the lungs and have them fill with blood, eventually drowning the victim. A bullet to the heart, the one-drop-shot, a favourite of thriller directors, would do the trick, but finding it was problematic. It wasn't a large organ and most people didn't know its exact location.

The second shot, to the head, near enough dead-centre in the temple, suggested a couple of scenarios. A hastily taken first shot to the chest to incapacitate the victim, followed by a 'dispatch' shot in the head to kill him. An alternative scenario sounded more chilling: a deliberate bullet in the chest to make the victim suffer or talk, followed by another to terminate the spectacle. Given the nature of McKinney's profession, she would bet on the latter.

She picked up the Drugs Unit's assessment of the dead man and here she could be reading about any number of characters she'd come across back in Manchester. McKinney kicked off selling marijuana to schoolmates. As soon as he realised he could make more money dealing than staying on at school and hoping for a good job at the end of it, he dropped out. Like all entrepreneurs with a good idea, he set about building the foundations of his future business with vigour and innovation.

He then disappeared off the police radar for a couple of years, no doubt still dealing, but employing kids and 'clean skins' to do the street work. If any of them were nabbed by the police, they would be found with only small quantities of drugs in their possession, and not having yet accumulated a long criminal record, they would most likely be let off with a caution.

McKinney reappeared on the radar some time later as number-two to Charlie McQueen, a big-time drug dealer, more remote from the street business than McKinney. In the smart part of Hove where McQueen lived, his neighbours would be under the impression the guy living in the large house with several expensive cars parked outside was a respectable businessman.

Vicky sat back. What if she could not only find McKinney's killer, but could tie the killing back to Charlie McQueen? What a scalp he would be. Good enough to seal her promotion up to DI in the not too distant future. She could but dream, and as her old desk sergeant in Manchester used to say, 'if you ain't got ambition, darlin', what the fuck are you doing here?'

TWENTY-FIVE

Henderson got up from behind his desk, walked out of the office and headed over to the staff restaurant. He hadn't slept well the previous night, many of the things Rachel said ping-ponging around his head. He didn't feel much like breakfast before leaving the house first thing this morning, but now at a few minutes past eleven, he felt ravenous.

The team at Longhurst Studio had been wound down and Castle Hill Girl's DNA and fingerprints had been sent to European police forces through Europol. All he could do now was sit and wait. They'd been led down so many blind alleys with this case. Try as he may, he couldn't recall another so frustrating.

It didn't help that Cindy's abduction took place at a rural location with only two partially-helpful witnesses, while the second victim didn't possess any identification and her fingerprints and DNA didn't appear on the national database. A comb of the Missing Persons Database came up with nothing, and despite a wide-ranging search which included a newspaper appeal, they still couldn't identify her.

He stood at the back of a small queue of people waiting for hot food, a bottleneck that didn't change much throughout the day, due to the Malling House building complex housing such a large number of officers and civilians, most working shifts and unsociable hours. His turn soon came and, armed with two slices of toast and a cup of coffee plus a chocolate bar which he put in his pocket, he made his way back to his office.

'Hello Angus.'

He turned to see DI Gerry Hobbs walking towards him.

'Hi Gerry, how are you doing? How's the new job?'

'Good to see you. It's not bad, although I've never attended so many meetings. I'm off to one now. If we're not meeting civic leaders concerned about the number of needles on the seafront, it's members of a charity annoyed with the heavy-hand we're showing to some of their customers.'

Henderson laughed. 'Serious Crime doesn't look so bad now, does it?'

'I needed a move, a change is as good as a rest, so they say. What I wanted to tell you is, we've located Liam McKinney's car. The call came in about twenty minutes ago. Uniform found it burned out in Shoreham.'

'Right. I'll tell Vicky Neal.'

'You need to watch yourself there.'

'What, with Vicky?' Henderson asked.

'Yeah.'

'What makes you say that?'

'I hear she's a bit of a man-eater. Ambitious too.'

'Gerry, I think I can look after myself. What do you make of McKinney's murder? Did he have many enemies or is someone trying to muscle in on his business?'

'I heard from one source,' Hobbs said, 'which I'll take with a pinch of salt until I hear it from someone else, but he says McKinney and Charlie McQueen fell out.'

'Charlie McQueen, the Brighton drug dealer?'

'Oh, he's a bit more than that, Angus. We reckon he's one of the biggest players on the Brighton drug scene.'

'That big? Why don't you...ah, but you can't touch him, can you?'

'Nah, he's never been one to get his hands dirty.' He looked at his watch. 'It's been good seeing you again, Angus, but I need to go. Catch up with you sometime over a beer.'

'I'll call you and arrange something.'

'Excellent. See you later.'

Henderson went one way and Hobbs the other. He didn't know if it was due to the new job, the promotion, or a combination of both, but it had re-energised Hobbs. Henderson couldn't criticise his performance when they worked together, but Serious Crime affected people in different ways and often by the end of a two or three-year stint, they needed a change. A move to another specialism such as drugs or fraud wouldn't solve Henderson's own dilemma, and put a stop to working fewer hours and not being called out to attend crime scenes during important dinner parties. Hobbs didn't seem to work any less hours than he did before.

He arrived back at his office, the smell of decent coffee and buttered toast playing havoc with his grumbling stomach, such that if he'd spotted a place where he could sit on his journey back, he would have stopped and scoffed the lot.

He sat down, uncapped the coffee and took a sip, but it was still too hot. Two bites into his first slice of toast, the phone rang.

'Bloody hell!'

With some reluctance, he picked it up. 'Good morning, is this Detective Inspector Henderson?' a guttural, East European voice asked.

'It is.'

'Excellent. Good morning Inspector, I am Principal Agent Gabriel Albescu of the Poliția Română, the Romanian Police. How are you today?'

'I'm fine,' he said, but thought, *If you'd only let me eat my toast, I'd feel a lot better.* 'How are you?'

'I am excellent, except when bureaucrats in Brussels give me all their money and expect me to fill in their stupid forms in return. Ha, ha.'

'It's different here, we fill in the forms, but they don't give us any money.'

'Ha, we could teach you some tricks.'

'I bet you could. You speak very good English, Agent Albescu. Have you ever lived in the UK or America?'

'Myself and another officer from Bucharest were seconded to the Boston Police Department for one year and, in return, they sent some American officers over to Interpol in Bucharest. I liked America, the wide, open spaces and the large parking bays, but I hated the food. Chips with everything and, in some places, the only alcohol on sale is beer.'

'The US can be liberal about some things but straight-laced about others. After all, their porn industry is larger than their legitimate film business.'

'I agree. I am calling you because we received here in Bucharest the fingerprints of a murder victim you have there in the UK.'

At the start of the call he thought he was talking to someone he'd met last year at the international police symposium in Amsterdam, but now he realised it wasn't. He pushed the distractions of toast and coffee to one side and gave Principal Agent Gabriel Albescu his full attention.

'Yes, you're right, I sent them out. Have you found her?'

'Thanks to our friends in Interpol, we have a fine digital fingerprint system. They have a unit based near our offices here in Bucharest and I think they like to keep us local boys sweet, you know?'

'I see,' Henderson said, willing the detective to speed up, but realising he would only move at his own pace.

'Your victim's name is Elena Iliesc, she is nineteen years old and comes from a town in Romania called Oradea which is close to our border with Hungary.'

'How do you spell her name?' he asked.

The Romanian detective spelled it out for him and he noted it down. 'She worked at a local factory in Oradea and was arrested in the town centre for assaulting a tourist. She claimed this person spilled red wine over her dress but, in return, Miss Iliesc scratched the tourist before punching her in the face. She only received a fine. She was lucky, in my opinion, not to go to prison. The courts here do not like the tourist industry damaged in such a way.'

'Do you know why she came to the UK?'

'I have already instructed the local police in Oradea to talk to her family.'

'Thank you, I appreciate you doing this. Have the local police reported back to you?'

'Yes, indeed they did. She disappeared six months ago as she walked home from work. She didn't have a car and so a colleague often gave her a lift, leaving her with about a two-kilometre walk to her home. She lives in a rural part of the town.'

'Disappeared how?'

'The family do not know, but we believe it is the work of traffickers. They kidnap girls walking along the road or standing waiting at a bus stop. It not only takes place here in Romania, but also in Hungary and Bulgaria too. These girls are taken to Germany, France and the UK to become prostitutes or slaves on farms and in houses and factories. I am disgusted to know this trade goes on in my country.'

Henderson knew a little about it, dubbed by many commentators 'modern day slavery', but he had no direct experience.

'So,' Henderson said, 'if she was kidnapped in Romania six months ago and we find her body in the UK only a few days ago, it sounds like she must have been working for the traffickers all this time and fell out with them or tried to escape and they caught her.'

'Yes, six months is not enough time to earn enough money to satisfy her kidnappers. If she cannot work or will not work, they would have no choice but to kill her.'

'Thank you very much for calling me,' Henderson said. 'What you've told me will be a huge help in trying to find her killer.'

'I would like to thank you, Inspector, on behalf of Elena's family, for investigating this case. The family would like to find out who killed their daughter and have made a generous donation to the police benevolence fund to ensure we keep them fully informed.'

TWENTY-SIX

The train arrived at Victoria Station and, trying hard not to show it, Henderson couldn't wait to get off. From Brighton up to about East Croydon he and Walters discussed the Longhurst case, keeping to non-contentious issues as there was always lots of movement and noise on any train from the south coast.

Now, with the name of Castle Hill Girl, Elena Iliesc, he set the murder team the task of finding anything else they could about her. Having been in the UK for less than six months and, assuming she had been in the hands of traffickers all this time, there was little chance she would appear on national databases like the DVLA or Inland Revenue, but they would look nevertheless. They would also look on social media, make contact with other agencies and charities, and talk to Border Force.

He didn't understand enough about human trafficking in the UK to know if they used commercial sea ports such as Calais to Dover or Zeebrugge to Hull, or brought people over to the UK in private yachts and trawlers as used by many drug dealers. If using the official sea crossings and bringing the girls into the UK by bus disguised as a school trip or cultural exchange, everyone on board would still need some form of identification and, with a bit of luck, the details would be recorded somewhere.

The underground train felt hot and clammy despite the cold February day outside where the thermometer wouldn't shift from about six Celsius. It was noisy too, buskers playing in a carriage up ahead, and the rumble of the wheels as it thundered through a narrow tunnel. The bustle of the crowd prevented much conversation taking place between himself and Walters which suited him, as the earlier discussion on the train had exhausted everything they knew about Cindy and Elena's murders before it turned to relationships.

Henderson was a keen poker player, although he hadn't played for several weeks, and believed he could hold a straight face when many would crack. For some reason, his uncommitted expression didn't fool Walters and she probed and poked like a well-drilled detective.

They exited Vauxhall Station and walked along Albert Embankment. He liked this part of London, busy without the cloying crowds of Oxford Street or Covent Garden. There was plenty around to spark his interest, although people-watchers would be having a harder time with everyone wrapped up in warm coats, scarves and hats to ward off the biting wind whipping off the Thames.

'Isn't that the MI6 building?' Walters said, jerking a thumb at the brown-faced building with green windows, dominating an enormous corner plot overlooking Vauxhall Bridge.

'It is, but they're now called SIS, so I suppose we

should call it the SIS Building.'

'What's SIS?'

'Secret Intelligence Service.'

'It's not much of a secret if they're housed in such a prominent building and everyone knows where it is.'

'It used to be called the worst kept secret in London as all the cabbies knew where to find it. I see it's been repaired after Raoul Silva's bomb blew it up.'

'What? When did this happen?'

'In the James Bond film, *Spectre*.'

'Oh. I don't watch that rubbish.'

'What do you call *Fifty Shades*?'

'It's not the same thing.'

They turned down Tinworth Street and it didn't take long to reach the headquarters of the National Crime Agency. They were housed in a glass and brown-brick building, looking more like the scientific research unit of a major university than a crime-fighting agency.

Ten minutes later, after passing through an elaborate security system, they both took a seat in the office of NCA Officer, Rebecca Gregson.

'Smart office, shame about the view,' Walters said after they were seated.

'It is. Watching the people in the building across the street sit at computers holds no fascination for anyone. Perhaps to distance themselves from us, they don't use the institutional furniture you see in our place and every other police office you visit.'

'It's a funny organisation, the NCA. It's a police force, but not having any powers of arrest, it isn't really.'

'You can ask Rebecca about it now, here she comes.'

'Angus Henderson,' she said as she walked into her office. 'I've haven't seen you for ages.'

Henderson stood and found himself in a hug rather than the handshake he expected.

They broke away and, after taking another look at his face, she turned to Walters. 'You must be Detective Sergeant Walters. Pleased to meet you.' Walters made do with a handshake.

Gregson walked around her desk to take a seat, as Walters shot him a look. He shrugged as if to say, '*did I not mention that I knew her?*'

'Welcome to the National Crime Agency. I hope I can be of some help. So, where are you now, Angus?'

'Still in Sussex, although we've moved offices from Brighton to Lewes.'

'You might not be aware, Carol, but Angus and I go back a long way. We were both officers in Glasgow in the same unit. He stayed on to chase murderers, I went into drugs. To be honest, a personal vendetta against the scum responsible for killing my cousin.'

'What made you join the NCA?' Walters asked.

'The short answer is they were recruiting and I quite fancied a change. The longer explanation is more about the approach of the NCA versus the police. Like you and every officer I know, I got really fed up with the paperwork, the procedures we're required to follow for doing something simple, like booking in a suspect, and policy directives for everything else. Here, there's greater emphasis on gathering intelligence and using computers to analyse detail before bringing in you guys to make the arrests.'

'And leaving us with all the paperwork and dealing with the CPS,' Henderson said.

'You got it. Our role has changed since the days of SOCA, our predecessors at the Serious Organised Crime Agency. We now have the power to compel you, Detective Inspector Angus Henderson, or your ultimate boss, the Chief Constable of Sussex, to undertake a specific operation. SOCA didn't have such authority.'

'It's a good position to be in,' he said.

'You interested? I could put in a good word.'

Henderson hesitated. He'd left Glasgow after he shot and killed a well-known drug dealer. The consequent rumpus, fed to the press by the dead dealer's family, piled too much pressure on his marriage and work, but his domestic situation at the moment was nowhere near as bad. Moving here wouldn't be the get-out Rachel so desired as he doubted the NCA was any less pressurised.

'No, I'm happy where I am.'

'If you ever change your mind, you know where I am. Now to business. You said on the phone you're investigating two murders with suspicions they're connected to human trafficking?'

He went on to explain about his call from **Principal Agent Gabriel Albescu who first raised the suspicion that Elena Iliesc had been trafficked.**

'What I'd like to know,' Henderson said, 'is how it works. How do they bring girls into the country, what they do with them when they get here and how the commercial side works. Also, I'd like to find out if you're in possession of any intel to suggest how much of this activity is taking place in Sussex.'

'We class human trafficking under six broad headings: sexual exploitation, forced labour, domestic servitude, organ harvesting, forced marriage and child-related. How old are your victims?'

'The latest one is nineteen.'

'Take your pick of the categories excluding the last one.'

'I imagine our victim's role is sex-related,' Walters, said. 'She looks young and pretty, but I can also see how she might work in a factory or someone's house or even be forced to donate her organs.'

'You asked how they get into the country, Angus, well the answer to that question is in every way imaginable. Many are duped by people they like or trust. They respond to an advert in a newspaper promising a better life in the UK, something like working in an office or au-pairing for a good family. They are driven away from the airport or ferry port by an 'agent' who takes their passport. He tells them they are now five thousand pounds in debt and are forced to work in potato fields in Norfolk, brothels in London or in the kitchens of large hotels and restaurants in Manchester to pay back what they owe.'

'Which I imagine they never do.'

'Which they never do, you're right. The other way they arrive here is when they're kidnapped, like your victim, a common occurrence in rural parts of Romania, Albania, Bulgaria and Hungary. They are either smuggled into the UK on lorries or provided with fake papers and turn up at the border like so many school groups who do so every week.'

'I think you already answered one of my questions, Rebecca, which was how the business worked. I can see if traffickers are bringing people into the UK to work as prostitutes or as domestic help, money will be changing hands with the person they end up working for.'

'Yes, but don't forget, the people they bring into this country are considered no more than commodities by the trackers. They can be bought and sold like a bag of heroin or a stolen laptop. Some traffickers may not work in prostitution or the labour side, but are only handling people they can sell to whoever needs them.'

'It's a sickening business,' Walters said.

'It really is and it's one of our main priorities to try and stop it wherever we find it going on.'

'I suppose the hold they have over the victims is confiscating their passports and bringing them into a strange country where they don't speak the language.'

'Yes, but they also use violence. Despite the kidnappers needing slaves to work, say as prostitutes, they think nothing of breaking bones, smashing faces and injuring organs.'

'A lesson to others who are thinking of resisting,' Walters said.

'Right, and another hold they have is telling the women they know their sister or their mother and threatening to kill them if they try to escape. It's a growing problem We have hundreds of cases going on at the moment.'

'So many?'

'It's shocking, I know.'

'What intel do you have specific to Sussex?' Henderson asked.

Gregson picked up a computer printout from her desk. 'Your victim was found where?'

'The first came from a village called Hurstpierpoint, about twenty-five miles north of Brighton, and the second, in a field about four miles to the north-east of Brighton.'

'We currently have three cases going on in Sussex: a clothes factory in Crawley where we believe the Indian workers are beaten regularly, a private clinic in Uckfield where we have some doubts about the source of their organ donations, and another case in Worthing concerning a chain of brothels.

'I don't suppose you'd be willing to share this intel?'

'We will, but not at such an early stage in the investigations. As I said earlier, when we've gathered enough information to make arrests, you'll hear from us.'

'That's a pity, as I'd like to get a heads-up as to who could be behind these murders.'

'If you can identify them, I promise you this. You'll receive the full support of the NCA in closing them down.'

TWENTY-SEVEN

Vicky Neal looked down at the paper in her hand. The number seemed to match the sign on the door, although the sign was held on by only one screw so it was lopsided, leaving callers unsure if the house was 61 or 19.

'This is the place,' she said to DC Deepak Sunderam beside her.

She shoved the paper back into her jacket pocket and pressed the 'call' button on the grubby intercom pad.

They were standing outside a house in Buckingham Street, a wide street in Brighton not far from the station, sectioned off on either side to allow the parking of cars. Although it was a fair distance from the seafront, a more typical seaside scene she couldn't imagine, made more realistic with the loud cawing of numerous seagulls perched or hovering over the rooftops. Most of the houses on the road were painted white, some cream, with bay windows, no gardens and one side catching the early evening sun, making her feel all she needed to do now was turn a corner and buy an ice cream and she would feel the warm sea breeze on her face.

'Yeah?' a voice on the intercom crackled.

'Nick Scanlon? Police, open the door.'

'Police? What? Nick's not here, he went out about an hour ago.'

'Nick, don't mess with me, I know it's you. Open the bloody door.' She was bluffing, she didn't know Nick Scanlon from Old Nick. In fact, she didn't know many people in Brighton full stop.

'What do you want?'

'To read your bloody gas meter, what do you think?'

'Eh?'

'We'd like to ask you some questions.'

'That's what you lot always say before you drag me down to John Street.'

'We're not here to drag you off anywhere, Nick. Just open the door.'

She heard an electronic click and nothing more.

'Maybe we've panicked him,' she said to Sunderam, 'and now he's sprinting down the fire escape before jumping over his neighbours' fences.'

'No, I think he's probably scooping up all the needles and his stash and dumping the whole lot down the toilet. If we don't hear anything else from him, at least we've done some good today.'

'He might still be in there. In my experience, these guys are wary of people like us, but if they can see a way of gaining some advantage, curiosity often gets the better of them.'

A minute or so later they heard a door slam and in between the noise of a car driving past, the sound of shuffling feet coming closer.

The door was hauled open and a bedraggled figure in a crumpled white t-shirt and black stained jeans stood before them. His eyes looked bloodshot and his thick black hair was such a mess, a magpie would refuse to bed there.

'Yeah, what d'ya want?'

'We want to talk to you about some people you might know. Can we come in?'

'Are you gonna arrest me?'

'No. We just want to ask you some questions.'

'If you're not gonna arrest me, why don't you ask your questions someplace else. There's a decent pub around the corner. I could do with a drink.'

Neal thought for moment. The detectives didn't come here looking for drugs inside what could turn out to be a skanky house with filthy carpets and stained walls, and she quite fancied a drink. 'Fine, get your jacket.'

Scanlon wandered back the way he'd come, his pace faster, no doubt brought on by the allure of free booze.

'I wouldn't mind a glass of something,' she said to Sunderam, 'just to make Mr Scanlon feel comfortable. Are you okay driving us back to the office? I wouldn't want to get busted by Sussex police before I've got my feet under the desk.'

'No problem. I don't drink much in any case.'

'Why, because of your religious beliefs?'

'A bit, but I'm third generation and my family aren't deeply religious.'

'What then, are you one of those lightweights who blabs out all their secrets after only a couple of pints?' she said smiling. 'It's obviously not to control your weight, there's hardly an ounce of fat on you.'

'No, I'm on a course of antibiotics after a suspect cut me with a rusty knife. Anyway, I don't mind drinking any non-alcoholic drink they can offer. I've done it often enough.'

Neal's old DI in Manchester was suspicious of anyone who didn't drink, and gauged an officer's ability to carry out work, how reliable they would be and those who would have his back, on their capacity for booze. As a result, he was surrounded with a cadre of large fat men who could sink four pints of beer at lunchtime and not fall asleep in the afternoon. Those who were slim, a non-drinker or a woman, and God-help anyone who was gay, didn't get a look in.

The door opened and to her relief Scanlon was wearing a stylish Berghaus jacket, as many of the young Turks in his line of work around her old manor would swan around in tasteless tracksuits and 'look at me' yellow and orange jackets.

The *Battle of Trafalgar* had a narrow frontage but like the Doctor's Tardis, it felt spacious inside, perhaps the paucity of early evening drinkers adding to the effect. They took a seat at the back, beside a door leading outside to a beer garden. Its position, shielded by the pub itself and the houses opposite, she imagined would turn into a suntrap in summer, evidenced by the tables and the number of shrubs growing against the wall. Neal walked to the bar for drinks.

She was renting a flat in Lower Rock Gardens in Brighton while trying to decide where to live. She liked Brighton and wanted to stay there. This was a change of heart, as at one time, she believed she would never leave Manchester. However, unlike the seaside resorts she knew on the Yorkshire coast, such as Bridlington and Scarborough, the refuge of the elderly and dodgy retired businessmen, Brighton felt like a vibrant town on the one hand, and a young, lively holiday resort on the other. Although she realised her opinion might change once she'd experienced the crowds who, she'd been told, descended here in their thousands in the summer and on bank holidays, clogging roads, filling pubs and making any journey along pavements exasperating.

She returned to the table with the drinks: double whisky and water for Scanlon, a gin and tonic for her and a Diet Coke for Sunderam. She sat down.

'Cheers,' the druggie said lifting his glass. She noticed a slight tremble in his hand, more likely the result of a bender the night before than any fear he had of the two detectives sitting opposite. She didn't think Scanlon was wary of being seen talking to two cops, as Neal was a new face in town and Sunderam looked too young to be a cop.

'I needed that,' he said, depositing a half-empty glass on the table with a thump.

'Nick, we're investigating the murder of Liam McKinney.'

She looked at his face and it registered some movement. He knew McKinney, so any subsequent attempt to deny it would be met with stoic resistance from her.

'You know who he is?' she asked, testing the water.

'Maybe I've heard the name, you know, but nothing more. I don't move in those circles anymore.'

He reached for his glass but Neal's hand snaked out and grabbed his wrist. 'Don't fuck with us, Nick. We know you work for Chris Hooper, but that's not why we're here. Liam McKinney worked for Charlie McQueen, rivals of Hooper and I know you guys talk. Give us a flavour of what you've been yakking about.'

She removed her hand and he lifted his glass, this time sipping it like a whisky connoisseur. 'You folks are only investigating Liam McKinney's murder?'

She nodded.

'Nothing more?'

'Nope.'

'You're not interested in Chris Hooper or any of his stuff?'

She shook her head.

Scanlon smiled for the first time and she saw the yellow and rotting teeth of a regular user. The people who succeeded in the drugs business were those who didn't slip their mitts into the merchandise. Doing so not only cost them money, consuming product they could sell, but chances were they would be out of their heads when they did their dealing and it could lead to mistakes.

They could also be careless with their stash, the main dealers in essence had access to an unlimited supply of gear. With such temptation lying around, it was easy for a sloppy addict to inject an overdose, imbibe too pure a product or do something foolish like steal money or make deals with rivals. People like that were usually found floating in a river or with a bullet in their head, just like Liam McKinney.

'It's not good to speak ill of the dead,' Scanlon said,

the wisp of a grin on his face, 'but if I'm being honest, McKinney was an aggressive Irish shite. He bullied the guys working for him and beat up addicts who messed him around or owed him money. He threatened me with a knife once when he found me talking to one of his dealers. I was only saved from being slashed or stabbed when one of my mates turned up.'

'Did McKinney fall out with McQueen?'

Scanlon lifted his empty whisky glass and waggled it from side to side.

'I'll buy you another when you answer my question,' Neal said.

'Fair enough.' He put the glass down and stared at the wall for a few moments. 'As I said, McKinney was an aggressive little toad and always carried a knife. It didn't take much for him to produce it, you know what I'm saying?'

She nodded. 'Carry on.'

'He used his knife on somebody, a friend of McQueen's by all accounts, and Charlie didn't like it. The rest is history, as they say.'

'Who's this friend?'

'You're asking a different question. How about that drink?'

She went to the bar again, but only for Scanlon's drink, as she didn't want any more and Sunderam had barely touched his.

She put the glass down and retook her seat. 'It's the last you're getting from us, so this time I want some answers.'

'Okay, okay,' he said lifting the glass to his lips.

'I'll ask you the same question I asked before. Who did McKinney use his knife on?'

'I don't know his name, some guy McQueen was friendly with is all I know.'

'I was conned into buying you that drink, I thought you knew his name. You're not holding out on us, Nick, are you?'

'Me? No way. It's all I heard.'

'My, it was worth waiting for. What about his killers? Who killed him?'

'I'm told they brought in an out-of-town crew. Two shooters came down to Brighton from London.'

'Their names?'

He shook his head.

The detectives left the *Battle of Trafalgar* five minutes later and walked back to the pool car.

'I'm not sure we learned much from him,' Deepak Sunderam said. 'I think his head's too screwed up with dope.'

'You're right there, but I think we can put some meat on the bones. We didn't know why McKinney was killed, but if we believe what Scanlon told us, we do now. We also didn't know who killed him and, again if we trust Scanlon, we sort of do now.'

'Trouble is, we don't know how reliable his recollection is.'

'I think the whisky oiled his brain and he told us all he knew. I agree it's only the word of one man but cases like this are jigsaws. It's not often we're given the outer edges so we can see the scale and extent of the investigation, but random pieces scattered across the middle. Our job is to continue to collect as many of them as it takes to make a picture we recognise.'

'Very allegorical. I like it.'

'It's funny though, we start off looking at the stabbing of a Newhaven businessman, done by a mugger he says, and days later, we find a drug dealer murdered for knifing a friend of Charlie McQueen. Am I making connections where there aren't any, or is Ted Mathieson the key to this whole case?'

TWENTY-EIGHT

Henderson walked away from the Interview Suite, DS Walters alongside him. The naming of the second murder victim, Elena Iliesc, lifted his mood and that of everyone else working on the investigation.

Searching through the photographs at Longhurst Studios might have been considered by some a mind-numbing exercise, but the work yielded the pictures of their latest victim, allowing them to make the connection between her and Cindy Longhurst. They now believed both victims were in some way connected to human trafficking.

If Rebecca Gregson at the National Crime Agency couldn't share the information she had with him, Henderson had to develop some of his own. What he needed was a name, or several names, of the main traffickers in the Sussex area; in particular, those operating close to the geographic areas where the bodies were found.

Unlike the drugs business where the names of the key players were often known to the police, human traffickers were secretive and unfamiliar. The 'goods' they traded couldn't be concealed so easily as a kilo of heroin, and discovering the place where the victims were housed or working would give the game away.

These last few days, they'd interviewed several

workers from human trafficking charities, government-funded agencies and those involved in Sussex Police, in a bid to try and understand the situation in the region. It felt like opening a Pandora's box of crime. He had no idea how much was going on and originally believed it to be limited to the vegetable fields of East Anglia and large textile companies in the Midlands and Yorkshire. In the Sussex area, he now knew, human slaves were suspected of being involved in such activities as cannabis cultivation, office cleaning, car washing and prostitution.

Many of the women the charity workers assisted were from Vietnam and China, but one told them the story of a Hungarian girl who'd been kidnapped on her way home from work. Like Elena, she had also come from a poor background and lived in a rural area. She'd been taken to the UK in a minibus, her head full of threats made by the kidnappers if she opened her mouth and her body woozy from some drug slipped into her drink as they approached the border crossing.

She'd been kept in a house the charity worker believed to be near the seafront in Brighton and forced to satisfy the sexual needs of between ten to fifteen men per day. One night, when the guard drank himself into a stupor, she stole the keys to the front door, manned and locked 24/7 except when admitting a punter. When she opened the door, she was surprised to find the brothel didn't empty of the twelve girls in the large town house. Many were too frightened of what the gang would do to their families back home.

'Some of the stories we heard in there,' Walters said, jerking her thumb in the direction of the Interview Suite, 'would take your breath away.'

'The more I deal with evil,' Henderson said, 'the more I believe there is a breed of men, as it's predominately men, who can set all feelings of empathy and sympathy for their victims aside in the pursuit of money and power.'

'Do you think they're born evil and behave so for most of the time?'

'Whether they're born or made is debated endlessly in psychology circles, but as to how they behave, I think some of them can turn it off and on. In some of the cases we've looked at, the guys involved were married with kids. Did they fake it and pretend to love their wives and children, while at the same time offering no sympathy whatsoever for the women they'd locked up and were abusing in their brothels?'

'We'll never find out until we grab some of those animals ourselves.'

They stopped outside Henderson's office. 'I'd like an update this afternoon about the database search for information on Elena.'

'No problem, I'll talk to our Indexers.'

'Let's see what we've got at,' he looked at his watch, 'four. Okay?'

'Will do, catch you later.'

After the last interview, Henderson had planned to walk over to the staff restaurant and buy a late lunch. Like Walters, having heard what a charity worker had to say about the conditions in one brothel, it not only took his breath away, but his appetite too.

He sat down but before starting work on anything new his phone rang.

'Henderson.'

'Ted Mathieson here. Do you know what your fucking detectives are doing? Upsetting all my bloody staff, is what.'

'Whoa, hold on a minute, Ted. Where are you?'

'At work in Newhaven. Why?'

'When did you get out of hospital?'

'Tuesday.'

'What are you doing in there at work? You should be convalescing. Stab wounds like yours take weeks to heal.'

'How can I convalesce with so much going on here?'

'I'm sure you've got people who can handle it for you.'

'I thought so too until I saw this.'

'Going back to your opening statement, something about my detectives.'

'About half an hour ago, two of your detectives, Neal and Young, came in here and started asking questions about drug shipments and the murder of Liam McKinney, two things I know bugger all about.'

'What did they say?'

'They accused me of orchestrating McKinney's death in retaliation for him stabbing me. I don't know where they got the information from, a drug dealer so they say, but it was a bloody mugger who stabbed me. I don't know who Liam McKinney is, and I had nothing to do with his murder.'

'In the hospital it sounded like you wanted to take

revenge on your attacker. Perhaps Liam McKinney is that man.'

'Yeah, if you put two and two together and make five. I told you at the hospital, it was just a figure of speech. I had no intention of seeking revenge on anyone and I don't know if this dead guy is the person who attacked me or not. How could I attack someone I don't know?'

Henderson could hear that the injury Mathieson suffered had not softened his crusty exterior, and knew he would not budge from his exaggerated pleas of innocence. Instead, he asked, 'Where are the detectives now?'

'This is the problem. They said they wanted to take a look around and I thought what's the harm, but they're upsetting the boys down in the loading bay and keeping them off their work.'

'I'll call Detective Sergeant Neal, and if she hasn't a good reason for doing what she's doing, I'll instruct her to come back to the office. How does that sound?'

'You do that and— agh!'

'Are you okay?'

'I moved a bit too fast in my seat and this bloody wound gave me a jolt. I'm fine. Okay, so you'll move them out. Job done. I would say now, 'Be seeing you' but I hope I bloody won't.'

After putting the phone down to Mathieson, Henderson called Neal.

'Are you still at Mathieson's?'

'Yes sir, I am. I have reason to suspect Ted Mathieson is complicit in the importation of Class A drugs.'

'What evidence do you have?'

'The statement given to myself and DC Sunderam by a Brighton drug dealer, Nick Scanlon.'

'I've read the statement, Vicky, and it says nothing about Ted Mathieson. It's also common practice when we obtain the word of a nark, we try and obtain some corroboration of their story and then apply for a search warrant. You've gone stomping in there with your boots and all guns blazing. I'd be more inclined to overlook your cavalier approach if you'd discovered anything new, but the absence of a phone call into this office suggests otherwise.'

'Everything looks normal with the exception of a locked strong box in the loading bay for which Ted Mathieson has the only key. I'm sure it's where he keeps the drugs. If I could just get the key to open it and–'

'It's not going to happen without more evidence and a search warrant. I want you and whoever's with you to terminate what you're doing and return to the office at once.'

'But, sir–'

'No buts, DS Neal. You don't have grounds for what you're doing and you're upsetting Ted Mathieson, who, as far as we know, is guilty of possessing nothing more than a bad temper. Back here. Now.'

Henderson dropped the handset into its cradle, resisting the temptation to slam it down. On listening to Mathieson, he believed he'd given DS Neal too much rope and the impetuous sergeant had choked on it. On thinking through the incident, he realised it was a mistake often made by more experienced officers. When their enthusiasm for nabbing a seemingly obvious criminal encouraged them to ignore the policies and procedures designed to protect the innocent.

It was an error of judgement nevertheless, and he would reprimand her for it. This didn't mean Ted Mathieson would be left alone since Henderson didn't believe the company business owner had been mugged at Devil's Dyke. A mugger would have taken something, like his phone or car, and the stabbing would only happen if the victim had attacked his assailant.

Henderson noticed Mathieson's phone when he first went to see him, a crack in the screen and the distinctive blue and white Brighton and Hove Albion bumper. He still had the same phone when the DI went to see him at the Belvedere Hospital.

In DS Neal's interview with Nick Scanlon, he said he believed Charlie McQueen was behind the murder of Liam McKinney because the Irishman had stabbed an acquaintance of his. It was too much of a coincidence to ignore. The DI believed it was McKinney who met and stuck a knife into Ted Mathieson at Devil's Dyke.

His supposition still didn't explain what was going on between Mathieson and McQueen's organisation, but if it was Mathieson's stabbing that got McKinney killed, it had to be something big and important. Scanlon told DS Neal that McKinney had become something of a loose cannon, a view corroborated by DI Hobbs, but in Henderson's view this didn't sound like sufficient justification for the action he took.

Mathieson owned a fleet of lorries which criss-crossed East and West Europe every day. The business card found at McQueen's house and Scanlon's statement connected Mathieson to Charlie McQueen, but did this mean Mathieson was importing drugs or was he simply a user of McQueen's products? Mathieson also had connections to Cindy Longhurst.

He was about to pick up the phone and talk to Hobbs again when DC Sally Graham walked in carrying her laptop.

'Can I interrupt, sir?'

'You can. What's on your mind?'

'Can we sit at the meeting table? It might be easier to show you what I've got on my laptop.'

Henderson stood, headed to the meeting table and took a seat.

'I don't know if I mentioned it before, but on one of the files on the portable hard disk drive at Cindy's studio was found to be encrypted.'

'I think I remember you saying something about it.'

'Well, I sent it off to the High-Tech Unit and they managed to open it.'

'Good. What did it contain?'

'Take a look.'

She pushed the laptop round so they could both look and Henderson's mouth dropped open. There had to be over a hundred pictures, this time not posed head shots and smiling families, but photographs of what looked like low stone buildings out in the woods, perhaps some Second World War barracks or unusual-looking storage depots.

'This is what we've been looking for!' Henderson said. 'I knew we'd recognise it as soon as we saw it.'

Among them, the pictures he'd seen before of the girl they now knew to be Elena, standing outside a house somewhere. She looked relaxed and carefree, her mind unaware of the subsequent fate that would soon befall her.

Scrolling down, he saw her again, walking in the countryside and throwing sticks into a river. The pictures of her and the other girls didn't look as posed as Cindy's photographs often did, but natural, the girls' smiles easy and unforced.

'Is there some meaning in the images included in this file?' he said. 'They appear to be chronicling something, but I'm not sure what.'

'Me neither, but if we assume, and I know it's a big assumption, this is all about human traffickers, these pictures could be the victim's journey from the time they arrived in the UK. They start off in those stone buildings, say until the kidnappers decide where to take them. The photographs of streets and buildings, could be the places where the abducted women are required to work. The pictures at the bottom maybe are photographs of those who escaped.'

'It fits, and with such scant information available on this case, I'm tempted to believe it, but I must introduce a note of caution. If we make an erroneous assumption and head down the wrong path it could bugger up this investigation for good. With the pressure for a result from upstairs and the media, we would find ourselves on the street before the end of the day. We need to proceed with care until we can collect more evidence.'

'I understand, and I think I know how we can get it. Click on this picture of Elena,' she said pointing at one of the images.

Elena was standing outside a house, a large semi-detached post-war house, well maintained evidenced by the blemish-free driveway and new-looking garden wall.

'If you look to the right I think you can see a street sign.'

'Good God, so there is! If we can find out where this was taken, we might be able establish the link between Elena and Cindy. Can you enlarge the picture?'

She rolled the wheel on the mouse and the photograph grew in size. She slid the image across the screen until the focus of their attention, what looked like a street sign, moved into the centre.

'Right, we can see it better now, for sure it's a street sign.'

'It's hard to distinguish any detail.'

'Maybe the High-Tech Unit can clean it up.'

Henderson leaned back and took control of the mouse, enlarging the image and shrinking it. He did this several times. 'I think I can make something out. The first letter of the first word is definitely a 'B and the last an 'N'. What do you think the middle one is, 'B' or 'D'?'

'I think it's 'D'.'

'So, we've got 'B' something 'D' something 'N'. It could be Bodan or Bedon.' He thought for a moment then it came to him. 'It's Baden, Baden Powell. Which would make the squiggly last word 'Drive.' Baden Powell Drive.'

'It fits with the shape of the letters, but what does it mean? What or who is Baden Powell?'

'Robert Baden Powell, the founder of the Scout movement. The road is named after him.'

'You should be on *Mastermind* knowing something like that.'

'It wasn't so difficult, I used to be in the Scouts. One of the first things you learn is the name of the person who founded it.'

'Just a sec.' She moved the mouse and Google appeared on the screen. She tapped in 'Baden Powell Drive'. A few moments later she said, 'There's a street in Colchester with the same name.'

TWENTY-NINE

Leaving the A12 and heading towards Colchester, DI Henderson and DC Graham soon hit traffic. A few minutes later he realised why when he spotted a Sainsbury's supermarket on the far side of the roundabout. He'd never studied town planning but even he knew it wasn't a sensible idea building such a large retail outlet there. People entering and departing supermarkets often had their brains on their shopping list or on the great bargains they'd bagged. For sure, they didn't have it on the car in front or the ones they were holding up behind with their slow driving.

They turned down the aptly-named Straight Road. Colchester, a former Roman regional capital, contained many remains of those industrious people and he suspected this road was one of them. Not since the Romans left Britain in the fifth century had A and B-roads been constructed along straight lines. Instead, most were built upon existing droving trails that circumvented hills, skirted rivers and avoided any other obstacles that sheep couldn't be bothered facing.

They turned off Straight Road into Baden Powell Drive, named after the founder of the Scout Movement, a man with more African connections, he suspected, than with this Essex town. Spotting a good place to park, he pulled into the side of the road and switched off the engine. He turned to his passenger. 'It would be better if we walk. If vulnerable women are living here, they might be spooked at seeing a strange car cruising back and forth outside their window.'

'Can't argue with you there.'

Armed with the picture of Elena standing in front of a house, they got out of the car and started walking. The photograph had been taken in summer, although they weren't sure in which year. However, by looking at the picture they had of the victim and comparing it to those of her contained in the encrypted file, she hadn't aged, making them think it was the previous summer.

They walked along the road looking at houses, trying to find one similar to the house in the photograph. Even allowing for gardens to alter due to seasonal change, some owners may have made significant modifications. Instead, they were relying on those things not easily modified, for example, the position of the garage, chimney and television aerial.

A few minutes later they stopped outside a semi-detached house: small garden out front, brick construction with white windows and a white door,

'This looks like it,' Graham said, 'but the garden wall looks recent and the door is different.'

'The alarm box is in the same position, so is the satellite dish, and look, there's the bracket for the hanging basket we see in the picture. Without a door number we can't be certain, but I think this is the place.'

'What do we do now?'

'We knock on the door and see if anyone is at

home.'

Walking down the path he spotted the neighbour in the house next door looking over. The DI was holding a photograph of the house in his hand and the woman would most likely conclude they were viewing the house with a view to buying it. The age difference between the detectives might give her pause to ponder, but if she concluded they were father and daughter he wouldn't be best pleased.

Henderson rang the bell, sounding loud in the quiet of a lazy Monday afternoon in this suburban part of Colchester.

'The house is well secured,' Graham said. 'There's locks on the windows, an alarm, and the door looks solid and protected by three locks.'

'Are you utilising knowledge gained in uniform, or are you itching for a move back there?'

'The former. I don't hear any movement inside.'

'Me neither.' He rang again.

A minute or so later, he stepped back and examined each window in turn, but couldn't see the flicker of the television or lights and no faint shudder from the blinds or curtains. 'I don't think anyone's at home. Let's try the house next door.'

They approached the house, the other half of the semi-detached and the one containing the inquisitive neighbour. Her curiosity was about to be sated.

'The woman in here can't pretend it's an empty house,' Henderson said, as he pressed the doorbell.

'Good afternoon, madam,' Henderson said when the door opened. 'Police.' He held up his ID for her to see. 'We'd like to ask you some questions about your neighbour if we may.'

'Yes, of course. Do come in. I'm Celia Bannerman by the way.'

'I am Detective Inspector Angus Henderson and this is Detective Constable Sally Graham,' he said, omitting to add, 'of Surrey and Sussex Police'. No sense in muddying the waters.

Celia Bannerman from a distance looked older than Henderson, early fifties would have been his first guess. However, on closer inspection he could see he was wide of the mark. She was no more than thirty-five with thick brown hair, a trim figure and a round, pretty face. The pink sweater and tweed skirt fooled him and was perhaps her way of looking older. If she combined her cherub-features with the right clothes she could, without too much trouble, transform back into being a teenager.

'Can I offer you something to drink? Tea, coffee?'

'It's very kind of you. Coffee for me,' Henderson said.

'Me too,' Graham said.

'Please, sit down wherever you like.'

The fawn leather settee looked inviting and the soft back a welcome change from the upright seat in the car.

'It's a lovely house,' Graham said after they were both seated.

'It is. I like the wooden flooring, the fancy rug and look at those huge windows.'

'Yes, but you're a fan of older houses, are you not?'

'I am. No matter what you do to a new house like this one, you can't get away from straight walls and square or rectangular rooms.'

'A lot of people like it.'

'I'm sure they do, coupled with the reliability of utilities like the heating, plumbing and electricity all of which in an older house can cause problems.'

'I prefer older houses too. I like how previous alterations can leave little alcoves and odd-shaped rooms.'

'Here we are,' Celia Bannerman said as she re-entered the room bearing a large tray.

Henderson stood, took the tray from her and placed it on the coffee table.

A short time later, Henderson was drinking a mighty fine Americano, as good as anything he could buy in Starbucks or Costa. By the sounds coming out of the kitchen ten minutes before, she had to be using one of the expensive Italian machines used by many restaurants.

'You wanted to ask me about my neighbours.'

'Yes, we did... is it Ms or Mrs Bannerman?'

'Mrs, but please call me Celia. You're lucky to get me here today, I work with my husband in our little manufacturing business and I only slipped away as I'm expecting a delivery. Most times we ask a neighbour to take in deliveries for us, but this one is a heavy item and old George would put his back out trying to lift the thing.'

'Does George live in the house we were standing outside?'

'Oh no, three young women live there.'

'What do you know about them?'

'Are they involved in doing something illegal?'

'Oh no, nothing to worry about. Their address came up in a minor investigation we're undertaking. We just wanted to have a word with them about it.'

'Well, what can I tell you? I think they're all employed in office jobs as I sometimes see all three of them heading out first thing in the morning and they're always well dressed. I wish the people who worked in our business were as diligent at turning up for work on time and wore something other than an old sweatshirt and jeans.'

'How long have they lived here?'

'About nine months.'

'And before them?'

'Four other young women.'

'Is the house rented?'

'I don't know for certain, but I think it must be. I mean, what are the chances of a group of young women selling a house to another group of young women? I don't know the stats, but when I walk through the town I see plenty of teenage girls. Colchester is quite a young place, but even still.'

'It sounds to me like it's owned by something like a housing association or a charity who only rent it out to young women who otherwise couldn't afford to buy. Perhaps trying to give them a leg-up in the housing ladder.'

Henderson was couching his thoughts in everyday language, not wishing to alarm householders like Celia Bannerman, concerned about falling house prices and standards in their neighbourhood. The spectre of a house containing a small group of battered women or, as the detectives believed, trafficked women, would certainly concern them. Not only about the plight of the women themselves, whose stories couldn't fail to elicit sympathy from the most cold-blooded of people, but also about the husbands and traffickers who might come looking for them.

'This is what my husband Barry says, although I don't think he cares where they're from or why they're here. He just likes to ogle them when they're out doing the garden or washing the windows.'

Henderson smiled but Celia didn't break from her previous serious frown. To him, this suggested that a house containing three pretty young women was a sore topic in the Bannerman household, although perhaps not with Mr Bannerman.

'Do you or your husband ever speak to the women?'

'We do when we're bringing in the shopping or going out for walk, but not so much at the moment with all the frosts in the morning and dark nights. No one likes to linger in the winter, do they? He speaks to them more than me. They're not British, that much is clear. He says they're from Eastern Europe, but I wouldn't trust his judgement, he often gets the names and nationality of his own staff wrong.'

'You've been very helpful, Celia, I think we've asked all the questions we came to ask. How about you Sally, anything you'd like to add?'

'Just one thing,' she said. 'What time do the women return at night?'

'Oh, at various times, I think, between about six and seven in the evening. The woman who used to live there must have been a teaching assistant or something as she came home at different hours of the day, sometimes early afternoon. I only work part-time in our business, you see, so I know most of the goings-on in this part of the road.'

'The woman you're talking about,' Henderson said. 'Is she one of the previous group of four before the current occupants?'

'No. Didn't I say? At one time, there were four women living in the house, not three as there is now. The fourth girl went out to work one day and didn't return. I don't know if my husband knows where she went, I can ask him if you like.'

Henderson reached into his pocket and extracted a photograph of Elena. Not the pale mortuary image, displayed at the press conference a few days after her body had been discovered and published in various newspapers, but one from Cindy's collection.

'Is this her?' he said passing the photograph over.

She took one look before raising her head. 'Yes, it's her. This picture was taken over there,' she said pointing, 'outside their house last summer. I remember the delightful hanging basket.'

THIRTY

The day following their trip to Colchester, Henderson and Sally Graham were heading north once again, this time on a train to East Croydon. Research done by the murder team discovered that the house in Baden Powell Drive where Elena used to live in Colchester was owned by a charity, Action for Trafficked Women. According to their website, ATW provided a comprehensive help package for victims of trafficking: medical assistance, moving them to safe accommodation, assisting them to settle in the UK or, if preferred, paying for their passage home.

It was a short walk from East Croydon station to Sydenham Road and they soon found the squat two-storey building matching the address on the slip of paper in his hand. The building was constructed of brick with large white painted windows, giving the impression it was solid and reliable, as if owned by a reputable firm of family lawyers.

'Impressive,' Graham said as they approached. 'Any charities I've dealt with are more often than not crammed into a couple of small rooms above an Indian restaurant.'

'There's a lot like that while others, particularly the animal ones are awash with money. Not only are people happy to drop spare cash into their collection tins in shopping centres but now and again a cat or dog lover dies and leaves millions to their favourite pet charity.'

He turned the handle on the door and walked in to a bright and warm interior, a pleasant change from the dull and dreary day outside.

A few minutes later they were seated in the office of ATW director, Linda Herschel. It was obvious she was either an extremely busy or inefficient person as stuffed folders were stacked on her desk, on cabinets and several large piles stood on the floor. The word 'fire hazard' didn't seem adequate.

'Smart offices you have here,' Henderson said.

'Yes,' Herschel said, 'it belonged to a firm of surveyors but the lure of the high-rise offices you can see all round Croydon got to them in the end.'

The striking thing about Linda Herschel, after her dazzling white teeth, was her hair. It wasn't the style that caught his eye, but the colour; a strange shade of red, something he suspected was not found in nature.

Coffee was served in mugs which he liked, but floral-patterned china cups and silver teaspoons would have been more appropriate alongside the wood-panelled walls and sash windows.

'Can you tell me something about the charity and what you do, Ms Herschel?' Henderson asked.

'Of course,' she said in strong Surrey tones.

'It was founded by myself and Virginia Mason three years ago to try and assist the thousands of women who are trafficked into this country every year.'

'Do you confine your activities to the UK?'

'Oh, no. Our aim is to help women wherever human trafficking takes place. We have operations in Germany, France and Sweden. We rehouse the women and give them a safe place to stay until they feel able to move on. If they wish to remain in the country they have been trafficked to, we will help with visas, learning the language, job hunting, housing and anything else they need. If they prefer to return to their home country, which can be problematic as you can imagine, the traffickers still being there, we will assist with their onward passage.'

'Impressive.'

'Thank you.'

'It sounds like an expensive operation.'

'Oh, it is, but we couldn't do it without the backing of our benefactor.'

'Who is it?'

'Joshua Lindberg.'

'The mobile phone entrepreneur?'

'Yes, the same. He gives us a generous allowance every year and, like any other charity, we also receive donations from people who support what we do and from the women we've helped once they get back on their feet.'

It all clicked into place – the large offices, the range and scope of work they did. Lindberg started his mobile phone company at the beginning, before the indispensable little devices became as ubiquitous as fries in a MacDonald's restaurant. Back then, queues would develop outside Lindberg's shops whenever they received a new delivery; they couldn't sell them fast enough. As a result, Lindberg didn't become an ordinary millionaire, limping into the lower reaches of the *Sunday Times Rich List*, but a billionaire, regularly vying for top place alongside property developers, industrialists and software entrepreneurs.

The super-rich bought football clubs or retired to a yacht moored in Monaco, to bask in Mediterranean sunshine and benefit from a low tax regime which ensured they couldn't spend their fortune, no matter how hard they tried. Lindberg was different, son of an émigré from Poland, he never forgot his roots and vowed to donate all his money to charitable causes and leave nothing to any of his four children.

'As I said on the phone,' Henderson said, 'we are interested in a house you own in Baden Powell Drive, Colchester.'

'After you called, I looked the house up. When we were a much smaller organisation I knew all the properties and the names of all the women living there, but now,' she said with a shrug and turning her palms skyward, 'we've become too big.'

She turned to her computer and shook the mouse to wake it. After a few minutes tapping on the keyboard she said, 'There are three women living in that house.'

'What can you tell me about them?'

'We originally put four women into that house, all brought to us by a good friend of the charity.'

'What's this friend's name?'

'I'm afraid I can't tell you, although I don't think it would do any harm to say as she's dead now, but she came from Sussex.'

'Was her name Cindy Longhurst?'

'My God,' she said. 'How did you know?'

Henderson would have punched his palm in satisfaction if he wasn't facing such a stony face which might misinterpret his exuberance. It was the connection he had been looking for.

'Her name came up in our investigation.'

'If you need to speak to her, I'm sorry to say, Inspector, Cindy was killed several weeks ago.'

'I know,' Henderson said.

'I suppose you do, being the police. Do you know if anyone has been arrested yet?'

'No, I'm afraid they haven't.'

'I hope you do find someone soon. Cindy was such a lovely person.'

'Did you know her well?'

'Yes, for a number of years. We got together after meeting one another on various marches and demonstrations.'

'What's the connection between Cindy and the women in Colchester?'

'She came to me, it must be about four or five months ago. She said she found in the course of her work as a photographer a place where trafficked women were being held when they first arrived in this country.'

The photograph they'd seen on Cindy's portable hard disk drive of a series of low concrete buildings, nestled out in the woods popped into Henderson's mind.

'We tried to interest the police here in Croydon. I have a good relationship with them but Sergeant Halliday said they were too busy with a murder and a fatal bus crash. So, Cindy went ahead on her own.'

'To do what?'

'She went to the place where the women were being held and I'm not sure how, managed to get some of them out.'

'It's a dangerous activity for any member of the public to undertake on their own.'

'A lot of the activities my staff get involved in are dangerous, Inspector. We deal day in, day out with evil people. It doesn't mean I condone unnecessary risks. You must understand, I don't regard anyone who works here as an employee, I consider them members of my extended family.'

'Did Cindy bring the women to you?'

'Yes, she did. If my memory serves me right, she released ten. Four decided to return home and the other six have settled here in the UK.'

'You help them settle by doing what, providing them with a house...'

'We moved four of the Sussex women into Baden Powell Drive and applied for visas to allow them to stay and work here. In time, they'll apply for full UK citizenship. At some stage in the future when they're ready, they'll move on and other trafficked women will take their place.'

'Do you know anything about the place in Sussex where these women were being held?'

'No, and I didn't ask Cindy about it. You see in this business, Inspector, we try to compartmentalise information. The less people know about something important the lower the chance they might blab about it to friends or, God forbid, be forced to reveal it at the point of a knife or gun.'

'Does this happen often?' Graham asked.

'More than I care to think about, to be truthful.'

'Did Cindy know the identity of the traffickers?'

'She was trying to find that out when she was kidnapped. She believed the gang was being led by a local businessman, but she wouldn't reveal his name without further confirmation. She didn't want to blacken his name without better evidence, that's how principled Cindy could be.'

'It's all credit to her that she didn't. Most people are only too happy to put the first thing they find up on social media and worry about the consequences later.'

'I agree, it's much too prevalent nowadays. In situations where we know the name of one of the traffickers, we, and all the people we work with, are encouraged only to reveal the perpetrator's name with a police officer or someone from the National Crime Agency present. It's safer for all of us this way.'

Henderson realised he would not find out anything more. He could understand the reluctance of anyone working in this field not to expose themselves any more than they needed to, but he felt cheated. One word, one name or address from Linda and he felt confident they would get their hands on the killers of Cindy Longhurst and Elena Iliesc. It felt like he'd gone fishing for trout and a pike had snapped his line.

'You said there are three women in the house, but there used to be four.'

'Yes, the fourth left a few weeks ago and she didn't come back. No phone call, not so much as a 'thank you' email. We tried to find out what had happened to her, but the other girls said she'd been unhappy and, in their opinion, had gone back to Romania.'

'Is this her?' Henderson said, passing over Elena's photograph.

She picked it up and looked at it. 'Yes, it is. This is Elena. Such a lovely girl.' She looked at him suspiciously. 'Where did you get this?'

'I'm sorry to say, but Elena was found murdered three weeks ago.'

'What?' she said, dropping the photograph and her hand moving to cover her mouth. 'This is terrible news.'

No one spoke for the next minute or so, the quiet of the room pervaded only by cars passing outside, the whir of the desk computer fan and the sobs of the ATW director in front of them.

'Did you not see her picture in the paper?' Henderson asked. 'It was widely circulated.'

'I don't read many newspapers or watch news programmes,' Linda Herschel said, dabbing her eyes with a paper handkerchief. 'This work is harrowing enough without adding to it.'

'I understand.'

'How did she die?'

Henderson went on to explain about Elena's death and the connection they'd made to Cindy's.

'You think the traffickers killed both women?'

'Before coming here today I had some doubts, but I don't now.'

'I told Cindy what she was doing was dangerous. She said, no, the place where they were being kept was

258

out in the country and mostly unguarded. The guards lived in a house nearby and only went near the place when they brought food or dragged one of the women back to their house for sex.'

'I think Cindy was killed for releasing the women and Elena for escaping. I also think they will kill the remaining three women in Baden Powell Drive if they can locate them.'

She nodded, but this time her voice sounded weary. 'This is how they work, they like to send a message to the others to stay in line. If you study history as I do, it makes me sad to say, but they operate in much the same way as the Nazis did with their prisoners.'

'Bearing in mind this increased risk, we and your charity need to think about how we can protect them. Also, I would like to speak to the women and try and find out more about the place where they were being held.'

'I agree we need to do everything to protect them although I'm confident their location is still secret or they'd all be missing or dead by now.'

'Elena was beaten before being killed.'

'She was? How awful. Why did they do this? To reveal the location of the other women?'

'I believe so. Is it a risk you're willing to take?'

'No, no it's not. I'll move them as soon as I can, but I can't let you speak to them and they would refuse to talk to you if approached.'

'I can offer them protective custody until the traffickers are caught.'

'The answer is still no, I'm afraid.'

'If you don't mind me saying, I think this is a crazy decision. If we can find the place where the kidnapped women were being held, we can close this operation down. With a bit of luck, we'll also arrest the traffickers. Don't you think this would be in the best interests of the charity and the women housed at Baden Powell Drive?'

'I can understand your frustration, Inspector, I really can, but I can't let you near them. It's a policy enshrined in the very fabric of this charity. The less people know about these women and their backgrounds, the safer and more able they are to get on with their lives.'

THIRTY-ONE

'She said she wouldn't let you speak to any of the women?' CI Edwards said, her expression aghast. 'I haven't heard anything so stupid for a long time. She wouldn't take such a bloody pious tone if we put her in handcuffs and dragged her down to the station for obstructing a murder investigation.'

Henderson was sitting opposite Chief Inspector Edwards in her spacious office although the gap between the two of them didn't half feel small when she was like this. She was in a bullish mood, as frustrated as everyone else on the team at the obdurate attitude of Linda Herschel at ATW.

'On the one hand, I can understand her trying to protect the women,' Henderson said. 'One slip of the tongue in the wrong company and it could endanger any one of them in their secure houses. On the other, when the danger is so imminent for those women at the house in Colchester, it looks as if she's following procedures just for the hell of it.'

'Something still bothers me.'

'What?'

'They beat up Cindy, we think, so she would reveal the location of the photos she took of the women in order to destroy them. Agreed?'

'Yes,' he said, 'although now we have them, their

only use will be in confirming the place where the kidnapped women are being held once we know where it is. The photographs don't tell us much more as they don't contain any location information.'

'Did the kidnappers believe the photos were more damaging than they are, or are we missing something?'

'Maybe they're paranoid about leaks, because as Linda said, Cindy suspected the guy running the show is a local businessman.'

'He won't be a businessman much longer when we get hold of him.'

'I don't think we're missing anything,' Henderson said, 'unless there's some pictures we haven't seen. Even then, I don't think this is the case as we saw the place where Cindy stored the back-up disk drives and we've examined them all.'

'Let's park that issue for the moment. We know they beat Cindy for the reason we said, but they also did the same to Elena. This time, to reveal the location of the house where she and the other escapees were living.'

'Agreed.'

'This is what's bothering me. Why haven't the kidnappers come for them?'

'I don't know, as I don't see how a young woman like Elena could hold out after all the abuse she must have suffered.'

'Me neither. I think she must have told them.'

'In which case the attack on the women could happen any day now.'

'If it hasn't happened already.'

'What makes you think that?'

'You didn't see them when you went there, did you?'

'No, according to a neighbour, they were all at work.'

'I don't imagine the people at ATW keep daily tabs on the women so there might only be two in the house or none at all.'

'I'll contact Linda and ask her to do a check on their whereabouts, and find out when they intend moving them to a different location.'

'Did Linda tell you any more than simply filling in the blanks in Cindy's story? I feel for Cindy, you know? Here's a woman with a good business, two kids and a smart house, putting herself on the line to try and save those unfortunate women.'

'Getting killed for it too.'

'Aye, but I'm sure she was aware of the dangers. You said Linda Herschel warned her?'

'She did, for all the good it did.'

'Cindy sounds like a head-strong woman with strong principles, not something you find on every street corner. In which case, it wouldn't make a difference what Linda Herschel said, I think she would have gone there regardless.'

Henderson walked back to his office in sombre mood. CI Edwards didn't often wear her heart on her sleeve, but this case had got to her as well, making Henderson feel no matter what resources he required, she would authorise it. In fact, he didn't need any more resources than were in place. The paucity of leads didn't fully occupy his team at the moment.

**

Henderson walked over to the bar and bought the drinks; vodka and lime for Rachel and a pint for himself. He didn't need to savour his drink this evening as, for once, he wasn't on-call. Despite a wish to stay at the office to try and find an opening in the Cindy Longhurst case, he decided he fancied a night in the pub. Also, based on the mood Rachel had been in lately, no way did he want to work late or sit indoors.

'You've never taken me to this place before. It's small but neatly formed.'

'Are you angling for a job as your paper's restaurant and pub critic?'

'No, I'm just saying.'

They were seated in a pub called *The Hand in Hand* on Bristol Road, a short walk from their house. Small it was and would feel crowded with more than twenty people inside. Early evening on a cold Tuesday, he counted six customers including them, so there was no need for anyone to encroach into their space just yet.

'When we go out it's often at the weekend,' Henderson said. 'Friday and Saturday nights this place is packed, we would never get in. It's not so bad in the summer as people stand outside in the street drinking, but not at this time of year, only smokers are so foolhardy.'

'Good choice,' she said lifting her drink. 'I meant to ask. How's your dad?'

'He's fine. I told you about his chronic inability to

cook?'

'Yes.'

'I meant what I said it. He couldn't knock up a plate of beans and toast or scrambled eggs. I suspect if he tried making a sandwich, he'd chop one of his fingers off.'

'I thought they taught you all those things in the navy?'

'No, it's the opposite. Unless you work in the kitchens, all meals are served.'

'How does he survive on his own?'

'When mum went into hospital last time, about six or seven years ago, Mrs Carmichael across the road brought in food for him. She's too old now but her daughter does it and stops him starving to death.'

Henderson's parents lived in Fort William in the north of Scotland and yesterday his mother, Mary, was admitted into Belford Hospital for a gallstones operation. Back in the day, this involved serious open surgery with the attendant risk of infection and long recovery times. Nowadays, they used keyhole techniques, requiring no more than a series of small cuts to the abdomen. Most patients were allowed home the same day. His mother was spending an extra day in hospital due to complications and would require about ten days recuperation.

He'd instructed his father not to expect his wife to look after him during her convalescence period. A few years back, his father had taken up carpentry, refitting the shed at the back of the house and converting it into a workshop. To give his dad something to do and to give his mother some peace, he'd recently sent him a picture of a bedside table from the John Lewis catalogue and asked him to reproduce it.

'You learned to cook when you lived on your own.'

'There was no Mrs Carmichael living across the road for me, that's for sure. It's partly true. When I was married, Laura didn't mollycoddle me like my mum does to my dad. If I came in late from a shift there might be something left for me to eat, but sometimes she would be out taxiing the kids to ballet or swimming and I had to make it myself.'

Henderson picked up his beer and slowly took a drink, his way of indicating he didn't want to talk any more about his former marriage.

'Oh, did I tell you Marnie's leaving?'

'Which one is she?'

'The large lady in my office who always wears black except for her specs which come in every colour of the rainbow.'

'I remember her now, large and loud.'

'The very one, and if booze is thrown into the mix, she becomes many decibels louder. She's jumping ship and moving to ITV.'

'Not fronting a television programme, I hope.'

'Oh no, unless they can find a camera wide enough and they don't mind their ratings plummeting. She's joining them as a researcher in current affairs.'

'Not fancy a move into television yourself?'

'Maybe. I'll keep in touch with her and see how it pans out. It might be fun being on first-name terms with a bunch of celebrities.'

'Or not, if you find the work they do in front of the camera is all a bit of a show and they behave like spoiled brats when they're away from it.'

'Trust you to be so cynical. How are you getting on with finding out who killed Cindy Longhurst?'

'Are you asking in a professional or personal capacity?'

'Personal.'

'None of this will appear in print?'

'Nope.'

'We now believe she was killed for helping trafficked women escape from their kidnappers.'

'What? I knew she was an ardent campaigner against fracking and building power stations, but I never believed anything she campaigned against would result in her being murdered.'

'Trafficking is in a different league from standing outside a field in Balcombe trying to stop lorries moving in and out with fifty like-minded companions. The men operating trafficking businesses are evil and ruthless beyond measure.'

'I imagine it goes with the territory.'

'How do you mean?'

'With drugs, it's attractive to kids and young people with no future and they see a bit of buying and selling as a way of getting out of their situation. The only people attracted to a business involving the slaving of another human being have got to be twisted individuals in the first place. They must be sociopathic, or even psychopathic.'

'Fair point, but I believe Cindy was aware of the dangers she faced.'

'How can you say such a thing? She's a middle-class mum with her own business and a kid at private school. How could she possibly comprehend it?'

'There's no need to raise your voice.'

'Well, your arrogant attitude winds me up. You're blaming her for getting herself into this situation, not the evil people who killed her.'

'No I'm not. Don't be soft.'

'Don't call me soft.'

'I meant–'

'I know what you meant. You're patronising me.'

'Look, can you calm down and talk about this like a reasonable person?'

She stood and towered over him. 'Is this what you call it? Well, you can stick your bloody drink, I'm going home.'

THIRTY-TWO

Eric Stansfield didn't realise he was singing until a car drove past, the first this morning. Most days if a car approached, the driver would offer a wave, but this time the guy inside laughed. He didn't have his fly open and Dusty, the Golden Retriever ambling on the lead beside him, wasn't doing anything daft like pissing on his wellington boots. It had to be the sight of a white-haired old geezer singing and moving his head in time to the music.

For his birthday three weeks past, he had treated himself to an iPod. Neither his miserable son nor his daughter would buy it for him and all he got from them was a bottle of wine and a pair of welly boot socks, same as last year. With help from a younger member of the tennis club, he managed to convert all his vinyl albums and cassettes to digital, or whatever the young generation called it when an LP popped up on his iPod. He called it magic and something a 16th century Sussex witch would be proud of and burned at the stake for her efforts.

Now, whenever he took Dusty for a walk he could listen to the music he would never throw away; Marillion, U2 and the incomparable Thin Lizzy. No longer was he required to suffer his ears being assailed by the cackle of arguing crows, the cawing of hawks overhead as they hunted for small animals in the frosted grass or the endless *thrum-thrum* of his welly boots as he strode along the tarmac road.

Despite giving the dog a daily walk and living not a mile from this place, King's Lane to the south-east of Cowfold, he hadn't adapted well to living in the country. It was his wife who wanted to move here as she believed the fresh air would be better for her asthma. It seemed to be doing the trick as she didn't wheeze as much as she used to when they lived in Falmer. He missed being close to Brighton, especially now with so many bands he liked all those years ago re-forming and back touring.

He hated the journey too. A lecturer in Medieval History at Sussex University, he cycled to work from the old house, but living out here, he was forced to endure a tortuous drive through narrow and pot-holed country lanes, and to battle for road space with speed hogs on the A23. If Rod at the tennis club could manage to make his iPod play through his car's speakers, he would become a friend for life, and no longer would he subject him to a complimentary bottle of his wife's ghastly nettle wine.

The dog was feeling frisky, not often a trait associated with elderly retrievers, so he decided to enter the field at the point where King's Lane changed into Moatfield Lane. Gates and big dogs didn't mix, in particular those secured with a chain, as no way could he lift the heavy mutt over. This one, thank goodness, wasn't locked and so they entered the field without drama from the dog at being lifted, or him trying to make it home with a slipped disc.

He understood enough about farming to know that at this time of the year, if the farmer intended cultivating this field, something would already be planted there. He skirted the edge of the field for a minute or so and, seeing only grass, he unclipped the lead and let Dusty roam free.

Five minutes later he couldn't see the dog and assumed she was foraging in the row of trees he could see twenty or so metres in the distance. He reached the trees as his favourite track of all time popped up on the *Dad's Faves* playlist, *Waiting for an Alibi* by Thin Lizzy. Scott Gorham's beautiful guitar intro had him smiling, but before the voice of the late but legendary Phil Lynott stormed into his ears and reawakened sleeping goose bumps, he ripped the ear buds from his head.

Dusty was sitting there in the rough grass wearing the dog equivalent of a smile on her face that said, 'hey, pop, see what I've found.' Facing Eric was the naked body of a young girl.

A girl of model-type proportions he would say later in the pub, her gorgeous face only spoiled by the bullet wound to her skull. He omitted to tell his friends he threw up at this point and had to hang on to the nearest tree to stop him falling, his knees as wobbly and unsteady as his wife's overweight nurse on her bicycle.

THIRTY-THREE

Henderson parked on the road behind Grafton
Rawlings's Austin Healey 3000. He could have chosen
to drive into the field as his Audi was equipped with
four-wheel drive, but not only did the surface look
bumpy, the mid-morning sun had melted the frost
and the movement of support vehicles had turned it
into a quagmire.

He took a pair of wellingtons and an oversuit out of
the boot. Walters did the same. Walking across the
field to the small cluster of vehicles and people in the
distance, he was too preoccupied to notice much of his
surroundings: green fields, birds chirping their hearts
out and a couple of pheasants pecking at the ground
twenty metres away. He did, however, take note that
the remote location had kept neighbours and the
press away for the moment.

He pulled out his ID and presented it to the
constable, positioned there to keep the public and
media away from the crime scene. With no rowdy
crowd to deal with, it wasn't surprising to find him
examining the proffered document with exaggerated
importance.

The first thing Henderson spotted was the body,
only about a metre inside the tree line. The killer
could have moved it further in, making its discovery

less likely, but chose not to do so. Why? The second thing he noticed, the body was naked, same with Cindy, same for Elena. He bent down beside the pathologist, his heart heavy and his mood sombre.

'Morning Angus.'

'Morning Grafton, what do we have here?'

'You're not going to like it. Naked, only a little bruising this time, young, pretty, and a bullet to the head. Sound familiar?'

'All too familiar, if you ask me.'

'Of course, you can't quote me until I can get her back to the mortuary, but first indications are not encouraging.'

Henderson suppressed an urge to punch or kick someone, not the man in front of him or any of the other people here, but whoever was responsible for doing this.

'I would estimate the time of death as sometime last night, I would guess between ten and three in the morning.'

Looking closely at her face now, straight collar-length brown hair parted to the right of centre, a young almost elfin face, he recognised her. He'd seen so many photographs of young women these past few weeks, but when Sally Graham came up with the encrypted file, the low concrete building, the barn conversion, the women enjoying themselves, he'd memorised the faces. This lifeless individual in front of him was one of them.

'Thanks Grafton,' Henderson said a few minutes later. 'I'll see you again at the P-M.'

'It's one of the trafficked women, isn't it?' Walters

said as they stood at the edge of the copse of trees looking out. At times like this Henderson wished he smoked, something to soothe jangled nerves and take the edge off frayed emotions.

'I'm sure I've seen her picture in the file. To confirm, we'll take her picture down to the P-M.'

'We'll need to get the bullet analysed.'

'Even if it's not the same shooter, if her photo checks out, it's the same team.'

'It's a funny case this,' Walters said, kicking a clod of turf with her boot. 'The murder of three women will cause the papers apoplexy and they'll start printing dire warnings to all women not to go out and not to get into cars with strange men, but we know they're not in any danger.'

'Yes, but we're not going to enlighten them, are we?'

'Why not?'

'Why give the traffickers a heads-up? Let them think we're clueless, but we'll get them, we're getting closer.'

'You seem very sure, but from where I'm sitting, it feels like we're adding scraps. I can't see the whole picture.'

'I think we're at the stage now when one piece of information will clinch it. If we can discover the name of the businessman behind the traffickers, the location of those low concrete buildings we've seen in the photographs or the address of a house being used as a brothel, we'll be on to them.'

'I wish I shared your conviction.'

'Would you rather hear me say that I wasn't

confident of catching them, or throw my hands up in the air and say I don't have a clue and we should give up now?'

'Goes without saying.'

'I tell you though, if I did say it Youngman would replace me like that,' he said snapping his fingers together.

'Why would he? We've made progress, albeit slow and with no clear idea about the final goal, but progress nevertheless.'

'Because he told me he would.'

'Not in so many words, surely? Perhaps you misread the signals.'

'There's no mistake. He told me unequivocally.'

'I'm gobsmacked. You should have said something.'

'Would it have made any difference? C'mon, let's get back to the office.'

**

Henderson returned to his office after the team meeting. He left his folders in the office and walked over to the staff restaurant for something to eat. He brought it back to his desk without seeing anyone he knew. At this time of night, thoughts of going home often surfaced, but heading back to an empty house for the first time in almost a year, didn't hold much appeal.

Rachel had moved out of the house they shared in College Place and had gone back to live with her parents, a move she would not have considered without some careful thought. Her mother would be on her case from the moment she arrived. It shouldn't have come as a surprise. The tension between them had been simmering for months, but like the anticipation of a slap, it still stung when it occurred.

The murder team kicked around what little information they had about the new victim. After the P-M, if the photograph in Cindy's files matched their latest victim, Sally would email a copy to Linda Herschel at AWE and await confirmation of her identity.

He was convinced without confirming the girl's photograph or receiving a ballistic match for the bullet lodged in her skull, the same group of human traffickers were responsible, but they would undertake the necessary checks nevertheless. They'd killed this victim for the crime of escaping from their evil grasp. This was a sign, if one was needed, they were dealing with people who came from the bottom of a cess pit with no real concept of what it felt like to be human.

This meant when he finally cornered them, and he had to think positive here as he wanted to believe he would catch them, the team needed to be prepared for a vicious shoot-out. If they thought so little of the girls bringing them pots of money, they wouldn't hesitate to gun down a couple of cops, armed only with extendable batons.

Henderson chewed the toasted ham sandwich but it tasted bland in his mouth. It wasn't the fault of the sandwich, although it didn't come away entirely without blame, but this case. It had buggered up his relationship with Rachel and now it had turned him away from food.

No, he couldn't blame the case for everything, harrowing and disturbing as it might be. Rachel had been unhappy for some time. The worst aspect was he couldn't do anything about it. His job, like many he could name: accountant, computer programmer, sales staff, all experienced periods of intense activity followed by a lull. In his case, and anyone employed within the emergency services, they also carried the burden of the horror of what they faced, a lot more disconcerting than a monthly balance sheet or a terse round of contract negotiations.

'Working late, boss?' Walters asked.

Henderson looked up to see Carol Walters standing in the doorway. 'Hi Carol, on your way home?'

'Yep, feet up with a glass of wine for me. My brain and everything else works better with a glass of wine in my hand.'

'I can't agree with you there,' Henderson said, his attention already on a large glass of Glenmorangie. 'Mind you, you've only got a couple of things to think about—'

'I know, I know. We want the name of the local businessman, the location of the low buildings, the address of a brothel. See, I do listen. Don't stay too late. See you tomorrow.'

He picked up the analysis done by Phil Bentley of Sussex businessmen, those who had been to Longhurst Studios to shoot a video or television advert. Phil Bentley had run all the names through the

Police National Computer and it threw up a fair number possessing a criminal record.

Henderson went through them one at a time and put a line through those whose crimes were purely financial or involved insignificant sums of money. His pen went through those who had been disqualified from acting as a director for embezzling investors' funds, another who'd done time for a drink driving offence and another for selling houses in Spain that had never been built.

He then outlined work he would ask Bentley to undertake on the remaining twenty-seven. It was hard to imagine a businessman becoming actively involved in a human trafficking operation from Eastern Europe, if not from Eastern Europe themselves, or having strong ties in the region.

Based on names alone, he could see a few fitted the criteria, but more work would be required to try and uncover if the others in the list also had connections. He jotted down some criteria for Phil to consider: having an Eastern European partner, family living there, a change of name to hide Eastern European origins. It was all he could think of at the moment, and left PC Bentley to fill in anything he wanted to add.

Two names, not on his Phil's list came into Henderson's head: Constantin Petrescu and Ted Mathieson. Petrescu, the owner of Regency Wines and the house where Mike Harrison first met Cindy, was born in Romania, and Mathieson was married to a woman from Lithuania. They had examined Mathieson in detail, too much detail in DS Vicky

Neal's case, but not Petrescu. Why would they? There were plenty of businessmen in Sussex from Hungary, Romania and Bulgaria, the countries named by the Bucharest police officer who had called Henderson, so why would they target him?

Of course, the analysis of this list would be futile if the businessman in question didn't have a criminal record. However, the optimist inside always believed the next lead would be the one to supply the breakthrough and he would pursue it regardless.

He pushed the paperwork to one side, his mind on a glass of the good stuff, when his phone rang.

'Good evening, this is Detective Inspector Henderson,' he said, looking at his watch; eight-fifteen.

'Inspector, the women are gone.'

'Who is this?'

'Linda Herschel at Action for Trafficked Women. I received the email today from Detective Graham. What's it about?'

'It's in connection with an enquiry we're undertaking. Is she one of the three women you housed at the Baden Powell Drive address in Colchester?'

'Yes, she is. Her name is Ivona Lupei. She's dead, isn't she?'

'We found a body this morning and we believe it to be Ivona.'

The phone went quiet at Linda's end, except for the occasional loud, distressing sob. Perhaps, if Linda felt the loss of one of her clients so keenly, she was in the wrong profession. It was obvious she was a good person and a fantastic fundraiser to have encouraged a philanthropic billionaire to back the charity, but human trafficking was the dirtiest business he'd ever encountered. Those involved in the drug, money laundering and gun running trade all had a choice, these women didn't.

'I'm sorry Inspector,' Linda said. 'I don't know what came over me. In truth, I didn't know Ivona that well.'

'No problem. You said at the beginning of our call about the girls...'

'Yes. When I got the email from Detective Graham, I called the house in Colchester. I received no response from the house phone or from any of their mobiles which is unforgiveable. At that time of the evening, they all should have been at home after returning from work. You have to appreciate, all the women in our houses are required to follow the charity's communication protocols. They are forbidden to be out of contact with this office, ever.'

'I understand.'

'When I received no response, I sent someone around to the house. When they got there, the house was locked up, but the person I sent had keys so they went inside. The breakfast dishes were lying unwashed on the worktop. They've been taken, Inspector Henderson, the traffickers have taken back my girls.'

THIRTY-FOUR

Henderson carried a cup of black coffee up to CI Edwards's office. When he finally made it home last night, he took a seat in the lounge with a large glass of Glenmorangie in one hand and the case notes on his lap. The next time he looked at the clock it was almost two in the morning.

'Come in Angus and close the door behind you,' Edwards said as he approached.

'Morning gov.'

'What's the latest?'

'After I spoke to you last night, I called the Colchester police. Someone from ATW went to the house in Baden Powell Drive with a couple of officers. When they got inside they confirmed there was no evidence to suggest there had been any form of a struggle, but there was no sign of the women.'

'It looks like the traffickers grabbed them elsewhere.'

'This is what the cops think. They checked their call register and asked their patrol cars for any reports of a street altercation or someone struggling to haul another person into a vehicle. As yet, no one has informed them of seeing anything amiss.'

'They might have approached them at their place of work, telling them one of their friends was ill or grabbed them on their lunch break.'

'Colchester are following this up. If they find CCTV of the women with their abductors we'll be the first to know.'

'A car or van registration would be better.'

'It would, but don't forget Maggie Hyatt, the woman Cindy was photographing the day she was kidnapped. She got a good look at both kidnappers but didn't manage to identify their faces when we gave her mug shots to look at. She might be able to recognise someone from a CCTV picture.'

'Was the woman from ATW any more open with information, now that a couple more of her clients are missing?'

'She gave us the names of the two missing women.' He opened his notebook. 'Marina Vasilescu, aged twenty, and Felicia Marinca, aged eighteen.'

'Eighteen? Bloody hell. Only a few years ago we'd be calling her a child.'

'She also sent us photographs which, to no one's surprise, matched pictures in Cindy's collection.'

'When you think about it, Cindy went to all that bother of freeing those women, and got killed in the process, but for what? Nothing. The four she freed who were living in Colchester are either dead or back working for the traffickers.'

'Don't write off everything she achieved. According to Linda Hershel, she released ten women, the four we know about and another six who went elsewhere.'

'Where they'll be picked off again by the traffickers if they're not careful.'

'Plus, don't forget, the pictures Cindy left behind

put us on to the traffickers.'

'Although I suspect it wasn't her original intention. So, Angus, any good news to tell me?'

He explained about the analysis conducted of Sussex businessmen.

'I understand where you're coming from with this, but my advice is to take care. There's a lot of business people out there with the same mentality as Ted Mathieson. Rub them up the wrong way, and in a couple of days' time they'll be interviewed on South Today, complaining of police harassment or bending the Police and Crime Commissioner's ear. Next thing we know the issue will be sitting on the Chief Constable's desk.'

'I'll bear it in mind.'

'This businessman Cindy told Linda Hershel about might be one of Cindy's customers. It would be a good idea to check the list against something like the top fifty businessmen in Sussex.'

'Good idea.' Henderson had thought of doing it late last night and asked Phil Bentley to follow it up, but he didn't want to discourage the Chief Inspector as she often thought of things he didn't.

'Anything else?' she asked.

'I'm hopeful the P-M this afternoon will offer us something.'

'Why should it? We didn't get anything from the other two. The traffickers are being pretty thorough, divesting the corpses of their clothes to avoid incriminating fibres and dumping the bodies in rural spots in the middle of the night, away from cameras and in places where no one will spot what they're doing.'

'Yes, but this is the first victim not to be beaten which makes me think they also have the other two. Why bother bashing up Ivona to reveal the whereabouts of the missing women when they already have them in their custody?'

'We can hope they got away, but chances are you're right, they've grabbed all three.'

'The traffickers maybe gave Ivona a choice, become a prostitute, drug mule or whatever business they're involved in, or be killed.'

'She must have refused to be part of it.'

'If you think how this scenario might have played out: she's captured and they drive her back to their base. They drag her out of the car and ask her, what's it to be, work for us or face the consequences? She refuses to do their bidding and they shoot her.'

'Most likely raped her first.'

'Maybe, but my point is, they might have carried out this murder quickly and maybe in a state of anger. I'm hoping they made a mistake this time.'

'Let's hope so as I fear for those missing girls.'

'I do too. It could be they're not giving them a choice at all but killing them and dumping their bodies for some dog-walker or farmer to find.'

'Which means the clock is ticking. We need to find them and it needs to be done soon.'

He looked at his watch. 'Hell, is that the time? I better get a move on or the P-M will start without me.'

**

Henderson's thoughts glazed over as the rasping buzz of the bone saw filled the mortuary air, cutting through Ivona Lupei's skull with the ease of a chainsaw slicing into a log. He doubted if anyone in the room, except maybe the pathologist and his assistant, maintained their concentration throughout a post-mortem, not him, DS Walters, the photographer or the young lady from the coroner's office looking a bit peaky and green around the gills.

The P-M wasn't such a long and arduous procedure that it couldn't command his attention for the whole of its duration. However, many of the procedures the pathologist undertook, cutting into the skull, running a sharp knife down the cadaver's chest and emptying the remains of their last meal into a bowl, would turn anyone's stomach if they looked too closely.

When Henderson first saw the body at the crime scene, he noticed Ivona didn't display the extensive bruising seen on the other two victims: broken noses and depressed cheekbones, smashed and bruised ribs, damage to kidneys and deep cuts on both arms and legs. Grafton had spotted this too and examined the dead woman's organs thoroughly to ensure the traffickers hadn't changed tactics and were now using less visible forms of torture, such as waterboarding or electric shocks.

He found no evidence of any maltreatment beyond marks on her arms and legs, the result of rough handling, not systematic cruelty. If the traffickers hadn't kidnapped the other two women as they suspected, he felt sure the woman lying here would have been tortured to reveal their whereabouts, reinforcing his view that all three had been kidnapped. In which case, he feared another two visits to the mortuary in the near future, unless of course, the ACC lost patience with the current lack of progress and replaced him with someone else.

He had stared at the faces of the two most recent victims and examined their backgrounds to see if he could understand any commonality in the traffickers' selection process. The technique worked in some serial killer and rapist cases, as the perpetrators often preyed on a type of woman with which the killer was familiar, be it nurses or students, or those with a certain characteristic such as tall, small or anyone who looked to be over thirty. The only distinguishing features he could find were the women all came from poor backgrounds, they were aged between eighteen and twenty-five and all came from rural areas.

Henderson's last hope of finding a breakthrough in the case lay with the genital examination. When talking to CI Edwards earlier, she said she wouldn't be surprised to find Ivona had been raped before being shot, a statement based more on the ruthless nature of traffickers than any information obtained from the crime scene. The pathologist confirmed she had indeed been raped, evidenced by bruising and several examples of tearing.

When no traces of sperm were found, Rawlings concluded that the rapist must have used a condom, but tissue samples would be extracted and examined just in case. Henderson tuned out now, as the pathologist moved through his tail-end checks.

By the time he would de-robe and drive back to the

office, it would be after four o'clock. Earlier in the day, SOCOs at the crime scene had discovered tyre tracks, those not trampled into the mud by their support vehicles, plus several fibres on nearby branches close to the site of the body, and Henderson wanted to make sure they were being followed up.

He was so deep in thought it was only when he looked up, he realised the pathologist was looking at him. To be fair, Rawlings spoke in such a soft voice it was often difficult to determine if he was talking into the head microphone he wore or to his assistant.

'DI Henderson, come and take a look at this,' he was saying.

Henderson walked towards the examination table, the smell of death, decay and disinfectant increasing with every step. He edged around the table, past Ivona's tagged feet and stood beside Grafton. In one hand, he held Ivona's hand and with the other he was using a small pointed instrument to scrape debris from under her fingernails into a petri dish.

'If I'm not mistaken,' Grafton said without taking his eyes away from what he was doing, 'these are skin cells. If we're lucky, they may belong to the man who raped her.'

THIRTY-FIVE

Henderson walked back into his office in buoyant mood. He'd told the team about the skin cells found by the pathologist and had relayed the news to CI Edwards. Without hesitation, she authorised for its analysis to be fast-tracked, an expensive process but easily justified in this case.

She also counselled caution. DNA was only useful if the suspect appeared on their records or if they had someone already in custody to compare it against. If the traffickers were being careful and hadn't picked up even a parking ticket in the UK, they would extend the search to European police forces, in particular, Hungary and Romania. This presented its own problems, but Henderson knew he had to try, no matter the time and effort required.

Ten minutes later, DS Vicky Neal came into his office carrying the Mathieson Transport file. Since her run-in with Ted Mathieson, she'd taken a step back, but still convinced of his guilt, kept a close eye on him and his business. Through Henderson's contact at the National Crime Agency, Officer Rebecca Gregson, Vicky had been put in touch with their drugs team.

Neal sat down at the meeting table and opened her folder. 'There's been a couple of developments since we last spoke.'

'Okay.'

'I told you the NCA have been watching Mathieson for several months, after receiving a tip-off from a drug dealer?'

He nodded.

'Through contacts the NCA have in Germany, they believe Mathieson will be bringing into this country a substantial quantity of cocaine and heroin on Thursday. I've agreed with the NCA we'll mount a joint operation to intercept it.'

'At Dover, on the M20 motorway or when the lorry reaches its destination at Mathieson's Transport?'

'When it arrives at Mathieson's Newhaven depot.'

'I can understand why you'd want to do it there as you're likely to catch Ted Mathieson with his hands on the merchandise, but in some ways I think you've picked the most difficult spot.'

'How do you mean?'

'Have you seen the massive steel door they have at the end of the loading bay? Once a lorry's inside and it's closed, you'll never get in. By the time you bash in the front door and make your way through the Reception area, he could have poured the whole lot down the nearest drain.'

'I'll mention it to my contact at the NCA, but I'm sure they've got it covered.'

'I hope so.'

'There's more. The NCA also found out the name of the person he sells it to.'

'Surprise me.'

'Charlie McQueen.'

'I'm not surprised.'

She smiled. She didn't do it often and when she did, her face softened and even he had to admit, she did look attractive. 'Here's the good bit. They've watched Mathieson a couple of times drive up to Devil's Dyke and hand the drugs over to Charlie McQueen.'

'Watched how?'

'They had a bloke observing the scene through binoculars from some distance away.'

'You know what I'm going to ask you now. Were they in position at the time when Mathieson got stabbed?'

'No, I did ask, but their informant only finds out a few days before a shipment is due to arrive. It doesn't leave a wide enough window to get someone in place.'

'Nevertheless, what you said strongly suggests the little toad was lying when he said he'd been mugged, as we both suspected.'

'Yeah, and the whole thing makes sense if the person Mathieson was meeting at Devil's Dyke was Liam McKinney.'

'Now I get it,' Henderson said, as he watched a number of disparate strands coming together, a result of hearing that Ted Mathieson was involved in the importation of drugs. 'McKinney gets leery with Mathieson for reasons we don't know, maybe he was trying to rip him off or doing the dirty on McQueen and attempting to start his own business. Either way, they argue, maybe exchange a few blows before McKinney pulls out a knife and stabs him.'

'Right.'

'Charlie McQueen, upset at the prospect of losing a good supplier, decides he's had enough of McKinney and decides to top him. With him out of the way, a recovered Ted Mathieson is happy to go back and sell to McQueen.'

'That's what the NCA think.'

'It all hangs together well, except it doesn't sound to me like a good enough reason for Charlie McQueen to top one of his team. Does he have anger issues or something?'

'I think McQueen experienced other problems with McKinney going back months, according to Nick Scanlon, the dealer we talked to. The stabbing of Mathieson was the last straw as far as McQueen was concerned.'

'Have you passed this intel on to Gerry Hobbs?'

'I have.'

'Is he pulling Charlie McQueen in for questioning? If he is, I'd like to be a fly on the wall of the interview room.'

'I'm afraid not.'

'Why the hell not?'

'The NCA believe that due to the pressure McQueen is feeling after a few successful drugs busts and attacks on his business by a Russian gang, his business is contracting. As a result, they think McQueen needs Mathieson badly. In a bid to restore his faith, Charlie McQueen might be doing the pick-up himself at the next get-together on Devil's Dyke.'

'Interesting. Why don't you do the stop there and arrest both of them? It's a better place to mount an operation than the Newhaven depot.'

'We considered it, but if we do Newhaven first, we can nab Mathieson and also the drivers involved. Then, the next day when Mathieson id due to meet Charlie McQueen, an NCA officer, who I'm assured is as portly as Ted Mathieson and about the same height, will drive a similar car to the one Mathieson uses for his trips to Devil's Dyke. With a bit of luck, Charlie McQueen himself will show up, and if he does, we'll nab him as well.'

**

'Thanks for the beer, Angus, cheers,' Gerry Hobbs said lifting the glass to his lips.

'Cheers,' Henderson said.

'How are you getting with your big murder case?'

Henderson and Hobbs were sitting in the *Hove Place*, a pub not far from where Hobbs lived. They were squeezing in a quick drink before heading home, Henderson to a quick-cook lasagne for one and Hobbs to wish his kids goodnight before taking a seat and listening to what his exuberant wife did with her day.

'Christ, three dead and two missing,' Hobbs said, 'it's like the plot of one of those serial killer books my missus reads.'

'Aye, it doesn't make good reading. If it wasn't confined to a small group of people, we'd have mass panic on our hands.'

'Any worse than it is now? Look at this place,' Hobbs said looking around the lounge of the pub. 'There's hardly any women here.'

'I could take the pressure off by telling the press

what we know, or think we know, but I don't want to alert the traffickers that we're getting closer. They probably think the cops here are as corrupt and incompetent as the ones in their own country. Well, let them. When we turn up I want it to be a big surprise.'

'They haven't given you much to go on, have they?'

'You know as well as I do even the most careful killers make mistakes. Our job is to find them.'

'Locard's Exchange Principle and all that.'

'The very man. Can you manage another?'

'Sure, but only the one.'

Henderson went to the bar for refills. Hobbs was right, he could see plenty of people in the pub, but the few women around were in the company of men and they didn't look relaxed. It wouldn't keep everyone at home at night, there were still those who were blasé about their chances, those who didn't read newspapers and others who deliberately ignored what they believed to be Big Brother telling them what to do.

He returned to the table. It was in the corner with a good view of the room, a habit ingrained into drug dealers, ex-cons and police officers.

'Cheers,' Hobbs said, lifting a fresh pint of lager to his lips. 'It's not like me to pry into other people's lives, Christ knows I get my fill of drama at home, but it's usually you who's heading home first, not me. Everything all right between you and Rachel?'

'No, it's not, Gerry. She's left me.'

'She's what?'

'She hasn't moved all her stuff out, only a suitcase

full, but she's gone back to live with her parents where she'll, and I quote, 'reconsider her future.' Whatever that means.'

'I'm really sorry to hear it, Angus.'

'Ach, these things happen, but thanks.'

'She doesn't get on with her mother, I seem to remember.'

'You're right there. They're too similar in so many ways and argue over everything.'

'I warned you, mate, that Vicky Neal is a real ball breaker.'

Henderson laughed. 'You think I'd go out with someone I work beside? No way. It's nothing to do with Vicky. It's the job, Gerry, nothing else.'

'You're stuffed then. If she said you had questionable toilet habits or smelly feet, you could do something about it, but the job's the job. It can't be changed. In fact, without getting too poetic, it's more than a job, it's a... a calling.'

'You must have seen this with Catalina, but when you first meet a new woman, you explain the kind of work you do and any time you're called away it's okay, they're not too bothered. Then, when you move in together, it all of a sudden becomes a major problem.'

'It's the same with alcoholics. When the couple go out, she loves the fact they're forever in the pub and, after sinking a few down his neck, he's the life and soul. Then, when they get married it's like one of those Christmas records by Slade or Shakin' Stevens. Once you've heard the same song a hundred times, you could take a hammer to it.'

Henderson said goodbye to Hobbs ten minutes

later, Hobbs walking towards Church Road and home, Henderson heading towards the seafront to the place where he'd parked the car.

He decided he would eat his lasagne beside a roaring gas fire and have a couple of glasses of Glenmorangie to ward off the blues. He could take his pick of the cause: Rachel leaving, him not solving this murder case, or the sight of a lovely young woman being dissected with the pathologist's knife.

He started the car and remembered he was low on whisky. He could drive back to College Place and buy it from the local pub, but they added at least ten pounds to the price. He racked his memory, trying to recall a decent off-licence in Hove, and then remembered his favourite booze shop, the Regency Wine Warehouse, was close by in Portslade.

Once inside the warehouse, he wasted no time admiring the comprehensive wine selection and headed straight for the whisky. Regency dabbled in Irish, included a few of the American big brands and even one or two Japanese, but it majored on Scottish whisky. Henderson didn't stop to ponder if he'd like a peaty malt from Islay or a single blend from Orkney, and instead reached for his favourite tipple and took it to the counter.

'The boss not in tonight?' he asked the male assistant as he wrapped his purchase.

'No, he doesn't often stay beyond five.'

'Family man?'

'Have you met his missus?'

'No.'

'You know him like? I'm not talking out of school?'

Henderson had spoken to him a few times but he wouldn't say he knew him well. 'Whatever you say won't get back to him.'

'She comes in here quite a lot, but she's too fond of the stuff we sell, if you know what I mean. Her antics drive him potty.'

'Really?'

'Yeah, I think he avoids going straight home after work and tries instead to visit some of the other branches most day. I know if I was married to a woman like that I would do the same.'

Henderson walked back to his car, the assistant's little tale playing on his mind. Well, well, everything in Constantin Petrescu's garden wasn't as golden as the owner would have everyone believe.

His thoughts were interrupted when his phone rang.

'Hello, DI Henderson here.'

'Ah, good evening, DI Henderson, I hope I haven't caught you at a bad time. It's Hal Anderson from the DNA and Forensics Unit.'

'No, it's fine. You're obviously working late.'

'Well, we knew this was a rush job and you would want a result as soon as possible. We've analysed the skin cell samples from the body of Ivona Lupei you sent us and found a match on the system. It belongs to a man by the name of Vasile Lazar.'

THIRTY-SIX

Veronika Kardos woke, her head thick and woozy as if she'd downed six shots at her favourite nightclub, *Peaches and Cream* in the centre of Budapest. Not that she ever drank that much as the salary she received as a shop assistant didn't allow it.

On Tuesday night, she stepped off the bus into a downpour, looking miserable and feeling sorry for herself. Why did she take the lift from the handsome stranger in the Toyota? She'd read in newspapers of girls being kidnapped and taken to foreign countries to work in filthy factories and serve in the houses of abusive and ignorant people. She liked to joke with a girl at work that she wouldn't find it so bad. Veronika had once worked in a dirty tyre factory and didn't she wait hand on foot on her alcoholic father?

The one thing she feared was becoming a sex worker. She was catholic and, unlike her father and neighbours who pretended to be pious when the occasion demanded it, she believed she was the real deal. Not a bible-thumping maniac who gave all her earthly goods away to the poor and couldn't wait to get to heaven. One who liked to have a good time as far as her money would allow but lived by the teachings of Christ. She regularly visited an elderly neighbour, assisted the priest on Sundays and didn't believe in sex before marriage.

The other girls in the minibus, those she could speak to when they weren't sleeping under a drug-induced haze, had depressingly familiar stories like her own. What they had in common was they all did low-level jobs, not a difficult thing to find across Eastern Europe, and came from poorer backgrounds. As a result, their families could not afford to bribe the police and newspapers to conduct a concerted effort to find their missing children. They knew it, the traffickers knew it.

Her eyes opened at the border and she believed she saw signs in English making her think they were in the UK. The scenery passing the windows was of fields and trees, but with darkness all around she couldn't see anything to give her any idea of the direction they were travelling.

She must have dozed off for a spell and when she awoke, her head was clear. She felt the bus slowing and moments later it turned to the left and into a narrow path between dark trees. The trees surrounded them as they drove, making her think they were in the middle of a forest.

In the gap between the seats in front she had an oblique view of the windscreen. The dancing headlights picked out a long low concrete building to the left, and a brightly-lit house in the shape of a very large hay barn about one hundred metres on the right. She hoped they would be told to go right, but somehow knew it would be left.

'Everybody out,' the driver's mate said in broken Hungarian. The man speaking was thin and wiry and had the eyes of a weasel, while the driver was a bull of a man with little or no neck, reminding her of big Erik, a worker on a neighbouring farm who had the strength of two and the intellect of an eight-year-old. Neither man resembled the Toyota driver who had lured her into his car. She assumed he was back in her home country looking for other girls to kidnap; the evil swine.

They trundled out of the minibus slowly and moodily, some annoyed to be woken up from a dreamless sleep, others quietly weeping. They stood close by the bus, their presence illuminated by the lights of the vehicle and a bright light on top of the concrete building. Away from the noises inside the minibus, she could now hear the sounds of dogs barking and realised it was coming from the far side of the concrete building. She liked dogs, but she didn't like the sound of those ones.

'This will be your home for the next few days,' the little weasel said. He spoke Hungarian, badly, but then most Hungarians believed Romanians did most things badly.

'What happens after then?' Veronika asked.

Weasel-eyes walked over and punched her in the face. His fist hit her on the cheek and even though she saw it late due to the shadows formed by the lights, she still managed to deflect her head and diminish some of the force. It hurt, but the runt wasn't strong enough to break bones. She was sure glad the driver didn't punch her as she wouldn't hear the rest of the arrival speech.

Weasel-eyes raised a finger and pointed it round

the bedraggled group of girls. 'None of you ask me any questions, understand? Where was I? Ah, yes. Do not think of trying to escape. This area is surrounded by a high fence and if we find you we will use these,' he said, pulling a gun from his waistband and holding it up for them to see. 'If you try and hide, we will release the dogs you can hear barking and they will come looking for you. These are not friendly little pooches but big hungry, hunting dogs. You will hope we find you before they tear you to pieces. Come,' he said waving his gun in a 'follow me' gesture, 'this way.'

THIRTY-SEVEN

At eight-seventeen on a cold, clear Thursday evening, the gates of Mathieson Transport slid open and a huge Volvo truck reversed into the yard. The brakes let out an ear-shuddering hiss as the truck slowed before disappearing inside the jaws of the loading bay. Once it had come to a halt, the heavy steel loading bay door started its descent with a loud rattle and shake, disturbing the peace and calm of a quiet Newhaven night.

When the door reached the halfway point and Ted Mathieson had left his observation spot at the window on the first floor, two armed officers, one from the NCA and DS Vicky Neal from Sussex Police, nipped under the rapidly closing door. They were both wearing black clothes, black flak jackets and black baseball caps, and snuck into the shadows of the partially-lit loading bay on the opposite side of the truck from the driver to await this evening's expected entertainment.

A minute or so later, the door leading from the office area opened and Ted Mathieson walked in carrying a can of Coke and, down at his side what looked to Neal in the dim light like a gun.

'Steve, good to see you,' Mathieson said to the truck driver as he climbed down from the cab. 'I'd give you a hug but my gut would give me dog's abuse.'

'Are you taking anything for it?'

'Nah, just some paracetamol if it plays up, but I tell you, it doesn't half pep up your sex life.'

'How? I would have thought an injury like that would put something as boisterous as shagging on the back burner for a couple of months at least.'

'No way. My young missus felt so sorry for me after being stabbed, so she did, all I have to do now is just lie there and let her mouth do all the work.'

'I must try that some time. Her indoors thinks her tongue's for licking the bottom of crisp packets.'

They both started laughing and the shoulders of the NCA officer in front of Neal shook. She hoped it wouldn't spoil the recording he was making, the voices of Mathieson and Steve coming over loud and clear. The two men moved around to the front of the truck and from there, the officers could see them. If one of them looked in their direction they could duck behind the truck or stay still and let the shadows and dull light keep them hidden.

'Here's your Coke, but there's no Snickers left, only a Bounty.'

'What happened?' Steve said, holding up the 'gun' which she realised now was the dark shape of the chocolate bar, bent over in the middle to form an 'L'.

'Just before you arrived I heard a noise outside in the yard and thought it might be those thieves who've been breaking into warehouses around here. I must have turned too quickly and tweaked my wound. It screamed bloody blue murder at me. I put my hand against a wall for support and realised I was still holding your Bounty bar. Sorry mate.'

'No worries, it still tastes the same,' Steve said, tearing off the wrapper and starting to munch.

'How's Otto?'

'Jolly as ever even when he's telling me bad news. He says the next batch will cost us more, maybe an additional ten per cent as his sources are feeling the heat from the DEA. Market forces, he says.'

'Market forces my arse. He probably needs the money for the shopping mall he's planning to build in Strasbourg. Doesn't he know the EC are talking about moving it all back to Brussels? Let me make some enquiries and I'll get back to you before you see him again. If he's playing us for silly buggers, don't you worry, I'll call his bluff.'

'Do you want to deal with the stuff now?'

'Nah, we'll do it in a mo. I want to show you something first. Walk this way.'

'What, walk like you do with one hand over my gut?'

'Fuck off, you cheeky git.'

The two men walked back to the door leading to the offices, opened it and disappeared inside. The door snapped closed behind them on the strong spring of a fire door.

NCA Officer Gary Walker turned to face Neal. 'So far, so good,' Walker whispered. 'We've got on tape what they've been talking about and it's obviously about drugs–'

'I'm not totally convinced,' Neal said. 'I'm sure a good lawyer could persuade a jury otherwise.'

'I suppose what they said could be twisted out of

context, but it won't matter if we catch them with their hands on the goods.'

She nodded, she wanted it too.

'So now, we either wait and see if they come back and bring out the merchandise, or if they've called it a day and gone home.'

'It won't be much fun staying in here all night.'

'You're right but if I'm not mistaken, that big black button by the door opens the loading bay door. If it doesn't work, there's an access door beside it and if it's locked we, or the guys outside, can force it open.'

'Thank god for that. I didn't bring anything to eat and I like my food.'

Walker removed his NCA cap to reveal thinning grey hair and drew his sleeve across the sweat dotted on his brow. She felt hot but not under her hat, under her flak jacket. No way would she take it off, because if she did, as sure as eggs were eggs, shooting would start.

Walker replaced his cap. 'If they do bugger off home, we'll search the truck.'

'Up there,' she said, indicating the ceiling, 'I can see a couple of PIRs. This place is alarmed. They'll set the thing before they go, I'm sure.'

'If they do,' Walker said 'we've got twenty, twenty-five minutes to pull this lorry apart and find the drugs before the key holder or the local plod shows up. It's my least preferred option. See, we might find the stash, but we've only got the tape as evidence against Mathieson and his driver.'

Most of what Walker just talked about had been covered already in the briefing. The NCA guys were ex-coppers and top-notch at analysing what-ifs and undertaking risk assessments. They'd looked at the 'going home' scenario and thought it unlikely. If Steve's truck contained a stash of Class A drugs as they anticipated, no way would he or Ted Mathieson want it going back on the road the following day.

In addition, they wouldn't want regular staff unloading the truck in the morning and making a chance discovery. The NCA expected the truck to be divested of its illegal cargo tonight, the question was, when?

Neal sat in silence for several minutes, wondering if the men had gone out for a beer to celebrate their good fortune or were sitting upstairs, tucking into a curry take-away. She liked take-aways but preferred the real thing, especially with Nan bread and cold beer. She had to stop thinking about food, this could be a long night.

A short time later Walker said, 'I hear movement.'

They ducked down, peering around the bumper of the truck for thirty seconds or so before the door opened. Ted Mathieson and Steve walked in, jabbering on like a couple of old women as they discussed a video Mathieson had obviously been showing his driver.

They stood talking guy's stuff for a few minutes before Steve clapped his hands together. 'Right mate, let's press on. It's been a long day and I'd like to go home. I'll get the gear.'

Now came the tricky stage. They'd debated in the briefing about where Steve would stash the drugs, but with no knowledge of the truck he drove they instead pooled their experience. This ranged from dummy fuel tanks, to hollow body panels and fake spare wheels. It could also be hidden within the load. However, with only two guys in attendance and one of those not fit to lift anything heavier than a pen, the officers didn't believe they would be capable of unloading a large lorry most likely stacked with heavy pallets.

They heard the noise of an aluminium ladder being moved and being erected on the driver's side of the truck. Seconds later, the dull thud of someone, probably Steve, climbing up. Neal breathed a sigh of relief. The officers wanted to make a move at their choosing and not when Steve walked towards them, forcing them to roll under the truck.

They were now blind to the activity taking place and could only use their ears to make sense of what the two men were doing. A whirring noise started, not as loud as a drill but similar in nature to an electric toothbrush or screwdriver. She heard it again, in total four sets of whirrs, before what sounded like a body panel being removed and placed to one side.

It went quiet for a moment or two before Steve's strained voice said, 'I tucked the buggers right at the back to be on the safe side, now I'm having trouble reaching them.'

'Can't help you there, mate,' Mathieson said. 'I'm shorter than you and I'm not climbing any bloody ladder. Do you want to use the grab hook?'

'No way. It'll burst the bags and we'll not only lose money, it'll leave traces for the fucking dogs to find.'

'I suppose.'

'Give us a sec and I'll climb on the cab roof and try and get a better angle.'

They heard the ladder rattle and the thump of Steve's boots on the roof of his truck. The officers instinctively ducked under the chassis in case Steve decided to take a gander down the other side.

'Right, mate, this is good. I can reach them now. Right, I've got the first. How do you want to play this?'

'How do you mean?'

'I mean, what I usually do is lob one of these to you and you catch it. With you in your, erm, condition, if you don't catch it right, it could do you some lasting damage.'

'I'm not a fucking cripple yet, Hedland. Throw away.'

'No fucking way, mate, we're not doing it like that. Tell you what, if you can you come part-way up the ladder, say a couple of steps, I'll lean over the side and hand the bags to you. You seem to forget, these fuckers are two kilos each. One dodgy catch and the stuff will be all over the loading bay and you'll be back in the Belvedere. You'll also be as high as a kite and that's before they give you any tranquillizers.'

Mathieson laughed. 'I'm not going back in that bloody place. Fair enough, have it your way. Just take it easy, okay?'

'Okay.'

The officers waited until all the bags were unloaded and, more importantly, Steve's feet were on the ground. No way did they want to be chasing him over the roof of the truck. The two men were cackling like a couple of hyenas about all the money they would make and what they intended doing with it as they pawed and fingered the heavy bags. The officers eased themselves out from their hiding place and walked to the rear of truck, weapons pointed.

They stopped in the space between the end of the truck's trailer and the platform on the loading bay. Mathieson and Hedland were three of four metres distant, facing a desk with their backs to them, the strong box DI Henderson refused to let her have a warrant to search, now open.

Walker called out in a clear, authoritative voice, 'Police! Put your hands where we can see them!'

Mathieson turned around and clocked them and if Neal was carrying a camera she would have loved to have taken a picture. The aura of the cocky, self-confident businessman gone, now a schoolboy caught with his hands down his trousers.

'It's not what you think,' Mathieson jabbered, 'I can explain.'

'Hands! I want to see them!' Walker bellowed as he levelled his scratched and well-used weapon.

Steve was still bending over the strong box, moving the bags inside. When he straightened and turned, in his hand he held a gun. He pointed it at the two officers. 'Come and get me, coppers,' he said.

Walker laughed, a surprising response, as Neal couldn't see anything funny about the situation.

'We have two automatic weapons aimed at you son. What chance have you got?'

'I'll take my chances.'

'Steve, put it down,' Mathieson said.

'What? We'll do time, Ted. I don't want to go to

prison.'

'Better that than coming out of this place in a box.'

'I can't believe you're not backing me, mate.'

'Too right I'm backing you. All the way. But I don't want to see you killed. Think of Sue and your boy.'

Mathieson reached out and placed his hand on top of the gun and pushed it down. Believing it was all over Neal relaxed her grip on the weapon. Steve took a step to the side and lifted the gun again.

'No way, Ted, you don't understand. I can't do time.' Almost in slow motion the gun moved up, not in the direction of the police officers, but towards Steve's head. He opened his mouth as if to say something, but instead shoved the barrel inside. He then pulled the trigger.

THIRTY-EIGHT

The heater in the car was set high to combat the early morning frost and chill. It wasn't quite dark as DC Phil Bentley, with DC Lisa Newman in the passenger seat, drove towards a house in Brighton. With every minute that passed the light levels seemed to increase a little more.

The last known address of Vasile Lazar, the man whose DNA had been found underneath the fingernails of Ivona Lupei, was at Sandown Road, a road leading off Elm Grove. Bentley found a place to park, not outside the pleasant-looking red brick semi, but further down, still with a good view of the house. He switched off the engine and reached for the flask lying on the back seat.

'Do you think he still lives here?' she asked.

'We'll find out soon enough if he comes out the door, but it's the only address we've got. Sally found it in the Council Tax Register.'

'You don't think of criminals paying Council Tax and doing ordinary things, do you? Behaving like an upstanding member of the public by day and changing into a heartless trafficker at night? It doesn't make sense to me.'

'I imagine people like him don't pay income tax and parking fines, but if they don't pay Council Tax, a council official will come to the door. If they still refuse, they won't get their bins emptied and they'll be taken to court. I'm sure criminals produce as much rubbish as the rest of us.'

'I suppose they do.' She took a drink from her plastic cup. 'So, all the boss wants us to do is follow him? Why don't we arrest him?'

'All we're doing is locating him and then we're to follow. The boss doesn't want him arrested yet. Even though they found traces of him on the dead girl, he could claim she was a prostitute or the sex they had was consensual.'

'I can't say I like it, but it makes sense.'

'As one of the last people to see Ivona alive, it still leaves him as a suspect, but without further evidence, we'd never have a hope in hell of convicting him.'

'The bit I don't get is, what's the point of following him?'

'If we assume the house we're waiting outside is the place where he lives, and not a brothel or the place where he keeps the girls when he first brings them into this country, chances are we won't find much incriminating evidence inside. If we follow him, he might lead us to somewhere more interesting.'

'Right, as he heads off to work, or whatever human traffickers call their day job. DS Walters pulled me up for calling it 'people trafficking'. Do you know the difference?'

'Yeah, of course, I do.'

'I sure hope you don't play poker, Phil Bentley, because I can read your lying face. What is it then?'

'I don't know but I'm sure you're about to tell me.'

'People trafficking is what happens when lorries, like at Calais, bring refugees into this country. The drivers are not bringing the refugees here to work for them, but they get paid by the refugees or someone else for transporting them.'

'I see, and human trafficking is when you bring people here to work on something you want them to do, like becoming domestic slaves or prostitutes?'

'Right.'

'I'm up to date now,' he said, as he reached into his pocket and pulled out a breakfast bar. 'I was going to save this for elevenses, but I need something to eat now.'

'Which kid did you pinch that from?'

'What do you mean?'

'Those are the things harassed mothers buy when their kids won't eat cereal or drink milk.'

'How do you know? You're too young to have kids.'

'I watch what people do when I go shopping, you should do it too.'

'No, I didn't nick it off any kid. I buy these because I like them.'

The street was rousing from slumber. Bleary-faced people were out walking dogs, yawning faces at the window were trying to assess the weather prospects, and others in dressing gowns reached for the door-step milk delivery looking as though they wouldn't be awake until they'd consumed their first hot beverage of the day.

Fifteen minutes later came the school run. First it was the kids at far-flung schools requiring transport in a car. Twenty minutes later, the kids from the local school, freshly-washed faces and smartly-attired, they walked with purpose, keen to get there early. Fifteen minutes after them, doors slamming, ties askew and toast partly eaten in their hand, the latecomers, running all the way down the road.

'Did you walk to school, Phil or did your parents drive you?'

'Walked.'

'What were you like when you came back home and your mum asked about your day? Were you one of those sulky boys I went to school with who answered every question with 'fine' or 'okay', or were you one of the more voluble kind?'

'What does voluble mean? Hang on, I see movement.'

The door of the house they were watching opened and a giant of a man emerged. He looked six-two or three and weighed about one-hundred-and-ten kilos. Bentley, a keen rugby follower and player equated his frame to that of a front-row forward.

'He's a big fella,' Newman said.

'What car do you think is his? The Mini or the Smart car?'

'A man his size could lift a Smart car and put it in his pocket. It has to be that monster Jeep, it's the only car in the street big enough to accommodate that large frame.'

Sure enough, the lights of the Jeep Grand Cherokee flashed and a few moments later Lazar climbed in, his considerable bulk causing the car to rock. It looked as innocuous as other large 4x4's, but Bentley knew about cars and could tell by the wheels and the custom colour scheme it would have cost him upwards of seventy-thousand. It wasn't as showy on the outside as some vehicles used by drug dealers, but sufficiently understated to keep Lazar's head below the parapet.

Lisa called the office to let them know they'd made contact with the target, while Phil slipped the dirty, nondescript Vauxhall Vectra into gear and followed the Jeep.

The Jeep didn't go far, across Elm Grove and down Queen's Park Road where it stopped about half-way down, making Bentley think the lazy bugger could have walked. However, most of the front row forwards he knew, big guys with thighs so large they rubbed together when they walked, were like Lazar. They owned a large 4x4 and drove it everywhere.

Lazar walked towards a white-washed terraced house. Bentley wound down the window to try and hear any conversation between the visitor and the householder, but all he heard was the sliding of a couple of deadlocks before the door opened. He disappeared inside.

'Are there a lot of burglaries around here?' Newman asked as she noted the address on a 'List of Contacts' sheet.

'Not that I was aware of, why do you ask?'

'They have what looks to me like over-elaborate security for a normal end-of-terrace house.'

'I see what you mean.'

For the next half an hour, they sat there, discussing the raid DS Vicky Neal carried out on Mathieson Transport, and DI Henderson's quiet demeanour making everyone suspect things were not tickety-boo on the home front.

They set off again and arrived at another end-terrace house half-a-dozen streets away. Like before, Lazar repeated the same disappearing act. Thirty-five minutes later, they set off and at a house in Southwick, he did the same again. Lazar's absences became so predictable, sometimes taking forty minutes or over an hour, the officers managed to fit in toilet breaks and buy something for lunch, all without rushing back to the car in a panic.

By seven-thirty in the evening, Lazar had visited six properties, and Bentley was sure what they all had in common were they were large, four or five bedrooms and end of terrace, or detached, less noise to interest or annoy nosy neighbours. Darkness had descended and just when Bentley was considering calling the office and asking DI Henderson to relieve them, the Jeep headed out of town. He didn't make the call. Having spent the day following him, Bentley wanted to see where he ended up. Lisa did too.

The car was easy to follow in the daytime, as it was big and burgundy and stood out among a sea of grey and silver cars, but now at night it became more difficult. In their favour was the volume of traffic, busy with those heading home after working late at the office, or parents picking kids up after football practice.

They headed north on the A23, the Jeep never travelling faster than seventy-five miles an hour, a man careful not to be stopped by the numerous unmarked cars patrolling this road. Many motorists believed they were easy to spot, a Volvo with two male occupants inside was often cited, but the traffic team liked to vary it and often used BMWs, VWs or a Skoda.

The Jeep signalled left and joined the slip-road sign-posted to the Hickstead Showground.

'Do you know this area?' he asked.

'I've been to the Showground a few times to see the show jumping.'

'I don't think there's a horse large enough to accommodate this guy.'

'He wouldn't be able to find one to jump over fences, but he could have a carthorse if all he wanted to do was go for a trot.'

The Jeep took a left at the junction, away from the Showground. Bentley could have followed straight afterwards as the road wasn't busy, but he waited instead for a car to come before pulling out. At another junction a few miles further on, Lazar turned right and joined the A281. This suited Bentley as he knew this area. He used to date a girl from the village they were heading towards, Henfield.

They followed him through the village, not an easy task due to a number of new housing developments in the area. Those developments had increased the amount of road traffic, the number of parked cars at the side of the road and the frequency of roundabouts, transforming the village into a small town.

Shortly after passing the turn-off to Partridge Green Road, the Jeep turned down a narrow country lane. Bentley had widened the gap between their car and the Jeep, but when he made the same turn into the lane, there was no sign of the Jeep. He accelerated harder than he wanted to as the lane was suitable only for one car and if a deer or fox stepped out, it would be curtains for them and the poor animal. He rounded a corner and, there in the distance, he spotted the Jeep's dancing red lights, glowing bright as if braking. Seconds later, the lights disappeared. For a moment, Bentley felt sure they'd lost him, but then they saw the white lights of his main beam cutting through the trees.

Seconds later, they arrived at the turn-off to the lane. Before doing so, Bentley reached out and switched off the car's headlights leaving the road lit only by sidelights.

'What's happened? Have you buggered up the electrics?' Newman asked, her voice raised in alarm.

'No, I haven't buggered up anything, I switched them off. Unless Lazar is taking us down here to lose us, I reckon his destination must be along this road. I'm sure it doesn't lead anywhere. With so few houses, I don't think too many people live in the area, so if he saw a light close behind him, he would soon twig he was being followed.'

'Fair enough, but I'm worried in case we end up in a ditch.'

Lisa started calling out a warning if he veered too close to the side of the road and, a few minutes later, they made it to a straight stretch where they could relax for a few moments. Up ahead, he could see the lights of a large house and beyond, the sight of the Jeep turning into a driveway through a thick copse of trees.

'What did I tell you, Lisa?'

'Spot on Mr Bentley.'

He drove past the driveway and two hundred metres further on, parked beside a farm gate. He switched off the engine.

'What now?' Newman asked. 'We call the office and ask someone to relieve us?'

'When I can summon the energy, as it's been a long day, I'll go over there and take a quick look at this place. When I know what we're looking at, I'll come back and we'll call the boss.'

'Hang on. Didn't we say in all those meetings how ruthless this gang were and how they shot their last victim for trying to escape? It's too dangerous, Phil. We should wait for reinforcements.'

'Yeah, and when they get here, they find it's the home of Lazar's grandmother. No, let me take a quick look and confirm what's there first.'

'I'm not sure.'

'Tell you what, if I'm not back in say, twenty minutes, you can call out the cavalry. Okay?'

THIRTY-NINE

Veronika Kardos paced up and down in her 'cell', a large dog kennel converted to house humans. The walls were concrete, as was the roof and floor, the only evidence a dog didn't sleep there was a mattress big enough for her and a bucket into which she could pee.

It was now Saturday night. She'd arrived in this place two days ago, on Thursday. She'd spent most of the previous day sleeping and vomiting, the crap the kidnappers gave her making her feel unwell. It also had the benefit of keeping the kidnappers away, unlike many of the girls beside her in neighbouring cells. They had been taken away to the building nearby, which the kidnappers called the bunkhouse. In there, the four guys she'd now seen did with them what they wanted.

She was sure it would be her turn in the morning and no way could she put up with it. She'd decided not to make a move until nightfall, which was also the time when one or two of the kidnappers came down to the cells and selected a girl for their evening's entertainment.

A few minutes before, a girl a few cells down was carried kicking and screaming towards the bunkhouse. As they came past her cell, Mr Weasel-Face, the skinny guy who had doctored their drinking water on the bus coming here, stopped and looked at her through the bars.

'I'm looking forward to having this one, Dmitri, aren't you? We are going to have such fun. Have sweet dreams darling thinking of me naked.'

'Come on Nicholae, Vasile will be becoming impatient and you know what he's like when he becomes angry.'

'I can handle Vasile and his moods, I'm just having a little chat with this lovely one here. See you later, my love.'

After they left, Veronika waited ten minutes before removing a hairgrip from her hair and walking towards the cell door. Like many of the women on her bus, she didn't have a grand job like working in an office or the warm cafeteria of a factory, she worked in a shop. Not a mindless place like a supermarket, selling bottles of strong vodka to people like her father, but an ironmonger.

Her shop stocked the usual selection of mouse bait, clothes cleaners and various electrical plugs and cables, but also a large range of security equipment including burglar alarms and locks. In her spare time, she taught herself how to open locks without a key and to disable alarms without knowing the code.

The stupid kidnappers only saw bars and a lock and believed their captives were secure, not realising the cell was fitted with one of the simplest two-lever locks you could buy. A lock of this type was ideal for kennels as dogs couldn't pick locks, but no barrier to someone who could.

She bent the hairgrip and inserted a prong into the

lock. When she made contact with the levers she twisted her wrist sharply and heard the lock slide back. She stopped to listen. This place didn't often fall silent, if it wasn't the guards standing outside the bunkhouse smoking and baiting one another, it was girls sobbing or the dogs at the far end of the cell building barking. They seemed to bark at their own shadow and they were barking now, making it difficult for Veronika to hear any other noises.

In planning her escape, she dreaded walking out of this building, tasting the fresh air of freedom for thirty seconds, only for a heavy fist to knock her to the ground before dragging her back.

If she could open her cell door and providing her hairgrip would last the pace, did it make sense to open all the other cell doors? It would be the Christian thing to do, but she decided not to. She would stand a better chance of getting away on her own and, when free, she would alert the authorities as to the plight of the other women here. If she did try and open the other cell doors, it would take time and be more difficult for ten women to escape than one. It would also waste time in which the kidnappers could return, perhaps intent on finding another woman. Maybe the one they took away earlier tonight was now exhausted or didn't meet their expectations as she cried too much.

She pushed open the cell door, stepped outside and closed it. Luckily for her, she was in the cell at the start of the line and didn't have to walk past the other women. Their shrieks and shouts would surely raise the alarm.

The cells opened out into a corridor, more concrete, with a door at the end leading outside. She could see the light switch but didn't switch it on, instead feeling for the door handle in the dark. No need to use the hairgrip here; the door was open, no doubt to allow the guards easy access, and complacency derived from the sight of a row of barred cells.

She stepped outside and froze when a security light switched on, flooding the yard in front of her in a stark white light.

'These fucking foxes again,' a voice at the door of the bunkhouse said. 'Why doesn't Nicholae let us shoot them?'

'Because he knows how good a shot you are, you stupid motherfucker. You'd miss and kill someone.'

The men traded insults for several minutes which, to Veronika felt like hours, before the security light switched off and, a minute or so later, the door of the bunkhouse door slammed shut. From her position, out of sight of the men at the door, she'd used the illumination offered by the light to plan her escape route.

She recognised the yard where they had assembled on the evening of their arrival, and could see the track they had travelled on and knew it led to a public road. The bonus of the light buoyed her spirits as she didn't have a good sense of direction and may have blundered into the copse of trees bordering both sides of the track.

She made sure the door behind her was shut and, after taking a deep breath, ran towards the track. As soon as she stepped out, the security light switched on, but a quick glance in the direction of the bunkhouse told her no one was looking. She now knew what her grandmother felt like when she used to tell Veronika stories about how they smuggled food for her mother and sister under the noses of the Germans during the war.

Her lungs were aching as she flew down the track, but no way would she stop running until many kilometres were between her and this awful place. The ground was uneven and she had to look down as often as she looked up to ensure she didn't step into a pot hole or break her ankle on a loose rock.

From nowhere, a shadow appeared in front of her and before she could do anything to avoid it, they collided, knocking them both on the ground. Her heart sank when she realised it wasn't an animal or the fallen branch of a tree, but a man. She fought like a wild cat but his grip was strong and in seconds he had her on the ground with her arm behind her back. He put his knee on her back, stopping her moving.

He leaned over and said something in her ear but she couldn't hear for her own sobbing, a strange strangled noise as the man's knee was restricting her heaving chest. She then heard a word she recognised.

'What...what did you say?'

'Keep calm. You're safe now. My name is Phil Bentley, I'm a policeman.'

FORTY

'Oh, hello Vicky,' DI Henderson said looking up from the email he was writing. 'Come in and take a seat at the meeting table.' He walked over to join her.

She'd been on compassionate leave since the shooting at Mathieson Transport a couple of days ago, and looking at her now, he wasn't sure she was ready to return.

'How are you feeling?' he asked.

'Ah, I'm fine now. I'm annoyed with myself for taking it so bad as he didn't really threaten us. Well he did a bit, but I didn't feel at any time we were in danger.'

'I understand, but it's not a pleasant sight, seeing someone shoot themselves. It would spook anyone.'

'Not Ted Mathieson. He was upset at his mate being killed, yes, but he seemed unfazed by all the blood and gore.'

'There will obviously be an official inquiry into Steve Hedland's death and an internal inquiry here and at the NCA. In each of them, you will be required to give evidence, focussing on you and your fellow NCA officer's behaviour.'

'I understand.'

'In my opinion, you've got nothing to worry about, as I feel the operation was carried out by the book.

Steve Hedland's suicide could not have been anticipated in your risk assessment and there was nothing you or Officer Walker could have done differently to stop it.'

'Thank you, sir. It's good to know.'

'On the subject of Ted Mathieson,' Henderson said, changing the subject, 'he was interviewed yesterday. He lawyered-up but didn't give us a record number of 'no comments' as we expected, instead he admitted being an importer of drugs.'

'Excellent news.'

'He couldn't do much else with the weight of evidence against him. The way he tells it he was undertaking a public service, helping busy professional people like lawyers and television executives to function at their best.'

'What bollocks. He's forgetting something, his delivery wasn't all coke. There was some heroin in there too, and in any case, if he felt so public spirited, why didn't he donate all the profits to charity or the smart school his kid attended?'

'It's all flannel, designed to vindicate his champagne lifestyle. In fact, if not for the dope, the financial forensic guys I've got analysing his accounts say his business would have gone to the wall about three years ago.'

'He's been doing it for that long?'

'It seems so. Like we discussed before, I didn't want to bring him to trial just for the amount of drugs you and the NCA lads seized. If the accountants can prove he's been injecting cash into his company for a good few years, it will prove he's been a serious importer all this time. This should be enough for the CPS to mount a cast-iron case against him.'

'I'm glad to hear something good came out of the raid. It was starting to look like a PR disaster. One man dead and Mathieson bleating about underhand police tactics.'

'Don't you worry about that but there's more. When Mathieson started talking about how his side of the operation worked, he coughed up more information about Charlie McQueen's business than he intended.'

'How come?'

'He was happy to describe meetings with his buyer, without naming names, visits to Devil's Dyke and all the rest. When we asked him what happened to the drugs when he handed them over, he refused to say anything that would implicate his old pal Charlie McQueen.'

'Loyalty among thieves? I don't believe it.'

'Self-preservation more like. He doesn't need another enemy, especially one like Charlie McQueen. All he would say was he brought the goods into the country, took the money and thought no more about it until the next delivery. He didn't know what happened afterwards except his buyers took the bags to a place where the contents were diluted with some other white substance and divided into smaller packets.'

'Par for the course.'

'He didn't know where it was or who worked there, but said they called it the biscuit factory.'

She shook her head. 'Means nothing to me.'

'From Mathieson's perspective, he didn't think he

was ratting on his mates, after all, it could be a code word or a nickname for one of the processes they used. If it's a place, there could be a dozen or hundreds of old biscuit factories dotted around London and the south-east.'

'Fair enough, but I think you know what it means.'

'In Shoreham on an industrial estate near the port, there's an old building converted into dozens of small commercial units called *The Pinnacle*. Before the war, it was a biscuit factory making custard creams and digestive biscuits, but it closed in the 1960s when the company moved production to Poland. Biscuits haven't been made on the site for more than fifty years, but nobody locally or anyone working there calls it *The Pinnacle*. They all call it the biscuit factory.'

'How can you be sure it's the right place?'

'I informed the Drugs Unit and they put *The Pinnacle* under surveillance. In one particular unit, they noticed a number of small-time dealers going in and out in addition to several well-known faces who they assumed to be workers. Just when they were about to raid the place, Charlie McQueen rolled up and went inside. When they carried out the raid, McQueen couldn't plead innocence, that he was there simply to score a deal for himself, as there he was with his mitts all over the takings.'

'Brilliant,' Neal said smiling. 'I imagine he's pleading no comment.'

'Gerry's been dealing with him, but with his dabs all over the inside of the unit, no way can he plead that he made a mistake and wandered into the wrong

327

building, or that he went in there to talk to a mate.'

'He'll try.'

'Let him, but we've also got this: the crew working there had installed CCTV. This was to allow someone sitting in the office to monitor movement outside, give them early warning of the approach of rival gangs or police narks.'

'Did they use a recorder?'

'They did, and when the tapes were full, they chucked them in a box, unwrapped a new one and stuck it straight in.'

'The careless habits of the filthy rich.'

'We've now got a couple of months' worth and I'm sure we'll see Charlie McQueen's mug on camera a few more times.'

'A lot's happened since I've been away.'

'It's always the same at the tail-end of a large investigation, but that's enough for one week.'

'Right, I better crack on, there's a lot to be done.'

She left the office with a spring in her step, leaving Henderson surprised at the transformation he'd just witnessed. When he first saw her, he believed he would be sending her home for a few more days, but now it seemed like her old self had returned. He would watch her over the next few days as Post Traumatic Stress Disorder could strike without warning. Not every incident triggered it and not every person was affected by it, but he would keep a watchful eye nevertheless.

**

Ten minutes after Vicky Neal left Henderson's office, someone else walked in who equally could be suffering from PTSD: Veronika Kardos. She wasn't alone, but in the company of a woman from Action for Trafficked Women, Hilary Johns.

Veronika had colour in her cheeks, flesh on her bones, her short blonde hair looked glossy and on her pretty, unmarked face she wore a huge smile. She walked over and threw her arms around him and held him tight.

'Thank you so much for saving me.'

She pulled away from him, still smiling. Henderson showed her to a seat around the meeting table.

'How are you, Veronika, after your horrible ordeal?'

This was the first time Henderson had spoken to her since Phil Bentley picked her up on Saturday. He would have liked to have interviewed her yesterday, but Veronika didn't feel able and said she needed to go to church. Twice.

'I am so pleased to be free. I am now living with a good family where I have many hot showers and lovely meals.'

'You speak excellent English.'

'Thank you. My father taught English Literature at Budapest University for many years, but lost his job when he published some leaflets criticising the government. We moved to the country after my mother took ill. She died only two months later and he turned to alcohol, but he still made me speak English at every opportunity.'

He turned to the woman from ATW, Hilary Johns. 'It's good to meet you, Hilary and thanks for bringing Veronika along today.'

'Pleased to meet you too, Inspector.'

Henderson sorted out drinks and then got down to the real business of the day.

'I'd like you to tell me what happened to you, Veronika.'

She explained about the journey home from the ironmonger's shop in town and the long walk along country roads after the bus dropped her off in a downpour.

'It's a familiar story, I'm afraid, Inspector,' Johns said. 'These evil men prey on vulnerable women, kidnapping them, often in broad daylight, on quiet country roads.'

'When and how did they bring you here to the UK?'

'This is Monday, so I came here last Thursday, by minibus. They didn't give us much water on the journey and about half an hour before we reached the border they handed out water bottles. We all drank because we were thirsty and the next thing we know we are in the countryside and being told to get out of the bus.'

'You were drugged,' Henderson said, stating the obvious for everyone's benefit. 'What happened then?'

Veronika went on to describe the place they were held. Henderson got up, walked over to his desk and brought over some of Cindy Longhurst's photographs, now printed on A4 paper.

'Is this the place?' he said showing Veronika the photographs Cindy took of the low concrete buildings out in the woods.

She puzzled over the first picture for a few moments. 'I've never seen it before from a distance.' She picked up another picture. 'Yes, this one shows it better. There,' she said pointing at one end of the building in the photograph, 'this is the cell where I was kept.'

'How can you be sure?'

'I recognise the yard there, the track with the forest beside and through the trees you can just see the roof of the bunkhouse. Yes, I'm sure this is the correct place.'

'Where did you get these photographs, Inspector?' Johns asked. 'Have you known about this place for some time?'

He explained the source of the photographs but Hilary's suspicions remained. If the police knew about this place, why didn't they close it sooner?

'What will happen to the other women there?' Veronika said.

'Once we have finished our meeting, and you've told me everything you know about this place, we will mount a raid and close it down.'

'Good.'

'Why were you kept there? I assume this place wasn't your final destination.'

'They said the house we were supposed to go and work inside was having some building work done and wasn't ready yet. There were no vacancies in the other brothels,' she said, the disgust evident in her tone.

'They made no secret of what they wanted you to do?'

'No, we knew what they were intending to do with us. This is why I had to escape.' She went on to explain how the men in the bunkhouse came every night to the cells and selected a girl, 'to break her in' as they called it.

The anger he felt at the level of degradation and exploitation these women were suffering was on the point of boiling over, but he took several deep breaths to calm himself.

'So,' he said, 'the low building here in the picture currently contains the other women who came over from Hungary with you?'

'Yes.'

Henderson had left a surveillance team watching the site and instructed them to call at the first sign of movement. Veronika's escape could have caused panic among the traffickers and there was a good chance they were now making plans to evacuate, but his watchers had seen nothing yet. Perhaps with no place to send the women they had no choice but to wait it out or they assumed she was lying dead in a field after falling and breaking her leg.

'The guards, the kidnappers, they live in the bunkhouse?'

'Yes.'

'Can you tell me about it?'

Henderson assumed, and this was confirmed by Veronika, the bunkhouse was a temporary home for the men any time a group of women were occupying the kennels. After the women were dispersed to places where they would live and work, Vasile Lazar would go back to his house in Sandown Road and the others back to their own houses.

'I don't know much about the bunkhouse,' Veronika said, 'I have never been in there, but the girl in the next cell told me it is on three floors. There is living space at the bottom, beds in the middle floor where they sleep and at the top of the house, a games area with a big table. Like a pool table, but bigger.'

'Snooker?' Henderson said.

'Yes, snooker.'

'What do you remember about the men?'

'There are four of them.'

'Only four?'

'Yes.'

'Did anyone come to visit? Did you see anyone else?'

'No, I only see, saw the four men and they all live in the bunkhouse.'

'Tell me about them.'

She looked beyond Henderson, out of the window, trying to recall difficult memories. 'There's Vasile, he's a large man, twice as big as me but he doesn't say much.'

'We know about him,' Henderson said. 'We followed him and he led us to you.'

'I'm so glad you did,' she said smiling. 'Then, there's Nicholae. He small and thin with narrow, staring eyes that I call him Weasel-Face. He seems to be the boss and orders the other men around.'

'Ok.'

'The other two are called Dmitri and Stefan. Both are of average height and size. Neither of them made such an impression on me.'

'All the men are armed?'

'Yes, they all carry guns.'

'Is there anything else you can think of that might prove helpful?'

'I am not sure. Like what?'

'I don't know, if they go out often, if they receive deliveries, those sorts of things.'

She thought for a moment and then shook her head. 'I don't think I was there long enough to see everything.'

'Not a problem,' Henderson said, as he gathered his papers and photographs together. 'I'd like to thank you, Hilary, for bringing Veronika here today, especially after her experiencing such a terrible ordeal. Veronika, I'd like to thank you for being so brave in coming here and telling me everything you remembered. Now, with my officers, I'll work out the best way of closing this place for good.'

FORTY-ONE

Henderson pulled in behind the unmarked Ford van carrying six armed officers. They were close to the village of Shermanbury, more a hamlet than a village, and dwarfed by its near-neighbour Partridge Green. He'd instructed the other members of the team due here tonight to come from the north, as too many cars arriving from the south on such a quiet, rural road might raise suspicions with anyone watching.

A few minutes later, the release team arrived, and not long afterwards an empty minibus. The big lads in the Armed Response Team only made an appearance when everyone else was assembled. Despite being parked some distance from the bunkhouse, Henderson wanted all chatter, the slamming of car doors and the stamping of feet, kept to a minimum. Noises travelled far at night and the last thing he wanted was to lose the element of surprise.

They walked along the road sounding to Henderson like a small army but little could be done to mute the clanking of weapons against jacket buckles, boots striking tarmac and the sniffing from those with a runny nose. The surveillance team confirmed the gang had not evacuated the bunkhouse and kennels following Veronika's escape. It would be a large undertaking, with so much invested in the place and having a large number of kidnapped women to house. On the plus side for the traffickers, the escapee wouldn't have a clue as to her whereabouts, she couldn't speak English and with winter outside, a few months later someone would find her face-down in a ditch.

When they reached the track leading to the kennels, the group split in two and walked up both sides of the track, everyone ready to leap into the trees at the first sign of a vehicle or guard. It didn't take long before they heard the sound of dogs barking and, by the deep, throaty sounds they made, it didn't sound like a pack of West Highland Terriers.

At the top of the track they came to a yard, the kennels on the left, the bunkhouse over to the right. They stopped. The release team moved forward and, without speaking, Henderson pointed to the kennels, a long, low concrete building. The three officers nodded. Their role was to release and attend to the kidnapped women. Veronika had described how she had opened the lock of her cell door, and even though the release team expected to open them with the same level of ease, they would be using something more substantial than one of her hairgrips.

Two of the team set off while the third member waited. Five minutes later one of the officers appeared at the door at the end of the kennels with two women. As instructed, the women ran across the yard, triggering the security light, and into the arms of the third release team officer. The officer led the women down the track to the minibus.

He could hear the odd huff and puff from a couple

of guys in the Armed Response Team, keen as they were to get on to the main event of the night, but at the briefing they had been warned they needed to be patient. By the time women five and six had crossed the yard, Henderson's adrenaline was starting to rise, anticipating that they would soon see some action.

Out of the corner of his eye he spotted the bunkhouse door opening. Henderson instructed a member of the ART to move to a position opposite the kennel door and hide in the bushes. He then backed into the cover of trees and pulled out his radio. 'Dave, guard coming, repeat, guard coming.'

The man approaching from the bunkhouse was neither big like Vasile Lazar, nor short and skinny like Nicholae. This had to be either Stefan or Dmitri.

He was muttering something in his own language, no doubt about the stupid security light going off and on all the time. When the guard reached for the door handle and turned his back, Officer Wardle stepped forward and smacked him in the head with the butt of his Heckler & Koch MP5 carbine. The guard fell to the floor in an untidy heap. Wardle removed the gun from the guard's waistband and tied the hands of the unconscious man behind his back with plastic bindings, impossible to break and bloody uncomfortable to wear.

Following a signal from Henderson, Wardle dragged the dazed man across the yard and handed him over to a uniformed officer who led him down the track to a patrol car.

Henderson lifted his radio. 'Dave, threat neutralised. Cease evacuation, repeat, cease evacuation.'

If the guard didn't return to the bunkhouse in a timely manner, chances were another more alert guard would come out and, this time Wardle's surprise attack wouldn't be enough. He waved the ART forward, he and DS Walters, both armed with handguns, following at the rear.

No need for the 'Big Red' door opener this time as the guard had left the door of the bunkhouse unlocked when he came out. In a building like this, spread over three floors with several dangerous staircases, Henderson decided on stealth not shock, depriving Sergeant Bob Roberts at the front of using his deafening bellow, a familiar sound to anyone in the south stand at the Amex.

The bunkhouse, like many similar developments, was open-plan with a large lounge occupying most of the floor space. All the ground floor rooms were clear except for the lounge where they found a short, skinny guy, Nicholae, playing a PlayStation game on the giant television. He had big headphones clamped on his head, leaving him oblivious to their presence. A large gloved hand over his face soon caught his attention.

The team made their way upstairs, slow and steady, as it was potentially the most dangerous of all manoeuvres inside a house. If a gunman knew they were there, he could hold them at bay with a single weapon, and there would be little they could do about it. The group was now seven, one down as DS Walters had the job of escorting the handcuffed and gagged Nicholae, over to the officers in the yard.

They made the first-floor landing without incident

and discovered what gave the bunkhouse its name, as the whole floor consisted of a large room with eight beds, and off to one side, a large communal toilet and several private stalls. On one of the beds, the skinny, naked arse of someone he believed to be Dmitri or Stefan was bobbing up and down between the open legs of a naked woman. It had to be one of the women from the cells as it was obvious she wasn't there willingly, her face contorted in anguish and sobbing non-stop. Seconds later, her tormentor said something harshly in a language Henderson didn't understand before slapping the girl in the face.

Someone in the police group let out a gasp and the man turned.

'Put your hands where I can see 'em!' roared Sergeant Roberts.

The naked man moved as if to climb off the distraught woman, but instead, he reached under a pillow and pulled out a gun. He twisted round towards the group who were standing stock-still as if mesmerised by the spectacle and all bunched together at the door, making for an easy target. Before the gun reached its target, there was a short burst from Sergeant Roberts's carbine and the man's head exploded, showering the poor woman with blood and brain matter.

They left her screaming and made their way to the stairs. He saw Walters coming up and without speaking, pointed into the room with the dead man and the screaming girl. She gave him a thumbs-up in response.

They climbed the stairs with the same caution as

before, one step at a time. If Lazar, the last remaining member of the kidnapping group, heard the shots and the screaming, and they had no reason to think otherwise, he could lie behind the door of the games room and pick them off on the stairs. Instead, they heard a heavy thump and when they reached the top and looked inside the games room, he'd upended the snooker table and was taking refuge behind it.

The officers were standing partly on the stairs and partly on a small landing, the door to the left leading into the games room which, like the lounge, occupied most of the floor area at the top of the bunkhouse. In front of them and to the right, various toilets and store rooms.

Whenever anyone from ART tried to take a look inside the room, Lazar peppered the doorway with bullets. It was in their favour that the table wasn't in the centre of the room or they'd never be able to look inside, but instead it covered a corner at the far end. It looked as though he'd upended it and then dragged it into position. Henderson knew that Lazar was big, but if he could upend such a heavy item and drag it any distance, he had to be extremely strong as well.

'If what he's hiding behind is a proper snooker table, and sounded like it when it upended,' Sergeant Roberts said to Henderson, 'it's made out of thick slate to give it an even, flat surface.'

'Meaning?'

'Meaning from this distance, these,' he said tapping his H&K, 'won't put a dent in it.'

'So, in theory, he could hold out all night?'

'Yep, depending on how much ammo he's got.'

'Hang on. Let me try talking to him.'

'Don't get too close.'

Henderson moved to door. 'Vasile! Can you hear me?'

'I can hear.'

'We have many armed officers here. Put the gun down and walk out.'

'Get lost! Come and get me.'

Henderson spotted the movement of a gun at the top of the snooker table and ducked away before bullets splintered the door frame.

He turned to Roberts. 'That went well. What else can we do?' He looked at the ceiling for inspiration. 'We could crash through the windows, bring up a cherry picker with a sniper on board, throw in smoke, percussion, gas?'

'I'd favour CS myself,' Roberts said.

Henderson ran through the options in his mind. The first two would suit the military better than a group of big lads who could shoot straight but were better suited to standing on terra firma than abseiling down ropes.

'I do too. Do you guys carry anything in the van?'

'Nope.'

Henderson pulled out his phone and put an urgent call through to Lewes Control.

'They say they can get it here in about thirty minutes,' Henderson said after terminating the call.

Roberts nodded. He turned to his team. 'Lads, listen up. We're gonna smoke him out with CS gas but it won't be here for another thirty minutes. Okay?'

They nodded.

'Andy, you, Wardle and Butch keep your eye on him in there, the rest of us are taking a break, see if we can start a brew. If him inside does anything different, call me immediately. Understand?'

They nodded.

'After about fifteen minutes we'll come up and swap. Everybody all right with that?'

'Fine boss. Just don't eat all the bloody biscuits.'

'Andy, the boys in this place are Romanian. Any biscuits they have in here will likely be made from figs or lentils or some other shite.'

'In which case you're welcome to scoff the lot.'

Henderson walked downstairs with Roberts and two members of the ART. When they reached the next floor, the officers carried on to the ground floor while Henderson headed into the bunk room. There, Walters was comforting the woman they'd seen earlier. She was now wrapped in what looked like a former professional wrestler's dressing gown, a garish combination of black shiny material and gold braid dwarfing the woman's slight frame.

'How is she?' he said to Walters, nodding towards the head lying in Walters's lap.

'She's calmed but I can't tell her anything about what we're doing here as she doesn't speak any English. I think she's guessed we're cops from the body armour and the guns and the fact that the brains of the man tormenting her are splattered all over the bed. What's happening upstairs?'

'Lazar took refuge behind an upended snooker table. We can't go in as he's got the door covered. We'll try and flush him out with CS.'

'What was he doing up there on his own? You can't play snooker with only one person, can you?'

'No, but maybe it's like a young lad with a ball. If he can't find anyone to play with, he can practise various shots on his own and try to improve his technique. It's not to everyone's taste, but maybe he's the solitary type.'

'Three down and one to go, Walters said 'These things never go the way we plan them, do they?'

'It's not a bad result so far. Two kidnappers captured.'

'Plus, all the women are out of the kennels.'

'You restarted the evac?'

'Yeah, I figured with three down and seven against the last one, it would be safe to continue.'

'Good move. It was shaping up to be successful night if only the guy in here didn't take a gun to bed with him.'

'It's to be expected when everyone is armed.'

'True,' Henderson said levering himself up, 'but it still doesn't make me feel any better about someone being killed. I suggest you take this young woman over to the minibus and come back here for a brew. Sergeant Roberts is on kettle duty.'

'I will. See you in a minute.'

Henderson headed downstairs to the kitchen, thankful to be away from the bunks where the smell of death permeated the air. The body would need to lie there for some time longer as he couldn't allow a SOCO team or the pathologist to enter the building with a siege taking place upstairs. The walls and floor of the bunkhouse were made of wood and there was no telling how far a stray bullet would travel without the impediment of a brick wall to stop it.

The tea breaks over and the CS gas delivered, the armed officers gathered around the games room door and fitted their gas masks. The operator fired one canister further away from the snooker table than he would have liked and fired the other blind from behind the door frame, trying not to elicit a blast of gunfire from the holed-up man inside.

It was a big room and Henderson wondered if two canisters would be enough, but given that the gas was designed to be used with the obvious difficulties of the great outdoors, in the confined space of the room it filled every corner with astonishing alacrity.

Now came the tricky bit. There wasn't much cover inside the games room and if Lazar had mitigated some of the effects of the gas by deploying an effective face mask, as they couldn't hear him coughing or wheezing, the ART would be sitting ducks once visibility improved.

Roberts, as ever an officer who led from the front, went first. He instructed the team to fan out on as they entered the room. Henderson and Walters waited by the door. With all the officers now in the games room Henderson had a better view of the snooker table. Seconds later, movement caught his eye and he saw a handgun appear above the edge of the table. The team saw it too.

'Gun! Everyone down!' Roberts shouted, his voice muffled by the mask.

Lazar's handgun fired in random fashion, suggesting he had been blinded by the gas and had taken to shooting wildly, but it found its mark when two ART officers screeched in pain. Wardle, on the left side of the ART fan was making his way towards the snooker table, unseen by Lazar. When he reached it, he stepped behind to get a better view, his mask partially impeding his vision. He opened fire with a short burst and the clatter of the handgun ceased.

FORTY-TWO

Walters completed the preliminaries for the recording devices while Henderson took a good look at the man in front of him. At last, he'd got one of the human traffickers in an interview room, albeit with a duty solicitor sitting beside him. He would have liked to see all four in custody, but it wasn't to be.

They'd already interviewed Dmitri Manole and he had told them everything he knew which took a considerable time. Not that Manole had much to tell, but he didn't speak a word of English and they were forced to use an interpreter. By the end of the interview, they hadn't increased their knowledge by much, but enough to tell them that Nicholae Prodan was the boss.

They'd found plenty of evidence in the bunkhouse which was in the process of being analysed: weapons, laptops, phones, blood-stained clothes and bedding. Following on from Phil Bentley's tour of Brighton on the trail of Vasile Lazar, the Vice Unit called into each of the addresses where Lazar stopped. It came as no surprise to everyone involved in the case when they found each of the houses to be fully-functioning brothels.

Henderson had heard all the arguments about paid-for sex and took the view it was not something which could be easily halted. The demand was endless and, in some countries, their operation was sanctioned by the government. In a way, free movement within the EC took some of the responsibility. Itinerant workers on the whole were young and away from their families for long periods, and the chance to have sex with a young woman, perhaps someone from their homeland, sometimes proved irresistible.

Plenty of women willingly worked in the sex industry, but the traffickers didn't see why they should pay for something they could get for free. This form of exploitation turned Henderson's stomach, ruthless men enslaving women with only one objective in mind: to make themselves rich, like the arrogant sod in front of him.

'Mr Prodan, I assume you understand the charges against you?'

'Yes, I do. I am a very bad man, now deport me.'

'It's not going to happen.'

'What?' He turned to his lawyer. 'Tell him, I want to be deported back to Romania.'

The lawyer whispered something in his ear and while his angry expression didn't falter, it seemed to calm him.

'How did you start working in this business?' Henderson asked.

'A friend introduced me.'

'A friend here or in Romania?'

'In Romania.'

'Was everything already in place when you started? Were there kidnap teams established in Romania and

Hungary, were the bunkhouse and kennels already built, did the brothels exist?'

'I didn't have to do a thing, it was all there. This person wanted me to work there because he knew that I, Nicholae Prodan,' he said tapping his chest, 'would make it better.'

'Better how?' Walters asked.

He looked at the DS with disdain. Veronika's description of a man with weasel-like features was a good one. He was late thirties or early forties, with slicked-back hair, thick eyebrows and yellowing teeth. His small dark eyes darted back and forth, as if he was frightened of missing out on something or fearful of attack.

'I am good at making lots more money and I find more places for them to work.'

'What is the name of this person?' Henderson asked. 'The person who hired you.'

He turned to his brief and asked something.

Prodan turned back to face Henderson, a schoolboy-style smirk on his face. 'No comment,' he said.

'What happens to the money?'

He shrugged his bony shoulders. 'I don't know. I don't deal with it. If you didn't shoot Stefan you could ask him.'

The murder team and forensic accountants would try and follow the money once they'd mapped out its trail. To ordinary people, it sounded like a nice problem to have, the presence of lots of cash, but to the likes of drug dealers and bank robbers it was a perennial headache. Large deposits of cash and significant withdrawals from banks were reported, a process designed to stop criminals salting away millions in illegally obtained gains.

In response, criminals were forced to think up ingenious ways of circumventing the regulations. If not, they would be unable to use credit cards or pay bills and many organisations, such as those with retail websites and car hire companies, refused to do business without a credit card.

Henderson asked Prodan a few more questions about how the business was organised, but he deflected them every time, saying he didn't deal with this issue or he didn't know how this process operated. The DI decided to move on to a subject he would know something about.

'Why did you kidnap Cindy Longhurst?'

'I object to this leading line of questioning, Inspector. You are trying to implicate my client in a crime you have no evidence to connect him to,' the duty solicitor said.

'It's ok,' Prodan said, 'I reply. I have never heard of this woman.'

'We have a witness. The woman you threw out of Longhurst Studios has made a positive identification. She saw you and Vasile Lazar enter the studio and abduct photographer Cindy Longhurst.'

Henderson put Cindy's picture in front of him.

'Ah yes, I remember now. The photographer. She found out, I don't know how, but she came to the kennels and took photographs. Then she came back at night and freed some of our girls, the bitch.'

'You killed her for it.'

'No, I didn't kill anyone,' he said smiling, 'Vasile did. He's the killer, not me.'

'You think we'd fall for your lame excuse? It's easy to blame a dead man who isn't here to defend himself.'

'You will see when you look at his gun. He killed the photographer and the two girls who escaped.'

'Did you question her?'

'Yes, yes I questioned her. I wanted to know where my girls were. Is this so bad?'

The Vice Unit had discovered the two other girls who used to share the house at Baden Powell Drive, Marina and Felicia, were working in a brothel in Worthing.

'We found Cindy with heavy bruising, as if she'd suffered a severe beating.'

'Again,' he said shrugging, 'it's Vasile. I talk to them, then Vasile I don't know, loses his temper or something and hits them. Sometimes he doesn't know his own strength.'

'Same with the other two girls?'

'Yes. I questioned the first girl to find out where the others were hiding and then Vasile shot her. The other girl I did not need to question as we had the other two. Vasile shot her too.'

'Did you try and stop him?'

'Vasile is large man with vile temper. If I said something to try and stop him, he would shoot me too.'

Henderson let the issue lie for now as it wasn't possible to determine who actually delivered the blows. Even though ballistics could match the bullets to the gun, it wouldn't prove whose hand had been on the trigger. However, he could still wipe the smug smile off Prodan's face. Even if Vasile Lazar was responsible for killing all three women, under UK law if they could prove Prodan's presence there and his tacit approval of the deed, it would make him an accessory to murder.

They left the interview room ten minutes later.

'What a smug bastard,' Walters said.

'Yeah, he thinks we'll deport him back to Romania and that will be the end of it.'

'Maybe after he's served a couple of life sentences we will.'

'We'll talk to him again once we've got the full forensics. Maybe then he'll be more cooperative and willing to give up his backer.'

'You still think there's someone here in the UK?'

'There's no doubt in my mind.'

They'd arrived at his office and walked in, continuing a calm, rational discussion that could only be conducted at this stage of an investigation, not when they were mired with all the problems in the middle.

'The trafficking operation predates Prodan. The bunkhouse was built five years ago, Phil checked out the planning application. So, when Prodan arrived in this country three years ago, it was already there.'

'They might have bought the property with it already in place.'

'No, a limited company bought it ten years ago and the kennels date from the 60s at least, so they were already there but not the bunkhouse. Plus, why would anyone but traffickers build a bunkhouse out in the sticks?'

'I'm forced to agree with you. So, what you're saying is, if Prodan didn't oversee its construction, someone else did?'

'Yes, and the question that needs answering is, who?'

FORTY-THREE

The pub was heaving when Henderson arrived and when the crowd in the corner noticed him, a loud cheer went up. Was it because they were pleased to see him, or had they burned through the wad of drink money he'd given them earlier?

They were in the *Fortune of War* pub, a place often described as being on Brighton seafront. This was only partly true, as the pub was on the same level as the pebbles on the beach, several metres below the road.

The sea was calm tonight, but anyone coming here on a wild winter's night would hear the wind whip the pebbles off the beach and throw them at the pub window. For newcomers, the constant *tap-tapping* sound was like someone trying to get in the pub, but if they opened the door they would receive a lot more than just a gust of wind in their face.

'You lot got down here pretty sharpish,' he said to DS Walters. She was holding a drink. If her usual, it would be a vodka and lime. He took a seat beside her.

'Dragged down here more like. We'd finished with the interviews and I was waiting to see some forensic data, so I thought, why not? It's been a hell of a week.'

'I can't argue with you there. Plus, you could be waiting all night to see anything.'

'Or nothing, knowing that lot.'

He felt a nudge on the shoulder and Phil Bentley shoved a pint of something into his hand.

'It's IPA. I hope that's all right.'

'No problem. Thanks Phil.'

'It's your money boss, enjoy it,' he said as he walked back to the bar.

Henderson looked at the happy faces occupying the two corners at the end of the long pub. He took a long drink from his glass before pushing his chair back and standing. He held his hand up and said in a loud voice, 'Quiet please everybody. Let's have a bit of hush before we're all too drunk.'

When a modicum of peace had descended in their corner of the pub, he cleared his throat. 'I'd just like to thank you all for your hard work on this case, without it and all the long hours you've worked, the numerous, tasteless take-aways you've eaten and all the coffee you've drunk, we never would have cracked it.'

Loud cheers went up but he hadn't finished yet. He waited for calm to return before continuing. 'Thanks to everyone for all your efforts, we've not only smashed a large human trafficking operation, we've also closed six brothels all along the south coast. Every single one of you should be proud of your contribution. I certainly am. Cheers!' he said lifting his glass and toasting them. 'To every one of you.'

A huge cheer filled the air. There was a time in any bar in Brighton when the regulars would tell a loud group in the corner to shut-it, but with the growth of wild hen and bridegroom weekends they were well used to it.

Conversations restarted and Henderson resumed his seat.

'Hi boss, how are you doing?'

Henderson turned to see Phil Bentley standing beside him.

'It's great, Phil, a good excuse for everyone to let their hair down after so many weeks with our shoulders to the grindstone. What's this, the beer in this place not good enough for you or have you run out of cash?'

Bentley held up what looked like a soda water and lime. 'I'm alternating, one of these with a beer. My coach says I'm getting too fat and is threating to drop me from the team.'

Henderson laughed. 'It must be serious, as you've told me before he's lucky sometimes to have eighteen fit players.'

'It's true. It's hard to get youngsters interested in the game as I don't think many schools play it nowadays and, of course, football always has a higher appeal.'

'Aye, maybe here in the south, but around the borders of Scotland and even in football-mad Lancashire and Yorkshire there's still a strong rugby following.'

'Phil, come here!' he heard someone at the back of the throng shouting.

'I'm getting the call from Sam Richie over there as he wants to show me a video on his phone.'

'Phil!'

'I'll be there in a minute, Richie, stop shouting, I'm talking to the boss.'

'It's okay, Phil,' Henderson said, 'on you go. There's something I wanted to ask you, but it's about work and it can wait until tomorrow.'

'Sure thing boss, see you later.'

Henderson was listening to an animated discussion about computer viruses while he debated whether to stay or not. In the past, he often went to these celebrations just for a couple of drinks before going home. The presence of the boss could often inhibit the younger members of staff from enjoying themselves, and Rachel wasn't happy if he rolled back to the house stinking of booze. Now, he had nothing to go home for and he quite fancied a bit of a blow-out.

In the end, he stayed until pub chucking out time. It wasn't the 'end' for many of the younger members of the team as they had all decided to head off to a club. Even when younger, Henderson failed to see the attraction: deafening music, over-priced drinks and dancers behaving as if they were on speed, which many of them were. This, he would definitely leave to the youngsters.

The large group were milling around outside the pub aimlessly, everyone too drunk to take a decisive lead. He said his goodbyes and headed up the stairs to Marine Parade to start the lengthy walk home. Minutes later, he heard footsteps running behind him. He turned to look.

'It's not a mugger, it's only me,' Vicky Neal said.

'What a relief. I don't think I've got the energy to deal with one of them. Did you not fancy boogying the night away?'

'Not my style. Plus, I've got to get up for work in

the morning, lots to do.'

'Not anything to do with any after-effects from the Mathieson arrest?'

'What do you mean, PTSD?'

He nodded.

'No. The incident does come back to me now and again, but I think I can handle it. As you said, I can't go over my behaviour and say if I'd done something different I could have saved him.'

'Acknowledging that certainly makes a big difference. Did you enjoy the evening?'

'I really did. I'm getting to know Sally and Phil a lot better, although I still felt a bit of a fraud being here.'

'I know you arrived part-way through the investigation, but you're now part of the team.'

'I know, but I had nothing to do with closing the human trafficking operation.'

'Not in the end, for sure, but before we tracked them down we didn't know if Ted Mathieson was involved or not. We discovered he was importing drugs, but equally with his large transport fleet he could have been bringing in women too. Your work made sure we didn't waste time chasing him for the wrong reasons.'

'Fair enough. Thanks.'

They walked past the Palace Pier, dark and quiet at this time of night, but often when he passed in the afternoon or evening someone was usually standing outside. It was a good central point in the town for arranging to meet people or organising a lift.

Neal took his arm to steady herself as her heels were falling foul of the uneven and scarred pavements, and didn't release it when the surface improved. They talked about her time in Manchester and how it compared to Brighton.

It was a short walk along Marine Parade to Lower Rock Gardens, the place where Vicky was renting. Henderson walked up the road with her. It wasn't so far out of his way as he could cut along St James's Street at the top of the road, and at the same time, avoid the chilly night-time breeze blowing in off the sea.

They stopped outside a light-coloured building, sandwiched between two darker neighbours. There was a large bay window on the ground floor and simple sash windows on the first and upper floors. The residents appeared to be night owls as many lights were still burning.

'This is my place. Thanks for seeing me home, officer.'

'It's all right madam, we might be the hard-pressed employees of Sussex Police but we're only too happy to ensure unaccompanied women arrive home safely.'

'I'm on the top floor.' She turned and put her hands on the lapels of his coat. He could smell her breath, sweet and alcoholic. 'You can come up for a night-cap, if you like.'

FORTY-FOUR

On Thursday morning, Henderson interviewed Nicholae Prodan once again, this time armed with a ballistics report and other information. A single gun had been used to kill Cindy Longhurst and the two Romanian women, the ballistics analysis proved, and Vasile Lazar's prints and his DNA were all over it.

He told Prodan the good news: all three murders would be attributed to Lazar, and Henderson let the weasel wallow in the glow it gave him. It was his turn to feel pleased when he gave him the other news. He would be tried for the same crimes, but as an accessory. In addition, the witness statements given to them by the women rescued from the Shermanbury kennels and the brothels around Sussex, confirmed Prodan to be the chief torturer and rapist. If he was fit enough to climb the steps to a Romania-bound aircraft at the end of his sentence, Henderson would be most surprised.

With the list of charges against him and the prospect of spending most of his life in jail, the DI expected his offer of eliminating a charge or two if he gave up his backer would be better received. To his surprise, Prodan wouldn't give an inch, making him feel the backer wasn't a benevolent individual, happy to supply money as it gave him a good return on his investment, but a ruthless individual who ruled with a rod of fear. Henderson left the interview room, happy at last to be charging the two traffickers they had in custody, but frustrated at not knowing the name of the person behind the operation.

He returned to his office, only stopping to dump the files in his hand on the desk and grab his coat. He walked out the building and across the car park. When he arrived at work early this morning the weather was cold and misty, but now with the mist gone it revealed a bright, sunny spring morning. He knew it was nothing but a short interlude as winter hadn't yet run its course, so he would enjoy it while it lasted.

On the drive to Shermanbury, he listened to the last half hour of Woman's Hour on Radio Four. It included a studio discussion debating the question: Why Aren't More Women Business Leaders? They cited common complaints, the glass ceiling, too few women going into business, and those who were there being held back by men, worried about career breaks and child-care issues.

It wasn't a phone-in and he wouldn't have done so even if it was, but using the trafficking case as an example, he could have brought a different perspective to the discussion. If the way traffickers treated women was at some primeval level similar to the way many men thought, no wonder women had trouble progressing in business.

He arrived at the kennels in Shermanbury and got out of the car. He walked across the yard and rather than walk to the bunkhouse where the SOCO team were working, he headed instead for the kennels. In the daylight, it looked innocent enough, a long low building used for housing dogs, first as a commercial kennel some years before, and now a place where pit bulls were bred and kept.

Neither of the two traffickers in custody struck Henderson as dog lovers as they trotted out their well-worn mantra, 'Vasile did it.' Several of the incarcerated women were terrified of the beasts, and why wouldn't they be when something they really feared was living beside them and could be heard barking most nights? The traffickers played on this fear and threatened to release the dogs if they tried to escape. However, the handlers who took them away said the dogs were wild and ill-disciplined and would be just as likely to attack the traffickers as the incarcerated women.

The police dog handlers suspected they were being bred for dog-fighting, an illegal gambling activity which pitted dog against dog in a bloody fight to the death. In fact, it often led to the death of both dogs as the victor could end up so badly injured their owner would have no option but to put the dog down.

Henderson opened the door to the kennels and walked inside. Despite the warm spring sunshine outside, it felt cool in here, perhaps an asset in housing dogs as they wouldn't overheat in the summer months. He walked along the long corridor past the cells which were head-height and about four metres square, not a bad size for a short stay as it allowed a dog or person inside to walk around a little and stretch, but they were poorly furnished and included only the essentials. A puny wall heater provided a modicum of warmth, but concrete could be a cold material and it was hard to imagine how cold it would get in here when the thermometer outside dropped below zero degrees Celsius in deep winter.

The first twelve cells were intended for human habitation and those beyond for dogs, the beasts having the benefit of a small door at the back leading to a yard outside. He didn't like aggressive fighting dogs such as pit bulls, but the presence of so many dogs did interest him. In all the interviews, no one had given him a good reason why they were there and who owned them. The presence of one dog might suggest a stray or an impulse buy, but six dogs sounded to Henderson like someone's unbridled love for the breed, or a commercial operation.

He walked towards the bunkhouse hoping SOCO could answer some of those outstanding questions. If not, his one last hope was the HTCU, the High-Tech Crime Unit at Haywards Heath. All the electronic kit found in the bunkhouse, and there was plenty of it, phones, iPads and laptops had been sent there for analysis. Even if protected by passwords, the techs would worm their way inside and reveal its secrets.

He knew not to get his hopes up as many criminals were not IT savvy and could barely use a Pay-As-You-Go phone. However, the traffickers were younger than many local cons and might have been using the kit for something more than watching funny videos or playing games.

He walked through the bunkhouse, the first time he'd been back since Monday night, looking for what? It couldn't be something physical as anything of interest had been bagged and taken away for examination.

'Hello Angus,' Pat Davidson, Crime Scene Manager, said as he walked out of the kitchen. 'Back to see it before we finish up?'

'You finishing today?'

'Yep. It was an easy one, to be truthful. The people staying here were only doing so for short periods so they didn't have much stuff and what they had, clothes, sheets, electronic kit, we've bagged.'

He left Pat on the ground floor and climbed the stairs. He walked into the bunk room, the place where Stefan had met his end. Speaking later to the woman they discovered being raped by him, they learned he was at the bottom of the hierarchical ladder within the gang. He only got his hands on a woman when the other three were finished with her.

He climbed the stairs again and walked into the games room, the snooker table still upended and bearing the marks where the armed response team had tried shooting through it. He'd been told Officer Wardle would receive a commendation for his actions and the other two, both hit by Lazar's wild shooting, were at home convalescing. It was unlikely they would suffer any long-term effects as both wounds were superficial.

Walking downstairs and outside, Henderson decided he wasn't ready to leave the crime scene yet and headed towards the house next door to see if anyone was at home. An officer had called there on the night of the shooting and told the residents to remain indoors, but no one had spoken to them in any detail. He had no reason to suspect them of being involved and even though many referred to it as the house next door, the only one visible on either side of the kennels, it was at least a quarter of a mile distant.

The door of the house was opened by a housekeeper and after showing her his ID, she agreed to call the lady of the house. He was shown into a room overlooking the back garden and left there. The uninterrupted views were fantastic, fields rolling into the distance and no sign of any neighbours, due to a thick copse of trees on both sides. In fact, despite looking hard, he couldn't see any indications to suggest the kennels or the bunkhouse were there.

A woman walked into the room. She looked young, perhaps mid-thirties, with wavy, shoulder-length brown hair and a face which didn't strike him as beautiful, more distinctive, with a Roman nose, high cheek bones and piercing blue eyes.

'Good morning, detective, she said as she approached. 'I'm Julia Webster.' She held out her hand which he shook. It trembled, a sign perhaps of being fearful of the police, not likely he thought, more the result of a nervous complaint or drinking too much booze the night before; the DTs as his father used to call it.

'Please sit down.'

He took a seat on the settee, a style often seen in period dramas, a polished wooden frame with a sumptuous green velour seat. It looked elegant and fitted in perfectly with the other pieces of classical furniture in the room, but while his bottom appreciated the softness of the base, his back hated the knobbly bits in the frame.

The housekeeper walked in and he ordered coffee, so did his companion, but as the housekeeper walked away, Julia grasped her arm and said something to her. This little interchange revealed itself a few minutes later when the housekeeper returned with drinks, a coffee for him and one for Julia, with a large glass of white wine for the lady of the house on the side.

Henderson went on to explain about the previous Monday night's activity and the arrest of the human trafficking gang. He kept quiet about the shootings, not wishing to alarm a woman in what he believed to be a fragile state.

'Oh, it didn't bother me,' she said. 'I went to bed after your officer told me something was going on and I heard nothing more until nine, nine-thirty the next morning.'

'The men were operating a human trafficking business. They were bringing women over here from Eastern Europe and setting them to work in brothels which they owned all over Sussex.'

'You can't be serious?'

'It's true.'

'It sounds terrible. I wasn't aware, and for it to be happening so close to this house.'

'Have you ever noticed people coming and going, activity late at night?'

'No, I haven't. It's a quiet road outside and if they were coming and going after about ten at night, I wouldn't hear a thing. The walls of this place are thick and I sleep like a log.'

Henderson wasn't surprised because if she slugged wine as she was doing now from twelve noon until well into the evening, she'd be good for nothing by ten o'clock. No wonder she slept so well. Conked-out more like.

'Is there anyone else living in the house who might have?'

'No, the housekeeper, she goes to bed as early as me as she's up at the crack of dawn. Maybe my husband.'

'Is he around?'

'No,' she sighed. 'He leaves early in the morning and isn't often back until late at night.'

No wonder, Henderson thought. A house like this, staff, his wife's copious wine consumption, it all required a substantial income.

'I may come back as I'd like to talk to him. How long have you lived here?'

'About ten years, I think it is. It's the most time I've stayed in any house. You see, I spent my childhood living in places where the Army chose to send my father, often in parts of the world no one's ever heard about: Belize, Tristan da Cunha, Montserrat, to name a few.'

Henderson left Hillcrest House twenty minutes later, Julia Webster's monologues getting longer and becoming more spiced with bile from what sounded like the effects of a difficult childhood and a domineering father. She didn't add much to his sum of knowledge, but dispelled any notion the DI had about her owning the land where the kennels and bunkhouse were situated.

She didn't tell him in so many words, but her lack of knowledge about what was going on there was obvious. In fact, she didn't answer many of his direct questions, making him think she didn't know anything or was simply blotting what she did know. It didn't point her out as an out-and-out liar, but he knew many alcoholics and they had difficulty differentiating reality and their booze-soaked imaginations.

If he still needed more information, he would come back with details of who they believed owned the house and the land next door and see if she, or her husband, could enlighten him. He would also make sure they arrived no later than nine or ten in the morning, in the hope of finding her sober and a bit more compos mentis. He walked back to his car, resolving to treat himself to a decent lunch to make up for a frustrating morning. His phone rang.

'DI Henderson here.'

'Good morning DI Henderson, Dave here, HTCU. I've got some good news for you.'

Henderson paused. 'I was waiting for you to add, 'and I've got some bad news'. What's the good news?'

'We've cracked Nicholae Prodan's laptop. It's all in Romanian so I needed an interpreter by my side for most of the time, the reason it's taken so long. We're there now and I can tell you, sir, you're gonna like it. It's a gold mine of information.'

FORTY-FIVE

Henderson and Walters pulled into the car park at Regency Wines in Portslade. He'd been animated on the journey from Lewes, pleased at last to be bringing this case to a conclusion, but now in the car park, his mood darkened. He had come here often to buy beer, whisky and wine, and on his last visit the two bottles of wine he bought marked the end of his relationship with Rachel. The two of them had talked on the phone several times since she'd left, but the elephant in the room wasn't for shifting.

Proof that he wasn't ready for another relationship came on Wednesday night when Vicky Neal invited him up to her flat. He could see by the look on her face she intended their get-together wouldn't end with simply a coffee or a glass of whisky. She wasn't so drunk she was throwing caution to the wind, she knew exactly what she was doing.

He refused her invite for two reasons. One, he wasn't ready yet to move on and still harboured hopes of a reconciliation. Two, it would be a stupid action to take with a fellow member of his team, in fact with anyone working at Sussex Police. Not only would they see each other every day, but if the hours he worked could put the boot into his relationship with Rachel, dating another officer would only multiply the problem.

Documents found on Nicholae Prodan's laptop identified him as the leader of the trafficking operation team and the main liaison between the UK and two teams of three kidnappers, one in Hungary and another in Romania. Details had been sent to the relevant police forces in the hope they could strangle this odious trade at source. Prodan was also the main point of contact with the big boss over here, none other than a Sussex businessman by the name of Constantin Petrescu.

Henderson had talked to the owner of Regency Wines a number of times, a man he had marked out as a success after coming to this country in difficult circumstances. Little did he know about the real source of his wealth. And what wealth. The traffickers had been operating for years and raking in tens of millions from the numerous brothels they operated in Surrey and Sussex.

The money was being filtered into the banking system through a number of businesses owned by Petrescu: Regency Wines in front of him, a wine importing company, several bookmakers and a small chain of bureaux de change located in and around airports. The tainted businessman had also featured in several business magazines, the reason Cindy Longhurst first went to photograph him. Henderson believed the noise of the dogs piqued her interest and, after investigating, she hatched plans to free the kidnapped women.

Petrescu, it turned out, lived at Hillcrest House, the place where Henderson had talked to Julia

Webster, a lady who preferred using her maiden name. She'd been circumspect about who owned the kennels and the bunkhouse, as they had since discovered both were the property of her husband through companies which he controlled. Henderson would talk to the CPS about prosecuting Mrs Webster. Withholding information about the ownership of the kennels didn't stop the identification of Petrescu as its owner, but she had to know what had been going on next door and how she and her husband were benefitting.

Henderson wasn't taking any chances with this arrest. The gang Constantin Petrescu bankrolled, organised and led, didn't hesitate in using guns, and the DI didn't think the traffickers' boss would be any different. His caution didn't stretch to an armed response team this time, the sergeant of the team of the last one deployed not happy at losing two of his men, but he and Walters had come prepared.

Two patrol cars were also in the car park. He instructed two officers from one of the cars to accompany him and DS Walters and he left the other car to block any attempt at escape.

'Someone owns a smart car,' Walters said, nodding at the Porsche Panamera parked at the side of the building.

'Private reg as well, but at least it tells us he's here.'

The small team of four approached the large building and headed inside.

Polly was standing behind the desk and looked alarmed when she saw Henderson and Walters, two uniformed cops behind them. Henderson walked behind the desk and pushed open a door marked 'Private.'

'You can't go up there. It's private. Mr Petrescu doesn't like unexpected visitors.'

'He'll see us,' Henderson said.

'I must insist.'

'Go back to your customers,' he heard one of the officers say.

They walked upstairs and at the top, Henderson headed towards a door bearing the sign, 'Big Boss Man Works Here' and opened it. The office looked cavernous, the upper part of the back section of the warehouse. It contained a desk at the far end of the room and, close to the door, a well-worn black leather sofa and a row of filing cabinets.

Constantin Petrescu looked up, clocking the uniforms. 'What can I do...What the hell's this?'

Henderson walked closer. 'Constantin Petrescu I'm arresting you for–'

He didn't get time to finish. Petrescu pulled out a gun and started firing.

FORTY-SIX

When Henderson first saw the gun in Constantin Petrescu's hand, he didn't have time to unholster his own weapon. Instead he grabbed Walters and dived behind the settee. From their position, they could see one of the officers had been shot. The other was standing behind the door with the look of pure terror on his face.

Henderson heard rapid footsteps across the wooden floor. If Petrescu thought he was going to finish the officer off, or kill him and Walters, he had another think coming. Henderson now had his own gun ready and would have no compunction shooting Petrescu. No further shots were fired. Henderson risked a look around the side of the couch.

Seeing nothing, he crouched on his knees and looked over the settee. Petrescu wasn't at his desk or anywhere inside the room. Looking around, he spotted the open fire door. He stood and ran over to the injured officer. He opened the man's blood-soaked jacket. Walters knelt beside him.

The bullet had gone through his chest, close to his shoulder, but he couldn't be sure if it had hit any vital organs.

'Officer down, officer down,' Walters said into the radio. She relayed the address to the operator.

'They're five minutes away,' she said putting the radio down.

'Good.'

'Stay awake, stay with us Danny,' he said to the injured cop. Henderson tore off a piece of the man's shirt and folded it into a compress.

Henderson called the other officer over and told him to take hold of the material. The cop's hands were shaking so much, he couldn't grasp it. Henderson took his wrist, put the material in his hand and guided the make-shift compress towards his injured colleague's wound.

'Do this,' he instructed, 'and keep pressure on the wound until the ambulance arrives, understand? It's on its way.'

'Is he coming back? The guy with the gun?'

'No, he's gone, he's not coming back.' Henderson stood and put a hand on the officer's back. 'There's nothing to worry about, all you need to do is take care of Danny, okay?'

'Right sir, I will.'

'Good man. C'mon,' he said to Walters, 'let's get after Petrescu.'

They bolted down the fire escape. At the bottom, they found a large dry patch on the ground where Petrescu's car had been. They ran into the wine depot's main car park, looking for the patrol car but aside from the empty one belonging to the officers upstairs, it was nowhere to be seen.

'I'll call them,' Walters said.

'We're in pursuit of suspect's vehicle,' he heard the crackling voice of PC Dunn in the patrol car say, 'westbound on the A270. He's a fair distance in front and jumping red lights. Will keep you posted.'

Henderson ran over to his car and got in. Walters climbed inside and before the passenger door closed, they roared off.

'The patrol car was blocking the Regency Wines car park,' Walters said, 'but he nipped through the place next door.'

'He's had that escape route planned for a long time.'

Driving through back roads they soon hit the westbound A270.

Walters called the patrol car once again.

'We were close to him at the junction for the Shoreham Bypass but we lost him. We took the bypass but we can't see him.'

'Put his car on ANPR,' she said. 'It's a Porsche Panamera registration number, CON 15.'

'CON 15, got it. Will do.'

'What now?' Walters asked.

'I'm thinking. What if he didn't take the bypass and stayed on the A270. Where does it lead?'

'Shoreham Harbour and the Airport.'

'If he was heading for the harbour, he would have come off the A270 earlier. He must be heading for the airport.'

'Your guess is as good as any.'

A few minutes later Shoreham Airport, or Brighton City Airport as it was called now, came into view. It didn't compete in the same league as Gatwick, thirty-odd miles further north, as no commercial flights flew from there. Instead, it catered for private owners of planes and helicopters, local businessmen and those who used a plane to transport clients or their family on a day trip to France or Holland.

They left the car in the airport's car park and ran into the terminal building. He spotted an official-looking man and approached him, holding up his ID. 'We're looking for Constantin Petrescu, a tall, slim guy with curly jet-black hair. Have you seen him?'

'I know Constantin. He's a regular around here. I saw him not ten minutes ago. He said he'd left his briefcase on his plane and needed to fetch it.'

'Where does he keep it?'

'Come and I'll show you.'

They walked outside and strode past a number of hangers.

He pointed. 'There's his plane over there. Can you see it?'

'The one with the blue tail?'

'Yes, the Hawker 400XP. It's a beautiful aircraft but it wouldn't give you much change from two mill.'

Not for a rich man like Petrescu, something as simple and straightforward as a Cessna 172, a small plane with a single propeller. His was a twin-engined executive jet. If Henderson knew Petrescu owned such an asset as this when he believed him nothing more than a local businessman, it would have raised his suspicions about the sources of such cash.

He was about to run over to the plane when their helper said. 'Hold on a sec, I think it's moving. This is highly irregular because as far as I know, he isn't scheduled for take-off today and hasn't filed a flight plan.' He lifted the radio in his hand. 'Wait and I'll check.'

Henderson didn't hear the rest as he was now running. Instead of heading towards the aircraft as he first intended, he ran across the grass towards the runway. At this moment, another plane was landing.

Henderson had no idea how busy Shoreham Airport could be, if one plane took off every five minutes or five took off every day. If it was busy and a number of planes were circling above his head waiting to land, or several on the ground were ready to take-off, Petrescu forcing his plane onto the runway could cause a serious accident. Knowing the luck that seemed to follow the man, in the chaos, he would make his escape.

He would find out soon enough for as soon as the landed plane coasted past the Hawker, Petrescu moved his plane forward and moved into position at the start of the runaway. Henderson's lungs were bursting when he reached the edge of the runway. He withdrew the weapon he'd taken into Regency Wines and bent over double for a moment or two to catch his breath and to steady his hand.

He heard a roar as Petrescu gunned the engines and the sleek jet raced towards him. Henderson raised the gun and aimed at the windshield but realised it was designed to withstand strong air pressure and would be difficult to penetrate with only a handgun.

The plane sped towards him, getting larger, its acceleration getting faster, the noise louder and louder. He could see Petrescu at the controls, his face fixed in a determined stare. Henderson took aim. He counted 1-2-3 before firing – *bang, bang, bang*. He leapt to the side.

The port side tyre blew apart in spectacular fashion, firing large lumps of rubber at speed in all directions. Seconds before, Henderson had flattened himself on the grass to avoid being pulled over by the jet wash and now felt large pieces of rubber whizzing over his head. He turned to see the jet sway drunkenly across the runway, as if its fuel tanks were filled with alcohol and not jet fuel, before bumping over the rough ground at the side of the runway.

It was traveling at perhaps thirty or forty miles an hour when it hit something uneven, maybe a ditch, causing the plane to keel over and its nose to crash into the ground, making a loud crunching noise. It rocked from side to side for several seconds before tilting over but was prevented from turning over completely when a wing tip banged on the grass.

Henderson ran over. Getting closer, he inhaled a strong whiff of fuel. Perhaps the crash had ruptured fuel lines. He jumped on the wing and scrambled up to the cockpit. He hauled the cockpit door open. Petrescu was slumped forward, unconscious. The headphones were askew on his head, blood dripping down his face and his body hanging limp in the taut seat belt like a rag doll at a seafront show.

Henderson yanked the headphones off the pilot's head and undid the seat belt. Petrescu fell towards him, the dead weight of the big guy nearly knocking him over. He tugged and tugged, gradually pulling him away from the cockpit seat, the smell of fuel stronger than before.

He slid him down the wing and they both collapsed

on the grass. In spite of the noise from Henderson's own heavy breathing, he heard sirens as a fire crew and ambulance came speeding towards them. He got up, hoping for a second wind, and dragged Petrescu by the shoulders, pulling him further away from the plane.

Twenty metres away he slumped on the grass, exhausted, but he knew he had to get up and drag him some more. Before he could summon the energy to do so, he heard a loud *whoosh*, the sort of noise a big firework makes as it takes-off. He threw himself face-down in the grass as the fuel ignited and the plane erupted in a giant fireball. The heat was intense, searing his body through his clothes and sucking all the air out of his lungs.

The scorching temperatures vanished as rapidly as they'd erupted and when he dared look up, Petrescu's two-million-pound plane, bought through the suffering of countless young women, was engulfed in flames. A better metaphor for the collapse of his odious business he couldn't think of.

FORTY-SEVEN

Henderson walked into DCI Edwards's office and closed the door. He took a seat in the visitor's chair, facing her across the desk.

'I assume because you're in here today you're feeling better?' she asked.

'A little singed around the edges, but otherwise fine.'

'I have to say, you were a little cavalier out there at Shoreham Airport, Angus. One slip the wrong way and we would be having a different sort of conversation, that is, if you could still speak.'

'I acted on pure instinct. I knew I had to stop him as not only did he finance and manage the trafficking of those women, but he shot a cop.'

'How is Officer Carr doing? Do you know?'

'I went to see him this morning before I came in. Surgery was a success, although he might lose some mobility in his arm. He'll be off work for three, maybe four months and when he comes back, it will need to be in some administrative capacity, at least at first. He was lucky in a way that Petrescu shot him in his right shoulder, he's left-handed.'

'Petrescu is a ruthless man right enough, but what you did could have killed him and yourself.'

'Don't I know it. Any one of those bits from the

exploding tyre could have knocked my head off.'

'Aye, and if Petrescu hadn't been in such a big rush to get away, he might have filled the plane up with fuel before setting off, then where would you be?'

'Burnt toast, I think.'

'How's the man in question? Don't think I'm asking after his health, rather his ability to be questioned.'

'He'll live. He received a nasty bash on the head when the plane crashed, and broke two ribs. Before you ask, there are two armed guards outside his hospital room. I'm taking no chances. We'll see him in an interview room in a few days, pain or no pain.'

'Good, because I want this guy up in court. I want all the newspapers to report what he did to those poor women as a warning to others and I want the women you freed to see him in handcuffs.'

'I'm afraid it won't be good enough to deter others coming up behind as there's so much money to be made.'

'Talking of money, how are you getting on following it and uncovering his assets?'

'We've just about got our heads around his organisation. Most of them are shell companies with few assets, but bundles of cash, and a lot of the work is in trying to find its source. The real businesses, the wine warehouses for example, we've got the accountants looking over the financials to see if they were being funded by any of his prostitution money.'

'I'm sure they are as he expanded so rapidly, but you know me, I'll use any excuse to nab it. Stories involving large sums of cash recovered always go down well with the mandarins at the Home Office. It not only reminds them that what we do is important, but it also goes to prove that we don't cost as much as people think.'

'I'm glad to hear something pleases them.'

'The only outstanding issue is for me to offer you my congratulations at the successful closure of such a difficult case and give you a glass of the good stuff.'

Henderson glanced at the clock on the wall: two-thirty. It was a little early for him, but what the hell.

She reached into a drawer and pulled out a bottle of whisky and two glasses. She poured generous measures into each glass and passed one to him.

'Well done Angus,' Edwards said. 'Earlier comments aside, you did an excellent job. At least forty women have got you to thank for their freedom. This is for them.'

The End

About the Author

Iain Cameron was born in Glasgow and moved to Brighton in the early eighties. He has worked as a management accountant, business consultant and a nursery goods retailer. He is now a full-time writer and lives in a village outside Horsham in West Sussex with his wife, two daughters and a lively Collie dog.

Girls on Film is the seventh book to feature DI Angus Henderson, the Scottish cop at Sussex Police.

For more information about books and the author:
Visit the website at: www.iain-cameron.com
Follow him on Twitter: @IainsBooks
Follow him on Facebook @IaincameronAuthor

Also by Iain Cameron

All books are available from Amazon

A Small Request

If you have read any of my books, I would be grateful if you could leave a review on Amazon or Goodreads. All reviews are read and any comments noted. My thanks to every reader for your continued support.

Printed in Great Britain
by Amazon